I0526301

i

NEVER LEAVE MY ARMS

By Elizabeth H. Franklin

Published by Elizabeth H. Franklin Books in the United States of America.
Front cover designed by Billwyc at BookCovers.com
First Print 2026

ISBN (Print Edition): 979-8-9904227-2-8

Elizabeth H. Franklin
Greater Tampa Bay Area, Florida

ACKNOWLEDGEMENTS

Writing this book has been a journey of passion and perseverance. I could not have done it without the support and patience of my husband, Frank Muzio, and some very special people.

The keen insights and critiques of Richard Messina, Linda Kirnan, Jacquie Muzio, Sarah Keyes, Marianne Ostmann and Natalie Whitcomb helped me shape this story of Alexandra and Pierce and the entire Tennyson family's legacy. I cannot thank each of you enough for your generosity.

A special thank you to one of my stalworth cheerleaders, Lorrin Trifilo. Always there with words of encouragement and an unwavering belief in me and my stories.

"May we all find strength in the stories we share and hope in the love that endures beyond the page." *Unknown*

PROLOGUE
The Unlocked Drawer

Landon Estates
Middlesex, England
June 1811

Pierce Tennyson stood silently, gazing out the French doors of his study into the estate gardens. The sun hovered in the western sky, casting a warm glow over the well-groomed shrubs and plants. Tall and ruggedly handsome, the sixty-one-year-old British/Scotsman wore traditional Scottish attire: a kilt in his maternal family's tartan, a cream-colored shirt of saffron split at the neck with the long sleeves pushed up to his elbows, woolen knee socks with matching fasteners, and leather-laced shoes. Although half English, Pierce fully embraced his maternal Scottish heritage as a prominent descendant of the powerful Fraser Clan. His wavy silver-gray hair fell to his shoulders, pulled back neatly at the nape, while his equally light beard and mustache were cropped close, accentuating the sharp lines of his jaw.

Deep in thought, his eldest son, Reece, worked quietly at the large wooden desk, reviewing the ledger accounts for the family shipping business. Pierce had entrusted the company to Reece on the occasion of his twenty-fifth birthday. Reece possessed a keen business acumen, and Pierce saw much of himself in him, including a strong physical resemblance at the same age.

Much like his father, Reece's intensity and good looks made him the object of affection for many young women. He wore his dark, shoulder-length hair pulled back with a black leather tie, leaving an errant bang to fall over his right eye. It gave him a rakish air. His light blue eyes, inherited from his mother, Alexandra, held a steely power that unnerved many business opponents; when angered, the blue deepened in color.

In contrast to Reece, his younger brothers, Alex and Christopher, showed little interest in the family shipping business. Instead, they found fulfillment in collectively managing the estate's renowned thoroughbred stables. The brothers' partnership worked seamlessly. Alex handled the business side and scouted for new additions to the stables. His tall, athletic build and good looks, inherited from their father, combined with their mother's charm and knack for dealing with even the most difficult clients, made him the perfect complement to Christopher, who preferred to work directly with the horses.

While Alex was a blend of his parents in both demeanor and physical stature, the youngest Tennyson shared Alex's athletic stature, but their similarities ended there. Christopher favored his mother's light hair color and his paternal grandmother's striking green eyes. At a young age, he discovered his unusual ability to connect with horses in a way neither of his brothers nor his father could. It was not uncommon for neighbors or other breeders to call upon him for assistance, earning him a reputation for handling even the most challenging equestrian situations.

The Tennyson brothers, equally successful and exceptionally handsome, were considered the most desirable men by marriage-minded young debutantes. Until a few years ago, Pierce had his hands full with upset mothers and fathers about their lovelorn daughters. They felt they were not being considered seriously for marriage matches.

Thankfully, the marriages of Reece and Alex the past three years removed them from such considerations. Both men found their perfect partners in life, mirroring the exceptional fortune of Alexandra and Pierce in finding each other. However, her youngest son continued to be a source of occasional trouble, recently costing his father a fine bottle of scotch to quell the annoyance of an irate father. The man's daughter felt slighted that Christopher no longer called on the young gel. Alexandra prayed daily that he would find someone as special as her other two daughters-in-law.

Reece and his family had arrived at the estate the previous day for their summer stay. He and his wife Kat, an American from South Carolina and an international shipping owner in her own right, split their time between their London townhouse and the family's Middlesex estate, the childhood home of the brothers.

Shortly after their arrival, father and son retired to the study in the mid-afternoon to enjoy a glass or two of fine liquor and catch up on the events of the past two months. Before they got too far into their cups, Reece needed to complete some Fraser Shipping paperwork he had brought with him for the stay.

So deep in thought, Pierce did not hear his son's question until Reece cleared his throat loudly. Once he had his father's attention, Reece asked, "Where did you put the blank ledgers?"

Without turning, Pierce replied absently with a wave of his hand.

"In the bottom right," referring to his desk.

Reece frowned briefly when he looked down at the drawer, remembering that his father always kept that particular one locked. He paused, about to rouse his father from his thoughts again, when he tried the handle and found it open. The edge of a yellow ledger, partially concealed by a large, tattered, unusually thick folder, caught Reece's eye.

Reece reached to lift the oversized file aside when he read the bold, neatly printed words across the flap:

Annulment
Pierce Tennyson
and
Helene Cameron

Reece blinked several times as he processed the writing. The revelation that his father had been married before marrying his mother left him thunderstruck. He and his brothers presumed their parents were each other's one and only true love. They had always believed they were the most perfectly matched pair; their deep devotion and respect for each other were obvious. That neither had ever told them about their father's first marriage was unfathomable.

Pierce roused himself from his thoughts when he heard the thud of the heavy file being placed on the desk. He realized too late that he had failed

ix

to lock the lower drawer. Davis McCoy, the family's trusted investigator and legal counsel, had left only an hour ago. The two men had a standing monthly meeting to discuss Pierce's various investments and private interests. In his haste to greet his arriving son and his family, Pierce had placed the file in its usual secured drawer but forgot to lock it.

Based on Pierce's stunned expression, it was clear to Reece that his father had not intended for him to find the file. Before either man could speak, the rustle of skirts and soft footsteps coming down the corridor broke the awkward silence. Alexandra suddenly appeared in the doorway—a petite, beautiful woman in her mid-fifties with sparkling blue eyes and a bright white smile. She lit up every room she entered, and this evening was no exception.

"Dinner will be served in fifteen minutes you two," she said with her usual effervescence.

She loved having Reece and his family at the manor. Although Alex, his wife Sarah, and their two children were close by at the estate house down the road, and Christopher still lived in the manor, there was always a void when Reece, and his family were in London.

As Alexandra looked between her husband and son, her smile faded. There was an awkwardness in the air.

Stepping further into the room, she asked, "Is there something…?"

Her words trailed off as she spotted the large, tattered folder on the desk in front of Reece. She recognized it, and her eyes quickly darted to Pierce. He knew exactly what she was thinking. The two shared an indescribable connection since first meeting more than thirty-six years ago.

"I forgot to lock the drawer," Pierce said.

Alexandra let out a sigh of resignation; she knew this day would eventually arrive. It should have come long ago, but she and Pierce had decided then that it was a secret best kept between them. After all, they believed it had no effect on their life together, making it easy to maintain their silence.

Looking at her husband, Alexandra gave him a pleading look. "It's time to tell the family."

Reece's face, usually impossible to read, changed. He glanced at his mother and furrowed his brow.

"You know about this?" he asked.

Alexandra walked over to Pierce and looped a supportive arm through his as she addressed her son.

"Yes I do luv. Your father and I have no secrets from each other."

Pierce squeezed her arm affectionately and smiled down admiringly into her crystal blue eyes—a place he found himself lost in countless times.

"Son, I am certain you have many questions, as will your brothers," Pierce said. "Your mother is right. We have been holding onto this for too long."

Drawing strength from his wife, he took a deep breath.

"After dinner, we will gather here to explain everything."

Chapter One

Landon Estates
Middlesex England
June 1811
...later that evening

The Tennyson adult family members filled most of the seats at the large wooden dining table. The grandchildren were with their nanny and governess down the hall in the special playroom.

The dinner conversation was unusually subdued. Reece and Pierce were notably quiet. Reece's distracted behavior perplexed his wife. Although not normally a chatterbox, her husband usually contributed to the conversation, shedding his reserved, businesslike demeanor in the presence of his family. Tonight, however, he remained silent, which was out of character for him.

The same was true for her father-in-law, who typically enjoyed casual banter and often initiated discussions. Tonight, though, something weighed heavily on both men. Kat made a mental note to ask her husband about it when they returned to their wing of rooms following dinner.

After the final course, Alexandra and Pierce were the first to rise. Clearing his throat, Pierce wrapped his arm lovingly around his wife's shoulder and looked around at the group. They all gave him their rapt attention. There was an unusual tentativeness in his voice.

1

"Alexandra and I would like to discuss something with all of you this evening in the study."

The men and their wives exchanged questioning glances. This was not like their parents. They were usually fun-loving and lighthearted. Tonight, their tone and demeanor seemed distracted.

"Of course. Millie can help me with Landon and Alison, and I will be down directly," Kat offered.

She decided her conversation with Reece could wait until later.

Sarah chimed in as well.

"We can settle Maddie and Brenton quickly and be there in no time," she said, glancing at Alex.

Alexandra smiled brightly. "Splendid. We will see you all shortly."

Pierce nodded as everyone left the dinner table and made their way upstairs.

Alexandra looked up at her husband, her eyes filled with adoration and her voice thick with emotion.

"Once they know, they will understand and want to help in any way they can."

Pierce placed a gentle kiss on Alexandra's cheek.

"I hope so," he whispered before guiding her out of the dining room.

An hour later, the adults gathered in Pierce's study. The large, well-appointed room provided a warm and welcoming ambiance, with ample seating for everyone. A stone fireplace flanked by leather sofas on either side, along with comfortable wingback chairs positioned in front of Pierce's large, wooden desk, created an inviting atmosphere. Two additional chairs were situated just inside the doorway, and a set of French doors on either side of the desk led out to a private manicured garden.

Reece and Alex sat on the leather sofas alongside their wives, while Christopher moved a chair closer to the group. Pierce stood in front of the fireplace with a drink in his hand, Alexandra at his side. They surveyed their family, each member sitting quietly with questioning expressions on their faces.

Pierce struggled for a moment to find the right words to begin.

"I don't know where to start."

Alexandra could see the emotional toll this was taking on her husband. She placed her warm hand on his forearm and squeezed it reassuringly.

Pierce looked down at her and smiled. She knew when he needed her strength. Looking up at the group, he cleared his throat and steadied himself, trying to lighten the anxiety that hung in the air.

"The beginning is always a good place," he said with a nervous chuckle.

Kat offered a supportive smile to her father-in-law, her amber-flecked brown eyes soft with understanding. She sensed the weight of the burden he carried.

Pierce had taken an immediate shine to Kat when he first met her. The petite, raven-haired American beauty had turned Reece's world upside down. Before their serendipitous meeting, his son held tainted and antiquated views of women, believing they were only interested in his money and vain pursuits.

For years, Alexandra fretted Reece would remain married to his work, leaving no time for a wife and family. The fact that he kept a mistress annoyed her to no end. She desperately wanted grandchildren, and truth be told, so did Pierce.

The two quickly came to see that Kat was nothing like the women their son had known. She broke societal norms by pursuing and achieving a formal business education instead of a husband and family. She possessed a savvy for commerce that rivaled Reece's. Arriving in London with a plan to make her mark in the shipping industry, Kat purchased a small company and built it into her own successful international freight transportation line.

Initially, Reece found it difficult to take Kat's ambition seriously; he clung to his short-sighted stereotypes of women. Thankfully, with some candor from his father, nudging from Alexandra, and several sharp barbs from Kat, Reece eventually recognized her worth and exceptional capabilities. Although it took considerable effort for Reece to fully demonstrate that he regarded Kat as his equal, he eventually succeeded.

Pierce cleared his throat one last time and launched into his news.

"There is something I have been holding back from you all, and today I realized I should not keep you in the dark any longer."

Reece's expression remained inscrutable. Of those present, only he knew what his father referenced. His younger brothers, Alex and Christopher, exchanged concerned glances with each other and with Sarah. Kat noted her husband's lack of response; she knew him well enough to sense he had some insight into what Pierce was about to reveal. He refused to look at her when she glanced his way, a telltale sign that he knew more than he let on.

Alexandra sought to settle the rising anxiety in the room.

"It's nothing bad for our family."

Sensing the need to quicken the pace of the conversation, Pierce pressed on.

"As you know, my mother and maternal grandmother descend from the Scottish Fraser Clan."

Providing background, he explained that the Cameron clan, a neighboring group to the Frasers, held the land that provided access to the west coast of Scotland. Callum Fraser, Pierce's maternal grandfather, wanted to expand Fraser Shipping and needed access through Cameron lands to move goods to the port in Corran, located at the mouth of Loch Linnhe.

For his grandfather's dream of expansion to be realized, he needed Clan Cameron to grant him access to their lands. For years, Callum tried to broker a deal to no avail. Things changed, however, after Pierce's sixteenth birthday when Cameron relented under the condition the two groups enter into a marriage pact that would bind the two clans.

Never Leave My Arms

Unfortunately, Callum died unexpectedly before the negotiations were finalized. On his deathbed, he made his wife Maisie, Pierce's grandmother, promise to complete the pact.

Pierce paused for a moment to ensure his explanation had not confused the group. Scanning their faces, he saw expectation rather than puzzlement.

Satisfied with their reaction, he went on.

"My grandmother did as Callum asked and made the agreement, which included, among other terms, binding a marriage between the firstborn grandson of the Fraser Clan and the firstborn granddaughter of the Cameron Clan. I was the Fraser firstborn grandson, and Helene was the firstborn granddaughter of the Cameron Clan."

Alex and Sarah exchanged looks of disbelief. Reece only glanced briefly at Kat, his expression still unreadable. In that instant, she realized he had somehow known about this, explaining his reserve at dinner.

Christopher sat quietly in the winged chair, his head down, listening intently and concentrating on his every word. Learning his father could have been married to someone before his mother struck an angry cord in him. Uncertain if it was his sense of loyalty to his mother, or the fact his father had withheld such an important piece of information from his sons for so many years, Christopher took an immediate judgmental stance.

Looking up at his father, he asked with a stony expression, "Did you see the pact through and marry Helene?"

Pierce and his youngest son locked eyes. A lump formed in the older man's throat as he noticed the disappointment on Christopher's face. Alexandra saw it as well and frowned.

Releasing a sigh of resignation, Pierce nodded. "Yes son."

Alexandra squeezed Pierce's hand reassuringly. While the rest of the family remained calm and open to the details, Christopher's critical stance displeased his mother. Alexandra did not want her son to think less of his father, especially since he lacked all the information.

Addressing Christopher directly, she said firmly, "Your father was forced to marry Helene, and that was before he and I ever met."

Christopher's expression softened in response to his mother's subtle rebuke. He sat back and lowered his head in contrition.

Pressing against her husband, Alexandra squeezed his arm in encouragement.

"Dear, I think it's time we shared our story."

Chapter Two

Nathaniel and Larena Tennyson's Townhome,
Mayfair, London
Early January 1774

Larena Fraser Tennyson paced back and forth in the drawing room of their well-appointed home, her anxiety palpable. Nathaniel, her husband, stood by the fireplace, his elbow resting on the polished wooden mantel. He frowned as he stared absently into his empty glass.

Larena paused at the large window overlooking the park across the street. The bare trees looked stark against the white fluffy coating of snow on the ground, although some still had remnants of the wintery weather clingy to their branches.

Larena watched their son Pierce march angrily across the street before quickly disappearing into the park. His parting words as he angrily jerked the front door open were, "I need some air."

Close to tears, she turned back to her husband, desperation in her voice.

"Nathan, what are we to do? This is an impossible situation."

Nathaniel hated to see his wife so upset. Her crystal green eyes shimmered with tears. He calmly set his glass down and went to her, drawing her into his comforting arms. In all their twenty-seven years of marriage, he had never seen her so distressed. She was normally the voice of calm and reason, always looking for the positive side of a situation.

Squeezing her affectionately, he said, "He is a grown man. He needs to make this decision."

"He is so angry," Larena replied.

Stepping back while still in her husband's embrace, she looked up at him with a worried expression.

"How could my mother do this to him? Pierce has every reason to be furious."

Nathaniel softly ran his finger along her flawless creamy cheek as he took in her image. Not one to follow the current British fashion of having her hair dressed with powder and black pins or worn excessively high, she stayed true to her Scottish roots. She styled her thick, mahogany tresses into an artfully crafted coiffure. Using pins, she swept the sides off her face and secured them atop her head while the rest of her mane flowed in soft waves down her back. Those who mistook her petite stature for frailty or weakness quickly discovered she possessed an unbreakable fortitude, particularly when she knew she was right—which was often.

Smiling warmly, Nathaniel pulled her into his broad tall frame and gave her a comforting squeeze, pressing his chin to her forehead.

"Give him time. He will cool off."

As the words left his mouth, they felt hollow; even he did not believe them. In truth, Pierce had every right to be furious with his grandmother for binding him to a marriage pact. The older woman had said nothing to Nathaniel, Larena, or Pierce until today—Pierce's twenty-fifth birthday. Had she spoken up earlier, Nathaniel would have done everything in his power to break the commitment. He believed his son should have the right to choose his own bride, just as he had.

While Nathaniel's family adored and welcomed Larena immediately, it had not been an easy path for the Frasers to accept him. Larena's parents,

Never Leave My Arms

Maisie and Callum Fraser, liked Nathaniel well enough, but they struggled to accept his British heritage. They had hoped their daughter would marry within the Fraser Clan, but Larena dashed those hopes when she informed them of her choice to marry Nathaniel—a member of the British gentry. Over time, they seemed to accept the marriage, especially when they discovered Nathaniel and Larena were settling near her family in Scotland.

The young couple welcomed their first and only child two years after they wed. Their son thrived growing up among his Scottish Clan, fully embracing that side of his heritage. Although Nathaniel remained silent on the matter, he felt his son also needed exposure to his British family. An occasional holiday visit was not enough.

That opportunity arose when Nathaniel's father passed away suddenly, prompting him to relocate his wife and son to his family's business in Gloucester. Pierce was twelve at the time. Moving a great distance from his maternal grandparents and the clan and country he loved was a heavy burden for the young boy.

Early on, Callum set out to groom his grandson to take over Fraser Shipping when he came of age. He wanted to ensure he made Scotland his permanent home. Callum failed to consider that Pierce could not be easily manipulated. The young man loved his father and his British heritage just as much as his Scottish ancestry.

After much pressure from Larena and Maisie, Nathaniel agreed to allow Pierce to spend summers in Scotland with his grandparents, and return to London for the rest of the year.

Following her husband's death, and unbeknownst to Larena and Nathaniel, Maisie picked up Callum's torch and secretly completed the agreement between the Cameron and Fraser clans. The pact required Pierce to marry Helene Cameron, granddaughter of Clan Cameron's leader in exchange for access rights to Fraser Shipping.

Separate from the contract, Callum's testament included that Pierce would immediately assume running Fraser Shipping after he married. Further, upon reaching the age of thirty, he would receive full ownership of the company. The grandparents believed this would keep her their grandson permanently and fully tied to Scotland.

Maisie along with Helene's grandfather, kept the treaty secret until Pierce reached the specified age. On the day of his twenty-fifth birthday, Maisie delivered the news to her grandson, Larena, and Nathaniel of the impending nuptials. She knew that if she revealed the commitment earlier, Nathaniel would oppose it and try to prevent it from happening.

Her instincts proved correct. Her silence infuriated both Nathaniel and Larena. However, nothing could have prepared her for Pierce's extreme reaction. Her grandson exploded when he heard the news. Although he loved his grandmother and Scotland, Pierce wanted to make his own life decisions, especially regarding something as important as choosing a wife. Nathaniel and Larena stood in support of their son as he unleashed his fury towards his grandmother for what she had done to him and his future.

Maisie attempted to control his anger using every means possible, including guilt.

"Lad, your grandfather wanted this for ya and for Fraser Shipping. 'Tis your legacy. 'Tis Clan Fraser's legacy."

For Larena and Pierce's sake, Nathaniel bit his tongue at the older woman's audacity and blatant manipulation. Over the years, he had suspected that his in-laws' acceptance of their daughter's marriage to an Englishman was superficial. Out of love and respect for Larena, he never voiced his doubts about her parents' sincerity.

Unbeknownst to him, Larena also questioned their seemingly ready acceptance of her marriage as well, but it was not until today that Maisie revealed her hidden agenda, exposing what she and Callum had planned since Pierce's birth. They set out to entrench their grandson gradually and so deeply in his Scottish heritage that he would, without question, divest himself of his father's ancestry and wholly embrace his mother's culture.

Little did Nathaniel and Larena know that Maisie's manipulations were ineffective with Pierce, although he never let on. He loved his grandparents and Scotland, but he equally cherished his father's English heritage. No influence from Maisie would ever change that.

Larena nudged her husband to draw him from his thoughts.

"Nathan, I do not want him to marry out of obligation. It will make him miserable. I feel responsible for this mess because I pressured you to let him spend all that time in Scotland with my parents and the clan."

Nathaniel smiled lovingly at his wife and held her consolingly.

"Do not blame yourself. This is Maisie and Callum's doing."

Loosening his hold, he pulled her away enough to look reassuringly into her eyes.

"Our son is an honorable man and will not shame his grandmother. He is also decisive and not easily controlled. He needs some time to cool off. When he returns, I will try to talk to him again about his plans."

"Under the circumstances, I think it's best my mother return to Scotland immediately," Larena said.

It did not surprise her that within the hour, Maisie Fraser descended the stairs with her bags, ready to leave. With her face set sternly, she looked between her daughter and son-in-law and briskly announced, "I expect to see you two and my grandson in Fort William in two months for the wedding. Afterwards, we will celebrate the nuptials and the expansion of Fraser Shipping."

Nathaniel maintained a stoic expression and made no reply, while Larena simply said, "Goodbye Mother."

Pushing her way past the footman to the open door, the older woman scoffed as she cast one last glance at the couple before stepping unassisted into the hired hack.

Never Leave My Arms

Fort William, Scotland
March 14, 1774

Pierce Tennyson stood ramrod straight, his hands clasped behind his back and his broad chest thrust forward as he stared out the window of his room at the Fort William Inn. The marriage ceremony was to begin in one hour at the small church down the lane from Helene Cameron's grandparents' home.

Although Pierce maintained an impassive expression, his bearded jaw ticked; a sign to those close to him that he seethed inwardly. For the past two days, he had unsuccessfully tried to convince Helene Cameron to back out of the pact. They had met when Pierce arrived in Fort William. She seemed pleasant enough, but there was something about her that made him uneasy. Her interactions felt forced, as though she were putting on an act. Pierce chalked it up to nervousness; after all, she too, had just learned of the marriage contract a few months ago.

It surprised Pierce when his grandmother informed him of Helene's purity. The young woman was attractive and carried herself with a mature femininity not usually seen in someone her young age—six years younger than Pierce.

She wore her thick brown tresses pulled away from her perfectly oval-shaped face and braided down her back. Her brown doe eyes held a look of uncertainty in Pierce's presence, yet they sparkled when she was with others, particularly with Robbie Clyne, a childhood friend of hers. Initially, suspicions arose as Pierce noticed the amount of time they spent with each other. Then it occurred to him that perhaps they wanted to be together. If so, that would provide him the out he needed to cancel the agreement.

Alas, he felt crushed after sitting down to broach the subject with Helene.

"I can see you and Robbie enjoy each other's company very much," he said.

13

To his surprise, a look of panic crossed her face as she blurted out, "He's only a friend."

Pierce smiled sympathetically.

"You misunderstand Helene. I want us both to be happy. I see how he looks at you, and you at him. If you want to be together, I will not stand in your way."

Tears sprang into her big brown eyes, and her lower lip quivered. At first, Pierce thought they were tears of gratitude for the chance to be with Robbie. He was wrong.

"You do not want me? Am I not pretty enough for you?" she asked as a sob escaped her lips.

Pierce felt as though a mule had kicked him. He prided himself on his ability to gauge people and their motives, but clearly, Helene was the exception. He had completely misread her. Pierce would not lie, but he knew he needed to phrase his reply carefully.

"You misunderstand. It seemed as though you and Robbie had eyes for each other. I was simply trying to give you a path to him."

Helene's tears dried up immediately, and she managed a timid smile, dipping her eyes demurely as she daintily dabbed at their corners.

"Thank you, but as I said, he 'tis only a childhood friend. There is nothing between us. I am fully prepared to meet my obligation under the pact and marry you. My grandfather expects, nay, demands it of me."

Pierce nodded while he fought to suppress his disappointment.

"Aye. I understand. I shall see you at the church two days hence at noon."

The young woman, her eyes bright with a smile, nodded fervently.

Anger and disappointment consumed Pierce over the next two days as he struggled with the conflict between fulfilling his grandparents' wishes and prioritizing his own needs. If he backed out of the accord, he would shame his grandmother in the eyes of both clans, damage his clan's reputation, and shatter his grandfather's dream of expanding Fraser Shipping. Conversely,

Never Leave My Arms

if he went through with the marriage, he would be tied to a woman he likely could never love or trust, leading to a life of misery.

Pierce had never planned to marry. He wanted to travel to various countries with the Fraser ships and immerse himself in diverse cultures. The idea of finding a woman who would ignite his passion and be his partner, as his parents had experienced, was not at the forefront of his mind. But he knew without a doubt that Helene Cameron was not that woman.

Pierce spoke at length with his father about the impossibility of the situation. Father and son shared a close bond, which had grown even stronger since Maisie had delivered the news of the agreement. Nathaniel saw much of himself in Pierce; they both possessed a quiet temperament, rarely revealing their emotions except in the presence of loved ones. They were critical thinkers, capable of viewing situations from multiple angles and making informed decisions. Self-assured and principled, they both had a stellar moral compass.

The two men differed mainly in appearance. Although they were the same height at six feet, Pierce had a broader build and wore his thick dark hair loose just below his shoulders, complemented by a closely cropped beard and mustache. Nathaniel neatly clubbed his hair, so it skimmed his shoulders. He dressed in British gentry style—breeches, dress shirt, cravat, waistcoat, and stockings, finished with buckle-adorned leather shoes—while Pierce donned the attire of a Highland Scotsman. He wore a great plaid pleated and wrapped as a kilt in the Fraser clan tartan, with excess fabric draped over a saffron shirt and secured with a belt at his waist. The ensemble was completed with woolen knee socks and laced field shoes. With his strapping physique and Scottish regalia, he turned many a young maiden's head.

Nathaniel and Larena sat on the settee in the room eyeing their son as he stood silently, a distant look in his eyes.

"Pierce, are you certain you want to go through with this?" Larena asked.

15

Shaking himself mentally, Pierce nodded with a grim expression.

"I have to. I cannot ruin the Fraser clan's reputation by reneging."

Nathaniel remained silent, merely nodding in acknowledgment. He had spoken privately with Pierce that morning and knew his son planned to proceed with the marriage.

As Pierce prepared to leave to ready himself for the nuptials, Nathaniel said, "Son, if this marriage does not work out, do not stay in it for the sake of the clan or your grandmother. Just ask, and I will be there to help you escape your unhappiness."

Pierce nodded slowly, suppressing the hurt and anger threatening to surface.

"Remember, you should not sacrifice your happiness for the clan or your grandmother," Nathaniel added.

"Thank you. I will remember your promise."

Chapter Three

Landon Estates
Middlesex, England
June 1811
...that same evening

The family listened intently as Pierce recounted the story of what his grandmother Fraser had done. He paused briefly to look at each of them, gauging their reactions. The forced marriage and duplicity of his grandmother shocked his daughters-in-law. Alex and Christopher shook their heads in disbelief, while Reece frowned.

Christopher was the first to ask a question, directing it to his mother. He had quickly calculated his father's current age and compared it to the years of their parents' marriage.

"Mother, you said Helene and Father wed before you two met," Christopher said.

"That's right," she replied.

Pressing further, he asked, "If Father was twenty-five when he married the Cameron girl, you two have been married barely thirty-five years, and Reece will be turning thirty-five this month. That would mean…"

17

Reece and Alex recognized where Christopher was heading and cut him off. "Chris..." Reece warned.

Christopher's question did not cause Pierce or Alexandra any discomfort. They understood their son's question came from a place of disappointment in learning that his father had been married to someone so quickly before marrying his mother. Once armed with the full set of facts, he would see things differently.

"While I was coming to grips with having to marry Helene in Scotland, your mother had traveled to St. Kitts to stay with her aunt and uncle," Pierce began to explain.

Seizing the opportunity to lighten the mood, Sarah interjected, "Alexandra, that sounds like such an adventure. You must have been so excited."

Alex's wife not only made their son happy, but she brought a brightness and effervescence to the family. She always saw the excitement in life, letting her heart and instincts lead her. She even had a special ability to foretell certain things such as the gender of a baby before it was born. The family saw it firsthand when she predicted her friend's twins' gender and her sister's two children as well.

She complemented Alex perfectly in every way. She was as beautiful on the inside and outside. Tall, statuesque, with golden brown hair, and blue eyes, she turned his head the moment they met.

"Oh it was!" Alexandra exclaimed, her eyes glowing as she recalled those days.

"I convinced my parents to let me accompany my Aunt Annabelle to her home in the Leeward Isles and spend a year there before returning to London for my season."

She explained how she wanted to see life beyond Middlesex and London. Thankfully, neither of her parents arranged their daughters' futures. They wanted them to follow their own pursuits for happiness but tempered with the importance of learning certain cultural and societal norms.

Her mother, Cherisse, saw in her daughter the same hunger to explore she had at that age. Like Alexandra, she did not want her life to be a small box and was fortunate to have those freedoms that led her down a path of happiness and fulfillment.

Landon Estates
Middlesex, England
February 3, 1774

The light blue silk slipper sailed past Penelope Landon's head, narrowly missing her.

"Alexandra, there's no need to be hostile," she said with feigned indignation. "I was simply stating a fact. You have Mummy and Papa wrapped around your little finger. Whatever Alexandra wants, Alexandra gets," she mocked.

Grabbing the other slipper and glowering, Alexandra stopped short of throwing it at her sister but held it threateningly.

"Talk about hypocrisy," she scoffed. "All you have to do is pout those pretty pink lips, and they lay the world before you."

Penelope flounced off the oversized bed in a huff, tossing the slipper into the trunk Alexandra was neatly packing.

"It's not fair that you get to spend a year in a beautiful island paradise while I have to stay in this rainy, dreary countryside learning to stitch, read poetry, and play the harpsichord."

Alexandra's annoyance eased as she felt sorry for her only sibling. A little more than two years separated them in age; she was the oldest, turning nineteen soon, and Penelope, who preferred to be called Penny, had just turned sixteen. Alexandra had endured the same tedious lessons at her sister's age. Their mother touted these as societal necessities for all debutantes of the London *ton*.

"It's not as though I am going alone. Remember, I'm accompanying Aunt Annabelle on her return trip home to St. Kitts. Mummy and Papa only agreed to let me go if I stayed with her and Uncle Chester at their plantation under their supervision."

Never Leave My Arms

Annabelle MacKittrick was their father's younger sister. At thirty-eight, she and her husband, Chester, had relocated from the Middlesex family estate to St. Kitts two years prior. After years of trying to start a family, they finally gave up and made a major life change. Financial opportunities in trade and the year-round warm weather drew them to the tropics.

Once the novelty of their move wore off, Annabelle began to miss her family in England. With her husband Chester's support and insistence, she visited her brother and his family last summer to escape the hottest months of the year on the islands. When Annabelle announced her plan to return to St. Kitts, Alexandra begged her parents to allow her to accompany her aunt. The young woman had never traveled further than London and wanted the opportunity to see more of the world before having her season.

Knowing she needed her mother's support to convince her father, Alexandra grasped Cherisse's hands desperately.

"Oh Mummy, it's only a year."

Cherisse Landon looked at her oldest child sympathetically. Of her two children, Alexandra inherited her excitement and love for adventure. Cherisse had enjoyed her own wanderlust before marrying and starting a family; actually, that was how she met and fell in love with her husband, Brenton.

Trying to make a token effort to dissuade her daughter, Cherisse said, "Alex, St. Kitts is very far away. It's over six weeks at sea, and you know how you are with storms."

While not overly confident in her response, she replied, "Aunt Annabelle says the rainy season doesn't start for another four months. Besides, I have the constitution of a seasoned sailor."

Outwardly, Alexandra portrayed supreme self-assuredness, but inwardly, her anxiety twisted her stomach into knots. Storms had terrified her for as long as she could remember. On countless occasions, she had sought the safety and comfort of her parents' bed while rain, thunder, and lightning

21

rolled across their Middlesex estate. At times, it felt as if the storm would pull the large brick house from its foundation and toss it across the countryside.

Unlike Alexandra, her younger sister reveled in the storms. She would sit in the window seat of her room, watching the lights in the sky dance and flash as the sounds of thunder joined in like a symphony orchestra.

Determined not to let her fears prevent her from experiencing new places and trying new things, Alexandra held her chin up with confidence. Cherisse tried to suppress an admiring smile at her daughter's expressive fortitude. She knew it was an act but would not crush the young girl's efforts. Alexandra sensed that one more nudge would sway her mother to her side. Cherisse lifted her head as her daughter squeezed her hand pleadingly. The beautiful young girl's crystal blue eyes were wide and filled with emotion as she looked expectantly at her mother.

"Please Mummy."

Cherisse could not hold out any longer and slowly nodded.

"I will speak to your father tonight."

She laughed as Alexandra launched herself at her, hugging her tightly and whispering fervently, "Oh thank you Mummy. This means so much."

Pushing her daughter back enough to see her face, Cherisse said firmly, "Your father needs to agree to this as well."

Alexandra had confidence in her mother's ability to convince her father to let her make the trip. Cherisse Landon possessed persuasion skills that rivaled those of any man brokering a business deal. She knew how and when to nudge—a trait Alexandra had inherited from her mother.

Cherisse recognized her daughter's talent for inducing people to do what she wanted from an early age. When silently questioned about her actions by her mother's raised eyebrows, the young girl would shrug her shoulders and say, "I am just presenting opportunities."

Never Leave My Arms

Alexandra was certain her mother could persuade her father. Her parents loved each other deeply, and her father trusted her mother completely. Brenton Landon could not recall a single instance in which his wife's instincts had failed them.

Alexandra's intuition proved correct. The next morning, her mother delivered the exciting news: her father had agreed to the trip.

Penny broke her sister from her thoughts when she plopped down in the window chair and let out a heavy sigh. The younger sibling lightly fingered the hem of her sleeve as she pouted in disappointment.

"You will be gone an entire year, and I will be all alone while you walk barefoot on the beach with the sun in your face, listening to the ocean. It will be so romantic."

The young girl's eyes suddenly widened with excitement as she leaned forward and gushed at Alexandra.

"I'll bet you will meet a handsome man, you both will fall madly in love and he will whisk you away to a private island!"

Alexandra laughed at her younger sister's imagination.

"That sounds exciting, but I plan to spend my time exploring the island and its culture. Besides, having Aunt Annabelle and Uncle Chester as my shadows will make it impossible to be swept away by romance."

Penny eyed her older sister critically. The two resembled each other in height and stature—both petite and slender—but the likeness stopped there. Alexandra favored their mother's light blonde hair and crystal blue eyes, while Penny inherited their father's brown eyes and dark brown hair. It remained unclear where she got her wild imagination.

"Alex I'm telling you, I have a feeling about this trip. Something wonderful awaits you on that island."

Closing the trunk lid and clicking the latch, Alexandra rolled her eyes and let out a sigh of exasperation as she dropped onto the large wooden chest.

23

There was no getting through to her little sister, and she was not going to waste any more time trying.

Alexandra needed to ensure she had packed everything necessary for her trip. As she scanned the room, she took in every detail, committing it to memory. After tonight, it would be a year before she would see it again. Although she would miss her home and family, she wondered excitedly what her aunt and uncle's plantation in St. Kitts would be like. Penny believed they lived in a large thatched hut with monkeys swinging in and out of the windows and colorful birds flying about.

Alexandra found her sister's daydreams amusing.

"Aunt Annabelle says it's a simple plantation home with no animals joining us at the dinner table."

Penny sat in the window chair, quietly watching her sister move slowly around the room, touching each piece of furniture and various mementos. Even though the two bickered, as siblings do, she would miss her sister.

Rising from the chair, she approached Alexandra with her head down and whispered, "A year is an awful long time Alex."

Alexandra smiled warmly and pulled the young girl into a tight embrace. Both sisters' eyes brimmed with tears.

"It will go by fast. You will be busy with your lessons, and before you know it, I will be home," Alexandra said, her emotions surfacing.

Pushing herself slightly away, Penny forced a brave smile.

"Promise to write me weekly and tell me all about the journey and the island?"

A half-laugh, half-sob escaped Alexandra's lips as she placed a loving hand on her sister's soft cheek.

"I will make sure no package ship leaves St. Kitts without a letter from me to you," she promised.

The younger girl nodded, forcing back tears.

"Good. Leave nothing out. I want to know all the details."

Never Leave My Arms

The sisters hugged tightly before bidding each other goodnight.

Early the next morning, Alexandra and her Aunt Annabelle waved from the heavily laden carriage window as it pulled away from the manor. Despite packing lightly, they had four enormous trunks latched onto the top of the carriage behind the driver, along with a cart carrying six more cases.

The frigid February weather made it difficult for her parents and sister to stay outside very long to see them off. Unable to endure the cold for more than a few moments, her parents waved quickly and rushed back inside to warm themselves. Penny, with a heavy blanket wrapped around her shoulders, stood on the stoop in front of the massive wooden entry doors. She refused to return inside until her sister's carriage turned onto the main road and disappeared from sight.

Inside the vehicle, Alexandra and Annabelle chatted incessantly during their two-hour journey to the London docks. Annabelle chuckled at her niece's many questions about the climate, the people, the atmosphere, and her aunt and uncle's home. Although she would never admit it to her sister, Alexandra envisioned the island as primitive as well—just without monkeys hanging from the ceiling.

Before the duo knew it, they had arrived at their destination. The London docks were a flurry of activity, with cargo being loaded and unloaded from countless enormous ships, while sailors and passengers bustled about. In addition to two dozen passengers, their ship carried a load of textiles and supplies to the Leeward Islands.

Alexandra stepped onto the wooden walkway and paused, looking up in wonder at the vessel on which she and her aunt had booked passage. The massive craft had four large masts that jutted skyward so high that she almost tipped backward trying to see the top.

Annabelle smiled at her young niece's excitement. She did not want to dampen that enthusiasm, but their trunks were already being loaded, and it would not be long before they pulled the plank to launch.

25

"It is impressive. Wait until you see the inside," she said, gently urging Alexandra along behind the line of passengers boarding the vessel.

Two weeks into their voyage, Alexandra noticed a distinct change in the weather the further south they sailed. The cold biting winds they had left behind in London had transformed into warm soft breezes.

Shortly after setting sail, Alexandra had found she needed to limit her time above deck due to the freezing winter temperatures. Now, with the milder weather, she could spend most of the day wandering the finely polished wooden deck, laughing at the children playing and watching the crew work the sails as the winds shifted. From time to time, she would stop to admire the dark blue water sliding along the sides of the ship as it cut through the gently rolling sea. Her favorite spot was at the bow, where the southerly breeze and warm sun felt like a soft caress on her face.

As they drew closer to their destination, the captain spotted pirates through his spyglass late one morning off the coast of Tortola. The small island, along with several surrounding ones, had a reputation as a haunt for marauders. Out of an abundance of caution, he instructed the passengers to quickly return to their cabins below deck until the danger had passed, ensuring that they were not followed. It was an exciting and tense two hours before the travelers could return upstairs.

To pass the time, Alexandra brought her journal to document each day. Every night, she recorded her daily experiences, making special note of the pirate ship. *"Penny will love to hear about this,"* she thought to herself with an impish grin.

Never Leave My Arms

St. Kitts
Basseterre
March 18, 1774

Six weeks into their voyage, the duo made port at Basseterre, on the island of St. Kitts. Chester arranged for open-air transport to meet the two women. After loading their trunks into horse-drawn cargo carts, the small caravan set out toward the MacKittrick estate on the other side of the island. The well-worn path the transports traversed ran parallel to the coast, passing clusters of small thatched huts and expanses of sugarcane fields. The further they traveled, the lusher the vegetation became. Periodically, Alexandra spotted turnoffs leading to beautiful, whitewashed plantation-style homes atop small hills overlooking the coast.

As the sun began its descent into the western sky, the carriage turned off the main road onto a winding, well-worn path leading up a small hill. Palm trees and fragrant flowering vegetation lined the drive, obscuring any view of her aunt and uncle's home. A gasp escaped Alexandra's lips as their vehicle suddenly entered a large clearing, revealing a sprawling one-story plantation home.

The covered wooden front porch extended the full length of the expansive house, wrapping around both sides. Colorful flowering plants hung in decorative pots from the roof's edge like jeweled earrings. Wide mahogany stairs led up to the porch and a set of carved doors. Two massive windows flanked either side of the entry, each adorned with wooden shutters folded back to let in air and light.

"It is beautiful," Alexandra breathed in awe.

Uncle Chester and a lovely older native woman, her hair wrapped in an orange and yellow scarf, rushed out the front door to the porch, both smiling brightly.

"Welcome home," Chester said as he made his way down the stairs to greet his wife and niece.

27

Alexandra had not seen Chester since they moved to St. Kitts two years ago. Their relocation to the tropics seemed to have a positive effect on him. She remembered her uncle as polite yet reserved, not one to show his emotions. Time spent in the sun had lightened his thinning brown hair, and his five-and-a-half-foot frame had filled out slightly. Although his appearance had changed little, his face no longer looked drawn or weighed down. Instead, a distinct smile graced his suntanned face, and his eyes sparkled brightly, especially when he looked at his wife.

Though some might characterize the couple as plain, Alexandra would strenuously disagree. While he and Annabelle stood at the same height, her presence transformed him. In her company, the unassuming, middle-aged man shed his unassuming demeanor, radiating a newfound charm that was impossible to ignore. It was as if she unlocked a part of him no one else could touch, and the change was mesmerizing. His posture straightened, his presence grew, and he carried himself with such quiet authority that he seemed taller and more commanding than he truly was. Coupled with the radiance that overtook her from his attention, they made an attractive couple.

Chester and Annabelle MacKittrick shared something very special. Annabelle smiled warmly at her husband; the two celebrated sixteen years of marriage this past year. Their love and adoration for each other shone in their sparkling eyes as he extended his hand to help her alight from the carriage.

Aware of their surrounding audience, he placed a sweet kiss on her cheek.

"It is so good to see you my love," he whispered.

After sixteen years, Chester could still make his wife blush. A slight red stained her cheeks as she dipped her eyes demurely and murmured, "I have missed you as well."

The woman on the porch quickly descended to welcome them, her native accent prominent.

"Mistress Annabelle, da house not been da same since ya left."

Never Leave My Arms

Annabelle hugged the woman tightly.

"Lidy, it is so good to see you and to be home."

Stepping to the side, she gestured toward Alexandra.

"This is my niece, Alexandra."

"Alexandra, this is Lidy. She is our friend and keeper of our home. We were so lucky to have her and her husband join us shortly after our move here," Annabelle said.

Alexandra smiled brightly at the woman and nodded in greeting.

"Tis a pleasure to meet you, Lidy."

The island native appeared to be older than Annabelle, perhaps in her late forties. She had dark skin and exotic hazel brown eyes that slanted upward. The colorful scarf on her head covered most of her hair, but a few strands peeked through, black streaked with light gray.

"It's nice ta finally meet ya, miss," Lidy said brightly. "Ma husband is lendin' a hand to a neighbor. He can't wait ta meet ya."

Before Alexandra could reply, Chester interjected, "Let's not stand out here in the sun. Come inside for refreshments. You both must be parched from the ride."

He grasped Annabelle's hand and tucked it into his bent arm, patting it affectionately as he led her up the front steps.

Lidy slipped her hand into Alexandra's elbow, guiding her behind the couple.

"Ya gonna love ya visit here. Da island is beaut'ful. If ya like, ma daughta', Kishma, can show ya da island. She be bout as old as ya."

"What an excellent idea, Lidy," Annabelle said. Turning to her niece, she went on. "Kishma is a lovely young lady. I will bet you two will become fast friends."

Alexandra's smile brightened. She had initially feared she would be limited to the schedule and social circle of her aunt and uncle, but having

29

the company of someone around her age, particularly a native to the area who could expose her to the culture of the island gave her comfort.

Before entering the large home, she looked back across the lush tropical countryside. Taking a deep breath and exhaling to contain her excitement, she allowed the warm, relaxing island air to envelop her.

"I think I am going to love St. Kitts," she whispered as a smile touched her lips.

Chapter Four

Fort William, Scotland
Pierce and Helene's Wedding Day
March 15, 1774

Cameron and Fraser clan members filled the streets of the small village. The merger of the two families brought close and extended relatives together to celebrate.

The normally wet, and dreary weather held off, but dark ominous clouds loomed, threatening torrential rains at any moment. Larena took that as a sign this day should not be happening.

Pierce led the procession to the large stone church flanked by his father and mother. He walked stoically toward the minister set to perform the marriage ceremony, his expression indecipherable. Dressed in his finest traditional regalia, he presented an exceptionally handsome figure.

Two women followed behind the groom, scattering flower petals from their baskets for Helene to walk on. Unlike the groom, the bride wore a warm smile, her eyes glistening with emotion when she glanced at the crowd cheering for the couple. As she neared the church, she spotted Robbie Clyne standing in the back, behind her mother and grandfather. Her smile

31

brightened when their eyes met. Those watching attributed her radiant expression to her family, unaware of the man standing behind them.

The young bride looked lovely in a soft tan V-neck muslin gown adorned with light blue vertical lines woven into the fabric, complemented by a sheer ivory embroidered overlay that fell three inches shy of the ground, exposing her buckled shoes. The accompanying jacket featured a shawl collar that draped over her shoulders and wrapped around her bosom, secured with a large cameo. She tied a matching fabric band with a large bow around her head, keeping her curly brown tresses away from her face. Her mother and grandfather smiled proudly at her beauty and poise.

As his bride took her place on his left, Pierce briefly glanced down at her, their eyes locking for a few seconds. Although he maintained a stoic expression, he noted a flicker in her eyes that he could not identify, causing momentary unease. Shaking it off, he gave her a curt nod and turned his attention back to the clergyman.

They each spoke their wedding vows—Pierce's voice deep and emotionless, Helene's quiet and barely audible. Once their pledges were complete, family and friends followed the couple into the church for the blessing, then made their way to a close relative of Helene's grandfather's estate for the marriage celebration and bedding ceremony. Unbeknownst to all, including Helene, Pierce had decided to deviate from the day's plans. He had other intentions.

When they arrived at the estate, Pierce assisted Helene from the carriage, guiding her into the home with his hand on the small of her back. Upon entering the great hall, he asked his parents to stand off to the side, and they complied. Larena dabbed at the tears filling her eyes while Nathaniel watched his son intently. Pierce left Helene next to his parents while he sought out his grandmother who was conversing with Helene's mother and grandfather.

"Grandmother, I need a word with you," Pierce said.

Never Leave My Arms

Maisie glanced at her grandson briefly, replying absently, "Later. The celebration will start any moment now."

Except for the tick in his chiseled jaw, Pierce remained outwardly emotionless, but his tone indicated he would not be dismissed.

"Now Grandmother. This cannot wait."

Maisie's eyes widened at her grandson's demeanor and tone. Her first instinct was to reprimand him, but she thought better of it, considering the stakes.

Smiling brightly, she conceded, "Of course lad."

Pierce gestured for her to follow him to the study and motioned for his parents to accompany them, leaving Helene with her mother and grandfather.

Once ensconced in the room, Larena and Maisie looked at Pierce questioningly, while Nathaniel's expression remained flat.

"Lad, what is this all about? We have guests waiting for us," his grandmother asked impatiently.

Pierce looked down at her, his eyes burning with anger.

"Did Angus Cameron sign the agreement for Fraser Shipping?"

Maisie gave her grandson a blank expression.

"Aye," she replied slowly. "I have it here in my bag."

"I would like to see it," Pierce said firmly.

Uncertain about his insistence, she retrieved the parchment and handed it to him. Pierce read through the neatly handwritten document and noted the signatures of Angus and Maisie at the bottom. Nodding, he folded the agreement and tucked it into a pocket he had sewn into his plaid. Turning his attention back to his grandmother, he removed another parchment and laid it open on the desk for her to see. Picking up the quill, he dipped it in ink and handed it to her.

"Please sign at the bottom," he said coldly.

33

Maisie's eyes widened and then flared with anger as she read the document:

Assignation of Subjects

Maisie Fraser hereby transfers the full responsibility of operating Fraser Shipping to Pierce Fraser Tennyson. As such, he shall have complete and unrestricted authority to make all decisions for Fraser Shipping, without requirement of consultation, approval, or consent from any other party.

Moreover, upon the seventh day of April, 1779, formal ownership of Fraser Shipping shall transfer exclusively to Pierce Fraser Tennyson in accordance with the dictate of Callum Fraser's testament dated the eighth day of April, 1765. This agreement shall be effective upon execution by all parties.

_____   _____
Pierce Fraser Tennyson   Maisie Fraser

Dated this fifteenth day of March, 1774

"Lad, we don't have to do this now. There is plenty of time later," his grandmother stammered.

Pierce remained calm yet stern.

"Either you sign this now, or I leave without Helene, and there will be no marriage."

His grandmother looked at him incredulously. The implications of his threat would devastate not only Fraser Shipping but also Clan Fraser's reputation. Anger filled her eyes at her grandson's impertinence. Unable to direct her frustration at Pierce for fear he would follow through with his threat, she glared at her son-in-law.

"You put him up to this, you—"

Pierce sharply cut off his grandmother.

Never Leave My Arms

"This is my doing. Leave them out of this."

Blustering and muttering, the old woman yanked the pen from her grandson's hand and signed the agreement.

Pierce had his parents sign as witnesses to ensure she could not recant or claim the signature was a forgery. Once the ink dried, he folded the document carefully and placed it with the other agreement in his plaid. Opening the door, he gestured for his grandmother and parents to return to the grand entry.

Larena tried to make eye contact with her son as they walked down the hall, but he stared straight ahead with a stern expression. Maisie would not look back at Pierce; her frustration was too great. Nathaniel followed the three in silence.

Once in the main hall, Pierce approached Helene and pulled her aside.

"Quickly pack a week's worth of clothing. I will arrange for all your belongings to be sent to our new home."

Helene's eyes widened in surprise.

"Where are we going? Why do we have to leave now?" she asked loudly enough for those around them to hear.

The room fell silent.

Undaunted, Pierce looked directly at her. He did not love her, and she did not love him; to celebrate would be hypocritical.

"The pact required us to marry. We have done so. Now it is time to leave. Collect your things and return within the next thirty minutes."

Maisie and Helene's mother stepped forward to interject heatedly.

"You cannot leave now. There is to be a celebration and the bedding tradition."

Pierce turned toward both women, his jaw ticking and eyes burning with anger.

"I will not engage in such falsehoods. You three got what you wanted. Be thankful and let it be."

Helene remained rooted in place, her eyes wide and uncertain, tears welling up. She did not know what to do. She had assumed they would settle near her home; now it seemed Pierce had different plans.

Sensing her apprehension, Pierce said calmly, "If you refuse to leave with me, the pact will be void."

She looked fearfully between her grandfather and mother for guidance.

Her mother turned on Pierce.

"You would shame my daughter by not having the bedding confirmation?"

Nathaniel stepped up and placed his hand on his son's shoulder. Though his outward demeanor exhibited control, he felt the tension in Pierce's body. It was all he could do to tame his anger.

"Son, you must concede on this."

Pierce took a deep breath and gave his father a curt nod.

"We will stay tonight at Castle Stuart in Inverness. Two representatives may travel behind us and collect the bedding to bring back."

"That is outrageous," Helene's grandfather barked.

Giving him a steely glare, Pierce looked down at the old man, his voice crisp.

"That is my offer. It is up to you and your granddaughter. If you do not accept, the marriage contract will be void."

Helene's mother and grandfather exchanged looks of disbelief. They had no bargaining power. Supporting Helene to stay and forcing Pierce's hand, risked disgracing Clan Cameron and igniting a potential war with Clan Fraser.

Maisie glared accusingly at Nathaniel and Larena but remained silent.

Helene looked beseechingly at her mother, but the older woman shook her head.

"Do as he says lass. Gather your things."

"But I do not want to leave. I want to stay," Helene cried.

Never Leave My Arms

"Gather your things, Helene, and be quick about it," her mother said sharply.

A sob escaped the young bride's lips as she fled from the great hall, racing up the stairs to the living quarters to collect her belongings.

Enroute to Inverness
...immediately following the wedding

The trip to Inverness took six hours by carriage. Pierce only allowed one stop at a small inn to switch out the horses and to purchase bread, cheese, and meat for the remainder of the journey. The newlyweds barely spoke during the trip. Helene kept glancing back, anxiously searching for her grandfather's representatives, but they were nowhere to be found.

"Their carriage may have thrown a wheel. Perhaps we should go back and look for them," Helene suggested, dabbing at her reddened eyes.

Pierce stared stoically out the window, watching the rolling green hills pass and replied absently, "That is their problem."

Out of the corner of his eye, Pierce caught a flicker of anger cross Helene's face before she quickly returned to her sweet, demure demeanor. He attributed it to her frustration at being denied her wedding celebration and the uncertainty of traveling so far from home. However, he suspected Robbie Clyne was an important factor.

If confronted, she would deny it, but Pierce knew from the glances the two exchanged in the great hall after their arrival from the church that there was something between them. He secretly hoped that implementing his plan would force her hand, prompting her to break the marriage bonds and return to her clan and Robbie. Thus far, she had shown no wavering.

Several times, Helene pleaded with Pierce to turn around to look for her grandfather's representatives, but he refused to deviate from his plan—a plan he had only shared with his father. He insisted on keeping his mother in the dark, not wanting her to lie to Maisie if pressed for details.

Nathaniel waited until his and Larena's carriage had departed from the estate before beginning to explain, but his wife interrupted him.

"Nathaniel, what just happened?" Larena asked incredulously.

Never Leave My Arms

Nathaniel squeezed her hand comfortingly and spoke in a hushed tone. "This is what our son wanted."

He recounted how he and Pierce had spoken in the days following Maisie's announcement about the arranged marriage. Pierce recognized his grandmother's actions as a manipulation to keep him in Scotland and away from his father and paternal heritage.

Much to Nathaniel's surprise, Pierce had known for years that Maisie and Callum wanted him to turn his back on his father's British ancestry.

"They had pressured him to make Scotland his permanent home for as long as he could remember," Nathaniel said.

As their grandson matured, Callum and Maisie sensed their efforts were failing. They could see Pierce's eagerness to return to Gloucester at summer's end to be with his parents. Realizing they had to do something drastic to ensure their grandson would remain in Scotland, they hatched their plan.

The older couple believed that promising their grandson Fraser Shipping and tethering it to an alliance with the Cameron Clan through a marriage treaty would ensure his full devotion to Scotland and Clan Fraser. However, they underestimated him. Pierce had no desire to turn his back on his father or his English roots.

Just as Callum and Maisie had devised a plan to manipulate Pierce, he had also crafted one to turn the tables. He saw the marriage through and used the leverage of breaking the union to secure his grandmother's agreement to turn over the running of Fraser Shipping without interference. He also codified his right to ownership once he reached thirty years old, as promised to him by his grandfather.

"Pierce plans to move the Fraser Shipping offices to London and settle there," Nathaniel said.

39

Once Maisie had signed over the company operations to Pierce, he could do as he pleased, which did not include celebrating a marriage he did not want, or making Scotland his home.

Pierce set his plan in motion once the documents were signed. Inverness was the first stop, where Fraser's ships, not currently trading, await him before heading to their new base in London. He had already secured shipping offices and slips on the Thames.

The newlyweds are to stay the night in Inverness and then leave at first light leading the fleet to London. The arrangements were all made before Pierce and his parents left London for Fort William.

"It will initially look to Maisie as though he is moving to Fraser Clan land to settle. By the time she returns to her home in Inverness and realizes what has happened, it will be too late," Nathaniel said.

Larena sat silently, absorbing what she had witnessed and what her husband had told her. She knew her mother would be furious not only about Fraser Shipping's relocation to London but also about losing her grandson. Surprisingly, she felt a sense of pride in Pierce's actions. Maisie's own grandson had outmaneuvered her.

"We are to meet Pierce and Helene in Inverness and sail together," Nathaniel said. Continuing, "His friend, Alasdair Tweedie, arranged rooms at Castle Stuart for all of us. He has worked quietly within Fraser Shipping to help our son prepare for the move."

Squeezing her husband's hand, Larena nodded.

"Alasdair and Pierce have been as close as brothers. I trust him implicitly."

Nathaniel agreed.

"Alasdair is a good man. He felt Maisie and Callum did Pierce a great injustice and wanted to help his friend in any way possible."

Placing his arm lovingly across Larena's shoulder, he pulled her close.

Never Leave My Arms

"Try to relax. We have a long journey to Inverness. Hopefully, we will arrive shortly after Pierce and Helene."

Larena nodded and snuggled into her husband's side.

Unlike his parents' carriage, the temperature in Pierce and Helene's was much chillier. Helene tried to convince him to turn around several times, believing something had happened to her grandfather's representatives and that they needed help. Pierce remained unyielding.

"It is not my responsibility to see to their welfare," he said.

Tears filled Helene's eyes, and as she sniffed, Pierce let out an exasperated breath, dropped his head back, and closed his eyes to shut her out.

From the moment they met, he noted how she could weep on cue, then stop just as quickly. He had felt an unsettling sense of unease about Helene Cameron from their first encounter, and it had intensified every meeting thereafter. He hoped that when she realized they would not be returning from London, she would annul the marriage and set him free.

Realizing her tearful efforts were getting her nowhere, Helene turned away from her husband in a huff and glared out the window. She had tried everything to slow the trip to Inverness. She knew Robbie and his cousin Thane had volunteered to make the journey so they could put their own plan into motion.

As she went over the specifics in her head, a wicked smile touched her lips at the thought of deviating slightly from their strategy. While the pair's plan did not include her fulfilling the marriage bed obligation, Helene had other ideas.

The thought of lying with Pierce Tennyson sent a tingle through her entire body. There was something intoxicating about him. She wondered what his touch and taste would feel like. A man with such a powerful body and intensity had to be a great lover.

41

Before discovering the betrothal, she had given herself to Robbie, but always took precautions to ensure a child did not result. She justified her recklessness by believing they would eventually wed. The betrothal to Pierce changed everything.

Helene panicked. She needed to prove her chastity at the bedding ritual, not only to Pierce but also to her grandfather. Her mother knew of her dalliances with Robbie and helped her contrive a way to conceal her lack of purity.

She suggested Helene ply Pierce with as much liquor as possible until he becomes intoxicated. Then, she should discreetly leave a small amount of goat's blood on the sheets and him after he falls asleep. When he awakens the next morning, sees the blood, he will be none the wiser.

Helene decided to follow her mother's advice but use sedative herbs in his drink as well. She could not count on the fact he would consume enough brew to reach a level of intoxication. Between the two, she should be successful in rendering him unconscious. Once he passed out, she could follow her mother's suggestion, strip down to her shift, lay next to him, and await Robbie and his cousin to collect the linens. On the off chance he woke before they arrived, Pierce would see the evidence of her innocence.

Hopefully, he would not regain consciousness before Robbie and Thane's arrival. If so, that would hamper their ability to carry out their plan. They needed Pierce to be incapacitated so they could tie him up and dispose of him in the icy waters of Moray Firth. The three would then return to Fort William with the tragic tale that Pierce had imbibed to excess and wandered off near the water, fell in, and drowned. Helene would play the role of the grieving newlywed widow and claim Pierce's wealth, freeing her to marry Robbie after a brief, respectable period of mourning.

So lost in her thoughts, Helene did not realize the carriage had stopped until Pierce opened the door. As she mentally shook herself, she espied the remnants of the setting sun over her husband's shoulder. She reached out her hand for Pierce to assist her from the vehicle. He took it without hesitation and nodded gentlemanly as she stepped down.

Helene immediately looked around the large circular drive and saw no other carriages. She craned her neck to look down the long, empty, tree-lined road, neither seeing nor hearing any sound of other arriving transports. Turning with a questioning look, an older gentleman rushed from the front door to welcome the young couple.

"Welcome to ya, Mr. Tennyson," the cherub-faced Scotsman said. "Hope ya trip wasn't too taxing."

For the first time that day, Pierce smiled genuinely and shook the man's hand.

"Not at all Lachlan. We made excellent time."

"Wonderful to hear, sir. Me and the wife 'ave everythin' ready for ya two."

Helene's anxiety rose, and she looked questioningly at the Scotsman. "Are we the only ones here?"

"No lass. There is another couple here as well," he replied.

A flicker of annoyance crossed Helene's face. It did not go unnoticed by Pierce. Initially, he assumed her anxiety over her grandfather's delegates failing to keep up with them was simply virginal nervousness. However, he could not reconcile that with her irritation, which raised his suspicions.

Helene needed to stall a bit longer. Looking at her husband, she said demurely, "I am hungry. Might we have a nice supper after such a long ride?"

Pierce stared at her with an emotionless expression, trying to determine if she was sincerely hungry or if this was part of her manipulation. That uneasy feeling he experienced when with her never left him. Giving her the benefit of the doubt, he conceded to the request. Truth be told, he had an appetite as well.

Nodding, he said, "Certainly."

Looking to Lachlan, the older Scotsman beamed brightly.

"There is a fresh pot of stew and warm bread in the kitchen. Come inside and me and the wife will get ya settled."

Chapter Five

Inverness, Scotland
The Castle at Moray Firth
Pierce and Helene's Wedding Night
March 15, 1774

Even though the castle had fallen on hard times after the English war, it still exuded warmth and charm. The drawing room featured a massive fireplace, with the owner's coat of arms molded into the brick above the mantel. Costly furnishings placed strategically throughout the spacious room created a cozy atmosphere.

"'Tis beautiful," Helene breathed in awe.

Lachlan beamed with pride at the compliment.

"Thank ya, lass. My missus and staff work 'ard to keep things shinin'."

He gestured for the young couple to follow him into the dining room. The wall lanterns cast a warm yellow glow, highlighting the pristinely polished mahogany walls and the tapestries hung upon them. A heavy wooden table with twenty high-back chairs occupied the center of the room, resting atop a deep red rug.

A young maid hurriedly cleared the empty dishes left by the previous diners. When she looked up and saw Pierce, her face flushed scarlet; she had never encountered such a strapping, handsome man. Her perfect white teeth appeared as his eyes locked onto hers. Dropping her gaze, she mumbled an apology for taking so long and quickly exited the room, the dishes rattling in her wake.

As the maid departed, Helene's gaze followed her with an unmistakable hateful gleam in her eyes. She had not immediately realized that Pierce was observing her reaction to the girl, but she quickly lowered her head when she caught him looking at her. Although he maintained a carefully schooled expression, he knew in that moment that Helene was not someone he could trust.

Pierce pulled out a large dining chair and offered it to her. After she sat down, he took the seat across the table. The two barely spoke during their supper. While Pierce devoured two helpings of the delicious stew and bread, Helene ate only a spoonful or two, pushing the rest around her plate. She frowned as she contemplated her situation. Robbie had not arrived, and no opportunity had arisen for her to lace Pierce's drink with the sedative herbs.

Noticing her lack of appetite, Pierce asked, "Does it not taste good?"

Coming back to reality, she shook her head. "No. 'Tis delicious. I would just like some wine to help me relax. Perhaps you could find Lachlan and ask him for some?"

Pierce studied her for a moment before rising silently and disappearing down the hallway where Lachlan and the serving maid had gone. Wasting no time, Helene retrieved the herbs from the pouch tied to the inside of her skirt and sprinkled a generous amount into what remained of his stew. She stirred them into the mixture and quickly returned to her seat.

Seconds later, Pierce emerged from the hall with a long-stemmed crystal glass of wine in his hand. He set the drink in front of her and returned to his seat to finish his dinner. As she brought the rim of the vessel to her lips, she watched with hooded eyes as Pierce tore off a piece of bread and dipped it into the stew. A brief smile touched her lips as he shoved the bread into his mouth. After consuming the remainder of his meal, Pierce took a draught of his ale.

A frown appeared on his brow as he paused to listen.

"Sounds like more company is coming," he said.

Helene's face lit up. She jumped from her seat and rushed through the dining and drawing rooms to the front door. Although darkness had fallen, the lanterns flanking the entrance cast enough light to see down the front drive. Her shoulders slumped in disappointment when she saw Lachlan in a cart hauling firewood.

The older man spotted Helene and smiled brightly.

"Ev'nin, lass."

Helene managed a weak smile and half-heartedly waved before returning to the dining room, where she found her new husband pushing his empty bowl of food away.

After wiping his face with his napkin, Pierce stood and looked questioningly at her.

"Was it them?"

"No," she mumbled. "Twas Lachlan bringing in firewood."

"If you are done with your supper, we can retire to the room. Our bags are there."

Pierce stood next to her expectantly, hand extended. As she slipped her hand into his, an unexpected excitement surged through her. Surprised by her reaction, she glanced at him to see if he felt the same. Pierce's expression remained stoic, as it had throughout the day.

Helene allowed him to guide her down the red and green tartan carpet that lined the hallway to their room. The more she thought about Robbie and Thane abandoning her, the more annoyed she became. She had done everything to slow Pierce down so the two men could keep up, yet they had not arrived. There was no way she could see their plan through alone; she needed to rethink her strategy.

As she entered the small room and spotted the large, canopied bed, she clung to the hope that the herbs would take effect soon and that Robbie and Thane would arrive before dawn. Helene caught the first sign of success when Pierce yawned.

After closing the door, he casually commented, "Lachlan's wife arranged for you to have what you need to freshen up in that small chamber by the window."

While not overly spacious, the quaint room smelled of beeswax. A polished four-poster, fabric-draped bed sat across from the door on the far wall. Mahogany wood panels reached halfway up each wall. Two winged chairs with a small table and lantern sat underneath a set of windows overlooking a courtyard two floors below.

Pierce opened the window to let in the fresh air while Helene set her bag on one chair and removed her nightdress. Without looking at him, she turned and disappeared into the bathing chamber, quietly closing the door behind her. She let out a sigh of relief as she pressed her back against the door.

Distracted, Pierce inhaled the slight breeze of the night air to clear his head and called out to Helene, "I will be back shortly."

He heard her soft voice through the wooden chamber door respond, "Don't be long."

Pierce raised an eyebrow at her reply, then shook it off as he quietly left their room in search of Lachlan.

Helene pressed her ear to the bathing chamber door and sighed when she heard Pierce leave. It would not be long before he returned, expecting them to share the marriage bed. She nervously bit her nail as her mind raced. The herbs seemed ineffective at sedating him, and any attempts to delay their intimacy would raise Pierce's suspicions. She frowned sharply at the thought that Robbie and Thane had left her to handle the situation alone.

"It would serve Robbie right if I lay with Pierce Tennyson tonight," she thought. *"After all, what else can I do if the herbs do not work?"*

Never Leave My Arms

The more Helene considered it, the more excited she became at the prospect of sharing a marriage bed with such a virile man as Pierce Tennyson. Why not? If Robbie loved her as much as he claimed, he would never have let things get this far. She could play the inexperienced virgin for her husband, and she had the vial of goat's blood to conceal her lack of chastity and cover her deception.

The opening of the room door abruptly shook Helene from her thoughts. A small gasp escaped her lips as she realized she had not prepared herself for Pierce's return. She had hesitated too long about what to do. She now faced a decision: should she walk out of the chamber to tell Pierce she wanted to break the marriage pact and return home shamed and empty-handed, or should she go through with the consummation deception and hope Robbie and Thane arrived before dawn?

Pierce closed the door louder than he intended when he returned to the room. His head spun as he made his way to the edge of the bed to release his belt and unwrap his plaid from his shoulder and chest. The dim light made it difficult for him to focus. He shook his head sharply, trying to clear the sudden fog that had overtaken him. Pushing himself to his feet, he approached the side of the bed and removed his kilt. As he began unbuttoning his shirt, his arms grew weak, and he struggled to hold his head up. Darkness overtook him, and he fell back onto the bed.

Through flashes of light, Pierce saw Helene's face above him and heard her voice, though he could not make out her words. He tried to open his eyes but could not. Then darkness surrounded him again. Moments later, the sensation of soft hands running up and down his chest and abdomen heightened his senses, teasing him out of the blackness. His body instinctively responded to the stimulation. He desperately tried to reach the surface but fell back into darkness.

It felt like a dream when he heard Helene's voice whispering softly in his ear. Suddenly, his body tensed as he felt the pressure of his arousal invading her. For a few seconds, he found the strength to open his eyes and saw Helene sitting atop him; her head thrown back and her mouth slightly open, soft moans escaping her lips as she rode him. Pierce lacked the power to surface. His body went rigid as the urgency to release built, and the blood in his brain pulsed with intensity. Suddenly, he reached his peak. An uncontrollable shudder wracked his body as he reached his apex, sending him back into darkness.

Sometime later, Pierce slowly opened his eyes. Although he did not know how, he lay alone in bed, still wearing only his shirt. Glancing towards the window, he saw darkness outside with no sign of dawn. He must have been unconscious for a short time. Looking around the room, he did not see Helene.

Never Leave My Arms

Frowning, he carefully swung his legs over the side and sat for a moment on the edge collecting himself. He then donned his kilt, quickly pleating it and securing it with the belt. A sound from the closed bathing chamber caught his attention. As he walked around the bed to knock on the door, he espied the rumpled linens. The bright red specks of blood caught his eye. His scowl deepened, and when he reached to inspect the linen more closely, his foot struck something lying beneath the scattered bedding on the floor. Looking down, he pushed the fabric aside for a better view. A small empty vial with a string attached to a wooden stopper lay near the leg.

Still battling fogginess, Pierce sat down in the chair by the window to mentally gather himself. The small lantern on the side table burned low but cast enough brightness for him to examine the vial closely. He blinked to focus as he held it to the light. His brows drew down in a deep scowl, and his jaw began to tick. The vial contained blood.

Helene duped him. She must have slipped something into his stew or ale at dinner. Taking several deep breaths from the fresh air coming through the window, he steadied himself enough to finish dressing. He carefully secured the small stopper and concealed the vial in the sleeve of his shirt before he approached the bathing chamber door. Although outwardly he appeared calm, inwardly a furnace of anger ignited within him.

From the moment he met Helene, he had felt an unease but could never define its source. Her lack of chastity did not bother him as much as her blatant duplicity and attempt to possibly poison him. There was no way he would or could continue this farce of a marriage.

As he raised his hand to knock, Helene opened the chamber door, wearing her shift and a bright smile on her face. Her expression quickly turned to shock when she saw Pierce standing in front of her, filling the doorway. Recovering quickly, she smiled sweetly and brushed past him into the room, needing to put space between them.

51

Laughing nervously, she quipped, "I see you are awake. That ale must have been stronger than you realized."

Pierce did not make it easy for her. Although a fire raged within him, his expression remained bland. She shifted nervously as he approached her, pinning her with his eyes as he towered over her.

His voice was deadly calm.

"The ale was fine. Twas what you put in it."

Helene looked up at him and swallowed the lump in her throat. Stammering, she tried to explain.

"I, I, I don't know what you are talking about."

Pierce cut her off and demanded, "Why? Why the ruse?"

Helene's mind raced frantically. She had no idea the herbs would wear off so quickly. She should have taken into account Pierce's size and added more. Drawing deeply from her acting abilities, she looked at him pleadingly, her eyes filled with tears.

"I have never been with a man and was not ready to be your wife in that way. So, I thought we could wait one more night. I believed the herbs would help you sleep through the night, and when you awoke and saw the blood, you would think we had consummated our marriage."

She dropped her head in shame, unable to look at him.

He had to give it to her, Helene had a gift for telling tall tales convincingly. However, Pierce knew she had outright lied to him. Playing along, he gently lifted her chin with his finger until their eyes met. His expression remained unreadable, and the fire in his eyes had disappeared. Helene felt a sense of hope, believing he had bought her story.

"So, you are saying we did not consummate our marriage tonight?" he asked gently.

Unable to speak, Helene slowly nodded.

"And to cover that up, you put the blood on the sheets to lead me to believe we had?"

Never Leave My Arms

Still silent, Helene nodded.

"Did you know that the herbs you gave me put me into a sleep, but I was fully aware of everything that was being done to my body?"

Helene's eyes widened, and she jerked her chin from his hand.

Grabbing her roughly by the arm, he pulled her toward the bed, pointing at the linens.

"There is more than goat's blood on those coverings," he ground out in anger.

Helene tried to pull free, but Pierce was relentless.

"You say you have never been with a man. I saw you astride me, riding me in wanton abandon. You are a liar."

His last words struck a chord, and for the first time, Pierce saw the true Helene. She jerked free of his grip, stormed around the bed, and whirled to face him, fire blazing in her eyes and a sneer on her lips. She no longer looked like the sweet Scottish maid he had married less than a day ago.

"That's right. You are not my first. I was trying to protect myself from being shamed before my family and clan," she retorted.

Whether she was chaste mattered little to Pierce. His issue lay with her deception and drugging him to carry out her falsehood.

"If you deceived me about this, what else are you holding back?" he demanded.

Helene's mind raced. Robbie and Thane still had not arrived. If Pierce ended the pact and exposed what she had done, she would lose everything and become an outcast in her clan. She needed to change her tactic. Recovering her emotions, she schooled her features and returned to the sweet Scottish maid. Although he did not show it, Pierce wanted to applaud her acting abilities. She even squeezed out some tears as she looked up at him.

53

"Pierce, please forgive me. I am holding nothing more back from you. You know my secret, and I was wrong to withhold the truth from you. I am sorry. Can you ever forgive me?"

Pierce remained silent for a moment as he looked into his wife's eyes. Hope swelled within Helene as each second ticked by. She thought his silence meant he believed her story. Regrettably for her, she had misjudged her ability to manipulate him. He dashed her overconfidence with his reply.

"I cannot be in a marriage where there is no trust or love. We will leave within the hour to return to Fort William. Upon our arrival, you will tell them you have reconsidered and want to annul the marriage. If you do not agree to this, I will expose your deception. Do I make myself clear?"

Pierce frowned as Helene smiled brightly. The last thing he expected was acceptance.

"Perfectly," she said.

No sooner had he said, "Good," than Pierce's world went dark.

Robbie and Thane had arrived, striking the Scotsman about the back of his head and rendering him unconscious.

Robbie smirked as he looked down at the large Highlander out cold on the floor. Thane quickly shut the door to avoid drawing attention at the early hour.

"Where have you two been?" Helene snapped at the two men.

"We ran into trouble with a wheel on our carriage," Robbie said.

While Thane worked to collect the bedding and tie Pierce's hands, legs and feet, Robbie stepped over the unconscious Scot to reach Helene. His eyes burned with desire as he scanned every inch of her. She looked wanton with her hair loose about her shoulders, dressed only in her shift and barefoot. He stepped in close and slid his hands softly up her bare arms. Just as he bent to kiss her lips, he caught sight of specks of blood and Pierce's seed on the rumpled linens. Lifting his brow, he looked at Helene questioningly. Her face flamed scarlet.

Never Leave My Arms

"I tried to hold him off until you arrived," she stammered. "Robbie, the herbs didn't work well. I had no choice," she insisted.

Robbie was the one person Helene could never manipulate; he always saw through her lies. Helene's mouth went dry as his eyes bore into her. She struggled to find the words to assuage Robbie's growing ire.

Fumbling, she managed to croak out, "His excitement was so great…"

Her words trailed off as his expression turned thunderous. Instantly, Robbie turned on her.

"You willingly spread yourself for this man, didn't you?"

Before she could respond, he grabbed her roughly by the arm and pulled her close, his face inches from hers. The tears welling in her eyes had no effect on him. He knew her too well. She lied to suit her own purposes.

He knew he was not her first, even though she claimed such. She had an insatiable appetite for carnal pleasure. He thought he fulfilled those desires and even supported the celibacy she insisted upon once her family announced the pact. She did not want to take any chances to get with child before marrying Pierce. Apparently, he was wrong.

A blinding rage washed over him when she failed to answer. He knew she had done what he suspected. He slapped her viciously across the face. Helene fell to the floor, her lip split and bloody from the blow.

Thane, quickly stepped in to cool Robbie's temper.

"Come on, man, you don't want to wake anyone with the noise. We need to get to the Firth," he said in a hushed tone.

Robbie reined in his anger and nodded. He decided to deal with Helene later. He roughly pulled her from the floor by her arm and shoved her toward the bed.

Tossing a leather satchel on it, he snarled, "Put those linens in that, and when I signal you from below, drop it out the window to me."

A sob escaped her bloodied lip as she reached for the bag, her hands shaking.

55

Robbie approached her from behind and leaned over her shoulder, whispering dangerously in her ear.

"No delays. You follow the plan. Wait until sunrise to report him missing. Do you understand?"

Helene kept her head down and nodded.

Before walking away, he added, "When you get back, you will tell them he became drunk and beat you."

Robbie and Thane hurriedly rolled Pierce into the horse blanket they had brought and hefted him on their shoulders. The two men grunted and struggled with their burden as they carried the large Highlander down the narrow service entrance stairs to their waiting carriage. Both men breathed a sigh of relief as they roughly dumped Pierce onto the floor of the vehicle. Robbie stepped under the window of their room and let out a soft whistle. On cue, Helene appeared and dropped the leather satchel to him.

"We need to make haste to the Firth. Dawn will come soon," Robbie said.

They needed to be rid of Pierce and well on the road back to Fort William before daybreak to stick to their plan.

"Aye," Thane agreed with a nod.

The two set the carriage in motion and, at breakneck speed, reached the docks in less than a half hour. Between the swiftness of the horses and the roughness of the road, the carriage pitched and shifted, causing Pierce to bounce sharply. Thane checked to ensure he was still unconscious.

"Easy Robbie. Don't want to wake the giant," he said with a laugh.

Once they reached the docks, Robbie slowly steered the transport between a collection of stacked wooden crates near a ship anchored at the first slip. Due to the early hour, no one stirred about. However, once dawn broke, the area would buzz with activity. They needed to dispose of Pierce quickly and be on their way.

Robbie slipped from the carriage and crouched down, moving among the cargo cases to find an opening to put Pierce in the water. He decided on a gap between the two ships moored in the last two slips. The freight awaiting loading provided ample cover to get an unconscious Pierce out of the carriage and drop him into the water. The two men grunted and gasped as they struggled to get him onto the dock.

Before rolling him into the water, Thane looked tentatively at Robbie.

"Are you certain you want to do this?" he whispered.

Robbie nodded.

Then, quietly, the two cousins pushed Pierce into the icy Firth. The cloudless night sky, combined with the full moon, cast a soft white glow over the area, providing enough light for the two men to watch Pierce's body sink below the surface into the murky water.

The sound of someone moving nearby caught the men's attention; they did not want to be discovered. When the faint sound of melodic whistling drifted through the air, it spurred the two kidnappers to hurry back to the carriage.

Before snapping the reins, Robbie said cruelly, "'Tis done. Now we head back to Fort William so Helene can claim our inheritance."

Chapter Six

The Docks @ Moray Firth
March 16, 1774
...early morning hours

The rapid sound of horse hooves interrupted Alasdair Tweedie's whistling. The ship's mate could not sleep. He decided to venture out on deck for some fresh air. Alasdair worked on the largest vessel in the Fraser fleet, the Saltire Wind.

Six of the twelve vessels were docked, awaiting cargo loading at sunrise. They were to set sail to London initially and then on to port assignments in France and Italy. The Saltire's passengers included Pierce, his new bride, and his parents.

Although Alasdair was six years older than Pierce, the two men shared a close friendship forged through sailing. They had developed a brotherly bond when Pierce visited Scotland every summer. Physically, they were opposites: Alasdair was short and stocky, with unruly red hair and a long, shaggy beard, while Pierce towered over him by eight inches, fit and athletic, with long, thick, dark hair and a closely cropped beard and moustache. Alasdair's most charming quality was the constant twinkle in his eyes and the slight grin that gave the impression he carried a secret, in contrast to Pierce's unreadable and often brooding expressions.

Never Leave My Arms

Alasdair had spent a few more years at sea with Fraser Shipping than his friend. When Pierce was old enough, his grandfather Callum, took him under his wing to teach him about the business side of the shipping industry, a role Pierce embraced quickly. Before long, he and Callum were running the most successful shipping enterprise in Scotland. In addition to learning management, Pierce frequently sailed and became a skilled sailor. It was no surprise when Alasdair learned Pierce's grandparents chose to gift him the company.

In just a few short hours, Alasdair and Pierce would see each other for the first time in over two years. While Alasdair's life had remained constant. Pierce's had changed significantly this year. He was now newly married and preparing to move the Fraser Shipping lines from Inverness to London, seemingly eager to leave Scotland behind.

A thumping noise from the side of the ship interrupted Alasdair's thoughts. Leaning over the rail, he initially thought it was loose rigging banging against the wooden shiplap. Dawn had not yet broken, and the fog thickened the air, obscuring his vision. As he focused on the noise, he realized it was a steady, insistent thump, not a natural sound or rigging swaying in the breeze. Squinting, he leaned further over the rail and spotted something in the water below, near the ship in the slip next to the Saltire Wind. At first, he couldn't discern what it was, but as the ship shifted with the lapping waves, his breath caught, and he swore aloud. It was a man.

Alasdair quickly made his way below deck and woke one of his mates.

"'Tis a man overboard. Follow me," he said.

The two rushed across the gangplank. Halfway down, they spotted their target, his arm draped over a wooden pylon. The sailors tossed a rope to the man, who fed it over his head and around his chest, allowing Alasdair and his shipmate to pull him to the edge of the dock and haul him onto the decking.

When Alasdair saw the man's face, he gasped.

59

"Good lord, 'tis Captain Tennyson."

Despite the blow to his head and the lingering effects of the herbs, Pierce recognized Alasdair's voice.

Shaking violently from the frigid waters, his voice raspy, he asked, "Al, can you help me get up and onboard?"

In short order, both sailors helped Pierce to his feet, their shoulders under his arms, and brought him onto the ship, settling him into his cabin.

Before stripping off his drenched clothing and offering an explanation, Pierce downed a draught of whiskey to warm himself and ease his pounding head. Meanwhile, Alasdair lit two small heaters and retrieved a blanket for Pierce to wrap himself in. Once Pierce's focus returned, he quickly scribbled something on a piece of parchment, rolled it up, and handed it to Alasdair to take to Lachlan at the castle. Before leaving his cabin, he swore Alasdair and the shipmate to silence about finding him.

While Alasdair took care of the task, Pierce changed out of his soggy clothes into a robe. Thankfully, they had found him next to the Fraser ship he, his new wife, and parents were to travel on to London. Three days ago, they had brought aboard his and his parents' trunks, while Helene's were scheduled to arrive that morning. As he pulled off his shirt, he felt something in his sleeve: it was Helene's small vial, still intact. After tying off his robe, he slipped the little bottle into his pocket and poured himself a small amount of whiskey to warm himself as he awaited Alasdair's return.

The trusted sailor rode at breakneck speed to the castle, following Pierce's explicit instructions. He quickly returned to the ship as the eastern sky began to lighten. Pierce opened the door to find his father standing in the doorway, relief evident on his face. Nathaniel grabbed his son by the shoulders, concern etched across his features as he looked him over from head to toe.

Pierce sighed.

"I am fine. I have a knot on my skull, but I am fine."

Never Leave My Arms

Nathaniel let out a breath of relief and pulled his son into a tight bear hug. "Thank the lord."

Pierce poured drinks for himself and his father, and they sat at a small table. Nathaniel listened intently as Pierce recounted the events of the day after leaving Helene's grandfather's estate. Omitting the intimate details while under the influence of the herbs, he explained how Helene had concealed her lack of chastity, handing his father the vial as proof.

"I do not know who struck me from behind, but my guess would be Robbie Clyne," Pierce said, swirling the amber liquor in his glass.

Nathaniel gave his son a questioning look.

"How do you want to handle this?"

"Helene believes I am dead. She does not know you and Mother are at the castle. I never shared my future plans with her. I did not trust her, and for good reason," Pierce replied.

Nathaniel nodded, sharing his reservations about Helene and her suitability.

Pierce continued.

"I am glad I gave you the packet last night at the castle with the agreements signed by grandmother and Helene's grandfather. If Robbie or Helene had gotten their hands on them, it would have been disastrous."

He unrolled two pieces of parchment and handed them to his father. One document was a power of attorney designating Nathaniel as Pierce's representative in securing an annulment of his marriage to Helene. The second was a letter to Helene reiterating what he had told her after discovering her deception, stating he had instructed his father to release it to Helene's grandfather and mother if she did not agree to the dissolution. For good measure, he also gave Nathaniel the small vial for proof if needed. Nathaniel understood his son's wishes and agreed without question to follow them.

"Son what are your plans for now?" his father asked.

61

"I need some time away. As you know, this entire fleet, including this ship, are to sail to their new home in London today. I would like to make my stop brief and head out to sea. I hope you can get things set up for me at the office, and I will take over when I return."

Although his expression didn't show it, Nathaniel smiled inwardly. His mother-in-law would be furious when she discovered Fraser Shipping's headquarters were in London and her English son-in-law was heading up operations.

"Whatever you need son. Your mother and I will be there for you."

They embraced before Nathaniel set out for his return to the castle.

Prior to entering his carriage, he turned to his son.

"Where can I reach you? I presume you will want to know what transpired with Helene and the annulment outcome."

Pierce paused for a moment as he mulled over the question.

"I was thinking of somewhere in the Leeward Islands with a stop in France on the way."

Nathaniel offered a suggestion.

"I have a business associate in St. Kitts--Chester MacKittrick. He is always sending your mother and me invitations to visit his plantation. He says it's beautiful."

Pierce nodded.

"That is where you can reach me."

Nathaniel smiled brightly.

"Splendid. I will get word to him straight away."

Chapter Seven

Landon Estates
Middlesex, England
June 1811
...later that evening

Pierce rubbed the back of his neck, trying to ease the nagging ache that had developed. He had not realized how draining dredging up those old memories would be. Alexandra gently touched his forearm, sensing the difficulty her husband faced while reliving the past. Her eyes were soft and filled with emotion.

"It is late. Let's adjourn for the night and pick this up tomorrow after dinner," she suggested.

The rest of the family immediately agreed.

"Yes, that sounds like a wonderful idea," Kat said.

Although Reece remained quiet and stoic as his father shared his story, she could tell that certain moments, especially those involving Helene and Robbie, angered him. She hoped that once they were alone in their room, he would want to open up to her about his feelings on the matter.

Sarah and Alex echoed Kat's sentiment. They could see how deeply these memories hurt Pierce and did not want to burden him any further for the night.

"It has been a long day for everyone. A good night's sleep will do wonders," Sarah added.

Christopher surprised them all when he rose and approached his father. Pierce stood at his desk, looking at his son questioningly. He sensed something had shifted in his youngest son, though he couldn't pinpoint what. Without warning, he pulled his father into a tight embrace.

"Father, I am sorry for what they did to you." Pierce returned the embrace, his eyes moistening with emotion.

"Thank you son."

Alexandra pressed her lips together, desperately trying to maintain her composure. A silent tear slid down Sarah's cheek, while Kat, her eyes filled with compassion, smiled warmly as the group witnessed the moving exchange. Alex and Reece looked away, trying not to let their own emotions overwhelm them.

As father and son released each other, Christopher turned his face to hide the tears filling his eyes. He gave his mother a quick kiss on the cheek and slipped out the side door of the study, mumbling, "Goodnight," to his brothers and sisters-in-law. The remaining family members quietly left the study, making their way to their rooms.

Pierce and Alexandra knew that what they had disclosed this evening would be a topic of discussion for their sons and wives once they reached the privacy of their rooms. They were thankful that Reece and Alex had wonderful partners to lean on for support. Alexandra, however, worried about Christopher. She knew he would likely seek the comfort and quiet of the stable, checking on the horses as he considered what he had learned.

Never Leave My Arms

As expected, the youngest Tennyson son did just that. He sought the solitude and comfort of the quiet, cool night. Christopher needed to clear his head and regain control of his emotions.

The crunching of stones beneath his boots broke through the night's silence as he made his way down the path to the forward stables. While Reece found fulfillment in running Fraser Shipping and Alex enjoyed the business side of the thoroughbred farm, Christopher found joy and solace working with horses.

An hour passed as he walked from stall to stall, checking on each horse. The smell of fresh hay wafted throughout the barn, adding a soothing quality to the air. His father's story replayed in his mind.

Initially, when the family sat down in the study and his father revealed that he had been married before his mother, Christopher became angry. He felt betrayed that neither his father nor his mother had shared such an important piece of information with him and his brothers.

Learning about his father's struggles and the angst of having his life decided for him brought a lump to Christopher's throat. He could never imagine his parents doing such a thing to him and his brothers.

Letting out a sigh, Christopher dropped the wooden plank in place across the barn door and pressed his forehead to the cool wood. He closed his eyes and sent up a silent prayer for his parents, particularly his father, before pushing himself away to make the short walk back to the rear of the manor. With each step, he hoped that whatever the family was yet to learn tomorrow evening would not be as shocking as what his parents had revealed tonight.

Kat and Reece retired to their bed after ensuring their two children were fast asleep. Landon slept soundly in the nursery next door while Alison drifted off after Kat fed her and laid her down for the night in the bedside bassinet.

Kat climbed into their large bed. Reece had propped pillows behind him to cushion his back against the wooden headboard. He had been quiet all

65

evening, even since returning to their room. She could tell from the distant look in his eyes that what he had learned tonight deeply affected him.

Reece looked over at his wife. She sat with her legs folded underneath her, dressed in a soft yellow muslin nightdress that complemented the amber flecks in her eyes. Her shiny raven-black hair flowed about her shoulders and down her back to her waist. She smiled warmly and placed her hand over his as he gently stroked her cheek. Slipping his hand into hers, he pulled her forward to sit next to him and wrapped his arm around her.

The two sat in silence. Reece was not ready to talk, and she would not push. Kat laced her fingers through his and placed her head on his shoulder, knowing he needed time to digest what he had learned. Reece felt grateful for his wife's understanding and compassion. Although he had come far in learning to express his feelings thanks to her efforts, he still needed time to sort things out before he could discuss them.

He kissed her gently on the forehead and squeezed her hand as a sign of appreciation. Within minutes, he could hear Kat's soft, slow breathing. A smile played on his lips at the thought of his wife falling asleep in his arms. It was at least two hours later when Reece finally found his own slumber.

In the opposite wing, Sarah and Alex returned to their room. The children's nanny had left when the couple arrived. Alex looked in on their daughter asleep down the hall while Sarah checked on their son in his nursery next door. A loving smile spread across Sarah's lips as she gazed at the sleeping toddler in his bassinet. She placed a soft kiss on his forehead before slipping from the room, keeping the door ajar to ensure she could hear him if he awoke during the night.

While the couple readied themselves for bed, Alex broached the events of the evening.

"You know my parents have made cryptic comments over the years about their ability to keep secrets, and I wonder if what we learned tonight is what they were referencing," Alex mused.

Never Leave My Arms

Sarah sat at the dressing table brushing out her long, light golden-brown hair and smiled at her husband through his reflection in the mirror.

"It just may be, but that is a big secret to keep for so many years."

The young couple continued the conversation once they had settled into bed for the night. Alex explained how he recalled his father being estranged from his great-grandmother, Maisie.

"He didn't always embrace his Scottish heritage."

Sarah looked at Alex in surprise.

There was a time in Alex's childhood when his father turned his back on it. He vividly remembered when Maisie came for one particular visit. Alex snuck down the hall to the top of the grand staircase and overheard his great-grandmother arguing with his grandmother, Larena, and his father. He couldn't recall the details of the argument, but Maisie's visits always created discord with Pierce.

Then one day, Pierce received word that Maisie was gravely ill. He made the trip to Scotland to see her. Alexandra and their sons remained in England while Pierce journeyed north to Inverness. When he returned home, he had donned traditional Highlander regalia and had worn it ever since.

"My father stayed with Maisie during her last days. I presumed he made peace with her and wore it to honor her and my great-grandfather's memories," Alex said.

Sarah inhaled sharply and looked at Alex with wide, anxious eyes.

"You said they've made comments in the past about keeping secrets—as in multiple. Do you think there are more surprises to come?"

"Knowing them, it would not shock me," Alex replied with a nod.

Meanwhile, in Alexandra and Pierce's wing, the older Tennysons' nightly ritual was less chatty. Quietly closing the door to their suite, Alexandra paused, taking in the sight of her strappingly handsome husband. He stood silently at their large four-poster bed, his broad back to her, lost in thought.

67

After all their years together, Alexandra knew the source of her husband's silence. She stepped around him, drawing his attention, and slipped her arms around his waist, pulling him close. Resting her chin on his broad chest, she looked up, her eyes filled with emotion.

"Luv, Christopher will be fine. He has never been one to let things weigh him down. When the time is right, he will want to talk, and it will be with you."

Gazing down at his wife, he gave her an appreciative smile and squeezed her affectionately. She always knew what he was thinking and what he needed to hear. Pierce knew his life began the day he let Alexandra into his heart.

"As always, you are right," he said, his eyes taking on a familiar hunger as he admired her beauty.

"Just remember that," she said jokingly as she tried to pull away.

Drawing her back, he wrapped his arms around her. Alexandra looked up into his face and could see his desire as his lips formed a seductive smile, revealing an unspoken need in his eyes.

"I thought you were tired," she said.

As he lowered his lips to claim hers, he whispered, "I am never too tired to feel you."

Neither could explain it. Perhaps it was unearthing the ghosts of their past or the memories that made the years fall away, but a raging fire ignited, burning as hot as their first night as lovers. Sweeping Alexandra into his arms, he laid her down on their soft bed, ravaging her lips with demanding kisses as they each pulled at each other's clothing, fervently trying to feel the other's skin.

She threw propriety out the window, yanking the bodice of her gown and quickly popping the fasteners in the back to release the garment and expose her breasts. Pierce didn't give her a chance to push the dress down before he began a steady assault on each orb, kneading and suckling while she arched against him.

Once free of her clothing, she made quick work of pulling his shirt over his head and releasing his kilt, tossing the plaid aside as she reached for his engorged manhood. Pierce's body stiffened the moment he felt her warm, soft hand around his shaft and let out a groan. A smile of satisfaction flitted across her lips just before he captured them in a hungry kiss and pushed her back on the bed, covering her with his body.

Slipping her arms around his neck, she whispered seductively, "Can I lead?"

Letting out a playful growl, he replied as he entered her swiftly, "Only if you let me get you seated properly."

Alexandra's eyes flared with excitement at his invasion. Pierce planted himself deep inside her and rolled onto his back, bringing her with him. As she sat up astride him, he released her hair clips, allowing her silver-blonde hair to spill down her shoulders. He watched in fascination as his wife began a slow, undulating dance, her mouth partially open, and eyes deep pools of passion. She transformed into a seductive, uninhibited goddess before him, moving her hips back and forth, gasping and moaning softly while riding his erection. When he felt her body tighten around his member and her pace quicken, he instinctively grabbed her waist to slow her.

Then, placing his hands on either side of her face, they stared deeply into each other's eyes; no words were exchanged between them. Beyond the raw passion and excitement, they saw their love for one another. Overcome, tears welled up in Alexandra's eyes, and his glistened with emotion as well. He knew it was her love and devotion that healed his wounds of the past.

He pulled her in for a deep kiss and then growled, "I will take over the rest of the ride."

Even though he was in his very early sixties, Pierce Tennyson's physique had aged very little. He worked side-by-side with his sons daily at Landon

Stables exercising the thoroughbreds. Alexandra loved the feel of his taught, defined muscles, especially when they were wrapped around her.

Taken by surprise, she let out a gasp when, without breaking their connection, he rolled her onto her back, pinning her beneath him. Holding himself above her, he paused for a moment to take in her beauty. Her silver-golden hair spread out around her head and shoulders, framing her flawless oval face, flushed from their passion.

The tightening of her sheath around his arousal abruptly returned him to the moment, and a quick glance at Alexandra's full lips, bruised from their kisses, hinted at an impish smile. Realizing her game, Pierce gave her an equally mischievous grin as he set out to play along.

The cords of his neck bulged, and the muscles in his chest and arms rippled as he began a steady, seductive rhythm of driving deeply into her and creating friction by grinding against her womanly nub. As she squirmed beneath him, and lifted her hips to take him fully, he would withdraw his hard shaft to the edge of her womanly core and start the sweet ecstasy all over again. It drove her mad with frustration.

When Alexandra led the ride, she had control. Beneath him, her husband determined the speed and knew just the right tempo to bring her to the edge and then pull her back. She lifted her hips to meet his thrusts and pulled at his shoulders, silently begging him to increase the intensity, but he refused for as long as he could.

Finally, unable to hold back, he did as she asked and pushed her swiftly to her apex. The feel of her soft, satiny pouch contracting around his manhood brought about his own climax, and his body shuddered as he found his release.

Never Leave My Arms

Collapsing next to her, Pierce pulled her to his side, her hand resting on his chest and her head on his shoulder. It took some time for their world to right itself as they lay physically and emotionally exhausted in each other's arms.

Landon Estates
Middlesex, England
June 1811
...the next day

The day began like any other, and the family went about their respective plans and duties. Breakfast and dinner conversations revolved around mundane or benign topics, mostly led by Alex and Christopher about stable business and the horses in the presence of the children.

An unspoken agreement among the adults ensured that anything discussed the previous night in the study would remain there and not be rehashed with young ears in close proximity.

After dinner, the two young couples entrusted their children to their nannies for bedtime, and the family gathered once again in Pierce's study. Everyone reclaimed their seats from the previous night and settled in, eager to hear more.

Pierce leaned against his desk, hands braced along either side and faced the group. Alexandra seated herself beside him. Once again, Christopher sat by the door, away from the rest of the group. Alexandra had hoped their youngest son would be more receptive tonight, but he remained withdrawn and quiet.

The rest of the family patiently waited to hear what had transpired after Pierce decided to journey to St. Kitts and have his father deal with securing the annulment. Not wanting to delay further, he cleared his throat to capture his family's attention.

Looking among their faces, he said, "When we left off last night, Alasdair and I were preparing to set sail for the Leeward Islands."

However, before he could continue, Alex interrupted.

"What happened to Helene when Nathaniel returned to the castle? Did she admit what she and Robbie had contrived?"

Never Leave My Arms

Pierce had planned to address that part of the story later, when he received word from his father while in St. Kitts, but seeing the eagerness on their faces, he decided it wouldn't hurt to share it now.

Elizabeth H. Franklin

Inverness, Scotland
Castle Stuart @ Sunrise
Pierce and Helene's Room
March 16, 1774

Shock registered on Helene's face when she opened the door to find Nathaniel Tennyson standing in the doorway. She had never expected to come face-to-face with him today, the day after marrying his son, especially six hours away from Fort William. Her new father-in-law's presence made her uneasy, but she forced a smile.

"Good morning, Mr. Tennyson. What a lovely surprise. Pierce didn't mention you would stop by. I was just about to look for him. He left before dawn to go for a walk and has not returned. I am starting to worry."

Adept at concealing his emotions, Nathaniel remained stoic. However, an alarm went off inside him when he noticed her black eye and split lip. Helene shifted uncomfortably under his unyielding gaze, realizing where Pierce inherited his ability to be unreadable.

Attempting to engage him, she ventured sweetly, "Have you seen Pierce this morning? Is he well?"

Nathaniel took close note of her reaction as he replied.

"Actually, yes. I saw Pierce this morning, and he asked me to come here."

Helene's face turned ashen, and her jaw slackened. She shook herself mentally and placed her hand dramatically over her chest.

Feigning relief, she said, "Oh, I'm so glad. I was getting worried."

Looking beyond Nathaniel towards the hallway, she asked, "Is he far behind you?"

Nathaniel had to give Helene credit; she had a talent for acting.

Nathaniel cleared his throat.

"No. Pierce is not coming back. May I come in? What I have to discuss with you should not be done in the halls."

74

Never Leave My Arms

Despite a pit forming in her stomach, Helene stepped aside to let her father-in-law into the room. He turned as she was about to close the door.

"Helene, please leave it open."

Confused, she complied.

"I do not understand. You say Pierce is not coming back. What does that mean? Has something happened to him?"

Nathaniel paused before answering.

"Before I explain why I am here, what happened to your face?"

The blunt question took Helene by surprise, and she realized she needed to be careful with her response. Robbie had told her to use her injuries against Pierce when she returned to Fort William. If she admitted to Nathaniel that Robbie had hurt her, the chances of her playing the victim would be dashed. Conversely, if she claimed Pierce had beaten her as Robbie suggested, Nathaniel would likely call her a liar. She had to tread carefully.

Turning her face away in embarrassment, she clasped her hands tightly to her chest. Miraculously, tears filled her eyes.

"He didn't mean it. It was the ale. We quarreled, and he insisted on leaving. When I grabbed his arm to beg him to stay, he flung me off and struck my face."

By the time she finished her tale, she was sobbing. Her performance did not faze Nathaniel; he knew his son. No matter how angry or frustrated, Pierce would never lay a hand on a woman, intentional or accidental, regardless of how much ale he consumed.

Helene's sobs ceased when Nathaniel simply said, "I see."

Her demeanor quickly shifted from devastation to annoyance.

"You don't believe me?"

No longer hiding his feelings, Nathaniel pinned her with a piercing glare.

"No I do not. They pulled my son from the Firth before dawn, alive, with a knot on the back of his head. And before you attempt to act your way out

75

of this, claiming ignorance or some deep devotion to Pierce, let me stop you."

Nathaniel released the anger he had held in since discovering that his son had nearly been murdered at the hands of this conniving woman. Helene stood wide-eyed as he revealed that he knew about her deception and nefarious plan with Robbie and Thane to murder Pierce so she could lay claim as his heir.

Without giving her a chance to defend herself, he continued, insisting she would return to Fort William with him and Larena, where she would release Pierce from their marriage pact and grant him an annulment. If she refused, Nathaniel planned to expose her trickery, which would shame her before her family and clan, resulting in her being cast out.

"Your two cohorts should have kept their mouths shut during the ride from the castle to the Firth. Thanks to their carelessness on the rough road, Pierce regained enough awareness to hear their conversation. He recognized their voices—Robbie and Thane Clyne."

Helene's mind raced as she listened. Pierce hadn't drowned as they had expected, but Nathaniel had no proof of her deception. She could claim that Nathaniel was the one who attacked her when he found out Pierce was missing. A smug smile slowly appeared on her face as she formulated a new plan.

Flouncing onto the end of the bed, she met his look.

"You have no evidence of any such deception. The bedding showing proof of my chastity is on its way back to Fort William as we speak, and the vial that contained the goat's blood is at the bottom of the Firth."

Smoothing her skirt, her voice laced with confidence, she continued.

"No one will believe you because you are not of our kind. In fact, they will easily believe me when I tell them you beat me. You blamed me for your son getting so far into his cups that he stumbled into the water. It is

Never Leave My Arms

well known among the clans that you hate Scots, except for your wife, of course."

Although Helene's quick thinking had helped her manipulate situations in the past, it would not work this time. She did not realize it as Nathaniel walked over to the door and opened it wider. Crossing her arms, she smiled, believing Nathaniel recognized his loss and would leave. Her smile faded when Lachlan and Larena stepped out from either side of the door, having listened to the entire conversation.

The crowning blow came when Nathaniel pulled the small vial containing remnants of the goat's blood from his jacket pocket. He also showed her the parchment Pierce had given him before leaving that morning. It designated Nathaniel as his power of attorney for all his personal and business matters, particularly securing an annulment of his marriage to Helene. Pierce outlined, in graphic detail, the basis for the invalidation of the marriage, citing her deceit regarding her chastity and her culpability in his attempted murder to gain control of his inheritance.

"If you do not break the pact," Nathaniel warned, "I will expose all of this to your family and both clans."

The color drained from Helene's face as her plan disintegrated before her eyes. Pierce and Nathaniel had trapped her in her own lies.

"Collect your things now. We are leaving for Fort William in ten minutes," he said.

Conceding defeat, Helene complied. To ensure she made no effort to flee, Nathaniel instructed Lachlan to bring their carriage around while he and Larena watched over their soon-to-be ex-daughter-in-law pack her belongings. To their surprise, Helene made no effort to delay their departure. In fact, she made haste and the party of three were on their way back to Fort William forthwith.

Throughout the long ride back, Helene sat quietly. Nathaniel could not read minds, but he was sure Helene was plotting lies to avoid the consequences she and Robbie faced for their deceit and crimes.

Chapter Eight

Leeward Islands
Two days away from St. Kitts
Late May 1774

Pierce leaned casually against the ship's rail, soaking in the warm sun and ocean breeze. Nine weeks prior, he had docked briefly in London after leaving Scotland. He wanted to ensure the Fraser vessels arrived safely at their new home and to load his ship with cargo for a stop in France before continuing to St. Kitts.

His childhood friend, Llewelyn Greene, the son of the Tennyson family steward, had asked to join him on the voyage. Larena and Nathaniel thought it a splendid idea and arranged for the young man to meet Pierce's ship at the new Fraser Shipping docks. Greene and Pierce were close in age and had grown up together, forging a strong bond.

Greene's father had shared with him what Pierce endured while in Scotland, and he wanted to provide his friend with support. Seeing Greene cross the gangplank brought a broad smile to Pierce's face. The two men embraced heartily when he reached the main deck.

"'Tis wonderful to see you," Pierce said.

Although his expression did not show it, Greene noted that Pierce no longer dressed in his usual Scottish regalia. Instead of a kilt and plaid, he wore black fitted breeches with knee-high leather boots, a cream-colored muslin shirt open at the neck, and his long hair clubbed with a leather tie. Strap a saber to his belt, and he could have been mistaken for a pirate.

"I almost did not recognize you for a moment," Greene said.

The young Brit was a man of few words. Some who did not know him might say he came across as a snob due to his dry reserve, but Pierce knew the true Greene—a fiercely loyal lifelong friend.

Pierce took it in stride, smiling.

"Thought I would give the look of an English countryman a try to see how it feels."

Greene nodded in appreciation.

"You wear it well."

Pierce clapped his friend on the shoulder and laughed.

"Come along. I want to introduce you to a good friend, Alasdair Tweedie."

Greene and Alasdair were complete opposites, their very presence serving to juxtapose one another. Alasdair, short and stocky, with a distinct Scottish brogue and unruly red hair, had eyes that twinkled with mischief, and his gregarious personality made it difficult not to like him. In contrast, Greene was a stoic, tall, medium-built Englishman with a stiff British mien and a meticulously polished appearance. His dark, neatly combed back hair, tucked behind his ears, skimmed his shoulders. No one could characterize him as a dandy. Rather, his dark brown eyes gave nothing away and seemed to penetrate one's soul with silent judgment. Outside the presence of those who knew him best, he exuded an unnerving ability to intimidate.

Before turning south, Pierce took a detour to France to pick up his first mate, Nials Bissette, in Bordeaux. Nials and Pierce's friendship dated back to their mid-teens in Scotland when the young Frenchman worked his way onto one of the Fraser Ships heading to Marseilles, France. Pierce's grandfather had brought him along for the journey. The two teens bonded instantly.

Over the years, they remained in close contact, their paths crossing periodically. When Pierce decided to move Fraser Shipping to London, he knew he needed to be surrounded by reliable people such as Greene and Alasdair—Nials was also part of that group.

In short order, the four men forged a camaraderie as they set out on the journey to the Leeward Islands. Their voyage was not without its challenges. Once their ship cleared the northern Atlantic and turned toward the islands, they entered dangerous waters. Pirate ships preyed on vessels, lying in wait at smaller, less inhabited land masses.

The marauders searched to raid merchant vessels enroute to the Leeward Islands as the channel became narrower. The sea criminals concealed their boats in small coves and before their prey knew it, they would attack with no opportunity to prepare a defense. Most pirates simply relieved ships of their cargo and departed. However, some would seize the entire ship, tossing crew members overboard or killing those who refused to join them.

They were less than two days out from reaching St. Kitts when Pierce and his friends faced such an encounter as their ship reached the Greater Antilles. Inclement weather forced them to take a circuitous route around several islands west of the Bahamas which set them behind slightly.

Dawn had broken two hours prior as their ship cut through the blue water, quietly passing between two land masses. The small waves shimmered as the warm morning sun caught the tips of the water. Unbeknownst to Pierce, one island served as the base for a particularly well-known criminal and her small crew. As the Fraser merchant craft rounded the bend of the cay, a pirate ship greeted them in the center of the channel, its cannons pointed directly at them.

Pierce stood at the helm with Nials, Greene, and Alasdair, training the spyglass on the bandits. As Pierce shifted his view along their main deck, he counted at least a dozen sailors. His brows drew together in confusion as he surveyed the group; there was something different about them.

He pulled the piece away and blinked several times to refocus his vision. Putting the magnifier back to his eye, he could hardly believe what he saw. Scanning the bridge, he glimpsed the captain at the wheel. There was no doubt—standing at the helm was a woman, garbed in breeches with cuffed, knee-high boots, a shirt open at the neck, wearing a leather vest, and a cutlass tucked into her belt. She stared boldly back at him through her own spyglass.

The sailors on deck were also women. Like the captain, they wore pants but of varying lengths, long shirts, and what appeared to be ill-fitted men's jackets, along with different styles of hats and scarves to conceal their hair.

"You will not believe this," Pierce said, shaking his head.

He handed the magnifier to his Scottish friend.

"Here. Have a look."

Alasdair looked quizzically at Pierce but complied. As he placed the instrument to his eye, he let out a gasp.

"Glory be! 'Tis a bunch of women," he exclaimed.

Greene looked at the Scotsman skeptically. He took the spyglass from Alasdair's hand and looked for himself. His left brow instantly shot up when he espied the female pirate at the wheel. Even from a distance, he noted her womanly shape. The hat she wore hid most of her dark auburn hair, except for the waist-length thick braid draped over her shoulder.

Both Pierce and Alasdair noted that their proper British friend was taking an inordinate amount of time looking through the magnifier. Although Greene possessed the innate ability to maintain an unflappable affect, his companions noted a fleeting grin appeared on his face as he surveyed the ship's captain. Alasdair tried to conceal a smirk while Pierce cleared his throat to gain his friend's attention.

Never Leave My Arms

"I think we should find out what they would like from us," he said, trying to hide the smile on his face.

He turned to Greene and asked, "Don't you agree?"

Returning to his proper and stiff British mien, Greene gave a quick nod. Unbeknownst to the female marauders, Pierce had planned for such an encounter. He knew the dangers of pirates, particularly in warmer waters.

Years ago, brigands had seized two Fraser ships during voyages to France. They lost their vessels and cargo, and in one case, an entire crew perished. Shortly after these incidents, his grandfather acquired the ship they were currently sailing to the Caribbean from an old friend.

Although in a dilapidated state and modified from its original use as a cargo carrier, Pierce and his grandfather discovered that the previous owner had fitted it for weaponry. Callum saw it as a stroke of luck. He and Pierce worked with the shipbuilder to install concealed cannons on each side of the craft. By the time the thieves got close to the boat, it would be too late for them to realize their peril. This ship, full of women pirates, was about to discover they had picked the wrong vessel to rob.

Pierce ordered the crew to lower the masts as he slowly turned starboard and dropped anchor, wanting to ensure he had a clear shot at the marauders once he gave the order to fire. Meanwhile, Alasdair ran the white flag up to signal their acquiescence while Pierce had some crew members lower the skiff to row out to their ship.

"Nials, you take the wheel," Pierce ordered.

Carefully turning his head away from the view of the pirates in case they were looking through their spyglass and adept at reading lips, he said to Alasdair, . "You go below and wait for the signal to open the cannon doors."

"Aye," Alasdair said before making his way from the helm to the main deck.

83

Pierce, Greene and two Fraser crew members pulled their oars silently through the water in dance-like unison, propelling the small wooden skiff toward the pirate vessel. Pierce had brought Greene and two of his men with him to meet the thieves. Nials, Alasdair, and the remaining thirty member crew were left onboard to follow his orders should he signal things were becoming dicey aboard the pirate ship. He and Greene would board while the two crew would remain in small craft.

Six deckhands, their sabers drawn, greeted the two men as they easily climbed the rope and pulled themselves over the rail. Pierce scanned the assembly of female bandits, raising an eyebrow when he noticed the captain was not among them.

Fixing his hazel-green eyes on the tallest and possibly youngest woman, he demanded, "Where is your captain?"

The shortest among them, not quite five feet tall with a stocky build and fiery red hair, spoke up first. She wore baggy brown burlap pants tucked into low-cuffed boots that pointed at the toes, and a red striped shirt opened at the neck, exposing the tops of her large, swaying breasts. A wide, tightly cinched leather strap highlighted her narrow waist and ample hips. An overly long saber dangled from her waistband, dragging on the deck, and a badly aged tricorn sat atop her cropped locks.

"If'n ya want ta know sumtin, ya speak ta me, gov'na," she snapped.

Initially, Pierce looked around to locate the source of the surly voice, taking two glances before pinpointing it behind two deckhands. Comical surprise flickered on both his and Greene's faces as the short, plump female pirate pushed her way between her fellow crew members, glowering at the two men for their slow response to acknowledge her presence. Her head barely reached their shoulders. Quickly regaining his composure, Pierce glared at the irritable pirate.

"And who might you be?" he asked, struggling to keep a straight face.

Never Leave My Arms

Sticking her thumbs into her belt, she rocked back on her heels, critically examining both men. By the time her gaze reached their faces, she had to crane her neck back due to their height. She noted that the brawny man carried himself like a ship's captain, exuding a sense of danger that put her on edge, while his impeccable partner seemed almost bored with the entire situation.

"Name's Bert, and I'm first mate," she snapped irritably, deliberately tugging at the overly long saber in her belt to send a silent message.

Jerking her head toward the crew assembled behind her, she ordered, "You gents will need ta leave your weapons wit the crew here before ya go anywhere."

Pierce stared sharply at the stout pirate for what felt like minutes before slowly removing the large knife from its sheath on his belt. Greene followed suit, placing his weapon in the waiting hand of one of the crew members. Bert looked skeptically between the two men, finding it hard to believe that neither carried any other weapons.

"That be all you carry?" she asked, her eyes narrowed with suspicion.

Neither man intended to reveal that they both had daggers hidden in the calves of their boots.

Pierce raised an eyebrow in feigned indignation and quipped, "Care to have a look for yourself?"

Much to Pierce and Greene's surprise, the first mate's face turned dark red, and she began blustering and coughing as she dropped her head, adjusting the oversized saber for what seemed like the tenth time.

After a moment, she regained her composure and snapped, "Come along."

Taking two steps, she stopped and looked back at Pierce and Greene, warning, "Best mind yourself, or you won't be returning to your ship."

Although their expressions remained passive in response to the threat, Pierce slowly flexed his hands into fists at his sides as his jaw ticked.

85

As the chunky first mate escorted the two guests across the deck to the stairs leading to the helm and captain's quarters, the female crew boldly examined the men from head to toe. Several members gasped, while one let out a whistle of appreciation.

Both Pierce and Greene found it difficult to focus on the sounds around them due to the loud noise of the first mate's oversized saber dragging across the deck and clanking up the stairs. A fleeting smirk crossed Pierce's face as he imagined the first mate cutting her belt off while struggling to pull the saber from it.

When they reached the top deck, the female sailor stopped at a large cargo barrel next to the captain's cabin door. Before knocking for entry, she turned to scratch the head of the most bedraggled creature Pierce and Greene had ever seen. It appeared to have gray tiger markings, with large patches of fur missing, and wore an eyepatch. Both men looked suspiciously at the being, trying to identify it. When it caught sight of the two guests standing next to the first mate, it hissed sharply, providing an answer to their question.

As if the first mate knew what they were thinking, she said sharply, "It's me cat, Precious."

While Pierce said nothing, Greene lifted his British eyebrow in disdain and replied smoothly, "Apropos."

The cantankerous sailor shot the Englishman an annoyed glare.

"He's a friendly puss once he gets to know ya."

Still maintaining his bland demeanor, Greene replied, "But of course."

Scoffing at Greene's tone, she redirected her attention to the closed door of the captain's cabin and rapped sharply.

"Captain. Our company's aboard."

A soft voice from within granted them entry. Pierce noticed Greene's brows furrow fleetingly at the sound of the woman's voice. He quickly masked his surprise with his usual stiff demeanor before the first mate opened the door and stepped aside for the two men to enter.

Never Leave My Arms

As she was about to join them, the captain, standing in the shadows at the far side of the cabin, said, "Bert, I will be fine. Make sure the crew makes room for the new cargo."

The first mate looked confused by her orders. She knew the captain could take care of herself but felt it unwise for her to be alone with these two men. Moreover, she resented not being part of the conversation.

Readjusting her long saber for the umpteenth time, she looked between Greene and Pierce, but directed her comments to the Captain.

"But, Capt'n, are ya sure you don't need me ta keep these two gents in line?"

The captain's voice was firm, leaving no room for argument.

"Bert, take care of the crew. I will be fine."

After a brief nod, the first mate turned and walked out the doorway, grumbling as her long sword scraped on the wood floor while she closed the door behind her.

Pierce and Greene stood just inside, taking in the room. The space ran the entire length of the rear of the ship. Top windows on the back wall illuminated the main area, and the furnishings were well-appointed. For a ship, let alone a pirate vessel, the cabin was spotless and felt warm and welcoming.

A large wooden table with six chairs neatly arranged around it greeted them. To the right, an ornate wooden desk sat at an angle, with maps meticulously stacked in a pile on the corner and a large wooden chair behind it. On the far back wall was an oversized wood-framed bed with a carved headboard, crisp white linens and pillows, and decorative rugs on both sides and along the front. To the left, in the far corner, a folding screen concealed a bathing area.

Breaking the men from their thoughts, the captain stepped out of the shadows.

87

In the many years Pierce had known Greene, he had never witnessed his friend's demeanor as anything other than unflappable. Today, however, for the first time, Pierce saw his friend lose his composure when he came face-to-face with the female captain. Greene took a sharp breath.

"Maury Dresden," he whispered in disbelief.

Never Leave My Arms

"Now that is a name I have not heard in quite some time. Hello, Llewellyn," the Captain said with a smile as she crossed the cabin to the two men.

Pierce looked between his friend and the woman in confusion.

"Greene, you know her?"

Greene could not take his eyes off her.

It was no wonder—the spyglass hadn't done her justice. She was beautiful. Now that she had shed her coat and hat, her femininity was obvious. Tall and statuesque, she appeared to be in her early twenties. Her heart-shaped face was perfect and lightly sun-kissed, with high cheekbones and a patrician nose. Her clothing, unlike her crew's, was made of fine cloth and tailored to fit her athletic frame perfectly. She wore her thick, shiny auburn hair braided into a single plait draped over her right shoulder. Her dark blue eyes sparkled with excitement as she took in Greene from his polished boots to the top of his perfectly coiffed dark head.

"As I live and breathe. 'Tis truly you. I was uncertain if my spyglass was playing tricks on me."

Greene had recovered from the shock but had yet to regain his usual bland affect. Instead, he wore a softened expression as he looked at the beauty before him.

"Maury Dresden. How did you come to be here doing this?"

The Captain laughed softly and gestured to the chairs around the table.

"I go by the name Mame now. Come, sit down. 'Tis a long story. Can I get you two something to drink?"

Pierce finally shook off his confusion.

"Yes. Whiskey."

He needed it after this revelation.

Before Greene could reply, Mame eyed him critically.

"You look like your choice of drink is Scotch."

89

Greene nodded as he pulled out a chair and sat down. His eyes followed the young woman as she moved about the cabin, retrieving three glasses and two bottles of spirits. Both men noted she carried herself with feminine confidence. Rather than straddling her leg over the chair to sit down, she pulled the chair out and slipped into it with decorum. When Mame poured her guests' drinks, she did so slowly, without spilling a drop, and placed the glasses gently in front of them. Clearly, she had been well-groomed in manners.

Notably refusing to call her by her preferred name, Greene looked at her squarely.

"Maury, everyone thought you perished with your mother and sister at sea over seven years ago. How did you survive? How did you come to be here, living this existence?"

Mame stared silently into the glass of amber liquor as she pondered how to explain her life over the past years. Greene remembered her as a sweet teenage girl from an affluent Sussex family. His mother had been Maury and her sister's governess when they were much younger.

She had known him since she was a little girl and he was a young teen. A reflective smile touched her lips as she recalled the crush she had developed on him when she turned twelve and he seventeen. She believed that beneath his intensity and stuffiness lay a man who would protect her with an unwavering ferocity. *"The frivolity of a child's imagination," she thought to herself with a sigh.*

Taking a sip of her whiskey, she returned Greene's penetrating stare without flinching and recounted the details of when and where their ship sank. The sea took her mother and sister because they could not swim. Fortunately, Mame found a piece of debris to cling to.

She explained the aftermath of the wreck.

"A pirate vessel plucked me from the sea. Because I had lost my memory, I could not tell them who I was or where I was from."

Never Leave My Arms

The moment Greene heard who had rescued her, his eyebrows furrowed in a deep scowl. His mind immediately went to the likelihood that she had suffered unspeakable treatment at the hands of her miscreant rescuers. Nothing could have been farther from the truth. Mame reached across the table and placed her hand on his, giving him a reassuring smile.

"The captain was a woman about my mother's age. Her name was and still is Idalia. She took me in and helped me recover my memory."

Greene visibly relaxed, realizing his childhood friend had escaped a terrible fate. However, his curiosity had not yet been quenched.

"When you recovered, why didn't you go home to your father?"

Mame laughed lightly at his question. She could see his initial fear about what might have befallen her being rescued by pirates, but he did not know the true peril that loomed for her back in Sussex: the plan her father had laid out for her future. Mame took another sip of her whiskey to bolster herself before expounding.

"I had lived under the controlling thumb of my father and mother my entire life. My father wanted to marry me off to a wealthy older man I did not love or even like. The only reason he consented to the trip was because I agreed to marry the man when we returned. Once we reached France, I planned to disappear and start my own life, hopefully finding love. I knew I would be miserable if I returned to Sussex."

Greene did not seem to grasp the extent of her unhappiness at home.

"Maury, losing his family devastated your father. Finding out you were still alive would have eased some of his pain."

Mame's softened demeanor slipped as she released a caustic laugh.

"Llewellyn, my father's devastation extended to the loss of a wealthy son-in-law he could sponge off at my expense. The only person he cared about was himself. The one chance I had of finding any happiness was to remain dead."

Greene's expression hardened as he looked at the young woman.

91

"So, you found happiness in thievery?"

Mame did not take offense. She understood why Greene viewed things through a narrow lens. He remembered her as a shy young girl.

"I did what I had to survive and will not apologize to you or anyone else. Unlike some criminals that sail these waters, my crew and I take what we need to feed our people and their families. We don't traffic kidnapped women or kill for sport. You are fortunate you did not come across Lucrete. His base is not far north of us. He is a cruel butcher with a crew that is just as bad. I owe my life to these people. If not for them, I would have died with my mother and sister."

Rising from her seat, Mame stood behind her chair. Pinning Greene with an unwavering glare, she challenged him.

"Instead of castigating me and my crew, perhaps you should take some time from your holiday and see for yourself. Join us on Veilwind, our humble island."

Greene remained silent, staring intensely at her. Satisfied she had given him something to think about, she finally turned her attention to Pierce for the first time since they had entered her cabin.

"Captain, please accept my apologies for not giving you due attention."

Pierce's body tensed immediately. The last thing he wanted was a confrontation with this young woman. Her cannons were aimed at his ship, and while Greene and she had history, he was unsure how she or her crew would react if things turned unpleasant. Pierce held her gaze, his expression unwavering and impenetrable. To set him at ease, Mame softened her demeanor.

"Rest easy Captain. My people need grain and tea. If you have any on board, we will need to relieve you of that supply. After that, you are free to go."

Greene sucked in his breath and looked at her incredulously.

Never Leave My Arms

"Maury, you are stealing from my friend under threat of harm to him, me, the crew, and his ship?"

Mame's brows drew down sharply as she looked between the two men.

"Who has threatened harm to you?"

"The fact you have your cannons trained on my friend's ship to start, and then that cranky first mate of yours made our fate clear when we boarded," Greene retorted sharply.

"First, I have no intention of firing upon your ship. I needed to ensure I had your attention," she replied heatedly. "As for Bert, I will address that right now."

Mame stormed to the cabin door and yanked it open. Stepping outside, she called out sharply, "Bert. Get up here on the double."

While Greene and Pierce could not see what was happening, they both heard loud scraping sounds, accompanied by huffing and grunting. Both men exchanged glances, and Pierce tried to conceal a smirk as he imagined the irritable first mate desperately rushing up the stairs with her overly long heavy saber getting in her way.

Outside, Mame waited patiently as Bert climbed onto the top step outside her cabin door. The short woman held onto the rail until she caught her breath.

"Yes Captain?" she managed to squeak out between gasps.

"Bert, did you threaten our guests?" Mame demanded.

The sailor immediately stammered and nervously shifted her oversized saber.

"Well, ummm, I wouldn't say threatened. I just told them, ummm, the consequences if they tried anything."

Mame crossed her arms and looked down at her admonishingly.

"Bert. We have talked about this before."

The thin-skinned pirate dropped her head in contrition and attempted a weak explanation.

93

"Captain, I was just lookin out fer you and lettin' them know we don't tolerate no funny business. Besides, they didn't seem like they was takin' me serious."

Taking a breath, Mame released some of her annoyance at the sailor.

"Well, Bert, they did."

Although Greene and Pierce could not see the first mate from their vantage point in the cabin, Mame caught the smirk of satisfaction that flickered across her face. It was clear the stout tar took pride in the fact she intimidated the two giants, particularly the snob, Greene. Bert's joy was short-lived when she later learned her captain had issued an invitation to the man to join them on the island.

While Mame and her first mate were outside the cabin, Pierce and Greene remained seated at the table next to each other. Leaning in slightly, Pierce spoke quietly to his friend.

"Greene, we can accommodate her demands. We have plenty of tea and grain to spare. There is no expectation from the MacKittricks that we will bring them supplies. I had them loaded as a courtesy for their hosting us."

Greene seethed. It was difficult to reconcile how the sweet young girl he knew had grown into the leader of a band of thieves. To avoid drawing Mame's attention, he maintained a somber expression and kept his voice low.

"That is not the point. Maury is not only stealing, she is taking it from you, and that I cannot abide."

Pierce nodded, a fleeting grin crossing his face. He appreciated Greene's loyalty and outrage on his behalf but viewed things from a more practical standpoint.

"We have the supplies to spare. Besides, this is not a group of cutthroats. They are a crew of women just looking to survive."

Before Greene could respond, Pierce's tone brooked no argument.

Never Leave My Arms

"We will give them the tea and grain and be on our way. I want to get to St. Kitts by noon tomorrow."

Recognizing his friend had made his decision, Greene nodded in understanding. While he knew he could not change Pierce's mind, he could not walk away from Maury without trying to convince her to return to London and leave this life of crime behind her. No sooner had Greene made up his mind than Mame returned to the cabin with a look of satisfaction. Slipping easily into the chair she had momentarily vacated, she looked between Pierce and Greene with an engaging smile.

"I have spoken to my first mate and instructed her that no harm will come to you, your crew, or your ship."

After hearing the captain's reassurances, Pierce pushed himself from the table and stood, his expression guarded. Greene followed suit. While he remembered her as a well-bred young girl before this life, he did not know whether, after years at sea raiding ships, her word could be trusted. The telling moment was at hand.

"You are welcome to the load of tea and grain we have," Pierce said cautiously.

Greene remained silent, but his disapproval of Maury's conduct was evident in his glaring eyes.

Mame stood slowly, maintaining eye contact with Pierce, her expression friendly. Reaching across the table, she extended her hand in gratitude. Pierce accepted her gesture, and the two captains shook on the agreement. Not surprising, Pierce noted her grip was firm and confident; not feminine nor timid.

"Thank you Captain. Our small community is eternally grateful for your kindness."

Pierce did not immediately release her hand. Instead, he held her gaze, searching her eyes for something. Mame could see he wrestled with whether to trust her. She tried to assuage his reluctance.

95

"Captain you have my word."

Turning her attention to Greene, she smiled and once again extended the invitation for him to stay.

"Llewelyn, I stand by my offer for you to come with us and see our humble little island. I will ensure you are taken to St. Kitts to reunite with the captain as soon as you wish," she said.

It did not surprise Pierce that his friend accepted the offer. He could tell Greene felt an obligation to turn the female captain away from her life of crime.

Seething inwardly, he stared into the eyes of the shy young girl he once knew that had fallen away from civilized society.

"I accept."

Mame took no offense at Greene's demeanor. She had always known him to be stoic. Beneath that emotionless facade, she believed an intensity existed. Perhaps during his stay, he might allow his guard to drop, and she could glimpse what lay beneath.

Mame presented him with a beautiful white smile.

"Splendid. Shall we arrange to transfer the cargo, and then our respective ships can be on their way?"

Pierce nodded and the two men silently left the captain's cabin, making their way down to the skiff to return to the Saltire Wind.

In an uncharacteristic moment, Greene wore his infuriation openly but remained silent until they were out of earshot.

Once certain they could not hear him, he unleashed his annoyance.

"I cannot believe the unmitigated gall of stealing from you knowing that you are my friend."

The irritation in his voice turned to melancholy.

"Maury Dresden was one of the sweetest young ladies my mother ever mentored. How she could turn to a life of crime and thievery, in spite of her father's plans, is unfathomable to me."

Never Leave My Arms

Pierce had never seen this side of his friend. Greene always kept his feelings undetectable. Clearly, Maury Dresden had struck a nerve in him. His friend's safety concerned Pierce. Their interaction with her, although pleasant, might not be representative of her true nature. Of all people who could relate to that, Pierce could in light of what he endured from Helene.

"Are you certain it is a good idea for you to go with her to her island?"

Greene appreciated his close friend's concern for his welfare and sought to set him at ease.

"Yes. I need to try and help her see this is not the way. I know I can trust her and that no harm will come to me that is of her doing."

Pierce's hesitation was not alleviated.

"Still, you do not know what awaits you on that island, and I would never forgive myself if something happened to you because of this trip, my trip."

Greene felt compelled to do this. He needed to get through to Maury and that would likely take some time.

"If I decide not to stay, I will have Maury take me to St. Kitts straight away. My guess is, however, that I will be fine and hopefully successful in bringing her back to London where she belongs."

Pierce was not convinced Greene would achieve the outcome he wanted, but he understood.

"Before we continue to St. Kitts, I want the map coordinates to her island."

Greene smiled at his friend's determination to look out for him.

97

Chapter Nine

St. Kitts
The MacKittrick Estate
Mid-May 1774

Even with soft muslin curtains framing the bank of floor-to-ceiling windows, the morning sunlight filled the spacious bedroom. The delicate fabric swayed gently, stirred by the island breeze that carried the fragrance of tropical flowers from the courtyard just steps outside the door.

Alexandra's room overlooked a lush garden that stretched along the entire western section of the house. The wing consisted of her quarters and two additional guest rooms. It mirrored the eastern segment of the structure situated across the courtyard. A shaded veranda that ran the length of the two extensions connected them.

Since her arrival, she had made a ritual of retreating to the courtyard each evening after slipping into her nightdress and robe. As the only guest of her aunt and uncle, she enjoyed complete privacy. There, surrounded by the intoxicating scent of gardenia and plumeria, she wandered the stone pathways, her steps accompanied by the soft chirping of crickets. Later, she

Never Leave My Arms

would settle on the porch outside her room, gazing up at the night sky, awestruck by its brilliance. The stars on the island sparkled like scattered diamonds, more vivid than she had ever seen at her family's country estate in England.

"Hurry, Kishma! They'll leave without us!" Alexandra called, excitement brightening her voice.

Kishma laughed as she reached for the colorful scarf draped across Alexandra's whitewashed four-poster bed.

"I'm comin', I'm comin'! Don't forget ya scarf," she teased, her tone warm and familiar.

Only one year separated the young women. Annabelle had asked Kishma to serve as Alexandra's companion during her stay. In England, such a role would have involved preparing Alexandra for a whirlwind of balls and social engagements. But island life was simpler.

Here, there were no grand events, no elaborate gowns, or intricate hairstyles. Instead, her niece favored the practicality of loose skirts made from airy fabrics, paired with short-sleeved blouses tucked at the waist and cinched with colorful sashes. The climate demanded ease and comfort over opulence.

Initially, Annabelle had been cautious about her niece's safety. Alexandra's strikingly light blonde hair, vivid blue eyes, and fair complexion made her stand out among the locals. Her features were in stark contrast to their dark skin and exotic features. Marauding ships occasionally made port at St. Kitts, and there was always the lingering threat of young women being kidnapped and sold into slavery. Boris Lucrete, a notorious slaver, visited the island regularly, and whispers of his ship's arrival sent families scrambling to protect their daughters.

For weeks, Annabelle restricted her niece's excursions to the estate grounds. Alexandra, with Kishma's help, found a clever solution. One afternoon, her new friend dressed her in a native outfit. Because the white

99

creaminess of the English woman's skin had taken on a light brown tone from her time outdoors, her tanned complexion contributed to an indigenous look.

Shortly after her arrival on the island, Alexandra had discovered a small private lagoon on the far side of the property where she could enjoy a swim and dry herself under the island sun. She frequented the small paradise several times a week.

After wrapping the young woman's long blonde hair beneath a vibrant scarf, Kishma frowned.

"If ya scarf ever comes off, it will give ya away."

The two stood pondering the problem when a thought struck the young island native.

"I know. My ma has dis mixture she makes from berries dat temporarily darkens her hair. It washes out, and ya would neva' know it wasn't her true hair color."

Changing her hair color gave Alexandra pause. If something went awry, her aunt and mother would be furious, and she could end up looking freakish. After all, the combination of her eye color and light tresses defined her physical identity.

Sensing her friend's apprehension, Kishma tried to reassure her that her worries were unfounded.

"Da older women do it all da time. Me ma says it makes her feel and look younger, and it washes right out wit sum soap and a bucket of water."

Alexandra looked at her friend intensely.

"Are you sure it will wash out completely and I won't be bald or have sapphire hair?"

Kishma smiled kindly.

"I wouldn't say so it if it could cause ya harm."

The young woman's words eased Alexandra's concern, and she slowly nodded.

Never Leave My Arms

"Then let us get started."

Later that afternoon, the two young women had perfected her new look with Alexandra now fully disguised as a young native woman. They decided she should still wear the headscarf. The hair color would serve as protection should it come off or a tress escape.

The opportunity to test out the success of the disguise arose when Lidy asked Kishma to collect the evening's ham at the smokehouse. The two young women quickly complied, securing a ride with Kishma's father.

As they alighted from the small cart at the front of the home with the package for Lidy, Annabelle didn't recognize her niece at first.

"Good afta noon, Miss Annabelle," Kishma said brightly as the two climbed the porch steps.

Alexandra walked behind her friend, her eyes hooded and head dipped. Annabelle, seated in her favorite chair while working on her embroidery sampler, gave them a quick glance and returned to her task.

"Good afternoon, Kishma. And who is this? A new family member I haven't met?" she asked with a smile.

Kishma giggled, and Alexandra hid her smile behind her hand. Annabelle's brow furrowed at their shared amusement. When Alexandra reached the top of the steps, she paused, looking up to reveal her familiar cerulean eyes.

"It's me Aunt Annabelle," she said, her voice laced with laughter.

Annabelle gasped.

"Alexandra! I didn't recognize you!"

Her young niece's eyes lit up with excitement.

"Perfect! That's exactly what we were striving to achieve."

Annabelle looked quizzically at her niece. "I don't understand."

"You said I couldn't leave the estate because I didn't blend in as an island native. Now that I do, there's no reason for me not to be able to move about the island without you worrying," she replied hopefully.

Before Annabelle could respond, Alexandra launched into a two-minute dissertation on why she should be permitted to venture off the estate, properly escorted, of course. She gave her aunt no chance to interject an objection, specifically noting that the older woman initially thought she was a relative of Kishma's.

Annabelle sat quietly, listening to her niece. Outwardly, her expression remained attentive, but inwardly, she smiled with pride. Alexandra's mother would have been proud of her daughter's persuasive efforts; they rivaled her own. Once the young woman finished, Annabelle remained silent for a moment, considering her niece's plea. She took her responsibility for her brother's daughter very seriously.

Listening to her points of justification, she cautiously agreed to loosen, but not completely lift, her restrictions on Alexandra leaving the plantation. Before giving her blessing, Annabelle imposed firm guidelines. Trips off the property for anything other than venturing to Kishma's and her families homes required an escort of at least one groundskeeper and Kishma. Moreover, Alexandra had to wear the disguise at all times. Most importantly, the two young friends were to return immediately if any pirate ships were sighted or if word traveled of sightings. While not given full reign of the island, Alexandra appreciated her aunt relenting somewhat.

Squealing with excitement, she rushed forward and hugged her affectionately, causing the older woman to drop her sampler and laugh.

"Thank you Aunt Annabelle."

Her aunt laughed then took on a serious tone.

"If there's one incident where your safety is brought into question, we return to the previous arrangement. Do you understand?"

Alexandra nodded quickly.

"Yes. I promise it will be fine."

Turning to Kishma, Alexandra said, "Come along. We have to plan for a trip to shop at the port tomorrow."

Never Leave My Arms

The young friend rushed up the stairs and followed her into the house.

"I can't wait ta see what da ships bringin to da island," she said.

Annabelle watched with a smile as the two young women disappeared into the house, their excited chatter fading as the door closed behind them.

"I hope I do not regret this decision," she whispered to herself.

The next morning, Alexandra and Kishma rushed through breakfast to ensure they arrived at the village early. A ship had made port early in the morning with supplies from London and France. As the young women rushed past her on the porch, Annabelle concealed her apprehension from the two friends. She had, however, given their escort, two groundskeepers—one of whom was Kishma's brother-in-law—specific instructions to stay close to them at all times.

Kishma quietly surveyed her friend with an admiring gaze. She was unrecognizable. Dressed in her native Kittian attire, Alexandra would blend seamlessly with the locals. However, her captivating blue eyes brought concern to the young native.

As the cart pulled away from the estate, Alexandra instinctively adjusted the scarf around her head.

Leaning forward so only her friend could hear, Kishma whispered, "Dunt worry bout ya hair. Da berries did the trick. Jus dunt let anyone git a good view of ya eyes."

Alexandra nodded as she dropped her head, self-consciously running her hand along the scarf's edge once more. Settling back into her seat, she surrendered to the excitement of the day's adventure. She suppressed a grin as her intuition told her that today promised to be unlike any other.

103

Elizabeth H. Franklin

St. Kitts
Basseterre Port
June 1, 1774

The morning sun cast a warm golden glow over the emerald waters of the Caribbean, illuminating both the waves and the rugged figure of Pierce standing tall at the helm of the Saltire Wind. He took in the view of Basseterre while Alasdair and the crew tied the ship to its slip.

For a moment, as Pierce gazed toward the lush island mass of St. Kitts, he let his guard down, revealing a rare glimpse of vulnerability behind the steely exterior he typically wore. This new world, with its warm tropical breeze, colorful hills, and bright white sand, offered him a sense of hope. Perhaps he could find the peace needed to put the disastrous results of his forced marriage behind him and heal from the deep wound of his grandmother's manipulations.

Shaking himself mentally, Pierce took a deep breath as he surveyed the boxes of cargo on the deck. Summoning Alasdair to the wheel, he placed his hand on his friend's shoulder.

"Let's drop the gangplank to prepare for offloading. I see there's a package ship in port. Perhaps there's news from home."

Alasdair nodded.

The Saltire Wind had additional Fraser business, which included the delivery of cargo to three other islands. The ship carrying that merchandise was due to arrive within the next week. Once the freight was transferred to Pierce's ship, Nials would captain the vessel with Alasdair as his first mate. Pierce anticipated the journey would take approximately two to three months to complete, weather permitting. They would then return to St. Kitts to retrieve Pierce and then pick up Greene if he had not already joined them. All would return to London.

Never Leave My Arms

Alasdair and the crew quickly offloaded the supplies Pierce had brought for his hosts. Although he had told Pirate Mame she could have their stock of tea, Pierce secretly held back two cases tucked into a large munitions crate for the MacKittricks. English tea was scarce in the Leewards, and from what his father had told him, the family enjoyed the comforts of home while in St. Kitts.

Alasdair approached Pierce as he stepped onto the dock.

"The cargo is ready for transport."

Pierce looked around and scanned the crowd milling along the main street of the village. Most appeared to be locals, based on their sun-darkened skin and tropical attire. The men wore loose-fitting, light-colored, three-quarter-length muslin pants, shirts open at the neck, and no shoes, while the local women wore full skirts and fitted blouses with billowy sleeves of the same fabric, their hair captured by scarves or hats. Unlike the men, they wore roughly fashioned sandals.

The wealthy Englishmen were easy to spot in their linen breeches, white stockings with leather shoes, and long-sleeved cutaway dress jackets over high-necked shirts. Colorful parasols and fuller gowns of fine fabrics signaled the presence of well-off English women.

"Excellent. I want to stop at the mail office to see if word from my father has arrived, and then we need to find MacKittrick's supervisor to arrange for the transport of their cargo."

Elizabeth H. Franklin

Basseterre, St. Kitts
Market Square @ the Docks
...that same afternoon

The two young friends meandered through the crowd that had gathered near the port. The buyers waited eagerly while the vendors set out their wares and the freshly unloaded cargo from the arriving ships.

Suddenly, Kishma stopped abruptly, causing Alexandra to bump into her. Her friend's sharp intake of breath silenced Alexandra's impending rebuke. At first, she thought Kishma had stepped on something sharp or, worse, had spotted Lucrete. Alexandra's body tensed; she sensed something was awry.

She kept her gaze lowered as she leaned towards her friend, anxiety building.

"What is it?"

"He's beaut'ful," Kishma breathed in awe.

Unable to contain herself, Alexandra disregarded the strict orders to keep her eyes hooded and looked up to see what had captured her friend's attention. Initially, the sunlight made it difficult for Alexandra to focus, but once her eyes adjusted, she saw exactly what had caught Kishma's admiration. While her friend described him as beautiful, Alexandra thought a better term would be *dangerously handsome*—no, *dangerously ruggedly handsome.*

He stood at the helm of a large cargo ship, every bit the captain, feet braced apart, staring out across the square and Basseterre. His look was intense and unwavering as the soft sea breeze tousled his long, thick hair. A shallow groan escaped Alexandra's lips when he pulled his hair back and tied it at the nape, revealing a deeply tanned face and his chiseled jaw accentuated by a close-cropped beard and moustache. His loosely fitted, light-colored shirt split open at the neck exposed an equally tanned, muscular chest.

Never Leave My Arms

Alexandra immediately thought of Penny; this needed to be included in her next letter to her sister. Caught up in the moment, she conjured an image of him working on the ship's deck, effortlessly pulling the rigging to hoist a massive sail. His chest and arm muscles would bulge and glisten with sweat at each tug of the rope.

"I can't wait to tell Penny about this," she thought to herself.

Kishma heard her friend's groan and turned to see Alexandra openly gaping at the handsome sea captain. At first, she laughed lightly but quickly reconsidered when she realized her friend was putting herself at risk.

Stepping in front of Alexandra to block her view, she whispered firmly, "Drop ya head. People are all around."

As if physically shaken from a dream, Alexandra blinked twice, her eyes widening as she realized what she had done. How could she be so careless? If they drew any attention, they would have to leave immediately, ruining not only their day but also ensuring her aunt would never let her leave the plantation again. Quickly, she did as Kishma said and dropped her head.

"Did anyone notice?" she asked, anxiety rising in her stomach.

Kishma scanned the crowd and saw no one paying undue attention. Their escort maintained a respectable distance behind them and did not notice Alexandra's faux pas. The young woman let out a breath and assured her friend that all was well.

"It dunt look like anyone noticed. Jus' ta be safe, we should move furtha' to da square and 'way from the docks."

Alexandra nodded, careful to keep her gaze downward. The two young women slowly navigated through the crowd toward the row of harbor stores and office buildings flanking the open-air market. Once they crossed the main road, they roamed through the vendors who had already set up their merchandise on wagons used to transport goods to the square. Most were selling fresh vegetables, fruits, and homemade breads while a few offered

107

handmade scarves, necklaces, and bracelets made of seashells and colored stones.

The friends took their time stopping at each vendor to admire the items. Alexandra softly fingered the colorful fabrics and local jewelry. Much to her surprise, the ship that had arrived from England brought a supply of dyed muslin fabrics in soft lavenders and blues. The two friends took turns draping the fabric across each other, laughing, and suggesting clothing style ideas for the different colors.

Alexandra kept her gaze lowered. She remained mindful that her blue eyes could draw attention. However, neither she nor Kishma realized that her beautiful white smile would be distracting, particularly to Pierce Tennyson.

He spotted the two women immediately when he exited the postmaster's office. The petite one with the colorful scarf wrapped artfully around her head drew his attention. Her beguiling white smile made him pause.

Initially, his attempts to crane his neck and tip his head for a better look at her face were unsuccessful. However, just as he was about to step down into the crowd and make his way to them, something the dark-haired woman said to her friend made the smaller woman laugh. The melodic giggle carried on the breeze, feeling like a soft caress.

Pierce suddenly drew in a sharp breath when the young woman lifted her gaze enough for him to see a pair of piercing blue eyes on the most exquisite face he had ever encountered. Although he had only been in St. Kitts for less than two hours, he would bet she was not a local. While her skin suggested she had spent time in the sun, she did not possess the darkness of the island natives. He could not be absolutely certain because he could not hear their conversation and did not know if she had a Kittian accent.

Pierce saw her smile fade quickly, and she dropped her gaze when her friend whispered something in her ear. Whatever she said seemed to startle her. This raised Pierce's suspicion. The wounds of Helene's duplicity were still fresh, and something about these two—specifically the one with the headscarf—seemed off.

His reverie broke when he heard Alasdair calling for him down the boardwalk.

"Captain, the harbormaster is here."

Shaking himself to clear his thoughts, Pierce turned his attention to his trusted friend.

"Any word on MacKittrick's man?"

Alasdair nodded.

"Yes sir. He's at the harbormaster's office waiting for you."

"I have a slight change of plans," Pierce said.

Originally, he intended to ride out to the MacKittrick estate upon reaching St. Kitts, but he decided to give his crew some time off until the new cargo arrived. He, Nials and Alasdair would stay on the ship with a handful of sailors that would rotate time ashore. Pierce did not want the vessel left in an unfamiliar harbor, out of his watchful eye, with only a skeleton crew.

After taking one last glance at the mysterious young woman with the colorful kerchief, Pierce followed Alasdair to the Harbor Master's office to secure a slip for two nights. After the second night, Pierce would move the vessel into the bay and anchor there until the merchant ship arrived for their rendezvous.

The representative sent by the MacKittricks to meet Pierce, arranged transport of the cargo saved from Pirate Mame to the estate. After making the delivery, he agreed to return when Pierce sent word to collect him.

Following their meeting, Pierce retrieved a letter from his father at the postmaster's office. He cautiously opened the letter hoping Nathaniel had been successful in securing the annulment from Helene. To his disappointment, however, his communication conveyed the opposite message.

Helene's family demanded financial reparations before they would agree to release Pierce from the marriage bond. Apparently, her mother knew of her daughter's lack of chastity and advised her to use goat's blood on their wedding night. Regardless of their efforts to stall the dissolution of the marriage contract, Nathaniel assured his son he would not rest until he successfully freed him from all obligations to Helene and her family.

Pierce neatly refolded the letter, slipped it back into the envelope, and tucked it into his pocket. Although he remained composed on the outside, his stomach churned at the thought that he was still married to Helene.

Never Leave My Arms

St. Kitts
The MacKittrick Estate
June 5, 1774

The merchant ship arrived sooner than expected, and the Saltire Wind set sail the following day. Pierce had sent word to the MacKittricks that his arrival would be delayed the week until his ship was loaded and set off on its next leg. While staying on the moored vessel, Pierce, Nials and Alasdair took a small skiff and ventured ashore to enjoy a mug or two of brew at a local pub.

Pierce always scanned the crowds, hoping for a glimpse of the beautiful young woman with the colorful headscarf. Since initially seeing her, she was never far from his thoughts. Truth be told, he dreamed of her at night as well. Those beautiful blue eyes haunted him. Alas, neither she nor her friend had returned to the village square since that first day.

Once the Saltire Wind was loaded with the additional cargo and Nials and Alasdair set sail, Pierce made contact with the MacKittrick's estate and a transport was sent to bring him to the home. The open-air carriage's turn up the plantation's long drive brought Pierce out of his thoughts of the mystery woman.

The vehicle creaked and swayed with the rhythmic plod of the sturdy horses pulling it along the winding drive. Evening light bathed the scene in hues of gold and amber. The descending sun painted the sky with streaks of fire as it hovered low over the horizon. The drive, a narrow ribbon of hard-packed dirt, snaked between towering walls of lush foliage.

Palm fronds and banana leaves framed the path like a living canopy, their edges catching the last glimmers of sunlight. The air was thick with the sweet aroma of jasmine and the faint scent of the salty sea that carried inland by the subtle ocean breeze. Although breathtaking in their own right, the English and Scottish countrysides were markedly different from this tropical Eden.

Elizabeth H. Franklin

Pierce sat next to the driver, a native Kittian man with sun-darkened skin, his rough linen shirt clinging to his back in the sticky heat. His hands held the reins loosely as he clicked his tongue, urging the two horses onward. The steady rhythm of the iron-rimmed wheels over the uneven track mingled with the chorus of chirping crickets.

As the drive began to widen, the dense vegetation gradually receded, revealing an open expanse bathed in twilight. The driver slowed the cart, lifting his wide-brimmed straw hat to wipe his brow as the plantation house emerged in majestic splendor before them. Pierce gave no outward reaction to the grand sprawling estate.

Its whitewashed facade glowed in the amber light bringing forth a wave of relaxation. The sweeping verandas were adorned with intricate fretwork. They offered a commanding view of the surrounding landscape. Hanging baskets of colorful flowers and ferns wrapped around their roof edge like delicate lace. Beyond the house, green lawns and open fields stretched toward the horizon. Lanterns flickered to life along the veranda and in the windows, casting a warm, welcoming glow.

The driver pulled the cart to a stop at the front stairs of the grand house. Before jumping down from his perch, Pierce took in the large home. Struck by the overwhelming beauty of its grandness, he felt an undercurrent of excitement and a renewal of spirit in the island air.

The driver tied off the horses' reins and alighted to fetch the trunk from the bed of the wagon. Pierce stepped off the platform to the ground and slung a satchel over his shoulder. Chester MacKittrick's boisterous voice from the veranda caught his attention.

"Welcome to our humble island abode, Mr. Tennyson. So glad to finally be able to thank you in person for the provisions you brought."

Pierce turned to see a short, balding man standing at the top of the wide wooden staircase leading to the home's entry. Even though the heat of the day had dissipated, the man's cheeks were bright red and the top of his

112

thinning pate glistened with perspiration. Chester smiled broadly and rocked back on his heels as he stuck his thumbs into the waistband of his breeches. Without an introduction, Pierce knew this had to be Chester MacKittrick. He was exactly as his father described.

Laughing softly, Pierce made his way up the stairs to his host, stopped at the last step, and shook his hand. He did not want to make the man feel self-conscious about the difference in height between the two. Although Chester did not let on, Pierce's gesture did not go unnoticed or unappreciated.

"Pleasure to meet you as well. My father told me you missed some of the finer things England offers."

Pierce smiled and gestured towards the grand tropical landscape.

"This is spectacular. Nothing like anything I have ever seen before."

Grasping Pierce's shoulder, Chester nodded and chuckled.

"This is only a sampling. Wait until you get to see the rest of the island. Come inside. You must have missed home cooking. My wife, Annabelle, made sure they kept a plate warm for you."

Before escorting his guest through the grand house's polished mahogany double doors, Chester signaled for the driver to take Pierce's trunks to his room at the south end of the home.

Chapter Ten

St. Kitts
The MacKittrick Estate
June 5, 1774
...later that evening

Although the exterior of the MacKittrick estate resembled an island plantation home, the interior combined bright colorful tropical hues with the darker richer tones characteristic of English tradition, particularly in Chester's study. After dinner, the two men retreated to the well-appointed room. The British transplant, an accomplished architect and engineer in his own right, designed and constructed the study adjoining the home's great room.

Island craft workers lined the walls with indigenous woods, creating a warm and inviting atmosphere. A local artisan constructed an oversized desk from wood salvaged from a shipwreck just off the coastline. Each time Annabelle traveled to London, she returned with boxes of first edition books, filling the bookcases with her husband's favorites.

To counterbalance the dark and heavy decor and invite fresh air, Chester had a bank of whitewashed wooden shuttered doors installed on the study's exterior wall. During the day, he would keep them open to air out the room and enjoy the landscape view from the private veranda. As dusk settled, he would close them and adjust the louvers so the cool night air could drift into the room along with the soft chirp of crickets.

Chester leaned back in his chair and casually surveyed Nathaniel's son. Pierce was deep in thought, swirling the amber liquor in his crystal glass, a pensive expression on his face. Fine whiskey was another English comfort that Chester appreciated, and Nathaniel made certain Pierce brought several cases to gift to his host.

His friend's letter regarding Pierce's visit had been cryptic. It simply stated he needed to address a business matter for his son while Pierce took a much-needed respite.

Chester felt no need for specifics. It pleased him to offer a place for the young man to relax and enjoy the rejuvenating effects of island living. Whatever reason had prompted Pierce to travel so far from England was none of his business, and he had no plans to pry.

"I would like to show you around the island and introduce you to my neighbor. We have been working on an irrigation system these past months in preparation for the rainy season. It's quite impressive," Chester said.

His voice pulled Pierce from his thoughts. Not wanting to seem inattentive, he looked up and nodded.

"That sounds fine."

Chester silently chuckled at the young man's attempt to hide his distraction. He could see something clearly weighed on him.

Chester pushed forward.

"I am an early riser and plan to head over directly after breakfast, if that's not too early for you."

Pierce gave him his full attention.

"I too am an early riser. That would work fine."

"Excellent! Regrettably, it will just be you and me for breakfast. My wife and her niece who is visiting from England, normally do not eat until late morning."

Since Pierce had arrived after the usual dinner hour, he hadn't had the chance to meet Alexandra. She had dined with Annabelle earlier. Afterward, Alexandra and Kishma helped her older sister bathe and put her children to bed before retiring for the night.

"You will likely meet Alexandra at dinner tomorrow," Chester said.

Pierce looked at Chester questioningly.

"Alexandra?"

Chester clarified.

"My wife's niece."

Nodding with understanding, Pierce mentally set that information aside and returned to absently staring into his drink.

After a moment of silence, Pierce raised his head and looked directly into Chester's eyes. The older man remained still and attentive as he returned his stare. Although Chester's expression was stoic, there was a heaviness he detected in the young man. The silence hung between them as Pierce debated whether his host knew the reason for his visit to St. Kitts.

After observing Chester's expression and demeanor and being mindful of his father's high regard for the older man, Pierce sighed.

"How much do you know about why I am here?"

Chester did not waver or break eye contact.

"Your father mentioned you were here for an extended holiday while he sorted out a business matter for you."

Pierce smiled with amusement and chuckled, shaking his head. His father certainly had a knack for framing his situation delicately.

Although Pierce was adept at presenting himself as engaging and stalwart during their discussions, Chester occasionally caught fleeting glimpses of sadness in the young man's eyes. Just as Nathaniel had the gift of eloquence when explaining the reason for his son's visit, Chester possessed the ability to read people's emotions. Based upon Pierce's distance, distraction, and questioning the content of his father's letter, he could tell something deeply personal had occurred to the young man. If he had to hazard a guess, he would say a woman was involved.

Leaning forward, he placed his glass on his desk.

Chester's eyes softened with compassion.

"My boy, I do not require the specificity of what brought you here, but please know, that should the time come you wish to discuss it with me, I am here to listen."

"Thank you," Pierce said.

Sensing it best to end their evening, Chester downed the remainder of his drink and rose from his chair. Pierce followed suit and moved toward the open doors leading to the veranda, inhaling the cool night air.

Placing a hand on the young man's shoulder, Chester said, "It's late, and we have an early start tomorrow. I'm going to get some rest."

Pierce shook the man's hand.

"I think I will take a walk before turning in. I can find my way to my room. See you in the morning."

Chester nodded and watched as his young guest walked out onto the veranda, down the stairs, and set out along the path leading to the southwest wing of the estate.

"She must have really hurt him," Chester thought, shaking his head.

While Chester joined Annabelle and retired to their room, Pierce enjoyed the cool night air. It felt refreshing on his face as he meandered along the worn path. Although he had no idea where the trail led when he first left the study, he quickly discovered it snaked parallel to the expansive plantation home then turned toward the back of the building.

Thankfully, the half-moon shone in the clear night sky. The myriad of bright stars helped light his way, creating a setting that looked like white sparks on the tips of various vegetation and grasses. He could see why Chester had traded the bustling, chilly dampness of London for the calm warmth of the island.

A rustling sound ahead broke through Pierce's musings and he abruptly stopped, alert and listening intently. He saw a set of glowing wall sconces ahead, illuminating the veranda that began near his room and wrapped around the back of the building. As his eyes followed the covered porch, a movement caught his attention in the back corner.

Suddenly, a flash of color emerged from behind some shrubs, rushed up the steps to the porch, and disappeared around the corner. Although fleeting, he could tell it was a woman. Dressed in native attire, she wore a flowy, cream-colored dress cinched at the waist with a fabric sash, and her dark hair was pulled back in a tight bun. His brow shot up in surprise. Out of curiosity, Pierce wandered further down to where she had slipped by. When he reached the back of the building, there was no sign of her.

Unlike the area he had just left, the rear of the estate had no obvious path, and large trees obstructed the moonlight from illuminating the space. Scanning the vicinity one last time before turning back toward his room, he made a mental note to explore the rear grounds more thoroughly in the daylight.

Pierce returned down the dirt path and ascended the stairs to the door where his hosts had left two wall lanterns burning. Windows with open shutters flanked either side of the entry. When he stepped inside, he felt the cool night air flowing through the openings, filling the expansive room with the night air.

The room's furnishings were a blend of British and native island woven rattan, with ornate area rugs placed strategically over the polished wood flooring. A large four poster bed occupied the far right wall, illuminated by a small table lantern nearby. Sheer netting draped over the top and across each corner post created a protective sleeping cocoon.

On the opposite side of the room, floor-to-ceiling curtains hung along the wall expanse. Pierce pulled them back to see what lay beyond and discovered a bank of doors similar to those in Chester's study. The panels opened onto a private covered porch overlooking a courtyard filled with lush greenery. The aroma of colorful tropical flowers drifted into his room, filling the air with a sweet scent.

He noticed a light flicker across the courtyard before going out. Presuming it was Chester or his wife's niece, he thought nothing of it and returned to his room, settling in for the night and seeking much-needed rest. Once again, as he drifted into the depth of sleep, he dreamed of the young woman with crystal blue eyes and a colorful headscarf.

Across the courtyard from Pierce's room, Alexandra was unaware of the new guest. She had planned to take her usual walk before retiring, but her late arrival home prevented it. Quickly, she removed her clothing, refreshed herself at the water basin, donned her nightgown, and slipped into bed. Much to her pleasant surprise, she too had a visitor in her dream—the strappingly handsome ship's captain she saw in Basseterre.

St. Kitts
The MacKittrick Estate
June 6, 1774

Alexandra had donned her native attire and stood ready to leave when Kishma knocked on the bedroom door shortly before the sun rose. She wrapped a bright yellow shawl around her hips and tied it at her trim waist while she followed the young woman toward the main house.

"Ya aunt is in da parlor and wants ta talk ta ya before we leave for ma sista's dis mornin," Kishma said.

Alexandra smothered a yawn as she followed her friend down the long hall. The smell of freshly baked biscuits wafted down the corridor, reminding her of her empty stomach. She and Kishma took a detour to the kitchen to investigate what delicious fare Lidy had prepared.

The large, bright white kitchen was a separate wing off the main living space. Unlike wealthier island homestead houses, Chester had the kitchen specifically designed and built as its own structure and connected to the dining room by a hallway. This kept the house cooler by isolating the heat of the ovens from the main building and provided direct covered access to the main house.

Lidy, dressed in a pristine white fitted top and flowy muslin skirt, greeted them with a beautiful smile that matched her dress. She had just placed a tray of hot, perfectly browned biscuits on the large wooden worktable in the center of the room.

"They smell heavenly," Alexandra said as she entered.

Wiping the flour from her hands on her matching apron, Lidy greeted her daughter's new friend.

"Mornin Miss Alexandra. Ow did ya sleep?"

Alexandra reached for a warm biscuit and smiled brightly.

"Good morning, Lidy. I slept like a babe."

Never Leave My Arms

Kishma greeted her mother with a soft kiss on the cheek.

"Mornin Mama."

Lidy smiled tenderly at her daughter, running her knuckle affectionately along the side of her face.

"Ya sista's time be close. Ya best not dawdle. She needs help wit doz little ones," she admonished lovingly.

Turning to Alexandra, Lidy added, "Ya aunt like ta speak wit ya before ya two leave for da village. She be in da parlor."

Alexandra quickly placed two biscuits in a towel, and wrapped them carefully.

"Let me see what Aunt Annabelle needs."

She called over her shoulder as she rushed out of the room, "Thank you, Lidy. Kishma, I will meet you on the path in a few moments. Walk slowly."

Lidy laughed lightly and shook her head in exasperation. She had never met a proper young British woman so excited about caring for small children.

Not only had Alexandra become Kishma's closest friend and confidante, but she had also found a place in the hearts of Lidy's family, particularly her oldest daughter, who was due to give birth to her third child.

If it were not for Kishma and Alexandra, the young mother would likely have lost the babe due to a difficult pregnancy. Thankfully, the two young women could care for the little ones from morning to bedtime, allowing her daughter to rest so she could carry a healthy full-term babe.

A sadness momentarily overcame Lidy. Little ones had been a blessing for her and her family, unlike the MacKittricks. Her heart broke for her employers. Fate had prevented them from having children. Before Annabelle left for England on her last trip, Lidy worried about her.

The emptiness her employer carried was evident in her eyes. Even Chester noticed it, which is why he suggested Annabelle extend her visit

121

with her brother and his family. He knew she missed them but also knew how much she enjoyed spending time with her nieces. When he suggested she try to convince Brenton and Cherisse to bring one or both back with her for a visit, she was over the moon with excitement.

Thankfully, a private letter from Chester to his brother-in-law and sister-in-law, pleading on Annabelle's behalf, helped clear the way for her request to be granted, at least in part. They had no choice when Alexandra squealed with delight at the offer and begged her parents to let her go. They felt their youngest needed to stay behind until she was a little older. Once Annabelle returned with Alexandra, the MacKittricks' home took on new life. Alexandra's presence brought a lightness that affected not only Annabelle but her usually solemn uncle as well.

Alexandra spotted her aunt in the parlor working on her sampler.

"Good morning Aunt Annabelle. Lidy said you wanted to speak with me."

Alexandra sat down on a small footstool across from her.

The older woman removed her dainty wire glasses and set them on the round table next to her, along with her project. Her niece always seemed to bring a soothing breeze into any room she entered.

Smiling warmly at her, she said, "Yes dear. I wanted to introduce you to Uncle Chester's guest before they left, but you just missed him."

Tucking a biscuit into the pocket of her colorful skirt, Alexandra frowned with feigned disappointment. She had overheard her aunt and uncle discussing a visitor arriving at the estate months earlier, but she had heard that something had delayed him. After committing to help Kishma and her sister in the village, Alexandra thought nothing more about the guest.

Honestly, she presumed the man would spend all his time with her uncle, talking business or designing some invention like the watering system he had built for a friend.

Never Leave My Arms

"Oh dear. How unfortunate. Perhaps another time," Alexandra said.

"How about tonight at dinner? What time will you be returning this evening?"

Alexandra nervously chewed her fingernail. She needed to phrase her response in a manner that avoided making it an obvious excuse to avoid meeting the visitor. Annabelle would think her rude if she shared her honest feelings: the gentleman was her uncle's guest, and she would have nothing in common with some old stuffy British businessman.

"Kishma's sister is very close to her time, so we have been staying late to get the children fed and tucked in for the night. Then of course, we have to wait for her husband to escort us home. I would not expect to be back for dinner tonight, or until well after the baby is born, and she is ready to resume her usual schedule."

Annabelle pressed her lips together to conceal her smile. She could tell her niece was doing her best to politely decline meeting Chester's guest. She understood why Alexandra might have assumed that her uncle's visitor would share similar interests. Little did Alexandra know that the two were not that far off in age and he was quite charming. Chester informed her last night that the young man is also from London. His parents live close to the Landon's city townhouse.

"I completely understand. The needs of Kishma's sister and children are more important than anything right now. I am certain there will be other opportunities for you to meet him."

Alexandra gave her aunt a bright smile before rising from the chair and quickly pecking her cheek.

"I knew you would understand."

Annabelle chuckled softly as she reached for her sampler and glasses.

"I will make your excuses. Now, you run along."

123

Her expression and tone turned serious as she addressed her niece before leaving the room.

"Alexandra. Make certain you wait for the escort home. Word is one of Lucrete's ships was seen passing by the island yesterday."

The smile faded from Alexandra's face as she nodded. The mention of the villainous pirate made her blood run cold. She had heard the stories about him and how he and his crew kidnapped young women from the islands, selling them into slavery in other countries or doing worse to them.

"Yes Aunt Annabelle. Kishma and I are always careful," she assured.

Never Leave My Arms

St. Kitts
Church Gutt
June 18, 1774

Three days after Pierce arrived, Kishma's sister gave birth to her third child. She and Alexandra stayed with the new mother and her children for two weeks. The delivery had been difficult, and the village midwife recommended bed rest for the new mother. Neither young woman minded. Kishma loved spending time with her niece and nephew, and Alexandra felt a sense of purpose in helping to care for the newborn.

On one particular day, dressed in the native clothing and colorful headscarf she had grown accustomed to wearing, she and Kishma went into the small village to purchase fruits and vegetables. Aside from her tanned skin and attire, which helped her blend in, she had also learned to adeptly mimic the Kittian accent.

For the most part, Alexandra tried to remain in the shadows in public and was never alone. Kishma shielded her from drawing attention. However, there were occasions when Alexandra had to communicate with merchants, and she needed to fully embrace the role of a young native. Such an occasion arose while the two young women were in the market square.

The bright morning sun climbed high in the sky on that warm June day, bathing the bustling village square in light. Although mostly locals frequented the market, a handful of well-dressed British were meandering about, carrying light-colored fabric parasols to protect their fair skin from the sun.

A business meeting with a plantation owner had brought Pierce and Chester to this area of the island. The older man wanted to purchase specific fruits that Annabelle enjoyed but were not easily obtainable at Basseterre.

125

Before disappearing into the throng of shoppers, Chester said to Pierce, "Give me a few moments, and we can be on our way to the Chamarelle estate."

Pierce nodded and wandered over to a less populated grassy area away from the hustle and bustle, where he could take in the view of the crowd and watch them mingle and haggle with the merchants. He caught the attention of several young women seated in a shaded area a few feet away. They watched him admiringly as he leaned against a large tree, crossing his muscular arms across his broad chest.

It was hard not to notice the tall, well-built foreigner. He embodied contradiction. Although not from the islands, his deeply tanned skin indicated he spent much time in the sun. His clothing combined a masculine, functional style with practical comfort for the climate. The fitted breeches and casually tailored linen shirt, made from fine fabrics perfectly suited for tropical weather, highlighted his muscular build.

As he casually rested against the tree trunk, Pierce's penetrating hazel-green eyes scanned his surroundings, briefly settling on the small group of women nearby. His fleeting attention elicited whispering and shy smiles among them. Extending a curt nod with an emotionless expression to the trio, he continued to observe the market crowd and took a sharp breath when he spotted a familiar colorful headscarf among the patrons.

He abruptly straightened and craned his neck to glimpse the young woman, but the gathering was too dense. Pierce kept his eyes trained on her head as he moved toward them, careful not to lose sight of her. She and her companion suddenly stepped away from a merchant cart and its crowd, turning to speak to each other. Pierce stopped in his tracks. It was her.

He recognized those striking blue eyes. Suddenly, a beautiful white smile formed on her face, framed with defined, plump pink lips. It appeared she responded to something clever or funny from her companion. Her friend leaned in close, and she immediately dropped her head and turned away.

Determined to meet her, Pierce set off toward the two women, but abruptly halted when Chester's familiar voice intruded his thoughts. Turning toward him, he tried to mask his annoyance.

It was too late; Chester could sense his young guest's irritation.

"Is something wrong?" his host asked with concern.

Pierce shook his head and quickly tried to reverse his impatience by enlisting Chester's help.

"Actually yes, you can be of assistance," he replied.

Feeling a renewed sense of purpose, Chester puffed out his chest with confidence.

"Absolutely. How can I help?"

"There is a young lady I saw on the day of my arrival in Basseterre. I could not catch her eye to speak with her, but I saw her just now in the market. Perhaps you might know who she is."

Eager to assist the young man, Chester scanned the crowd.

"Point her out to me. I know most of the people in this village."

Pierce looked back to the place where he had last seen the young woman. To his disappointment, both she and her companion had vanished. He quickly scanned the market but could not find either of them. The two had slipped away.

Turning to his host, he frowned. His frustration surfaced.

"It seems she has eluded me again."

"She can't have gone far. I'm sure she will appear again," Chester replied.

Pierce nodded, giving the older man an unconvincing half-smile before shaking off the incident.

"You are right."

Pierce mentally chided himself for allowing a woman to captivate him, especially after what he had gone through with Helene. Granted, he would soon be relieved of his ex-bride once word from his father reached him, he had sworn off allowing any woman into his life, let alone his heart, for a very long time. The bitterness of Helene's betrayal was still fresh, and he felt incapable of trusting any woman, no matter how beautiful or enticing.

Placing his hand on Pierce's shoulder, Chester squeezed it consolingly.

"Come along. I want you to meet Theodore Chamarelle. He has done remarkable things with the new system we designed for challenging topography. Afterwards, I will show you that small cove on the far end of my property where you can enjoy a swim and some solitude."

Since Pierce's arrival, Chester had monopolized his young guest from early morning to dinner, traveling around the island and leaving little time for himself. Similarly, their schedule had allowed few moments for Chester to spend with Annabelle. A few days of exploring the island on his own would be good for Pierce. Perhaps he would run into the young beauty who had caught his eye.

"Sounds good," Pierce said as the two men walked toward the waiting open carriage.

Once seated, Chester clicked the reins, and they set out for their destination. As he listened to his host chatter about their impending meeting, the face of the beauty with the colorful headscarf infiltrated his thoughts. He could not define it, but there was something unique about her. Although difficult to explain, from the day he arrived in St. Kitts and saw her, she had imprinted herself in his memory. No matter how hard he tried, he could not shake her from his thoughts and dreams. He needed to find her.

Pierce emerged from his musings as they arrived at the Chamarelle estate. Thankfully, the time spent being shown the expansive property and impressive irrigation system distracted him from thinking about her.

Never Leave My Arms

"Teddy," as Chester addressed his neighbor, proudly demonstrated how, thanks to Chester's design, he could harness fresh water from several strategically positioned drilled wells at certain points in the hillside to irrigate the tiered crops. The engineering impressed Pierce, and he made a mental note to share what he learned with his father upon his return to London.

While Fraser Shipping was his mother's family business, his father amassed his own wealth through a distant military connection to the British crown. It included extensive land ownership gifted to him by the monarchy. Nathaniel found immense personal and monetary satisfaction in cultivating and maximizing the use of his land for the betterment of his country and its citizens.

As the sun began its descent in the western sky, Pierce and Chester waved goodbye to the neighbor and began their journey home. The two men engaged in light chatter about their time at the plantation, omitting any mention of the young woman in the village, although she popped into Pierce's head throughout the return ride.

Chester quickly drew Pierce from his thoughts as he turned the carriage onto a less worn path at the far edge of his property. It led to a heavily vegetated area in the distance.

Pierce threw his host a brief questioning look at their deviation.

"I wanted to show you that cove I mentioned earlier. It isn't far from an abandoned mill on the outer fringes of my land," Chester said.

Pierce nodded, returning his focus to his host.

"Sounds interesting. In Scotland, I enjoyed the lakes near my grandparents' home."

His host laughed lightly. "My guess is they were much colder. I hope you like warm water."

129

Throughout the ride to the cove, Chester regaled his young guest with descriptions of the secluded paradise, emphasizing its privacy, solitude, and proximity to a pristine private beach.

"Feel free to take one of the horses anytime you wish and enjoy. No one comes here because it is so remote."

Such a paradise appealed to Pierce. He enjoyed spending time alone, surrounded by nature, especially near the water. His father's suggestion to visit the island provided the perfect environment for him to rejuvenate and prepare for his return to London.

Although he had spent most of his time with Chester traveling to various plantations and estates, it had been enjoyable meeting his neighbors. Many were English who sought the warmer climate like his host.

Experiencing island life and meeting many native Kittians made him feel welcome. There was just one particular local girl he had not yet had the pleasure of encountering, but he hoped that would change soon.

Chester pulled the carriage to a halt. They had arrived at a long line of trees with wide, billowy fronds and large bunches of green bananas hanging from thick cords attached to the trunks. Colorful, dense vegetation grew in between, creating a wall of privacy to what lay on the other side.

Noting no obvious entry through the trees, Pierce looked at Chester questioningly. Understanding his guest's hesitation, Chester motioned for Pierce to follow him as he carefully climbed down from the cart and tied off the horse's reins to a sturdy tree limb. Looking around, the older man's expression shifted to concern when he observed an area of grass that had been flattened, forming a subtle trail.

Pierce observed his host's expression.

"Is something wrong?"

"Looks as though someone has been here," Chester said absently. "I will need to speak with my overseer to ensure he checks this area for trespassers."

Never Leave My Arms

The two men made their way thirty yards down the tree line, where it turned left. Just past the curve, there was a small opening between the trees that Chester slipped through, motioning for Pierce to follow him. About twenty feet in, they emerged from the opening and were greeted by a large lagoon filled with crystal blue-green water. A carpet of lush green grass lined part of the shoreline. The remainder was surrounded by trees and colorful plants, except for a small opening on the far side.

Focusing on the passage, Pierce caught the faint scent of the ocean, along with the steady sound of waves washing ashore. Noting his young friend's interest, Chester smiled and pointed across the glassy water.

"A private beach is just a few feet over that knoll."

Pierce nodded as he bent down and ran his hand through the silky water. Although his expression did not show it, the warmth of the water took him by surprise. Even in the dead of summer, the lakes in Scotland were ice cold. Shaking off the water, he stood and glanced towards Chester.

"You were not exaggerating. The water is warm."

Chester explained that for most of the year, the water stayed tepid. During the rainy season, which was due to start soon, the ocean temperature became even warmer and set off serious tropical storms. Some were so severe they had wiped out small villages.

During the first two years after relocating to the island, he and Annabelle had structural modifications made to their home to ensure it could withstand high winds and excessive rains. Pierce had little knowledge of the island weather cycles—he had never sailed this far south. Most of his exposure at sea had been closer to England, Scotland, and France.

"How long does this season last?" Pierce questioned.

"Usually three to four months," Chester replied.

131

When Pierce raised an eyebrow in surprise, the older man guessed he had not planned to spend that much time in St. Kitts. He cautioned his young friend about attempting to sail during the season.

"I suggest that once your ship returns to Basseterre, you moor it on the north side of the island with some others until after the stormy season. It will be well protected, and you are welcome to stay with us as long as you would like. The more severe storms occur between September and November."

Pierce's trepidation about staying through the summer into early fall eased at Chester's suggestion and generosity. Although he did not want to burden his father with running Fraser Shipping for any longer than necessary, he also did not want to put his ship or crew at risk traveling in stormy weather.

Besides, Nathaniel had told him in his letter that everything was running smoothly and he should stay as long as he needed. Pierce trusted in his father implicitly and had no concerns about his ability to run Fraser Shipping effectively and successfully. Logic dictated he wait out the season.

"Perhaps we can journey to the north side tomorrow so I can inquire about repositioning the Saltire Wind when it returns."

His host gave him a pleased smile.

"Excellent. Now, let me show you that old mill. It is just off the path ahead."

Chapter Eleven

St. Kitts
The MacKittrick Estate Lagoon
June 24, 1774

The reprieve from Chester monopolizing Pierce's time allowed him to focus on his own pursuits, mainly a trip to Basseterre to check for news from his father. He hoped to hear something about the status of the annulment. Even though the purpose of his journey was to gain perspective and make peace with the past, he felt the emotional heaviness daily, reflected in his solemn demeanor.

Pierce had hoped the package ship that arrived in St. Kitts the day before would contain a letter from his father, announcing that he was free of Helene and could resume his life on his terms. Alas, no letter arrived, and he left the postmaster's office still burdened by the uncertainty of whether he would have the freedom to pursue the future he desired.

Releasing a sigh of resignation, he lifted his face to the bright afternoon sun. Its warmth permeated his sun-tanned skin and rejuvenated him. Knowing exactly what he needed, he unwrapped the reins of his horse, swung himself onto its back, and guided the steed adeptly through the streets toward the road leading back to the MacKittrick estate.

Instead of following the lane up to the house, Pierce directed the horse onto a smaller broken path that passed the home and opened into an enormous field stretching as far as the eye could see. Squeezing his muscular legs into the sides of his mount, it took the prompt and broke into a full run toward the far corner of the property where Chester had taken him the other day.

Pierce hoped the solitude of the cove and lagoon would help settle his thoughts. More importantly, he wanted to enjoy a leisurely swim. Water had always had a soothing effect on him since childhood.

Upon reaching the barrier of vegetation, he pulled the horse to a stop and jumped down. Looping the reins over its head, he led the large animal through the narrow opening into the cove. Once inside the concealed area, Pierce paused to take in its beauty.

The large round pool of clear blue-green water shimmered like a precious gem. In the distance, the faint hum of the surf washing against the shoreline drifted through the air. Taking a relaxing breath, Pierce turned and tied the horse's tether to a fallen tree where it promptly began grazing in the lush green grass.

After securing the animal, he quickly shed his boots and clothing, casually tossing them into a shaded spot under a large banana tree. Standing at the edge of the lagoon with his hands on his bare hips, he briefly surveyed the inviting water, and then slowly waded into its depth. With each step he felt its warm caress. It was markedly different from the bite of the frigid Scottish lakes he was accustomed to.

Taking a deep breath, he raised his hands above his head and launched himself over the glassy surface, his muscular arms propelling him underneath the water. Each stroke lessened the heaviness of his

Never Leave My Arms

grandmother's manipulations and Helene's betrayal. When his lungs could no longer keep him submerged, Pierce surfaced near the center of the lagoon with a sense of renewal and ease he had not felt in some time.

Unfettered by time and obligation, he floated aimlessly, allowing the warm sun to rain down on him. Occasionally, he would dive deep and admire the small colorful fish congregating near the stone masses at the bottom of the lagoon.

In the shallows, he would stand staring into the water and explore the various rock formations and vegetation that lined its edge and cascaded from the shoreline into the water. It fascinated him. Nothing like this existed in Scotland or England.

Based on the western position of the sun, Pierce estimated he had been at the lagoon for at least two hours. Before the day slipped away, he wanted to explore the beach on the other side of the cove. Making his way out of the water, he sat in the sun, allowing its warm rays to dry him before he dressed and sought out the beach.

As he approached the opposite side of the cove, the sound of the surf increased. When he reached the top of the dune, he stopped short. Pristine white sand stretched thirty yards before him to turquoise water as far as the eye could see. The surf softly caressed the shoreline. Its fingers gently pulled back the grains of sand with each wave.

The splash of the ocean muffled the sound of a young woman making her way through the narrow opening across the lagoon. Something instinctive drew Pierce's attention, and he quickly glanced around until his gaze landed on a familiar colorful headscarf.

Pierce's eyes traveled down to her face, and he released a sharp breath as their eyes locked. He would know those blue eyes anywhere. It was her. The elusive young woman from the village who had captured his thoughts and dreams since he arrived in St. Kitts.

Never Leave My Arms

Alexandra stood ramrod still, her eyes wide with shock. The last thing she had expected was to find someone at the cove—her private space. It had been her solitude since discovering it several days after arriving on the island. She had not been here in weeks because of her commitment to Kishma and her sister. Now that the family had settled in, she needed to spend some time enjoying the warm water and soothing sounds of the surf.

After breaking through the clearing, she had not immediately noticed the horse tethered off to the side. The inviting water was her focus. It was not until the creature whinnied and stomped a hoof that she realized she was not alone. Alarm bells rang in her head as she quickly glanced around and spotted the man standing across the lagoon at the top of the mound.

He stood with his back to her. His legs were braced apart and he wore dark fitted breeches, high black leather boots, and a white linen shirt that pulled taut across his broad back. The wind tugged at his damp long hair as he surveyed the beach and ocean before him.

Suddenly, as if he sensed her presence, he turned and saw her. Alexandra tried to look away, but his eyes held her captive—his gaze intense and penetrating. She recognized him immediately. It was the strapping, handsome man she had seen on the ship the morning she went to the village for the first time in disguise with Kishma.

Try as she might, Alexandra could not take her eyes off him. Her mother and aunt would disapprove of her unabashed admiration. A proper young lady did not gawk. They were to be demure and aloof, always keeping a gentleman guessing.

As her mind replayed the feminine etiquette teachings her governess had drilled into her for years, she did not realize Pierce had begun to close the distance between them. Alexandra gasped when she snapped out of her thoughts to find him walking towards her.

137

Her aunt's constant warnings about Lucrete rang in her ears. No young women were safe when he was about. What if this man was a trafficker too? He did not look like one at the port nor right now, but Annabelle's voice would not leave her head. She needed to get away from him, back to safety.

Alexandra suddenly turned and raced towards the opening to get to her horse.

Pierce called out to her, his voice rich and warm, pleading, "Lass, please don't leave. I saw you at the port in Basseterre and have wanted to meet you ever since."

His words did not give Alexandra pause, let alone stop her departure. Not wanting to scare her, Pierce did not follow. Disappointment washed over him as he stared at the opening in the tree line she had disappeared into. Although he wanted to follow her and explain he meant her no harm, he thought better of it, hoping their paths may cross again. Instead, he turned and ventured back towards the beach.

His elation at finally meeting the young woman who captured his attention weeks ago clouded his judgment. In his haste, he had not thought through how she might react under the circumstances of their encounter. He should have made a cautious approach so as to set her at ease and not scare her away. After all, she had never seen him before. He had heard about the traffickers that preyed on young island women, and she likely thought he was one of them.

While Pierce chastised himself, Alexandra quickly settled herself on the back of her horse. She was prepared to dig her heels into its sides and send the beast at breakneck speed down the path to the main road. Something made her delay. Even though her aunt's words replayed over and over in her head about Lucrete, something greater kept breaking through her thoughts. It was her intuition.

Never Leave My Arms

She did not believe, correction, or she did not want to believe this man could be a threat to her. First, he did not meet Lucrete's description, nor any pirates for that matter. He wore fine, tailored clothing and was well-groomed. Moreover, the ship she saw him on in Basseterre was a merchant vessel in excellent condition; nothing like the trafficking ships people watched for. Of equal if not more importance, he had not chased after her. If he meant to do her harm, he could have certainly caught her. His long legs could have easily outrun hers. More and more, her inner voice was telling her that she had nothing to fear from this man.

Just as he recognized her, she also remembered him as well. How could she not? Even though she only saw him from a distance, he had an unforgettable presence that set off a fluttering excitement in her, especially now that they were in close proximity of each other. As she pondered the situation, the warning bells in her head drifted off into the distance and her intuition urged her to go back. She needed to be cautious however, so she decided to remain on her horse in the event she needed a quick escape.

As Pierce started to climb the small mound, shaking his head at his own carelessness, a feminine voice carried across the water of the lagoon to him.

"What do ya mean ya be wantn ta meet me?" Alexandra called.

Pierce stopped in his tracks and his head snapped up. He dared not look for fear she would run again or worse, it would only be a dream. Taking a deep breath, he took a chance and slowly turned. His stomach dropped when he espied Alexandra. The beautiful island native was seated astride a golden brown horse framed in the opening of the tree line. She had returned.

The two remained in their respective locations, keeping the lagoon as a barrier between them. He did not want to startle her away again.

"Good afternoon Lass. I am glad to finally make your acquaintance," Pierce called to her.

139

Alexandra immediately detected a Scottish accent, but it had an unusual British clip. She frowned in confusion, uncertain if he was Scottish or British. It sounded like a London inflection.

Fortunately, in the much time Alexandra had spent with Kishma and her family, she had picked up a respectable amount of the local Creole and Western African expressions as well as the native accent. She had become proficient enough to sustain her through lengthy conversations without her true heritage being detected.

She urged her horse forward a few feet but stopped, still easily able to make a quick departure if the need arose.

"Ya say ya finally meet me. What ya mean by dat?"

Pierce remained in his spot. He sensed her apprehension and tried to put her at ease.

"I saw you the day I arrived in Basseterre. You were in the market square by the docks with another young woman. Then I saw you again in the village on the other side of the island a few days ago, but before I could catch your attention, you vanished."

Alexandra remained silent as she digested his words. She went over her visit to the village in her mind and did not recall seeing him there. If she had, she would have certainly remembered, especially after seeing him so close. This was a man a woman could not forget.

Trying to keep the conversation moving, he continued.

"My name is Pierce. What might your name be?"

Even though the rich timber of his voice eased her apprehension, Alexandra's mind raced at his question. If she gave him her true name, she could risk her safety, or if her aunt found out, her ability to move freely about the island. For a prolonged silence, she scrutinized Pierce, contemplating what she should do.

Never Leave My Arms

She had initially intended to leave and never see him or the cove again. But the more she looked at him, her inner voice encouraged her to stay. Or was it her sister's prediction: *"I'll bet you will meet a handsome man. You both will fall madly in love, and he will whisk you away to a private island!"*

A fleeting smile appeared on her lips as she thought of Penny's silliness. It did not go unnoticed by Pierce and hope rose anew for him.

She wanted to stay a little longer but was unwilling to take any risk by giving her real name. Thus, in a moment of panic, she blurted out the first name that came to mind.

"Kishma. Ma name is Kishma."

Pierce smiled.

"It is a pleasure to meet you Kishma."

Although the name rolled easily off his tongue, it did not seem to fit her. Her striking blue eyes contrasted sharply with those of the other natives he had met, most of whom had dark brown eyes to match their dark coloring. Regardless, it pleased him they had progressed to exchanging their first names.

Testing the waters for further progress, he asked, "Can you stay for a few moments?"

Alexandra stared hard at Pierce. He sensed she struggled with the decision but was encouraged that at least she was giving it serious consideration.

Offering her as much reassurance as possible, he said, "I swear to you I am not some nefarious villain. I came here because I enjoy the quiet and serenity of being at the water. In Scotland I used to swim in lakes that were ice cold. This is a pleasant respite."

Alexandra shuddered at the thought of jumping into something so frigid. She continued her critical assessment of his sincerity and let out a sigh.

"Ya not try nut'n wit me?" she asked suspiciously.

141

Pierce held up his hand as a pledge.

"I swear."

"Jus' fer a few minutes. Den I hafta leave," she warned as she slid off the back of her horse. She tied the creature off near a stump she could use to easily mount it if she had to leave in a rush. Then she perched herself on a fallen tree close to the animal.

Pierce, who had taken a seat on a boulder at the far corner of the water, asked, "Would you be amenable if I sat closer, so we did not have to shout to each other? I see there is a large rock at the edge that is closer."

The thought of him moving nearer did not alarm her. Rather, she found it exciting. The apprehension she had initially felt when they first discovered each other had been replaced with curiosity.

"Jus' remember ya promise," she warned.

Pierce nodded and casually made his way to a stone situated across from her on the water's edge.

He settled himself on the rock, one booted foot on the ground and the other on a nearby stone with his elbow casually resting on it. Joking with a lopsided grin, he said, "Much better. Now we don't have to bellow to be heard."

Alexandra returned his smile and nodded as the two made eye contact but then she quickly averted her gaze when she saw a trace of surprise cross his face. She bit her lip when she realized she had committed the one sin Kishma had warned her about—never let them see your eyes. It would be a giveaway that she was not an island native.

She quickly offered a preemptive explanation.

"I av me ma's eye colla. She wasn't from de islands."

Technically, Alexandra had not lied. She had inherited her mother's coloring, and Cherisse Landon was not from the islands. In an effort to divert his attention from her looks, Alexandra shot him a quick glance and then looked away.

Sensing her sudden discomfort, he allowed her to steer the conversation.

The richness of his voice and the slow casual delivery of each word in that unusual accent sent a tingling sensation throughout her body. It excited her and brought a flush to her face.

Although her interactions with male suitors were limited, the young men from Middlesex her father approved to call upon her had never evoked this type of reaction. This man was unlike any she had ever met. She found herself drawn to his maturity and intensity.

Even more, his admission that she had left such a lasting impression on him from afar touched her.

Careful in her reply, she gave him a shy smile before responding.

"I saw ya too dat day in da market. Ya was on a ship lookin bout."

Alexandra noted his relaxed expression, and he appeared pleased with her comment.

"What da ya want ta talk wit me bout?" she asked curiously.

Although Pierce remained at ease, he did not want to come on too strong and casually replied, "Your colorful headscarf initially caught my attention, but there was just something unique about you. When I saw your eyes and beautiful smile, I knew I had to meet you."

The mention of her eyes immediately reminded Alexandra to keep them averted.

"Please don't look away," he said warmly. "There is something behind that unusual blue that I would like to get to know if you would allow me."

She could not tell whether it was being caught in the moment with him so close or the soothing sound of his voice, but once again, Alexandra gave in to her instincts. They told her to stay and that she needed to get to know this man.

Following her intuition, she looked up and directly met his gaze.

"Let's start with ya. Ya not from da island, and ya sound like ya a Scotsman but ya no dress like one."

Pierce self-consciously looked down at his clothing. She was right; he dressed nothing like the Scottish nor the island colonials.

"Ya look like a cap'n of a ship," she observed.

Tilting her head to the side and giving him a quizzical expression, she asked, "That be yer ship I seen ya on dat day at the docks?"

Just as Alexandra had apprehensions about him, Pierce had his own about her. While she did not strike him as a duplicitous opportunist, he needed to be careful as well. Resorting to his guarded persona, Pierce replied cryptically, "Looks can be deceiving."

Although unfair to this beauty, he could not let go of the sharp pain of Helene's deceit. His wounds were still raw, and he was not ready to reveal too much about himself, particularly to a woman, until he was certain of her trustworthiness.

Alexandra noticed his expression turned guarded and his body tensed at her question. Sensing there was more behind his reply, she felt it best not to push, so she steered the conversation in a less personal direction.

Feeling more comfortable with him, Alexandra rose and walked down to the water's edge, calling over her shoulder, "Avn't seen ya 'ere before."

It took Pierce a few seconds to push down the feelings of anger and betrayal threatening to surface. He needed to return his focus to the present and the lovely woman just feet away from him.

His mother had admonished him on numerous occasions that his innate ability to be unreadable was fine for business dealings, but not when interacting with young ladies. It came across as brooding or dispassionate. After finally meeting her, he did not want to drive Kishma away.

Never Leave My Arms

Heeding his mother's advice, he took a mentally cleansing breath and relaxed his expression, adopting a friendly tone. He needed to remind himself that not all women were like Helene, presenting themselves as sweet and genuine, only to reveal themselves as deceptive and self-absorbed.

"I became aware of it a few days ago," Pierce said as he watched her wander along the water's edge a short distance away.

Espying a water flower off to the side, she plucked it and absently stroked the vibrant pink petals, turning it between her fingers.

"Where bouts ya be from? Ya dunt sound like the British dat live on the island," she said curiously.

Pierce gave her a mischievous grin that, unbeknownst to him, made him even more handsome and sent shivers of excitement up Alexandra's spine.

"I was born in England but spent a lot of time in the Highlands of Scotland," he said casually.

"Ow come ya go to Scotlan?" she asked.

To his surprise, Pierce found himself not shutting down her questions. He normally kept his personal information private, but for some reason felt comfortable with this young woman.

"My family was split between England and Scotland, so I tried to spend time between the two countries."

Turning the conversation toward Alexandra, he asked, "What about you? I know you are from the island, but you mentioned your mother was not. Where was she from?"

A pit began to develop in Alexandra's stomach. She had to be careful to keep the focus on him to avoid being caught in a lie.

Still maintaining a short distance between them and with her eyes directed anywhere but at him, she simply said, "Me ma dunt talk bout it much. She say she was born in England."

Technically, that was not a lie. Cherisse's birthplace was the same place where she married, settled with her husband, and raised Alexandra and her sister—Middlesex, England.

Before he could question her further, she looked up from her flower and captured his gaze. Flashing him a bright smile she asked, "What bring ya to da island?"

Pierce could not recall ever being so completely enamored by a young woman as lovely as the one before him. In his teens, there had been a few young lasses that caught his attention, and even Helene was pretty—at least on the outside. They all paled in comparison to this enchanting creature. There was a presence about her that made him feel safe. She genuinely wanted to know about him because it mattered to her—something he had never felt before with any woman.

"Hitched a ride to get a change of scenery and warm weather," he said.

Alexandra nodded as she digested his response. It was obvious he was not ready to divulge too much about himself, especially given their current proximity. Feeling more like herself and less guarded, she popped up from her perch, quickly moved past him, and called over her shoulder as she headed toward the beach.

"There's a change of scenery ova dat ridge. Da ocean and beach is sumtin to see and feel."

Pierce paused for a moment and then pushed himself off the boulder. He followed behind her and admired the soft sway of her hips and the peak of a bare calf as she lifted her skirt slightly to climb to the top of the dune.

Never Leave My Arms

Once on the white sand, Alexandra laughed as she put her arms out, embracing the soft breeze blowing across the ocean and beach. She looked over at Pierce as he stepped alongside her, his expression questioning with a smile playing on his lips as he looked down into those captivating eyes.

Giving him a mischievous grin, she said, "Come wit me."

Alexandra's exuberance captivated Pierce. He followed her to the soft white sand beach and fell into step beside her. An ease developed between the two as they walked along the surf, stopping every few feet to pick up a shiny colorful shell or watch a coquina burrow itself into the sand to escape the air when the tide receded.

At first, they strolled in silence, mesmerized by the foamy surf as it reached toward them and then slowly slipped back, absorbing into the next wave. Alexandra stood at the edge of the wakes, taunting it to wet her bare feet. She then rushed backward just as it came within inches of tickling her toes and giggled with satisfaction at each successful escape.

Finally, she surrendered to the temptation of the warm ocean water and allowed it to wash over her feet. With each pull of the wave, she sank slightly into the sand. A smile escaped Pierce's lips as he took in her playful antics. To his surprise, the tension slipped from his body as he allowed himself to enjoy her company. He had never experienced these types of moments with any woman.

The few women who had captured his attention had been purely physical with no desire to explore a relationship beyond that level. Helene, with whom he should have shared mutual companionship, especially since they were to marry, always presented a reserved demeanor.

On one occasion, after escorting her home, he had tried to kiss her, but she pushed him away in shock. Initially, he thought her rebuff stemmed from virginal inexperience but later learned that was not the case. There was nothing genuine about Helene.

Pushing his bitterness down, Pierce returned his focus to the young woman before him. She stood in the sand, the tide gently stroking her feet, staring out into the ocean. Tipping her face skyward, she closed her eyes and basked in the warm summer sun. As the water drifted back into the waves,

Never Leave My Arms

Pierce stepped up beside her. She immediately sensed his presence, and her pink, full lips curled upward.

"I love da ocean sun. It feels soft when ya by da water," she said.

Pierce had never thought about it, but she was right. The rays did not feel penetrating and hot. Rather, they had a silky quality. In all the times he had sailed—albeit in colder climates—he had never taken the time to stop, shut everything out, and actually feel the ocean and sun. The two stood silently next to each other, the massive ocean before them, their faces tilted upward and eyes closed.

So engrossed in the moment, Pierce did not notice the water seeping into his boots until it was too late. Unwilling to surrender the unusual peace he felt from the sound of the surf, the warmth of the sun, and her presence, he disregarded the state of his footwear and went with the moment.

Though uncertain how long they stood there, when he finally opened his eyes and looked down to assess the damage, the tide had receded enough that the water barely touched the toes of his soaked boots.

Glancing over at Alexandra, his breath caught when instead of seeing her profile, his gaze locked with her striking eyes. She had been silently watching him. For how long? He did not know.

In the short time Alexandra had observed Pierce, she could see shadows of pain flicker across his face, but as he took in the soothing sounds of the water, it seemed the troubling emotions lessened. After a few more moments, he appeared to relax. As she quietly watched him, she sensed he carried a heavy burden, and she wanted—no, needed—to help ease his hurt.

At first, Pierce stood motionless, staring at her. The waves crashed directly in front of them, sounding faint even though they were only feet away. Slowly, he turned to her, his eyes taking in every inch of her visage, keeping her rooted in place. She did not flinch. Instead, she maintained a soft expression, as if she knew something troubled him.

149

As his gaze traveled down her face and reached her plump pink lips, his mind insisted he must taste them. What was happening to him? He had never had such an intense reaction to a woman before. Not wanting to scare her, he slowly lifted his hand and placed it gently on her warm cheek. Alexandra's stomach fluttered at the excitement of his touch. The burning intensity in his eyes made her shiver.

A real man had never kissed her, and she was not ashamed to admit she wanted to experience it. The few kisses she had received were from young boys who had tried to steal them—landing either on her cheek or the side of her nose. Alexandra knew this would be different.

She held her breath in anticipation as he slowly lowered his mouth to hers. Pierce carefully slid his hand behind her head and pulled her toward him. As he pressed his lips to hers, Alexandra felt the brush of his mustache and beard. It tickled, but rather than making her giggle, it sent a warm sensation that washed over her and fueled her excitement.

Instinctively, she returned the kiss, leaning into him. Still maintaining his reserve, he slipped his arms around her and pulled her close. She slid her arms up his chest, around his neck, and pulled him down to her. Taking her cue, he deepened the kiss, nibbling at the tips of her lips and running his tongue along them, coaxing her to open her mouth.

Her limited experience impeded her briefly until she realized what he wanted her to do. She complied and was immediately swept into a vortex of passion she could never have imagined. His mouth slashed across hers as he held her tightly. Both breathed each other's breath.

A strange and exciting sensation developed between Alexandra's legs as their tongues danced seductively together. She clung to him, willingly accepting his assault and oblivious to the crashing surf. Pierce found himself similarly situated.

Never Leave My Arms

He had given up hope of ever meeting this beautiful creature, let alone holding and tasting her. Her abandonment stoked the fire ignited between them and encouraged him to explore her soft, shapely body.

Sliding one hand from around her waist, he slipped it between them and gently kneaded her breast. A soft moan escaped her lips. He could feel the hardened point through the thin linen fabric and ran his thumb back and forth over it. The sensation his touch created heightened Alexandra's arousal, and she felt an intense need in her womanly flesh.

Pierce's body also reacted to their passion. His excitement strained against the fabric of his breeches. With their lips still seared together, he slipped his hand over her soft, round bottom and pressed her against his arousal. The feel of her body against his rock hard member elicited a deep groan from within him.

Distant alarm bells sounded in Alexandra's head. Suddenly, the surf roared in her ears as she abruptly returned to the moment and realized what was happening.

Tearing her lips from his, she pushed away, her chest heaving as she tried to catch her breath. She held her arm out, as if to ward him off. Every inch of her felt scorched. Pierce released her and stepped back. They stood a few feet apart, unmoving, and silent. The only sound was the ocean. Filling his lungs with air, he closed his eyes and fought to regain control of his body. Neither said a word.

His mind raced with questions: *"What just happened?" "How could I lose control?"* Pierce Tennyson never lost control, especially with a woman. While he grappled with his thoughts, Alexandra realized she needed to put distance between them. She quickly dashed past him, rushing toward the dune that led down to the lagoon.

It took Pierce a few seconds to shake free of his thoughts, and he called to her just as she slipped out of sight at the top of the mound of earth.

151

"Kishma, wait! Please!" he called.

Alexandra ignored his plea. Lifting her skirt to her knees, she broke into a full run down to the lagoon to her horse. Quickly looping the reins over its neck, she stepped onto the tree stump and jumped onto its back. Swinging the beast around to the opening, she dug her heels sharply into its sides, sending it into a full run down the partially worn path back to the road.

Thankfully, Pierce had not followed her. The rush of the breeze in her face cooled her flush, but her body still tingled with excitement. She did not want to return to the plantation in her current state. When she reached the road, she turned in the opposite direction and headed to the village to seek out Kishma.

Alexandra needed to talk to her friend about what had happened—well, at least about meeting the handsome man from the ship. She need not disclose the intimate details.

Never Leave My Arms

Gutt Church
Kishma Sister's Home
...that same day - a short time later

"What was ya thinkin use'n ma name?" Kishma exclaimed.

"Shhh," Alexandra whispered fiercely. "I don't want your sister to hear."

Kishma stared at Alexandra in disbelief as she paced nervously in the small bedroom.

Upon arriving at Kishma's sister's home, Alexandra had grabbed her friend by the wrist and pulled her through the modest house. She quickly scanned the small space and found an empty room that provided the two friends privacy.

Kishma sensed something was wrong based on Alexandra's anxious behavior but was not prepared to hear its source. Learning that her friend had met that handsome man on the ship in Basseterre was titillating. To further hear he had become smitten with Alexandra and had been searching for her for weeks was even more exciting. However, discovering she had used Kishma's name as her own knocked the breath from the island native.

Alexandra looked at her confidant with dismay.

"I'm sorry. I panicked."

Kishma sat wide-eyed as she listened to her friend explain how her fear of revealing her true identity would prevent her from moving about the island.

Alexandra flopped down onto the bed dejectedly.

"Aunt Annabelle would most assuredly make me stay on the estate."

Turning to her close companion, her eyes filled with emotion.

"I am truly sorry, and I will make sure this does not reflect badly on you. I swear."

While still grappling with her shock at being dragged into this drama, Kishma understood how important it was for Alexandra to be free and enjoy

153

herself. She had watched her new friend grow miserable during her first two months on the island because Annabelle would not let her leave the property. Although the estate grounds were expansive, they mainly consisted of crops and fields, offering no outlet for a nineteen-year-old who enjoyed socializing.

Taking a deep breath, she clasped Alexandra's hands in hers and smiled.

"Dunt ya fret non. It be all right. Tis not like ya be seein him again."

Alexandra gave her a sheepish look that hinted at trouble.

"Right?" Kishma asked warily.

Dropping her head, Alexandra quietly whispered, "I don't know."

Kishma's mouth dropped open as she looked at her friend in disbelief.

"What ya mean ya dunt know? Ya cannot."

Alexandra had no intention of explaining every detail of what transpired between her and Pierce, but she needed her friend to understand the pull she felt toward him. She squeezed Kishma's hands and looked at her excitedly.

"I can't explain it in words, but there's a force that pulls me to him."

Kishma's eyebrow shot up as she looked at her friend skeptically.

Narrowing her eyes, she asked, suspicion lacing her words, "How did ya two meet?"

Waving off the question, Alexandra simply replied, "At the lagoon."

Her friend wasn't about to let the matter go that quickly.

"And who else was there?"

Again, feigning a dismissive response, Alexandra said abruptly, "Just the two of us."

It was obvious to Kishma that Alexandra was going to make her pull the information out of her. Two could play that game.

"So, ya two were alone at da lagoon. Did ya lay wit him?" Kishma asked bluntly.

Never Leave My Arms

Alexandra's face turned scarlet, and she shot off the bed, whirling around to face her friend.

"Absolutely not," she exclaimed with indignation. "I can't believe you asked such a private question."

Kishma could tell from Alexandra's reaction that she was being somewhat truthful. However, based on her flustered state when she arrived, she knew her friend was not sharing the entire story.

Nodding with satisfaction, she said, "Good. I'm glad ta hear dat ya did not give yourself ta dis man," Kishma said.

"Stop saying that," Alexandra whispered fiercely.

Kishma pressed her friend. "Den what did happen?" but before Alexandra could answer, she warned her, "And dunt tell me nut'n. I saw how ya come tear'n in here, all red and anx'us. Tell me da truth."

Alexandra was in awe of her friend. For a woman her own age, Kishma had an intuition that rivaled her own mother's when it came to reading her. Aunt Annabelle was easy to work around, but her mother and Kishma knew just the right strings to pull when Alexandra was trying to manipulate a situation.

Taking a breath, Alexandra calmed herself and sat down next to her friend to tell her the whole story—well, almost all of it. To Kishma's credit, she remained quiet and listened intently as Alexandra relayed her and Pierce's serendipitous meeting at the lagoon. She told her how she had captured his attention the day of his arrival in Basseterre. Alexandra had hoped Kishma would see the romance in it—being smitten from afar—but she kept her features schooled, giving nothing away.

Surging forward, Alexandra told her about their walk along the beach and their conversation about Pierce's heritage.

"He has this unusual accent. It's a blend of English and Scottish."

155

Again, Kishma expressed no opinion other than a nod of acknowledgment. Frowning at the benign reaction, Alexandra pressed on. She described how they watched the burrowing coquinas as the tide washed away, and their enjoyment of silently taking in the sounds and smells of the ocean.

"While we stood facing the ocean, I looked over to see if he was enjoying himself. I saw his eyes were closed. At first, flickers of what I could only describe as pain crossed his face. As we stood there in silence, they disappeared and he relaxed."

Kishma's expression softened slightly. Alexandra could tell she had cracked the hardened shell her friend had crawled into when she started the story. Seizing the moment, Alexandra continued.

"Kishma, I know you may find this difficult to believe, but with each breath he took, he seemed to shed whatever burdened him, and he relaxed. There's something troubling him, and I think I can help."

"Why do ya think ya help dis man, and what makes ya think he wants ya help?"

Her questions were no longer laced with mistrust, which gave Alexandra hope that she had made headway in bringing her friend around.

Encouraged, Alexandra said, "When he opened his eyes and saw me watching him, he no longer looked at me with a skeptical intensity. Instead, he looked like he trusted me."

Alexandra caught that Kishma's eyebrow immediately went up with her last statement.

"Please believe me," she pleaded. "I know how to read people just as well as you and my mother. I'm telling you, I know what I saw. There's a reason we crossed paths, and I believe it's because I can help him with whatever he's battling."

Never Leave My Arms

It was hard not to be affected by her friend's optimism. Since meeting the young English woman, Kishma had known her to be sweet, caring, and always willing to help someone in need. Kishma's family had benefited significantly from Alexandra's unwavering commitment to helping her sister prepare for the birth of her next child.

Regardless of her friend's altruism, Kishma still had concerns about Alexandra becoming involved with this man, especially if there was something in his life or background that could be dangerous. Lowering her eyebrow and softening her expression, Kishma gave her friend a loving smile.

"I admire ya for want'n to help him, but I feel ya are play'n wit fire. Please promise me ya won't see him again."

Feeling as though the inquisition was over, Alexandra squeezed her friend's hand affectionately. She knew Kishma was only looking out for her. She also realized she could not sway her friend to encourage or accept her continuing to see Pierce. When the native took a position, she held tight and would not relent.

If Alexandra told her she would continue to see Pierce, Kishma would most assuredly tell her aunt out of a sense of protection. Alexandra had to do the only thing she could—deceive her friend and tell her she would no longer see Pierce. She just needed to find a way to be convincing.

"I love you for looking out for me, but I swear, there's nothing to worry about. I can take care of myself, and he was nothing but a gentleman to me."

"Tis not what ya do I worry bout. Ya don't know what dis man gonna do. Don't make me tell ya aunt," Kishma warned, her tone becoming more urgent.

Alexandra seized the opening. Eyes wide with surprise and filling with tears, she shook her head vehemently and pleaded, "Please don't say anything. If you tell Aunt Annabelle, she'll send me back to England straight away. I swear, I will not see him again."

Kishma looked at Alexandra skeptically for a few seconds, trying to digest whether she could believe her. She didn't, and Kishma could give an equally convincing performance.

"Good. I'm only lookin out fer ya," she said sympathetically.

Nodding and wiping the tears from her eyes, Alexandra gave her friend a tremulous smile and asked, "You promise you won't tell Aunt Annabelle this?"

The young island native gave her a reassuring smile.

"Just between ya and me."

Alexandra hugged her friend tightly.

"Thank you for being such a good friend."

"I hope she feels dat way when I tell her aunt if I catch her seein dis man," Kishma thought to herself.

In the few short months the two young women had known each other, Kishma had come to think of Alexandra as a sister. As such, she would protect her from harm, whether from someone else or her own short-sightedness.

Chapter Twelve

St. Kitts
The MacKittrick Estate Lagoon
July 8, 1774

For the two weeks following Alexandra's visit to Kishma, the two friends were inseparable. This left no opportunity for the British beauty to slip away to the lagoon. Alexandra sought to demonstrate her commitment to avoiding Pierce, while Kishma pretended to believe Alexandra's promise. By the beginning of the third week, Kishma reluctantly conceded that Alexandra would keep her word. She hoped that her friend's absence had encouraged Pierce to give up and pursue another young woman.

"Someone has to save her from herself," Kishma thought.

This change of heart coincided with her sister's need for help caring for her children. Naturally, Alexandra volunteered to lend her assistance and spent her days in the small village looking after the little ones. Annabelle insisted that Alexandra return home before nightfall. Thus, shortly after the children were fed, Kishma's father would escort Alexandra back to the plantation.

In contrast, Alexandra's excitement grew each day she stayed away from the lagoon, but she could never share it with her friend. Kishma would disapprove. Pierce was never far from her thoughts. That passionate kiss they shared haunted her dreams and thoughts. Each night she went to bed, she would see his face, his smile, those penetrating eyes, and remember the feel of being held in his arms. She wished every day for Pierce to persist, hoping he would continue his visits to the lagoon in search of another chance encounter with her.

Almost three full weeks after their first meeting, an opportunity arose for Alexandra to return home early one afternoon. Aunt Annabelle needed her help hemming three dresses and asked if she would come back after lunch. Fortunately, the hemming project took much less time than expected, providing Alexandra the chance to slip away.

"Please be there," she thought excitedly to herself as she urged the horse along the path to the cove.

Guiding her mount to the usual stump, she slid off its back, looped the reins over its head, and led it through the narrow passage in the trees, emerging on the other side at the lagoon. She scanned the area and saw no one.

Disappointment quickly turned to excitement when she heard the stomp of a horse's hoof and its whinny. Following the sound, she spotted it tethered to a branch on her far left, concealed by a banana tree. Her heart raced, and her stomach fluttered.

"Pierce is here," she thought with exhilaration.

Alexandra quickly tied her mount to a tree and scanned the shoreline for any sign of him. Assuming he had climbed the hillside to reach the beach, she began to walk along the water's edge when she heard a splash. As her eyes skimmed the surface of the water, she saw him emerge at its center, flipping his soaking wet hair back, leaving a trail of water droplets behind him.

Alexandra could easily make out his muscular arms and bare chest in the crystal-clear water. So focused on his upper body, she let out a squeak when she heard his deep voice.

"Wasn't certain I would ever see you again," he said, not in a teasing manner, but sounding genuinely apologetic.

Alexandra noted this but remained outwardly unresponsive. Inside, however, she was in turmoil. She struggled with her conscience about breaking her promise to Kishma, but seeing him, especially in his current state of undress, sent waves of excitement through her.

Pierce attempted to gauge her feelings about their last encounter.

"I tried to get here sooner, but I had to take care of some business that tied me up these past weeks."

Still, Alexandra remained silent. He noticed her rigid stance, as if she were poised to flee at the slightest movement. Finally, he posed a question that could prompt her to run or respond in outrage.

"Are you still angry about what happened between us?"

Gathering herself, Alexandra shifted her focus from him to his question, careful to maintain her island dialect. She wanted him to know she had principles and deserved to be treated better.

"Ya made ya'self too friendly, and I ain't dat kind of girl," she said, lifting her chin with pride.

She half-expected him to laugh it off, but instead, he surprised her with an apology and a hopeful request.

"Kishma, it was rude of me to behave the way I did. I hope you can forgive me, and maybe we could start over?"

As the words left his lips, Pierce was surprised by his own vulnerability. He had not intended to apologize. Relationships with women had been strictly about fleshly needs.

Something about the young woman before him however, made Pierce reconsider his emotional barriers. It happened on the beach when he caught her staring at him. Logically, he knew she couldn't read his mind, but as he allowed himself, at her insistence, to close his eyes and take in the ocean, memories of the past months flooded him. The pain of betrayal and cruel manipulations welled up in him.

Until then, he had not revisited that time. Interestingly, she was right. Surrendering to the calming sounds and smells of the ocean eventually dulled the hurt. When he opened his eyes and saw her staring at him, he noticed something he had never seen before in a woman's eyes—trust and compassion.

Although Alexandra would never admit it to Pierce, aside from enjoying their kiss, she loved being held tightly in his arms. She felt safe, and when she looked into his penetrating hazel-green eyes, she saw an intensity that called to her very depths.

Kishma would say she was being foolish, tempting fate that would lead to pain and heartache. Alexandra disagreed. This man needed her. She felt it in her soul.

Pierce held his breath, waiting for her response.

Finally, she softened her expression and teased, "Do ya think ya could keep ya hands to ya'self?"

Relief flooded him as he chuckled. "I promise." Then, with a mischievous glint, he grinned, "Unless you tell me otherwise."

Alexandra waved dismissively. "Dunt be wait'n anytime for dat ta 'appen."

Never Leave My Arms

Knowing the uncertainty had passed, and the conversation had turned friendlier, Pierce remained submerged to his shoulders for modesty's sake but felt the effects of being waterlogged.

Giving her a lopsided grin he quipped, "Well, I know I can't wait any longer in this water. So, if you don't want me to test my promise, I best meet you on the beach, fully dressed."

Alexandra gasped at the thought of him emerging naked and hurried to make her way to the beach, but not without glancing back to see his broad naked back slowly emerging from the water. The liquid flowed like silk over his muscles and down past his waist. Alexandra's cheeks flushed as his perfectly shaped rounded buttocks came into view. Before he could catch her gawking, she rushed up the slope and disappeared on the other side just as Pierce stepped onto dry land.

Elizabeth H. Franklin

The MacKittrick Estate
The Cove
Late-August 1774

Almost two months had passed since their fresh start. Pierce and Alexandra met as often as possible. Sometimes they spent an hour together; other times, three or four. The couple walked along the beach and talked—well, Pierce did most of the talking.

Alexandra made it a point to keep him at the center of the conversation so she wouldn't have to fabricate stories to maintain her disguise. Instead, she shared what she had learned from Kishma about St. Kitts and its people.

She had continued to keep Penny posted on her island adventures, revealing in confidence that she had finally met a handsome sea captain. Adding levity, Alexandra assured her that she had not been swept away to a private island as her sister had predicted. However, she omitted the details of assuming a disguise, using a false name, and that she and Pierce shared a passionate kiss. Although she trusted Penny implicitly to keep her secrets, she knew her sister would find the kiss exciting but disapprove of her ruse. She would insist Alexandra tell Pierce her true name and heritage.

She could hear her sister's voice in her head.

"What if you fall in love? You will never be able to be together because of the lie."

Even though Alexandra was the older sibling, Penny had a maturity about her. She always looked at the long term possibilities of every situation. Her younger sister's words played in her head each time Alexandra and Pierce met. She could not deny that she felt herself being drawn closer to him with each moment they spent together.

On several occasions, she fell noticeably silent during their walks. The duplicity of her ruse pressed on her. The more she came to know him, the more she wanted to reveal her true self, but she quickly set aside that thought, knowing it would likely mean the end of their time together. The trust between the two would be broken, and her actions would hurt him deeply—something she could not bear.

Much like Alexandra, Pierce also held back a secret. During their time together, he spoke about his British-Scottish heritage and splitting his childhood between Scotland and England. Alexandra could see shadows of sorrow flicker across Pierce's face as he spoke about that part of his life. She sensed he carried something had occurred that caused deep wounds, but she never pushed him to discuss them.

She was unaware that the heaviest burden he bore was the uncertainty of the annulment of his marriage, a marriage he had not disclosed to her. Pierce had not yet received word from his father, and for all he knew, Helene refused to release him from their marital bonds. Like Alexandra, he feared that revealing his secret would cause him to lose her forever. Pierce needed confirmation that his father succeeded in freeing him before telling her.

Three days had passed since their last meeting. Alexandra sat at the top of the dune, overlooking the white sandy beach with her knees tucked under her chin and her long colorful skirt draped over her legs and bare feet. She had not been there long and was anxious for his arrival. Normally, the rhythm of the tide gently rolling across the shore assuaged her excitement. Her stomach flipped each time she heard the rich timbre of his voice greeting her. Today, however, the surf seemed rougher than usual—unsettled. It did little to soothe her nerves.

"Have you been waiting long?" he asked as he sat down next to her.

The warmth and friendliness of his voice made her tingle. Flashing her a grin, he leaned back on his hands, extended his long legs, and casually crossed his booted feet at the ankles.

Alexandra picked a piece of grass and rolled the dark green blade between her fingers inattentively.

"A bit."

She wanted, no she needed, to tell him the truth about herself. The time they had spent together over these past months convinced her of this.

She had come to genuinely like him and enjoyed his company. She found herself caring deeply for him and wanted to help him overcome whatever caused him so much pain that he felt the need to travel far from home to escape it.

Pierce seemed to reciprocate those feelings of closeness. He honored her wishes to refrain from kissing. Although every so often, while they walked along the surf, his hand would brush hers. The contact would send a jolt through her body as his long fingers momentarily weaved between hers in a soft caress before slipping free. Truth be told, they both wanted to feel each other. Although fleeting, it was meaningful.

The fear of losing him once he discovered her deception, however, gnawed at Alexandra. Before coming to meet him today, she had convinced herself that she must be honest and reveal her true self to him. She risked losing him, but he needed to know, and she could no longer carry on the charade.

Pierce sensed her distraction and frowned. Looking out across the ocean, he noticed the distant sky had darkened, and inclement weather brewed on the horizon.

This was no surprise. Chester told him that summers on the island were rainy, with fast-moving tropical storms. He had heard the locals speak of ones so destructive that they leveled homes and swept people away to their deaths. They did not happen often, but when they did, the impact could be devastating.

Using his sailing knowledge and experience, Pierce saw nothing catastrophic headed their way. But if they got caught in it, they would likely get drenched.

Never Leave My Arms

He could tell something troubled Alexandra, so he tried to draw her out.

"Looks like a summer storm is heading our way."

Alexandra had been so deeply engrossed in wrestling with her internal turmoil that she had not noticed the rapidly approaching weather. Her eyes widened as she saw how quickly the dark clouds advanced toward them. She jumped to her feet and felt the winds pick up and whip at her skirt. Her stomach dropped when she saw how angry the surf had become.

Panic-stricken, she turned to Pierce.

"I ave ta go now."

Seeing Alexandra's distress, Pierce leapt to his feet and grabbed her arms to steady her. Her eyes were wide with fear, and she trembled uncontrollably.

"Kishma, there is nothing to fear. It's just a quick summer squall. It will pass in no time," he said, trying to calm her.

Alexandra had never shared her fear of storms or much else about herself with him.

"I, I, I dunt like dem," she stuttered, attempting to break free of his grip. "I 'ave to leave."

Pierce glanced around the lagoon, searching for a safe place for them to ride out the storm. He could not let her leave in this state. He knew she would not reach the village before the rain started. Then a thought struck him as he recalled Chester showing him the old sugarcane mill. Taking her hand, he pulled her behind him toward their tethered horses.

"Come along. I know exactly where we can get out of this."

He easily helped her onto her horse and then swung himself onto his own.

"Follow me," he instructed as he guided them through the narrow opening onto the path.

Pierce surprised her when he took a sharp turn and urged his mount onto a barely visible trail. Alexandra held tight to the reins and followed closely behind. Her anxiety increased because she had never explored this part of the estate.

The line of trees on the left shielded them from the wind, but she could see the ominous clouds, now nearly black, creeping toward them. The smell of rain filled the air. She shook violently as a rumble of thunder boomed to her left. Pierce glanced back to check on her and saw she was leaning forward, gripping the horse's mane.

"We're almost there," he called over the wind.

Giving him a weak smile, she nodded.

Never Leave My Arms

A moment later, Alexandra spotted the top of an old brick building nestled in the trees. Hope welled up inside her. Pierce pulled his horse to a halt at the overgrown entry and jumped down.

"You stay up there. Hand me the reins, and I'll lead us in."

Without questioning him, Alexandra released her hold on the leather straps before he looped them over the horse's head. Standing between the two beasts, Pierce led them through the dense vegetation to the building. Once they cleared the trees, the remnants of the old brick structure became fully visible. He guided them around the side of the building through a large opening that once served for loading and unloading wagons.

Pierce quickly tied off the horses and turned his attention to Alexandra. Thankfully, they had reached the mill before the rain began, giving him only seconds to find a sheltered area. Most of the building's roof was missing except for a small section near the back corner.

Another clash of thunder roared as Pierce reached to help Alexandra down, startling both her and the horse. Alexandra gasped in fear and clung to its mane as it danced sideways, its eyes wide. Pierce quickly grabbed the halter and gently ran his hand down the mare's flank, speaking softly until he brought it under control.

Once the animal settled down, he reached for Alexandra, but she refused to move. Her eyes were tightly shut, and she clung to the horse's neck. Pierce had never seen her like this. In all their conversations, she had never mentioned a fear of storms. She carried herself as if she enjoyed every moment life offered without a care in the world.

"Kishma, you must let go," he said gently.

Tears escaped from under her long, light eyelashes, streaming down her sun-kissed face.

"I can't."

169

Grasping her trembling hands, he carefully detangled them from the horse's mane and placed them around his neck. He then slipped his arm around her waist and pulled her off the horse. Cradling her in his arms, her head tucked under his chin and her eyes still closed, he rushed to the dry area just as the first large drops of rain fell. A collection of wooden crates in various states of disrepair caught his eye, and he used his foot to push them together while holding Alexandra.

Once the boxes were stable, he asked softly, "Would you like to sit down?"

Alexandra nodded and opened her eyes. Pierce's arms tightened, as if reluctant to let her go before he slowly loosened his hold. He lowered her with care, his hands steadying her at the waist, their eyes locked.

"Easy," he murmured, his voice roughened by something deeper than concern.

She could feel her limbs tremble, uncertain whether it was from fear of the storm or the sensation of being in Pierce's arms. Freed from his embrace, she felt a profound loss of comfort and safety.

Another clap of thunder shook the old walls, followed by a piercing crack and flash of lightning that illuminated the shadows. Alexandra jumped and covered her ears. Rain battered the roof like a thousand fists, and the wind howled through the crumbling shutters. The storm unleashed its fury above, and the skies opened with torrential rain.

Pierce tucked her tightly to him and pressed against the back wall of the building, running his hands up and down her arms to soothe her. Alexandra shook uncontrollably as the sky rumbled angrily. No matter how hard she tried, she could not drown out the storm.

Memories of her as a small child, terrified and huddled in a corner of her room as storms passed over their estate, flashed through her mind. It wasn't until she entered her early teens that her mother realized how deeply they affected her. Cherisse assumed, like her younger sister, that the two enjoyed the sounds and sights of them.

That changed one afternoon when an unusually loud thunderstorm rolled through the English countryside of their home in Middlesex. Cherisse and the staff secured the windows when she heard a sound coming from Alexandra's room. Upon opening the door, she saw her daughter curled into a ball between her chifforobe and the wall, whimpering. Cherisse never forgot the terror in her daughter's eyes, and from then on, she and Brenton made sure Alexandra was never alone during a storm.

Pierce tried to calm Alexandra, but her anxiety deepened with each rumble from the sky. He attempted to comfort her with soft words of encouragement to no avail.

When a bolt of lightning struck a nearby tree, causing it to crash to the ground, she covered her ears and cried, "Stop! Please stop!"

"Kishma," Pierce's voice cut through the roar, low and gentle. He crouched before her. "You're safe. No harm will come to you, I swear it."

She shook her head, her lips trembling. Her mouth moved, but no words came out.

Pierce reached for her hands, slowly peeling them from her ears and enclosing them in his own, rough, and warm.

"Look at me," he murmured.

She opened her eyes, glassy and uncertain. He saw the childlike fear there, but also a trust she had not yet voiced. Another flash of lightning lit the contours of her delicate, pale face, and he knew he could not bear to see her suffer another moment.

With a suddenness that surprised even him, he leaned in and pressed his lips to hers. Tentative at first—just a whisper of a kiss, a desperate attempt to ground her. Her breath caught, and for a heartbeat, she went still. Pierce thought Alexandra would push him away, but she did not; she leaned in and accepted his closeness.

Her fingers, which moments ago had clutched her own head in panic, now curled into the fabric of his shirt. The kiss deepened, slow and searching, not urgent but alive. Her lips trembled against his but it was no longer from fear. The sound of the storm seemed faint. The roar in her ears had stopped. When they finally parted, the thunder still rolled above them, but Alexandra was no longer shaking. She exhaled, eyes wide, the storm forgotten for the moment.

"I—I didn't expect dat," she whispered, her voice unsteady.

"Forgive me," Pierce said. "I didn't know how else to pull you back to me."

Alexandra's chest still rose and fell with uneven rhythm, but the fear had dulled, overtaken by the warmth pulsing within her. Her heartbeat quickened, but not from fear. Not anymore. Encircled in Pierce's arms, she felt anchored. The storm had become something distant.

Chapter Thirteen

The MacKittrick Estate
The Abandoned Mill
Late-August 1774
...after the storm

The two sat in silence as the rumble of thunder faded and the rain slowed to a drizzle. The storm had passed and was moving across the island. Pierce reluctantly released his hold on Alexandra, and they peered through an opening in one wall to see what awaited them outside. Thankfully, the horses were where they had left them and none the worse for wear. Alexandra looked around the ramshackle structure, taking in its deplorable state.

"How did ya find dis place?" she asked.

"My friend brought me here shortly before you and I stumbled upon each other at the lagoon. He thought I would enjoy the privacy."

Alexandra continued to examine the vines and vegetation that had overtaken what was left of the walls.

"Best be careful

bout gettin caught here. An Englishman owns dis land."

Pierce chuckled lightly as he untied the horses from their tether.

"I'm not worried. He's the friend who is hosting my stay on the island, so I believe I'm safe."

Alexandra's back stiffened. Her mouth went dry, and a pit formed in her stomach.

"Oh God," she thought miserably. *"This cannot be Uncle Chester's guest from London. This cannot be that old, stuffy business friend!"*

She had to know for certain.

"Ya know dis Englishman?"

Unaware of her rising dismay, Pierce casually replied, "Chester MacKittrick."

Although Pierce did not see it, Alexandra turned away, her face draining of color. Anxiety surged in her throat like bile.

"How could I be so stupid?" she thought wretchedly.

This was the man she had avoided since his arrival, believing him to be an old, dry British businessman who likely enjoyed collecting bugs. Instead, he turned out to be the strikingly handsome man she had seen on the ship the first day he arrived at the port.

Alexandra took a sharp breath, her thoughts scattering in every direction. She had no choice; she had to tell him her true identity—but how? Discovering she was his host's niece would be a shock. How could she make him understand why she had taken up the charade? Would he still want to continue seeing her?

She couldn't collect her thoughts. She needed to talk to Kishma. Yes, Kishma would help her make sense of this. Her friend would undoubtedly be annoyed with her for continuing to see Pierce, but Alexandra knew Kishma would assist her.

Never Leave My Arms

To Pierce's surprise, Alexandra decided she wanted to leave immediately and took the reins of her horse from his hand. She looped the straps over the animal's head and turned to him.

"Can ya 'elp me up?" she asked.

Pierce looked at her questioningly.

"You want to leave this moment?"

"I need ta get 'back," she said.

Considering her extreme reaction to the storm, Pierce didn't want her to ride alone, especially if the weather changed direction and she found herself caught in it again.

"Very well, but I insist on escorting you," he said.

"Ya dunt need ta."

The chances of him finding out the truth were too great if he accompanied her to the village. He should learn it directly from her so she could make him understand.

"I be fine," she insisted, and before he could disagree, she warned, "I won't be comin' again if ya dunt respect ma wishes."

At first, Alexandra thought he would argue. He stared down at her with an intense expression. Even though he tried to conceal it, she could tell he was mentally debating whether to further the argument.

Finally, he nodded.

"Very well. But please be careful and go straight home."

Alexandra gave him a relieved smile.

Before turning to mount her horse, she said, "I see ya da day afta tomorrow when da sun is high."

Pierce stepped up to help her, but instead of lifting her from her foot, she squeaked in surprise as he gripped her waist and effortlessly lifted her onto the animal's back. His hand lingered at her side until she had positioned herself safely on the beast. Before taking the reins from him, Alexandra

175

captured his gaze with her striking blue eyes. She could see concern in them and gave him a reassuring smile.

"Dunt worry bout me."

Trying to ease his concern, Alexandra leaned down and placed a warm sweet kiss on his lips. Pulling away slightly, she searched his eyes.

"Thank you."

She wanted him to know how much his comforting her during the storm meant. She immediately realized she had not used her island accent. Giving him a quick glance, she saw no sign he had noticed her slip-up, but she couldn't take any chances. She needed to get away from him as soon as possible.

Swinging the horse around, she coaxed it out of the ruins and down the path leading toward the main road. Once she cleared the heavy vegetation, she set the animal out at a full run to find Kishma.

Never Leave My Arms

Church Gutt
Kishma's Sister's Home
...a short time later

Alexandra rode at breakneck speed to the village. Her thoughts raced as fast as her horse. She knew Kishma would be angry with her for reneging on her promise and continuing to meet Pierce. However, what would truly send her friend over the edge would be Pierce's identity. The very guest of her uncle's that Alexandra had spent months trying to avoid.

The moment Kishma answered the front door of her sister's home and saw Alexandra flushed and breathless, she knew something had happened. Surmising the obvious, she knew it must have something to do with Pierce. Grabbing her friend's wrist, Kishma pulled her inside and led her to the kitchen. The children were asleep in their room, and her sister had gone to the neighbors with her newborn for a visit.

Although small and crude, the space was clean and tidy. The fine wood counters shone from careful polishing. Above them, a long shelf stretched across the wall, housing neatly stacked dishes of various sizes and sacks of baking necessities. A roughly hewn table with four stools sat in the middle of the room.

Kishma impatiently pushed Alexandra onto a stool and took a seat across from her.

"What did ya do now?" she asked with exasperation.

Alexandra looked at her friend with surprise. She thought she could count on Kishma for support, not annoyance. She could not blame her for losing her patience. The last time she arrived unannounced and flustered, it had to do with the very man Kishma warned her to stay away from. She had cautioned Alexandra that no good would come of continuing to see this man.

177

Alexandra could not disagree more. Something good had come of it. She had fallen in love with Pierce Tennyson. It was nothing she planned to happen. She only wanted to help him deal with his burdens so he could be happy. At least that's what she kept telling herself.

If Alexandra were completely honest, she had to admit a powerful attraction to him. After all, aside from his handsome physical appearance, Pierce possessed an indescribable intensity she had only glimpsed briefly on two occasions: their first kiss on the beach and today at the old mill. Remembering, she absently touched her lips, still feeling his warmth.

A knot developed in Alexandra's throat, and her tear-filled eyes widened at the realization. She had never admitted that to herself until now. Although she should have been ecstatic, she could not be. In all the time they spent together, she had lied to him. He would likely never forgive her. What a mess she had created!

Upon seeing her friend's despondency, a wave of contrition washed over Kishma. She misread Alexandra's emotion as a response to her impatience, not realizing it was related to her feelings for Pierce and the consequences of her deception.

Reaching for her friend's hand, Kishma squeezed it warmly. "I'm sorry. I shouldn't 'ave said dat."

"Oh, Kishma, what have I done?" Alexandra said miserably.

Kishma became immediately concerned. She had never seen Alexandra in such distress. Taking both of her hands, she made Alexandra look at her.

"Ya are scar'n me."

Alexandra said nothing for a moment, staring wide-eyed at her friend as she tried to gather her thoughts. Just as Kishma was about to shake her, Alexandra blinked and took a deep breath.

"First, you must tell me you forgive me for breaking my promise."

Never Leave My Arms

Still on edge, Kishma looked at her friend questioningly. The only promise between them was that Alexandra would no longer see Pierce. Kishma had known from the moment she made that commitment that her friend would not keep it.

Giving her a tentative look, she asked slowly, "Ta stop see'n dat man?"

Alexandra nodded. "Yes."

Swallowing hard, she continued quickly, "I knew he needed a friend, and I swear that is all I planned for it to be."

Alarm bells rang in Kishma's head, but she didn't want to overreact before hearing everything Alexandra had to say.

Bracing herself for the worst, she squeezed the young woman's hand and calmly said, "Go on."

The room felt suffocating to Alexandra. She rose and quietly paced the small space. Each second of silence increased Kishma's anxiety.

Finally, in exasperation, she demanded, "Tell me."

Alexandra stunned her friend when she blurted out, "I have fallen in love with him."

Before Kishma could fully digest her friend's admission, the floodgates opened, and she sat with rapt attention as Alexandra laid out the entire story.

The two met at the lagoon almost daily, spending hours talking about everything—except Alexandra, of course. Pierce regaled her with stories of his British-Scottish heritage and his childhood in Scotland. Recently, before his trip to St. Kitts, he took charge of his maternal grandparent's shipping enterprise and relocated its headquarters to London.

Looking at Kishma with excitement in her eyes, she exclaimed, "Can you believe his family home is not far from our London residence?"

Kishma waited for Alexandra to take a breath before interjecting with her most important question.

"Did ya give yourself to him?"

Alexandra stopped in her tracks and glared at Kishma.

"Absolutely not!" she said heatedly, a blush creeping up her neck to her cheeks.

Kishma eyed her friend closely, trying to determine if she was telling the truth. Something nagged at her that Alexandra had more to say on the subject.

"Did he try to lay wit ya?" Kishma pressed, unwilling to let the issue go.

Alexandra's face flamed red with embarrassment. It was pointless to avoid the inevitable, but if she said it fast enough and launched into Pierce's identity, perhaps her friend would let it go.

"He kissed me twice, but nothing more. You will not believe..." Alexandra started to say before Kishma cut her off.

"When?" she asked with a mulish expression.

Alexandra threw up her hands in exasperation. She faced Kishma squarely and gave her a crisp explanation.

"Fine. If you must know, he kissed me on the first day we met and again today. And before you cut me off again, I told him after the first kiss that I was not that kind of girl and that he needed to respect his boundaries, which he did."

Kishma's eyebrow shot up, indicating she was waiting for an explanation of today's incident.

Alexandra's lips still tingled from their kiss, and her eyes softened as she remembered his tenderness and concern for her while she struggled with her demons.

"We got caught in a thunderstorm and took shelter in an old mill. You know how much storms terrify me. He tried to calm me, but I was so panicked I could not speak. He said he did not know what else to do, and that is why he kissed me."

Never Leave My Arms

Kishma slowly lowered her skeptical eyebrow. She knew about her friend's fear of storms and conceded that the one that had just blown through was intense. Alexandra took heart when she saw her friend relax.

"Sounds like ya two got ta be close," Kishma said, stressing the word "close."

The color drained from Alexandra's face, and she swallowed hard.

"Yes, we did. Closer than I ever thought or planned."

"Isn't dat good?" Kishma asked.

Alexandra began pacing again, her agitation rising as she quickly replied, "Yes," but then just as hastily countered, "No."

Kishma looked at her questioningly. "What duz dat mean? Is der sum'tn wrong wit him?"

Again, Alexandra confused her friend with her reply. "No," then correcting herself, "well yes."

Her annoyance building, Kishma threw her hands up in frustration.

"Stop pace'n girl. Tell me what's da problem."

Alexandra did as her friend asked and looked her squarely in the eyes. "It's because of who he is."

Again, the island native gave her friend a befuddled look.

"And who is he?" she asked.

What Alexandra said next caught Kishma off guard. "He is Uncle Chester's guest."

The already small room felt much smaller at the revelation.

With a stony expression, Kishma quietly asked, "Dat old English man ya been avoid'n deez past months?"

Alexandra nodded.

"Don't you see? That's why this is such a mess. When we met today, I had every intention of telling him my true identity but when I found out he is my uncle's houseguest, I lost my nerve."

181

Incredulous, Kishma asked, "Have ya forgott'n ya used ma name?"

Quickly taking a seat next to her friend, Alexandra grabbed her hands giving them a reassuring squeeze.

"I swear I will make this right."

Pulling free, Kishma looked accusingly at her.

"And how do ya tink ya gonna do dat?"

Alexandra chewed absently on her fingernail as her brain pieced together a plan, but no matter how hard she examined the situation, it always came back to the same answer. She needed to tell Pierce the truth as soon as possible. If it didn't come from her, or if he discovered it by accident, she would assuredly lose any chance of explaining and making him understand. He would shut her out.

"I would tell him tomorrow, but I remember Aunt Annabelle told me Uncle Chester and their houseguest were going to Basseterre. They are to be gone until well into the morning hours, so Pierce would not be able to meet me at the lagoon. That gives me another day to plan what I have to say, and I pray he will understand."

Giving Kishma a sheepish look, she asked, "In the meantime, can I stay here with you until after dark and then ride back with your father to the estate?"

She quickly explained. "I cannot risk running into him."

Even though Pierce stayed at the estate, likely in the wing opposite hers, the chance of them crossing paths was too great.

Giving her friend a supportive embrace, Kishma said, "Of course ya can."

Pushing her slightly away, she gave her a serious look. "Ya best be prepared ta do some fast convinc'n."

Never Leave My Arms

The MacKittrick Estate
Chester's Study
...that same evening

As with each of their meetings at the cove, Pierce's ride back to the estate provided an opportunity to reminisce about his time spent with Kishma. He had not realized until today how much her presence and company affected him. She gave him a sense of calm and made him feel grounded. She listened with rapt attention as he spoke about his life and the things that mattered to him, always asking or commenting at just the right moment.

Initially, the sound of his own laughter felt odd, as he could not recall the last time something had amused him. Now, with Kishma, humor and light-hearted moments filled their time together. Today, the ride was different; it felt invigorating. He allowed himself to relive the sensation of having her in his arms, his lips on hers, listening to her voice, touched by her smile, and captivated by those beautiful eyes. No woman had ever reached him the way she had, particularly Helene.

Pierce paused for a moment. It was the first time he had thought of Helene by name rather than using a pronoun laced with distaste. Thinking or saying her name aloud no longer affected him. The anger he once felt towards her had dulled; instead, the young island native with the colorful headscarf and captivating blue eyes monopolized his thoughts.

Chester noted his young houseguest's musical whistle drifting through the doors of his study. The path to the barn wound past the stairs to the older man's office, and he could hear Pierce making his way toward the main house. A smile touched Chester's lips as he stepped toward the open doorway and called to Pierce.

"Join me for a drink?"

Pierce chuckled. "I could use something to take the dryness from my throat."

183

His lightheartedness was a refreshing change from his usual serious demeanor. Chester wondered what was behind this transformation. He had seen it slowly coming on over the past two months. The older man poured a generous amount of the fine whiskey Pierce had brought from England into two crystal glasses and handed one to his guest.

"You seem to be having a good day," his host observed.

"Mmm," Pierce replied, taking a sip of the amber liquid.

"You can tell me it's none of my business, but there's been a notable change in you recently. Did you receive good news from home or meet someone here who might be responsible?"

Pierce pondered his host's comment, recalling their conversation in this very study on the first night he arrived at the estate. Chester had not pressed him for explanations about what had happened that led him to St. Kitts, but he had promised to discuss it when he felt ready.

Today, Pierce realized that much of the pain he had carried had subsided, largely thanks to the beautiful island native girl who had caught his eye. Moreover, a friendship had blossomed between him and Chester.

The older man had not only opened his home to Pierce but had also shown him unconditional friendship. He had given the young British-Scot a sense of belonging and safety, a gesture Pierce had not realized he needed. He now felt comfortable discussing what had happened with his new friend.

Chester sat quietly, maintaining an attentive yet serious demeanor as Pierce detailed everything that led him to St. Kitts. Only one specific event caused him to raise an eyebrow: the conspiracy to murder him.

"Thankfully, they dumped me in the Firth next to one of my ships. My friend and crew member heard me tapping on the ship's hull, and when they went to investigate, they found me," Pierce said.

"Unbelievable," Chester whispered.

Never Leave My Arms

It took Pierce a moment to gather his thoughts before continuing. Each word he spoke stoked the anger he had kept tamped down—not only over the attempt on his life but also the betrayal he felt from his grandmother and Helene.

He had given Helene an opportunity to back out before the marriage so she could be with the man she wanted, but she insisted on proceeding with the wedding. Had he known that money motivated their attempt to kill him, he would have gladly given her whatever sum she desired to avoid the marriage.

Initially, he thought reopening these wounds would offer no benefit and only deepen the pain. However, it was quite the opposite; he felt relief—freedom. Clearing his throat, he explained to Chester how he enlisted his father's help to turn the tables on Helene and her duplicity.

"When I told him I wanted to get away to a warm climate he insisted I come to St. Kitts. He thinks highly of you and knows you to be a trusted friend that I could count on. Before I left, I gave him legal rights to run Fraser Shipping and force Helene to end the marriage."

Chester swelled with pride and appreciation at Pierce's kind words. He also felt compassion for a young man who had been the victim of a cruel manipulation that almost cost him his life.

"I think just as highly of your father. He is a fine man. Has he sent word of any developments in resolving the matter?" Chester asked.

With his glass now empty for the second time, Pierce frowned at the bottom of the crystal vessel.

"In his last letter, he said Helene's family is not being cooperative, and he had to enlist the services of a barrister. It's going to take longer than expected."

Pierce shook off the negative thoughts that threatened to consume him and conjured an image of Kishma. It lightened his mood, and his lips curled as her striking blue eyes stared back at him. Chester noticed this.

"Seems there is something, or dare I say someone, easing your anxiety over the situation?" he said with a light chuckle.

An unexplained sense of chivalry overcame Pierce. His host's comment was not inappropriate, but he felt the need to champion the young woman's virtue and put things into proper perspective.

"It's only a friendship we share. She made it clear from the outset that is all she would allow, and I have come to see that's what I need due to my current situation."

Chester gave his young guest a thoughtful look. The man before him today bore no resemblance to the one who had sat in that exact seat months ago.

"I can see her effect. She must be quite special."

Pierce tried to conceal his smile but could not. "She is."

Relaxing further back in his chair, Chester took the last sip of his whiskey.

"Tell me about her. I know most of the people in this area. Where did you meet her?"

"I actually saw her in Basseterre when I first arrived. She and another woman were shopping at the street market. She had a colorful headscarf that stood out and the most unusual blue eyes for an island native."

"Was this the young lady you saw that day in the village at Church Gutt who slipped away?"

Pierce nodded. He went on to tell him that it was not a week later that he ran into her at the private cove at the far edge of the property. These past months they spent their time together walking on the beach and enjoying the lagoon. This piqued Chester's interest because most locals who reside in

Never Leave My Arms

Church Gutt work for his neighbors. Lidy, her husband, and their daughters live nearby.

"What is this young lady's name? I might know her."

"Her name is Kishma," Pierce said.

"Our cook's daughter's name is Kishma, but she doesn't match your young lady's description."

Chester took a moment to ponder any other young women who carried that name, but none immediately came to mind. It was not a common name.

"Well, no matter. Whoever she is, her effect on you is obvious. It's good to see you relaxed."

Setting his empty glass on his desk, Chester pushed himself out of his chair and reached across to shake Pierce's hand.

"I am truly sorry for what you have endured and thank you for trusting me enough to share. If there is anything I can do for you or your father to assist in resolving the situation, I am at your disposal. I have some contacts in that area of Scotland."

Pierce smiled warmly.

"Your friendship and opening your home to me has been incredibly generous and more than enough. I am truly enjoying my time here learning about St. Kitts and all of your efforts to improve life here."

Chester chuckled and joked, "You are welcome, but I think your lovely new friend deserves most of the credit for the enjoyment of your stay here."

Pierce smiled and did not argue the point. Chester was right.

"I will see you at dinner."

Catching Pierce's attention before his departure, Chester mentioned, "Before I forget, Annabelle has adjusted the time for serving breakfast tomorrow to accommodate our early departure for Basseterre to check on your ship's return. I informed her we would be returning around midnight. We can eat dinner in town."

The Saltire Wind had returned a day ago to Basseterre. The two men had scoped out an area Chester had recommended in Sandy Point to reposition the vessel until the stormy season passed. Before moving the ship, Pierce needed to meet with Alasdair and Nials and have a full inspection completed. Chester asked to tag along. Pierce welcomed his company and the opportunity to show him the ship.

Pierce nodded before he disappeared through the doorway to the veranda. His soft whistle drifted down the veranda as he made his way to his room.

Chester picked up the two empty crystal glasses and placed them on the polished mahogany sideboard. As he reflected on their conversation, his thoughts slowed when they discussed the young woman who had made such an impact on Pierce.

At the time, he had ignored a nagging feeling when he heard the name Kishma. Now alone, he focused more on it. Lidy's daughter shared the name. In fact, the young woman was about the same age as Alexandra and had been on the property daily since her arrival. The two young women had hit it off immediately and become close friends.

What confused Chester was Pierce's description of his new young lady friend. Although he had never looked closely at Kishma, he was certain she did not have striking blue eyes. She had the same coloring as her mother and father—brown eyes, and he had never seen her wear a colorful headscarf.

The only person he had ever seen wearing such a head covering was his niece Alexandra. When he first saw her dressed in island wear, neither he nor Annabelle recognized her. She and Kishma had contrived the outfit so she could move around the island without drawing attention. Dressed as a local, she looked like an island native—except for her eyes; their color gave her away.

Never Leave My Arms

Chester quickly shook off the notion as far-fetched. After all, she had light skin, but he had to concede it had darkened from her time in the sun. Besides, the impossible hurdle would entail concealing her light-blonde hair, which, now that he thought about it… she had colored dark brown and wore hidden underneath a colorful headscarf.

"Good lord. Could Alexandra be Kishma?," his inner voice whispered.

Elizabeth H. Franklin

Since before Pierce's arrival, Annabelle had expressed her frustration over Alexandra not spending at least one meal at home. Moreover, her niece had yet to meet their guest. She had never been home at the house long enough to learn anything about him. Instead, she spent all of her waking hours in Church Gutt with Kishma, helping her older sister with the children.

She desperately wanted them to meet. Annabelle sensed they would enjoy each other's company and possibly make a good match. Before leaving England, Chester recalled that Annabelle often engaged in matchmaking efforts with her friends. Although he frowned upon it, he had to give her credit, she was an excellent judge of compatibility. Many of her pairings ended resulted in matrimony.

After moving to St. Kitts however, her pastime fell by the wayside. There were no marriage markets like those in London. Pierce's arrival reignited her partnering efforts. She had told him spending a mere five minutes with the handsome British Scot convinced her that he and Alexandra would be a perfect match.

Unfortunately, Alexandra was making it difficult. Her niece constantly used excuses to avoid meeting the gentleman, claiming she was helping Lidy's older daughter with her children while preparing for the arrival of another baby.

Annabelle could not fault Alexandra for extending her help to someone in need. She loved that her niece cared so deeply for others' comfort and happiness. So, in the short term, she let it go, understanding that once the baby was born and settled, she needed to refocus on matters closer to home.

As Chester made his way from his study to their bedroom, his thoughts drifted. He wanted to tell Annabelle about the young lady who had caught their guest's eye and his suspicion that Alexandra was that person. No doubt this would please his wife, but he did not want to betray Pierce's confidence. The man had been through enough.

190

Never Leave My Arms

If Alexandra was Kishma, it puzzled Chester as to why she had not revealed her true identity when she met Pierce. It was not like her to play such games. Not one to judge without hearing her side, he surmised she would have a good reason, and he would soon hear it directly from her. This could not continue any longer. It had become cruel.

Annabelle had just sat down with her sampler when Chester entered their bedroom. Her face lit up at the sight of her husband.

"Hello dear," she said with a bright smile as she set the piece down on a small table. "You and Pierce were ensconced for quite some time. Is all well?" she asked, placing an affectionate kiss on his cheek.

Until that moment, Chester had not decided whether to tell Annabelle about part or all of his discussion with Pierce. It was a delicate balance. He did not want to break his young friend's confidence or reveal the torment that had brought him to St. Kitts, but he did want to mention the young woman he had met and his suspicions that she was Alexandra. The troubled expression on Chester's face raised concern in Annabelle.

"What is wrong? Something is amiss; I can tell. I know that look."

Chester motioned for her to sit in the chair she had just vacated. Annabelle sensed this was not a good sign.

"Chester, you are scaring me. What is wrong?"

The older man patted her hand reassuringly and softened his expression.

"Rest easy. Tis nothing bad."

Giving him a skeptical look, she asked slowly, "Then why such a serious expression?"

"I am sorry, my dear. It's not worry you see on my face. It is confusion. I hope you can help clear things up for me and our guest," he said.

Annabelle relaxed and brightened.

"Certainly! How can I help?"

191

Chester filled her in on part of his conversation with Pierce regarding a young island woman, how they had been meeting at the cove these past months, how he credited her with brightening his view of the world, and how he was quite taken with her. Pierce also pointed out that she was a young lady with morals and principles, offering nothing more than friendship.

"He said she is lighter-skinned, petite, with brown hair, and wears an unusually colorful headscarf."

Annabelle sat thoughtfully for a moment, trying to envision someone who fit that description, but drew a blank. Chester added more details.

"She has striking blue eyes…" he paused, then added, "… and her name is Kishma."

He gave Annabelle an intense, meaningful look. A look of confusion appeared as she processed the information.

"The only Kishma I know is Lidy's daughter — Alexandra's friend — and she does not fit that description."

"But Alexandra does when dressed in her island wear," Chester said.

He saw the moment his wife connected the dots.

"Good heavens!" Annabelle exclaimed. Vacating her seat, she took a few steps, stopped and turned back.

"Wait. That cannot be possible. The moment he said his name she would know him."

Chester looked at his wife questioningly.

"Are you certain she even knows the name of our guest? I have never told her, and you have barely spoken with her since we received word of his journey here."

Annabelle's mind raced as she tried to recall her few conversations with her niece and whether she had mentioned their visitor's name. She

Never Leave My Arms

remembered that her interactions with her niece had been brief and usually involved Alexandra rushing off with Kishma.

The only time she mentioned her husband's guest was when she intercepted Alexandra one morning as she tried to rush out. Annabelle recalled telling her that she had just missed meeting him, but did not remember giving her his name.

"Did you tell Pierce you believed Alexandra was his new friend?" Annabelle asked.

Chester shoved his hands in his pockets and shook his head.

"No. I am more interested in finding out why she did not tell him her true identity. If she had, Pierce would have known immediately, and this deception could have been avoidable."

Annabelle pursed her lips, her brows furrowed thoughtfully.

"Since her arrival, I have constantly impressed upon her the need to be cautious because of things that can happen to young women on this island, particularly someone like her whose coloring stands out."

Annabelle reminded Chester that she had kept her niece close at hand the first two months after her arrival. She had only agreed to let the young woman venture off once she proved she could maintain a disguise, and only with the understanding that she had to be in the company of Kishma or a family member.

"Alexandra likely deceived him because she did not know him or of him. She was being cautious."

Chester listened to his wife's explanations. She made sense. He had watched Alexandra grow up and knew her parents as fine, upstanding people who instilled good morals in their children. He refused to believe that Alexandra would be so cruel as to intentionally deceive someone while pledging her friendship.

193

Both Chester and Annabelle agreed that regardless of why she started the ruse, Alexandra needed to make things right with Pierce. She needed to explain and apologize.

Although she did not articulate this to her husband, all the makings of an "opportunity" existed for her to foster a budding romance between her niece and Pierce. First, Alexandra needed to admit her deception to him. She would need to employ her excellent skills of persuasion. Annabelle had every faith in her niece's ability to help him understand why she had initiated the subterfuge. If Pierce could forgive her, which Annabelle believed he would if he were as taken with her as Chester conveyed, then a future together was a real possibility.

From the moment her husband told her that Nathaniel and Larena's son would come for a visit, she had thought Alexandra would enjoy socializing with someone from similar roots. People spoke highly of the Tennyson family in London's social and political circles, and his Scottish maternal family were successful shipping magnates. When Pierce arrived and she saw how quickly he and her husband became friends, she immediately thought him a good match for Alexandra.

"Annabelle? Did you hear me?" Chester asked.

"Hmm. Oh. I am sorry. I was lost in my thoughts," she replied absently. "What did you say dear?"

"Alexandra needs to tell this young man her true identity as soon as possible. He deserves her honesty."

Annabelle carefully folded her husband's jacket and placed it across the silken slipper chair in front of her dressing table. She did not disagree with him, but would not immediately think the worst of Alexandra. She needed to provide an opportunity for her niece to explain herself and then figure out how to present it to Pierce in the best possible way.

Never Leave My Arms

Turning to help him remove his vest, she said, "Absolutely dear. I will speak with her tomorrow. You and Pierce will be gone until late, so that gives me an opportunity to spend some quality time with her."

Chester placed an affectionate kiss on her cheek and smiled lovingly at her. "Thank you."

Chapter Fourteen

The MacKittrick Estate
...later that night

Alexandra arrived home after dark. The entire ride she kept going over in her head how she would break the news to Pierce of her true identity. She expected his anger at being deceived, but she hoped she could convince him she did it out of necessity for her safety.

She had not been in her room more than a few moments when her aunt knocked at her door.

"Alexandra, it's me. May I come in?" she asked softly.

Alexandra opened the door ajar to let her in. She had not changed out of her clothing nor freshened up yet.

Annabelle chuckled at the sight of her young niece.

"I still cannot get over how different you look dressed like that and with dark hair."

Alexandra gave her aunt a weak smile and self-consciously ran her hand down the side of her brown tresses. She had planned to wash the coloring out tonight, but because she would meet Pierce the day after tomorrow, she had kept her hair dark until after they met. She felt the change in her appearance would add to the shock of her revelation.

"I have been so busy with Kishma, I have had little time to myself," she said with a nervous laugh.

Annabelle nodded. Her niece had been spending much time helping her friend. Lidy raved about how much her grandchildren enjoyed the young British girl and her innate ability to get them to behave for dinner and bath time.

"I think you and I should spend a little time together. Your uncle and his guest are off to Basseterre before sunrise tomorrow. They will be gone until almost midnight, and I would like you and me to have dinner together. I won't take no for an answer either," Annabelle said with a wink.

Alexandra could not deny her aunt's request. It was true. They had had little time together since she and Kishma had struck up their friendship. Annabelle had supported the union wholeheartedly. She loved the young island native. Of equal importance, Alexandra had no chance of running into Pierce due to their late return. She would be in bed long before they arrived home.

"That sounds wonderful."

"Splendid!" Annabelle exclaimed.

Before opening the door, she turned and chuckled as she asked, "Could you please don one of your lovely dresses so I can get a glimpse of my niece from Middlesex?"

Alexandra laughed lightly.

"Absolutely. I shall wear one of my best gowns."

Annabelle smiled warmly before slipping out of the door. As she walked down the long hall towards the main house, she hummed softly to herself.

197

The following evening…

Alexandra took one last look at herself in the mirror. It felt strange not to wear her flowy island outfit. The native attire gave her a sense of freedom from her tight, restrictive clothing and additional undergarments. Thankfully, a fresh evening breeze set in at sundown that cooled the expansive plantation home, making it bearable for her to wear one of the dresses she brought from England.

The satin light blue gown she selected accentuated her eyes. Its scoop neckline bodice, decorated with a V-shaped scalloped white lace inlay, narrowed to a point at her small waist. It sat perfectly on her hips, where the voluminous full-length skirt flared in countless folds to the floor. The fitted sleeves stopped at her elbows and were draped at their edges with matching bodice netting.

Because she planned to see Pierce tomorrow, she decided not to wash the color from her hair. Instead, she pulled it back off of her face with decorative hair combs she had purchased in the village and kept the back loose and flowing down her back.

Turning her head from side to side, she checked her appearance one last time. The image of the young woman before her was a blend between Alexandra Landon from Middlesex and her island native alter ego. Satisfied with her efforts, she smiled brightly and set out to meet her aunt in the dining room.

Although the hour was close to eight p.m., the late summer sun dipped in the western sky, diffused with a veil of soft clouds blocking its heat. Annabelle had the household staff lift the wooden louvered window shutters and open the doors. She wanted to capture as much light and fresh air as possible before the bright orange orb set.

Never Leave My Arms

Alexandra smiled at the sight of the beautiful table setting. Two long, cream-colored lit taper candles sat atop shiny crystal holders in the center flanking a small vase filled with fragrant tropical flowers of various colors. A lace tablecloth covered the round wood table, and two place settings of fine China sat across from each other. Lanterns placed strategically about the room provided ample lighting to illuminate the space once dusk set in.

"'Tis lovely," Alexandra said as she looked around the room.

Annabelle entered from the hallway that led to the kitchen and took in the sight of her young charge.

"You look stunning," she said. "Even though your hair is still dark, tis good to see my niece again."

Alexandra admired her aunt as well. She had pulled her hair up in an artfully crafted pile of curls atop her head and donned a square-neck dark green muslin gown. Since moving to the tropics, she had stored her satin and woolen dresses and chose light, breathable fabrics to fashion new frocks more appropriate for the warm climate.

"I wanted to do something special for us," Annabelle said as she gestured for Alexandra to sit down at the table.

The cook appeared in the doorway with a tray filled with a small roasted hen, vegetables, and a selection of warm breads.

Gesturing to the empty space she had cleared, Annabelle said, "Lidy, you can set the tray here. We can serve ourselves."

Giving the older woman an appreciative smile, she went on.

"You go on home and we will see you in the morning."

Lidy bobbed her head and flashed a bright white smile. "Yes Mistress Annabelle. Tank ya."

Alexandra had not realized how hungry she was until she smelled the delicious fare. She had only had a biscuit for breakfast and a banana after meeting up with Kishma.

199

The two women took no time sampling Lidy's efforts, their conversation limited as they enjoyed every morsel. Once satiated, Annabelle opened the floor for discussion.

"So, tell me all about everything you have been doing these past months. I know you and Kishma have helped her sister prepare for her new family addition. Is that all?"

Alexandra daintily wiped the corners of her mouth with her linen napkin and looked down at her plate as she answered her aunt.

"Taking care of the little ones kept Kishma and me busy, especially when they awaken shortly after dawn and don't go to sleep until after sundown. They are a handful," she said, shaking her head.

Annabelle chuckled.

"I can imagine. Tis a shame your commitment to Kishma and her sister has not permitted you to meet Chester's guest. He is a lovely man, and your uncle has taken quite a shine to him. Perhaps now that the babe has been born and is settling in you can spend more of your time here. It won't be long before we head back to Middlesex."

Alexandra's grip on the pitcher of water faltered at the mention of Pierce, and she promptly set it down. Her aunt caught the incident and dipped her head to conceal a threatening smile while her niece quickly placed her hands in her lap and clasped them tightly to stop them from shaking.

"Silly me. I don't think I have ever told you his name. But of course, how could I since we have barely spoken since his arrival," Annabelle said excitedly.

Alexandra kept her eyes hooded as her aunt continued.

"Interestingly, his father's family is from the Mayfair district of London, close to your parent's city residence. His mother's family are from the Scottish Highlands, a well-known clan. I believe it is the Fraser Clan."

Never Leave My Arms

Casting a glance to see Alexandra's reaction, she could see her niece's facade was about to crack.

"The moment I met him, I detected a certain clip to his English accent. Didn't you?" she asked deliberately.

Alexandra's eyes grew wide and shot up, locking with her aunt's. Her mouth went dry, and she reached for the water glass. The crystal vessel shook as she placed it to her lips and took several large gulps of the cold liquid, enjoying the feeling as it cooled her throat.

Annabelle kept her stare trained on her young charge and actually took pity on her. She saw the fear in her striking blue eyes, the same eyes that captivated Pierce.

The silence hung between the two until Alexandra finally croaked out, "How did you know?"

She did not know the extent of her aunt's knowledge of the situation but surmised it was likely most everything.

Reaching across to take her niece's hand supportively, Annabelle said warmly, "Pierce told your uncle."

Alexandra swallowed the lump in her throat and whispered, "Does he know the truth?"

Annabelle shook her head. "No. Nor is Chester going to tell him. Your uncle and I put the puzzle together last night."

Squeezing Alexandra's hand affectionately, she went on to say, "From what your uncle tells me, Pierce is quite taken with you."

Her aunt shared her discussion with Chester last night. Her husband told her how Pierce had disclosed he had met a lovely island native woman named Kishma. The two had struck up a friendship and developed a close bond. As the British Scot described the young woman, Chester realized she did not fit the description of the Kishma he knew. Rather, she bore a strong resemblance to Alexandra, the telltale, her unusual blue eyes and light skin.

201

"He and I put the pieces together," Annabelle said softly.

Her eyes still wide, Alexandra said quickly, "We are only friends. Nothing more. I told him that from the beginning when we met."

Annabelle nodded and squeezed Alexandra's hand reassuringly.

"I know that and he assured your uncle of the same."

Giving her niece a questioning look, she asked, "Why did you tell him your name was Kishma?"

Alexandra lowered her head in contrition.

"Because I panicked. I did not know him and what threat, if any, he posed. I was also afraid that if I gave him my real name, my disguise would be meaningless and I could not continue to move about the island or go to the village."

Taking a ragged breath, she added, "I know it sounds selfish, but there is so much to see and experience outside of the boundaries of the property, and I didn't want to miss out."

Annabelle had suspected the duplicity had something to do with her freedom.

"Do you think it is fair for Pierce to continue to be deceived?"

Tears filled Alexandra's eyes. The guilt over her deception overwhelmed her.

"I had planned to tell him the truth yesterday, but that is when I discovered he is Uncle Chester's guest. Then he told me the soonest we could meet again would be tomorrow. That worked out perfectly. I just needed one more day to figure out what to say that would make him understand. I plan to tell him tomorrow."

Wiping her tear-stained cheeks, she dropped her head.

"He should hear it from me."

Annabelle offered her encouragement and agreed.

"I am glad to hear of your commitment to correct this."

Never Leave My Arms

Relief flooded Alexandra, and she choked back a sob. So overcome with emotion, she could not immediately speak and only nodded.

Annabelle's eyes filled with tears as she saw how deeply this affected her. As the oldest of her two nieces, the two women had a special relationship, and she considered Alexandra the closest to a daughter she would ever have. She saw much of herself in her at that age and wanted to ensure she made decisions that would lead to happiness. Annabelle suspected her niece's feelings for Pierce ran much deeper than she even realized.

Gently nudging, she asked, "So, tell me how you two came to meet."

Alexandra gathered her emotions. Sniffing and dabbing her tears, she explained how the two had stumbled upon each other at the cove. Unbeknownst to them, both had captured each other's attention his first day in port. Alexandra saw him on his ship soon after he docked. Shortly thereafter, she caught Pierce's eye in the marketplace, but disappeared before he could meet her and introduce himself. Weeks later, he saw her again in Church Gutt shopping with Kishma. He tried to get her attention, but she and Kishma had moved on before he could reach her in the crowd.

Annabelle listened intently as Alexandra recounted the unfolding of her friendship with Pierce. She spoke openly, addressing all of her aunt's unasked questions. She explained how she had adopted the Kittian dialect and accent during their interactions, a subtle effort to blend in and communicate more naturally. Alexandra was careful, however, to keep their conversations centered on Pierce. The few details she did share about herself were technically true but vague enough to be easily attributed to anyone living on the island.

Their friendship developed through simple yet meaningful moments together. Much of their time was spent sitting quietly by the lagoon, talking, or strolling along the beach and the surf. They found comfort in the sound

203

of the ocean and the gentle rhythm of the waves, sometimes letting the silence speak for them as they walked side by side.

"That first day, when we went out to the ocean, I could see something weighed heavily on him," Alexandra said.

She described his intensity and attempts at being unreadable, but he never disclosed what burdened him. Alexandra withheld the fact that she and Pierce shared a passionate kiss.

Encouraged by her aunt's interest, she went on excitedly.

"Each time we met, he became more and more at ease. He told me about his heritage, childhood and how it was split between Scotland and England."

Annabelle smiled and nodded.

"Sounds like you discovered you have much in common," stressing the word "you" to remind her it was a one-sided relationship.

That did not go unnoticed by Alexandra.

"Each time we met, I would look at him, hear his voice, see his smile when I said something silly, and it affected me in a way I had never felt before. I realized I wanted him to know about the real me, my life, upbringing, likes and dislikes. I do not know when or what exactly happened that brought it on, but I knew I needed to tell him who I truly am."

Annabelle took careful note of her niece's reaction as she observed, "He is an exceptionally handsome man."

Even with her sun-tanned skin, Annabelle could see the blush creep up Alexandra's neck into her cheeks.

"Most assuredly, and to be honest, when Kishma and I saw him at the port in Basseterre, it was difficult to take my eyes off him. But after getting to know him, I discovered he is as pleasant on the inside as he is on the outside. He has been nothing but respectful of me."

Never Leave My Arms

It pleased Annabelle to hear her niece recognize the importance of a man's moral fiber. Giving her hand a gentle squeeze, she let go and went to push away from the table to get another pot of tea.

Alexandra rose quickly and took the fragile vessel from her aunt.

"Here, let me get you some more water."

"Thank you dear. There is no need to fill it up. The hour is getting late, and I only want one more cup," she said as she settled back into her chair.

Alexandra disappeared from the dining room and made her way down the long hallway towards the kitchen, using it as an opportunity to settle the flipping of her stomach. Releasing the anxiety she had held in these past few weeks had wreaked havoc on her. So wrapped up in figuring out how she would tell Pierce everything without driving him away, she did not hear the male voices that drifted from the front parlor.

As she emerged in the doorway of the dining room with the replenished teapot, she went perfectly still at the sight of her uncle and the large shadow of Pierce standing behind him.

"Good evening my dear," Chester said to his wife.

Annabelle smiled brightly and stood to greet her husband.

"What a wonderful and unexpected surprise! I thought you two wouldn't be back until after midnight," she said nervously.

Chester gave her a quizzical look. At first, he did not understand the cause of her anxiousness. Placing an affectionate peck on her cheek, he then caught sight of the source, his niece was standing in the doorway.

"Tis good to see you back to your normal self," Chester said. Looking at her dark brown hair, he frowned and corrected himself. "Well, mostly your normal self."

Alexandra, her trembling hands tightly wrapped around the porcelain teapot, leaned forward and carefully placed it on the table, averting her face from Pierce's direction.

"Good evening Uncle Chester," she murmured.

Annabelle sympathized with her niece. This impromptu revelation had to shake Alexandra to her core, but perhaps it was for the best. She did not want her to lose her nerve again.

When the couple discussed the situation, Chester had concerns about Pierce's reaction when Alexandra finally told him, particularly in light of what the young man had confided about his reasons for coming to St. Kitts. Out of respect for Pierce, Chester withheld that information from Annabelle. Regardless, Pierce needed to know Alexandra's true identity. Although a shock to them both, the two of them needed to work through this matter.

Annabelle saw Pierce lingering in the doorway and reached for his hand to draw him into the room.

"Pierce, please come in. I want you to meet my niece, Alexandra. I finally convinced her to join me for dinner. She has been preoccupied with other commitments these past months, but that has changed."

Directing her remark to the young woman, she said, "Isn't that right dear?"

Thankfully, the soft amber lanterns and candlelight casted shadows around the room that concealed much of Alexandra's face. For a fleeting moment, she entertained the idea of running. The knot in her stomach threatened to empty her dinner.

Still keeping her face averted, Alexandra quietly answered her aunt.

"Yes," she said.

Pierce noticed Alexandra the moment he stepped into the room. She struck a stunning petite figure. Her satin blue gown shimmered with the flickering light, while her long dark hair cascaded down her back and partially over her shoulder, shielding her face. There was something oddly familiar about her that he couldn't define. She appeared very shy. Little did

Never Leave My Arms

he know that the warm reverberation of his voice sent that familiar tingle of excitement down her spine each time they met.

Stepping toward her, he said, "Tis a pleasure to meet you Alexandra."

Annabelle could see her niece's trepidation. The young couple could not build a lasting relationship based on secrets.

Alexandra took a deep breath, mustered every ounce of strength she possessed.

"I will make him understand. He will forgive me. He must forgive me," she kept telling herself.

"Hello Pierce," she said warmly, a tentative smile played on her lips as she turned to face him.

The sound of her voice registered first. He recognized its sweet tone, but something was different. She spoke perfect English. A fleeting frown crossed his face at his confusion, then his eyes widened when she looked up at him.

You," he said softly.

Alexandra's eyes filled with tears. She caught the look of pain on his face. It was the same expression she had seen that first day they met at the beach while standing in the surf.

As the two young people stood silently staring at each other, Annabelle and Chester quietly slipped out and returned to their room. Pierce and Alexandra needed to speak in private. Although Annabelle wanted to stay in case the couple needed mediation, Chester felt it best for them to work this out on their own.

Closing their bedroom door, he gestured for Annabelle to sit on the bench at the end of the bed and took her hands in his.

"I know you're worried about Alexandra, but she can handle herself, and I trust Pierce implicitly to comport himself as a gentleman."

Tears filled his wife's eyes.

207

"It broke my heart to see Alexandra so torn."

Chester empathized and remained hopeful.

"He will be angry at first, and she will grapple with what she did, but I believe they can come out of this stronger. Let them figure out how to find their way back to each other, if that is meant to be."

Annabelle nodded. She knew Alexandra's power of persuasion and hoped she and Pierce would be able to talk this through. While Annabelle paced and Chester sat in his chair reading a book, in the dining room, Alexandra broke the silence between her and Pierce.

"Please let me explain."

Pierce cut her off, his eyes pinning her to her spot, his voice like ice.

"I presume your middle name is not Kishma."

A lone tear streamed down her cheek.

"I had planned to tell you yesterday, but then you told me who you were and I got rattled. I never meant to hurt you, nor for this to get so far out of hand. Please believe me."

Pierce reverted to his stoic, expressionless persona.

"Why didn't you tell me when we met?"

Alexandra tried to explain that initially fear for her safety and losing her ability to move about the island had held her back.

"My friend Kishma and I came up with the idea of the disguise before I met you."

"I presume that is how you arrived at your name," he said dispassionately.

Alexandra flinched. She could feel herself losing him with every word she uttered. She needed to regroup; change her approach.

Just as she was about to speak, Pierce cut her off. His expression filled with disgust. All of those feelings he carried from Helene's deception flooded him. Just as she duped him, so had Kishma, rather, Alexandra.

"I have heard enough.

Never Leave My Arms

He then turned and strode out of the room.

Alexandra stood perfectly still in stunned silence. She could not believe how easily he could set her aside. When she heard the front door close, a sob escaped her lips. She burst into tears and fled to her room.

When Annabelle heard the front door close, she checked the dining room and found it empty. Worried, she sought her niece out in her room. She listened for sounds from within as she tapped lightly on Alexandra's door.

"Alexandra, it's me. Can I come in?"

Rising from the large wingback chair in the corner, Alexandra dabbed her tear-stained cheeks and opened the door for her aunt. One look at her devastated young charge prompted Annabelle to wrap her in a warm embrace.

"It will all work out. You will see."

Alexandra's tears started anew as she pushed herself away and plopped down on the edge of her bed.

Shaking her head, she said miserably, "He hates me and wants nothing more to do with me."

Annabelle gently pushed a stray tendril back from Alexandra's face.

"He truly said those words to you?"

"He didn't have to. It was written on his face. My explanation meant nothing. He said he'd heard enough and just walked out."

"Once Pierce realizes that his anger is about what you did and not who you are, he will come to see that your ruse was for your safety and not to trick him with some cruel act. Give him some time," Annabelle soothed.

Alexandra didn't believe Pierce would ever forgive her, and she felt that nothing said or done could repair the damage she had caused. A sob escaped as she shook her head.

"He wouldn't let me explain. He just set me aside. I could see it in his eyes,"

Annabelle ran the back of her knuckles gently down Alexandra's cheek in a consoling gesture.

"Give him some time. From what he told your uncle, you are someone very special to him. I do not believe he could just walk away from you."

Never Leave My Arms

Alexandra did not respond. She sat quietly with her hands in her lap, staring blankly. Annabelle could see that she needed rest and bid her good night, placing a gentle kiss on her cheek.

"If you need me, you know where to find me," she said.

The tears threatened to surface if she spoke, so Alexandra just nodded. After Annabelle closed the bedroom door behind her, Alexandra changed into her nightdress and stepped out onto her veranda. She leaned against the railing and looked out across the garden, searching for any sign that Pierce had returned to his room. She saw nothing but darkness. Dejected, she returned to her room and curled up in the large chair.

"He is gone. I have lost him," she thought miserably.

The next day, Alexandra remained ensconced in her room. Annabelle stopped by to check on her. When the older woman told her that Pierce had sent word he was staying on his ship, Alexandra's flicker of hope vanished. Kishma had come by throughout the day only to be turned away.

"It's not you. I just need some time to myself," she called to her friend through the door.

After three days, Alexandra finally emerged from her room dressed in a simple muslin gown her aunt had made for her shortly after her arrival on the island. The cool fabric made the heat bearable. She had removed her native disguise and washed the brown dye from her hair, returning it to its light blonde color. She looked like the Alexandra Landon who had left London almost eight months ago. She didn't feel like that young woman; someone filled with excitement and hope. Instead, she felt empty.

Upon seeing her niece enter the dining room, Annabelle rushed from her chair and hugged her.

"Tis so good to see you up and about my dear," she said happily.

Gesturing towards a seat at the table, she continued.

You must have something substantial to eat."

211

Alexandra's appetite still waned.

Giving her aunt a weak smile she said, "I will just have some tea right now."

Annabelle frowned but felt encouraged when Alexandra reached for one of Lidy's tasty biscuits. Looking around the table, she noted one empty place setting. It did not go unnoticed by her aunt.

Pouring a bit of cream into her tea, Annabelle casually mentioned, "Your uncle has already eaten and is getting the carriage ready to go to Basseterre. We would love for you to join us. Two ships arrived yesterday, and the market should be full of wares."

Alexandra shook her head. She wanted to stay close to home and spend time with Kishma, who was due to arrive any minute.

"You and Uncle Chester enjoy your day. I will be fine."

Annabelle understood. Spending time with Kishma would do her niece good. She finished her tea just as Chester returned to collect her for their carriage ride to the port. Alexandra walked her aunt and uncle outside and waved as they set off down the long path, passing the cart with Kishma and her father. The young woman didn't wait for her father to help her down from her seat. She rushed up the front porch stairs and threw her arms around Alexandra in excitement.

"I am so glad ta see ya!" she gushed.

Kishma looked her friend up and down.

"I've been worried bout ya."

Kishma knew how to lighten her mood, and her exuberance brought a smile and a soft chuckle from Alexandra.

"I am fine," she said.

The young island native looked at her suspiciously. She knew how deep Alexandra's feelings for Pierce ran.

"Dunt ya try ta fool me. I know ow ya feel bout him."

Never Leave My Arms

Seeking privacy, the two friends walked down the path at the side of the home. Kishma looped her arm through Alexandra's as they strolled. She listened intently to how Pierce discovered Alexandra's ruse and his harsh reaction. Her heart ached for her friend. She knew she loved the man.

"Da man wouldn't let ya explain?" Kishma asked incredulously.

To avoid the threatening flood of tears, Alexandra could only shake her head.

Taking a ragged breath, she whispered, "I think I should go back to England."

Kishma stopped and shook her head vigorously.

"No. Ya can't let 'im drive ya off. 'sides, what if he comes around and forgives ya?"

Alexandra did not hold out much hope such would be the case. Each day that had passed and he did not return or even attempt to speak to her, that hope dwindled. More and more she believed that returning to Middlesex was the best way to get past this pain.

She could be with her parents and sister and become entrenched in her introduction to society for marriage. She needed to put Pierce Tennyson behind her. Leaving the island, her dear friend, and her aunt and uncle would be difficult, but staying just meant prolonging the torture of hoping for something that would never come.

Emotion welled up inside Alexandra as she choked out, "Pierce has set me aside. I saw it in his eyes, and I cannot stay here any longer. I plan to tell Annabelle I want to go home on the next available ship."

Tears gathered in Kishma's eyes. She cried for her friend's hurt and for herself; knowing she would have to say goodbye to her best friend.

213

Chapter Fifteen

St. Kitts
Basseterre Port
Early September 1774
...early afternoon, that same day

As expected, Basseterre bustled with the arrival of two merchant ships. Unlike London's cool September days, the islands stayed warm and sunny well into the new year. Today was no different. The vendors hurried to distribute their arriving supplies to new locations. Before stepping out of the carriage, Chester patted Annabelle's hand and smiled. He had arranged for their driver to take her to the market and accompany her while he attended to business at the wharf.

"I will meet you two at the market in about an hour."

Chester waited for the carriage to turn up the street and disappear from sight before walking down the dock to the Saltire Wind. The crews from the two merchant ships moored next to it had finished unloading crates of merchandise and stacked them neatly along the dock for transport.

Never Leave My Arms

A short man with wiry red hair, leaning against a large crate by the gangplank of Pierce's ship, spotted Chester and called out in a Scottish brogue, "Can I help ya, sir?"

Chester offered him a friendly smile.

"Perhaps. Is the captain of this vessel about?"

Alasdair felt a strong sense of loyalty to Pierce. Giving the man an examining look, he questioned, "Who be askin?"

Chester smiled, appreciating the man's dedication to his captain.

"My name is Chester MacKittrick. I am a friend of Captain Tennyson and his father."

Alasdair's demeanor softened immediately.

Nodding respectfully, he said, "Yes sir. The captain is aboard. Folla me sir."

Chester followed the sailor up the gangplank, into the ship, and then to the captain's quarters. Just as he was about to rap on the door, Nials Bissette opened it from within.

The Frenchman glanced between the two men and called over his shoulder, "I will check with ze merchant vessels to hear what zay saw and get back to you."

He nodded to the men in greeting, slipped around Alasdair and Chester, then rushed down the stairs to the main deck.

"Cap'n. Mr. MacKittrick is here ta see ya," Alasdair announced as he entered the cabin.

Pierce immediately appeared at the door, a welcoming expression on his face.

"Chester, please come in."

The older man smiled at Alasdair and shook his hand as the two men passed, one entering and the other exiting the cabin.

"Thank you."

215

The young Scot bobbed his head in appreciation and closed the door to give the two men privacy.

Chester took in the neatly kept quarters. Every wood plank shone, and the room smelled of beeswax. While not expansive, it lacked no comfort. In the far right corner of the space was a large wooden bed framed into the wall. The window above it provided fresh air, and books filled the wall shelves along its side. A folding privacy screen stood across from the bed for dressing and attending to personal matters. A large rectangular table with four chairs occupied the center of the dark polished wood floor. Two high-back upholstered armchairs were positioned under the large window to the right. The ornate mahogany desk in the far right corner had scattered papers on it, and judging by the chair's position, it appeared that Pierce had just vacated it.

"I hope I did not catch you at an inconvenient time," Chester said.

"Not at all," Pierce replied casually, gesturing for Chester to take a seat in one of the armchairs.

"Can I get you something to drink? It is noon, after all," he joked.

Chester paused momentarily before nodding.

"Sounds good. Perhaps some of that fine Scotch you brought me?"

Pierce chuckled as he opened a cabinet next to the chair, revealing a fully stocked selection of various liquors, including three bottles of fine Scotch.

"I'm certain there's a bottle or two in here."

After pouring generous amounts of the pale gold liquid for both of them, Pierce took the empty seat next to Chester. The two men sat in silence, savoring the taste of the fine spirits. Chester shifted his crystal glass from side to side, watching the liquid shimmer as the sunlight caught its golden hue while he collected his thoughts.

The older man broke the silence.

Never Leave My Arms

"It has been several days since we last spoke, and I wanted to check on you."

Pierce kept his eyes on his glass and nodded. His last communication was brief and only said he would be staying on his ship. He needed distance from Alexandra. The pain of her deception cut deeply.

He would never forget the humiliation and betrayal he felt when he locked eyes with her and realized she was not Kishma; the woman who had broken through the hard shell he had donned and helped him see he could be happy.

It puzzled Pierce that on the day he discovered Kishma, rather, Alexandra's true identity, he had spent the entire day with his host, yet the older man said nothing. Based on his and Annabelle's actions at the revelation, he sensed they knew of the deception.

"When did you realize Kishma and Alexandra were one and the same?"

Chester expected the question and did not shy away from answering.

"That evening you and I spoke, I suspected. When I talked with Annabelle later, we both put it together."

Before Pierce could ask the next logical question, Chester continued.

"Annabelle and I believed you needed to hear it directly from Alexandra for both your sakes."

Pierce could not help but let out a caustic laugh.

"Both our sakes," he echoed, stressing the word "both."

Chester did not fault Pierce for his anger. Alexandra should have told him long ago. In fairness, his niece had committed to making things right but allowed her fear of losing him to delay her. After returning from Alexandra's room that night and each subsequent day, Annabelle had shared Alexandra's regret and distress over hurting Pierce.

His rejection had crushed her so much that she even mentioned the possibility of returning early to England, which upset Annabelle. When his

217

wife began to suffer from the fallout, Chester felt compelled to intervene and mediate.

"Pierce, you may not want to hear this, but I say it as your friend. When you came to my home, you seemed withdrawn and unhappy. Over the months, I saw you shed that stiff, expressionless facade and actually begin to enjoy life and your time on the island. That evening in my study, when I questioned you about this change, you credited it to a young woman you had come to know and care deeply about. You regaled me with the wonder and attraction you felt for her and how she had pulled you up from an abyss that was slowly stripping you of joy and happiness."

Pierce sat quietly, absorbing the older man's words.

"That all changed when she intentionally deceived me."

Chester gave a lopsided grin, recognizing the young man's stubbornness. Taking a different approach, he summarized, "Alexandra is Kishma, not the other way around. The woman who is real and has stolen your heart is Alexandra."

Chester did not want to push further. Placing his empty glass on the table between them, he pushed himself out of the chair and shook Pierce's hand.

"I hope you come to realize that before it is too late."

Pierce could not be angry with Chester for his honesty. He knew he loved his niece, but the pain of her deception caused a deep wound.

Shaking Chester's hand, he said, "Thank you for stopping by. I will think about what you have said."

Chester smiled and nodded.

"I hope so." As he turned to leave, he paused and turned back to Pierce.

"I do have one more thing to leave you with."

Pierce looked at him expectantly.

"As an outsider looking in, I see two people who deceived each other for explainable reasons, and they need to come together to work through it."

Pierce regarded the man with surprise.

"I never deceived her."

"Didn't you? You have not told her you are married. You and I both know that the marriage will come to an end soon, but you are still married until you hear otherwise from your father. How is that any different?"

Pierce started to rebut the man's observations, but Chester stopped him with a friendly hand on his shoulder.

"Think about it, but not for too long," he said before taking his leave.

Elizabeth H. Franklin

St. Kitts
The MacKittrick Estate
Early-September 1774
...later that evening

The nighttime cloud cover obscured the normally twinkling stars. Alexandra set the pearl-handled brush on her dressing table after smoothing her long blonde hair. For the first time in weeks, she recognized her reflection in the mirror. She was back to her old self, at least physically.

Emotionally, she felt lost. Pierce Tennyson left her in knots one moment, swept her into a whirlwind of passion the next, and then abruptly rejected her, leaving her dazed and cold. His refusal to understand the reasons for her charade made her grind her teeth in frustration.

Pushing herself away from the table, she donned her robe and wandered out of her bedroom to the courtyard. Alexandra couldn't recall the last time she had enjoyed the solitude and fragrant scents of the outdoor retreat. Her long days with Kishma in the village caring for her sister's children, left Alexandra too exhausted to do anything except seek the comfort of her bed upon returning home late at night.

Usually, the bright clusters of stars and the radiating moon cast a warm glow to light her way. A soft tropical breeze would caress her face, gently pulling at her long hair and the hem of her robe as she explored every inch of the area. Tonight, however, the still air and dark skies made it less appealing to roam far. She decided to commandeer a heavy wooden bench in view of the steps leading to her veranda. Typically, she would sit in the comfortable chair outside her door, but the groundskeeper had moved the outdoor furniture inside in preparation of impending weather.

Word had spread quickly from two arriving ships in Basseterre that the seas had turned rough, signaling an approaching storm. While walking with Kishma earlier, the two friends even noticed flights of birds and animals moving away from the coastline toward the island's center, a sign the weather would be intense.

Before leaving the Saltire Wind, Chester had overheard Nials Bissette tell Pierce of an impending storm moving rapidly from the south. From all signs, the ships coming from the area reported it appeared to be gaining strength and was heading for St. Kitts.

Upon hearing the news, Chester sent a message to the plantation with his driver that he and Annabelle would stay in Basseterre overnight and to quickly prepare the estate for severe weather. When Kishma learned Alexandra would be alone at the plantation, she suggested her friend stay with her in Church Gutt. She knew how much she feared storms. Alexandra assured her she would be fine at the estate. Her uncle had made numerous enhancements to the home that enabled it to withstand the harshest of conditions.

Seated quietly on the bench, hands braced on each side of her hips, her slippered feet swinging softly, and her long, loose hair pushed back over her shoulders, Alexandra closed her eyes. She tried to distract herself from thoughts of the approaching weather. Apprehension grew at the thought of the small island being ravaged by winds and rain so destructive they could tear a home from the ground and wash it away. She had heard the groundskeepers discuss past storms that had done just that. The possibility of nature launching such an intense assault heightened her anxiety.

Her light blonde hair fell like a curtain around her as she shook her head to push away the building angst and replace it with pleasant thoughts. Suddenly, the image of the abandoned mill flashed before her. It was the day she and Pierce were caught in that fast-moving tempest at the cove. They had made it to the old structure to seek shelter.

Her skin tingled with excitement as she recalled the feeling of being held in Pierce's strong protective arms and the passionate kiss they shared.

Allowing herself to become lost in the memory, she relived every second. Caught up in the dreamlike moment, she actually felt his touch on her shoulder and heard his voice.

"Lass are you all right?"

It took a second for Alexandra to realize that what she felt and heard was not part of a memory or a dream. Gasping in surprise, she sat up abruptly, throwing her head back to find herself captured by Pierce's eyes.

Initially, he regarded her with concern. That quickly turned to shock and then fury, sucking the breath from her lungs. He released her shoulder as if she had scalded him and immediately stepped back. His reaction stunned her.

She understood his coldness about her charade, but she could not reconcile his recoiling at the very sight of her. Giving him a pleading look, she extended her hand as a gesture of apology, only to have him move back another step. His rejection registered clearly in her eyes.

The last thing Pierce had expected to see while looking out into the garden was a beautiful light-haired creature dressed in a flowing white robe. At first, he thought the shadows of the night were playing tricks on him. He had stepped onto the private terrace of his room, which overlooked the courtyard, to clear his head.

Alexandra had monopolized his thoughts. No matter where he turned, something reminded him of her. After mulling over his conversation with Chester, he decided she deserved the opportunity to explain her ruse. He also needed to tell her about Helene.

As he stood at the rail, a movement near the center of the garden caught his eye. He blinked twice to clear his vision and briefly glimpsed a woman before she disappeared among the flowers.

Pierce frowned in confusion. Chester had not indicated any new guests had arrived, and he knew it was not Alexandra because her hair was much darker. Intrigued, he descended the steps to search for her. After a few moments, he found the young woman seated on a bench with her head bowed and her face concealed by her long light blonde hair.

Concerned that something might be amiss, he called to her, but she did not respond. She must have been deep in thought, for when he touched her shoulder to gain her attention, she gasped in surprise and looked up at him. Nothing could have prepared Pierce for the shock. He recognized that perfect face and blue eyes instantly. It was Alexandra.

It took him a few seconds before shock turned to anger. Not only was she not the exotic dark-haired native beauty who lived in his thoughts every moment, but she was an even more stunning light blonde-haired goddess. For some reason, that infuriated him even more.

Looking at her now, he wanted to grab her, pull her to him, and kiss her. He felt drawn to her more than ever if that was possible. What spell had she cast on him? His eyes darkened as they bore into hers.

"Are you some kind of witch?" he asked in a husky voice.

At first, Alexandra felt confusion, then realized Pierce had never seen her hair in its natural color. Shame washed over her, and she closed her eyes, trying to find the right words. Before she could speak, he lashed out and cut her to the quick.

"Is there nothing real about you?" he asked coldly.

Rage welled up in Alexandra as she took a deep breath and rose slowly. Even though the cloud cover had dimmed the normally bright moonlight, her blue eyes snapped like shards of crystal. She had spent the last week berating herself for her deception. Seeing the hurt and then anger in his eyes when he discovered her ruse, knowing she was the cause, was unbearable. She wished she could do it all over again and let him see her true self from the beginning.

For him to attack her now without allowing her to explain was too much. She had had enough. Undaunted by his towering physique, she stepped forward, looked up at him, and poked her slender finger into his chest.

"You insufferable, pompous jack nape," she ground out.

Pierce's eyebrow raised in surprise at her attack. Although he remained silent with a stony expression, inwardly his ire cooled. He admired her temerity and found her anger exciting. Continuing in a tone laced with condescension, she pressed on.

"You are under the misguided and self-absorbed belief that my disguise came about because of you. Do not flatter yourself. I did it so my aunt would allow me to move about the island with my friend and help her family prepare for a new addition long before you landed on these shores."

Unwilling to grant him a word in edgewise, she stood on tiptoes, which did little to bridge their difference in height, and reminded him of a very important fact he seemed unwilling to acknowledge.

"I might also add that at no time did you ever tell me your last name or that you were a guest at my aunt and uncle's home."

Just as Pierce had cut her to the quick, Alexandra felt the need to return in kind before retreating to her room.

"For your reference, I deliberately avoided meeting their visitor, or even staying around long enough to learn his name. The reason being, I believed that they, that would be you, were some old stuffy milquetoast business associate of my uncle's. It appears I was right."

Alexandra knew she had struck a nerve when Pierce scowled sharply. Pleased with herself, she gave him a brittle smile, pushed past him, and quickly made her way down the path to her room, her robe and hair flowing dramatically behind her.

Pierce let out a snort of derision. The crack about his age and being weak stung. His first instinct was to go after her, but he fought the urge. Pierce allowed his pride to cloud his judgment, viewing this revelation about her appearance as a furtherance of her betrayal and deception. She had reopened the wound, and he refused to see the logic in her argument. *"She could have told me,"* he thought sharply to himself.

As he bathed himself in his own self-pity, a sobering thought suddenly occurred to him. He remembered his earlier conversation with Chester. Pierce had not told her something equally, if not far more important; he was married, albeit awaiting an annulment, but nonetheless married. He excused the concealment of his marital status as having no bearing on their relationship when he knew it was untrue. It would have everything to do with whether their relationship could move forward. Still, his pride and anger got in the way.

"She made me look like a fool," he thought angrily to himself.

Convinced he had made the right decision to let her leave, Pierce returned to his room, rubbing his chest where she had poked him, mumbling something about being strong and not even in his prime yet.

Not two hours later, the tropical storm unleashed against the island. Thunder rumbled like a war drum. Sheets of rain lashed the courtyard of the plantation home, and lightning illuminated the night sky, highlighting the colorful garden.

Pierce lay awake in his netted bed, his arm bent and tucked under his head, staring at the wooden plank ceiling of his room, unwilling to let go of his thoughts of Alexandra. His pride stood as a wall between them. He used her deception about her identity as an excuse to shut her out. Yet he too, had been deceitful by not revealing his marriage and annulment efforts to her. He had stalked away, angry more with himself than with her.

As the storm roared with fury over the MacKittricks estate, Pierce suddenly remembered Alexandra's worst fear. He had witnessed how they gripped her in terror, leaving her inconsolable. The thought of her in that state propelled him from the bed. He threw back the covers, pulled on his breeches, tugged his shirt over his head, and ran barefoot across the rain-slicked courtyard to her room. The storm soaked him instantly. Warm rain clung to his skin, and his linen shirt molded against the hard planes of his chest.

Reaching her door, he knocked. No answer.

"Perhaps she is somewhere else in the house," he thought.

Concern tightened his chest. Pierce needed to ensure she was safe. He pushed the door open, scanning the dimly lit room. The thunder crashed relentlessly, drowning out any sounds. At first, he saw nothing. Then, a movement in the corner caught his eye. A flash of lightning briefly illuminated the room, revealing the shimmer of light golden hair. A small figure was tucked into the corner on the floor against the wall. She had her hands clamped over her ears and her head bowed.

"Alexandra."

Never Leave My Arms

His voice was low but firm. She didn't respond. The storm drowned his words, and her body shuddered, betraying the depth of her fear. He crossed the room in three long strides and crouched beside her. Gently, he grasped her shoulders, forcing her to look up. Her wide, stricken eyes were filled with terror and something else, vulnerability. His anger at their earlier quarrel vanished.

"It's all right. I am here."

She blinked at him, as though uncertain whether he was real. A great clap of thunder shook the house, and she flinched violently, pressing her face to his chest. He reacted without thinking, wrapping his arms around her, and pulling her close. His warmth surrounded her. His scent calmed the erratic beat of her heart.

He reached for a blanket draped over a nearby chair and wrapped it around her shoulders, then sat down next to her and settled her onto his lap. She nestled against him, seeking his strength. His hands gently stroked her back, and his lips brushed her temple. The storm raged outside, but inside, a different tempest began to brew.

Slowly, her trembling eased. She pulled back just enough to look up at him, and in that moment, something shifted between them. The heat of his body, the roughness of his breath mingling with hers, the way her fingers clung to him, it all spoke of something neither could ignore any longer.

"Pierce…"

Her voice was barely a whisper, but it carried more weight than any words spoken between them before. He cupped her face, his thumb grazing her cheek.

"Alexandra. There is something I must tell you—" She silenced him with her lips, a kiss filled with urgency, longing, and surrender. He groaned softly, his arms tightening around her and drawing her closer. The blanket

227

slipped from her shoulders as her hands moved, tangling in his wet hair and pulling him deeper into the kiss.

Still holding her close, he gently lifted her and placed her on the cool sheets of the bed. The flickering candlelight cast golden shadows over her skin. Her lips were red and plump from their kiss, and her breath came in soft, uneven gasps. He hovered over her, drinking in the sight of her.

"You are exquisite," he murmured, tracing the curve of her jaw and the delicate line of her throat with his finger.

She reached for him, tugging at his soaked shirt. He pulled it over his head and tossed it aside. Alexandra's breath caught as her fingers outlined the hard ridges of his chest, following the trail of dark hair that disappeared beneath the waistband of his breeches. He dipped his head, pressing heated kisses along the column of her throat, trailing lower to the delicate hollow between her collarbones and then to the soft mounds of her breasts.

His hands kneaded one breast as the other teased its hardened nipple between his fingers, pulling a gasp from her lips. She arched beneath him, her hands tracing his hard, muscular sides. Lightning flashed, momentarily, bathing the room in brilliant white. He saw her lips parted in anticipation and felt the rapid rise and fall of her chest beneath his fingers.

"I want to see all of you," he whispered.

She tingled with excitement as he untied the ribbon of her nightdress. The fabric slipped from her shoulders, revealing her smooth, sun-kissed skin. A deep groan escaped him as he drank in the sight of her. Leaning in, he kissed her again, but this time with a possessiveness that drew her into the center of their own storm. Every touch and each caress spoke of desire and passion neither could fight any longer. His hands traveled along the delicate slope of her waist and the soft curves he had only imagined in his dreams. Her fingers fumbled with the laces of his breeches, pushing them down and freeing him, exposing his excitement.

Never Leave My Arms

There was a hesitation, a moment of stillness between them. He met her gaze, searching for uncertainty. Instead, he found trust and a need that matched his own. His hand moved down her flat stomach to her womanly apex, his fingers gently encouraging her to open her legs. He teased the sensitive bud of her core, and her body instinctively jerked at the stimulation. She felt the heat race through her as he easily slid his finger inside her.

Cognizant of her petite stature compared to his strapping build, he moved with care over her and settled his hips between her legs, holding himself above her. His neck and shoulder muscles bulged and rippled. She should have felt smothered by him, but she did not. Instead, she felt safe. She ran her hands up his sides, feeling the tautness of his body, and looped her arms around his neck, pulling his lips to hers for a deep kiss. Reading her signals, Pierce eased himself into her, breaking her virginal barrier. Alexandra gasped softly. Her body tensed at his invasion then relaxed as he kissed away her hesitation, and the two moved as one.

With each whispered plea, each stroke, each shared breath, they created their own tempest and found their release amidst nature's fury outside. As dawn broke and the island storm finally subsided, the two lay with their bodies entwined and their hearts forever changed.

Chapter Sixteen

St. Kitts
The MacKittrick Estate
Early September 1774
...morning after the storm

Shortly after the sun broke in the eastern sky, Pierce awoke to the feel of Alexandra's soft warm body pressed against him. Her arm was slung across his chest and her bent knee rested provocatively on his hip. The two had spent hours making love and whispering their thoughts and passions. They had set aside what had transpired this past week with an unspoken truce.

Pierce had come to Alexandra's room last night with the intention to not only comfort her from the storm, but to tell her about the secret he had kept from her and ask for forgiveness. In part, that was why he returned to the estate last night.

He also wanted to give her a chance to explain herself. Although he let his pride get in the way when he discovered her in the garden, he later realized her reasons were valid for the charade. Her initial reaction when meeting him supported such.

Never Leave My Arms

He had been unfair to her as well by not telling her about Helene. Pierce tried to at first, but could see her fear of the storm had taken over. Then suddenly, things quickly turned to a need like neither had ever experienced before. In that moment, he finally admitted to himself how much she meant to him. He needed her as much as she needed him.

Lying beside Alexandra, savoring the feel of her, Pierce debated whether to wake her and share everything. She deserved to know the truth. Pierce knew they could not move forward together with this secret hanging over them.

However, something within him made him pause. He needed to be able to tell her that the marriage had been annulled when he disclosed his secret. Having confirmation of his freedom would hopefully assuage Alexandra's shock at the news. If he were honest with himself, the weight he bore was more shame for allowing himself to be controlled. Thus, he decided he would hold off a little longer.

Pierce let Alexandra continue to sleep. He quietly slipped from the bed, placed a soft kiss on her forehead, dressed and returned to his room. Changing his clothes, he then set out to Basseterre to check on his ship. He planned to return to the estate as soon as its repositioning was in place. Then, he would tell Alexandra everything, regardless of whether he had an answer from his father.

Once he received word of the storm, Pierce moved the Saltire Wind out of its slip and anchored it in the bay until the weather cleared. Nials and Alasdair, along with a small crew, remained onboard to secure the vessel and mitigate any damage.

Upon Pierce's arrival at the port, Alasdair greeted him at the docks. Although the ship had not come through unscathed, the repairs needed were not extensive and could be completed within a few days.

231

"I've fetched some supplies and leavin on the skiff. Do ya need a ride?" Alasdair asked.

Pierce did not immediately respond. His eyebrow shot up as he spotted a vessel in a slip.

"I am surprised to see a package ship is in port. They must have just arrived this morning."

Alasdair eyed the weathered vessel.

"Lookin at their tattered main sail, I'd say they had a rough ride."

Pierce agreed. Then a hopeful thought struck him.

I need to make a stop first. Comeback for me after you drop off the supplies."

Alasdair nodded and the two men parted company.

A short time later, Pierce left the postmaster's office and ran into Chester and Annabelle in their carriage near the docks. Hailing them he learned they had stayed in town for the night to ride out the storm. They had just received word the roads were passable for the carriage.

"I hope we'll see you at the house soon," Annabelle said, optimism apparent in her voice.

Pierce nodded.

"I have some repairs to make on the ship that should not take more than a couple of days, but I plan to return once they're completed. Can you please let Alexandra know my plans?"

Pierce wanted to return sooner, but needed to ensure the repairs were completed posthaste. He needed to get the ship repositioned to Sandy Pointe to protect it from any future storms.

Chester smiled broadly at his young friend.

"I am pleased to hear we will see you soon. I am certain Alexandra will be happy to hear of your return."

Never Leave My Arms

Pierce waved at the couple just before the driver set the carriage in motion.

Once inside his cabin, Pierce quickly flipped through the mail and spotted an envelope with his father's handwriting. He inhaled deeply before opening it, and as he read each line, relief washed over him.

July 7, 1774

Dear Son,

I will keep this brief. Helene and her clan have capitulated. You are relieved of the marriage bonds.

Furthermore, Helene and Robbie Clyne have disappeared. According to sources, they married in Gretna Green and have left for the Americas.

The new Fraser headquarters is functioning at full capacity, and there are currently contracts for all vessels. There is no need for you to hurry home.

Enjoy your time in St. Kitts..

Your mother and I send our love,

Father

Pierce let out a halting breath and allowed himself to feel liberated. A clean slate lay before him. He could not wait to share the news with Alexandra. He finally shed the heavy cloak of his grandmother's manipulations and Helene's nefarious agenda.

Back at the MacKittrick estate, Alexandra awoke to bright late morning sunlight and discovered Pierce was gone. She stretched languidly before throwing back the sheet to get out of bed. When the cool morning air caressed her body, her face flushed. She had slept naked in Pierce's arms.

As memories of their night together flooded her, she spotted her nightgown lying on the floor. A smile touched her lips, and her skin tingled

233

as she recalled the passion they had shared well into the early morning hours: the excitement of his touch, the taste of his kisses, the feel of him.

Quickly donning her dress, Alexandra rushed barefoot through the courtyard to Pierce's room. She surmised he had returned there before dawn to ensure they were not caught together. Rapping lightly on the door, she quietly called for him. Frowning at the silence, she pushed the door open and looked around the room. Stepping inside, she closed the door and wandered about the large space. As she ran her hand softly along the top of the white eyelet bedcover, she espied the clothes he had worn last night draped across it. Glancing around, she caught sight of a piece of paper sitting on the bureau. She thought Pierce might have left her a note. Nothing could have prepared her for what she read:

May 2, 1774

Dear Son,

I have mixed news to share with you. The pleasant: the London office is running smoothly with contracts for sixty percent of the vessels. I hope to secure the remaining agreements over the next month.

The unpleasant: regrettably Helene insists she will not release you from the marriage and that she wants to reconcile. Her family is standing by her decision.

As such, I have a consultation with a barrister in London to discuss the options available.

I will keep you abreast of my progress. In the meantime, try to enjoy your stay in St. Kitts.

Your mother and I send our love,

Father

Alexandra stared in horror at the missive. She could not believe its contents.

"Pierce is married!" her mind screamed.

Never Leave My Arms

He had never told her; had never even hinted at it. She tried to re-read the letter, but the words began to blur as tears filled her eyes. Suddenly, the space closed in on her, and the air became stale. A sob escaped her. She needed to get out of his room, out of this house, off this island, and away from Pierce Tennyson. Dropping the letter, she rushed out the door and back to her room, closing and locking it in case he returned.

As she pulled her clothes from the wardrobe to begin packing, she noticed the small bloodstains on the white linens, evidence of her lost virginity. A fury swelled within Alexandra. She ripped the sheets from the bed and threw them in the corner, trying to hide them from sight, and began sorting through her belongings.

Annabelle and Chester arrived home a short while later. When Alexandra heard the knock on the door, she went rigid but relaxed upon hearing her aunt's voice.

"Alexandra, tis me. May I come in?"

Taking a calming breath, Alexandra opened the door and returned to sorting through her things. Annabelle looked incredulous at the sight of her niece's belongings strewn across the room.

"What is going on here?" she asked.

"I have decided to return to England as soon as possible."

Before she and Chester had gone to Basseterre, her young charge had expressed a desire to return to England, but she had not anticipated it would be so soon. Annabelle could see her upset and tried to be calm and reasonable.

"Dear, it will take time to book passage."

Alexandra would not be put off.

"There must be a package ship in port. They arrive at least twice weekly. I plan to book passage on the next one. I know they accept passengers."

Annabelle did not understand Alexandra's sudden urgency.

235

"This is true, but why do you have to leave so soon? Don't you want to try to work things out with Pierce?"

Then adding, "Besides, no ships are going anywhere because of the storm."

Alexandra could not meet her aunt's gaze for fear of crying.

"Pierce has set me aside. It's best that I leave as soon as one of the ships are ready."

"But your uncle and I ran into him this morning in town," Annabelle said. Alexandra cut her off.

"Pierce and I have nothing more to say to one another. I want to go home. Promise me neither you nor Uncle Chester will tell him."

Not wanting to push any further, Annabelle conceded.

"Very well. But you will not go alone. I will tell your uncle to return to Basseterre and book our passage for the next departure."

Alexandra gave her aunt a quick hug. "Thank you."

Annabelle made her niece look at her. She could see the redness in her eyes from crying, and her heart ached for her.

"We will get you home as quickly as possible"

"Thank you," Alexandra whispered.

Never Leave My Arms

St. Kitts
The MacKittrick Estate
September 10, 1774

Chester worked miracles securing passage for his niece and wife on such short notice. Neither he nor Annabelle understood why Alexandra insisted on leaving so quickly, especially since Pierce seemed to have come around. He had planned to return to the estate after completing repairs to his ship and specifically asked for them to relay his plans to Alexandra. It seemed obvious he wanted to work things out.

"She wouldn't tell me the reason for the rush and had no interest in hearing anything about Pierce," Annabelle said as she placed a pile of clothes into one of the three trunks she was packing.

Chester shook his head in confusion. He had hoped Pierce would arrive before the two women set sail but had received word repairs were taking longer than expected. Perhaps if they could speak, Alexandra would change her mind, and he wouldn't have to say goodbye to his wife for six months.

Not to mention, they were setting sail at the height of hurricane season. The seas were extremely dangerous. He had considered telling Pierce about their plans, but his wife had made him promise not to say anything. Alexandra was firm that she did not want to see or speak to Pierce Tennyson, and he had to respect her wishes.

"The carriage will be here at noon. Will you be ready by then?" he asked.

Annabelle stepped back and surveyed the three large steamer trunks filled with her clothes and various sundries. Surprisingly, this accounted for only one-third of her wardrobe.

"I believe so," she said as she began latching each trunk.

Chester lowered his head and let out a sigh.

"I'll have the driver and Lidy's husband help to load them."

237

Annabelle had been so wrapped up in preparing for the trip that she hadn't considered how her absence would affect her husband.

"Wait," she said as he reached for the door. Chester turned and gave her an expectant look. She took his warm hand in hers and searched his eyes, her own shimmering with tears.

"I wish you could come with us," she said.

Pulling her into his arms, he hugged her tightly.

"I do too, but we know that isn't possible right now."

Pushing herself slightly away, she placed a tender kiss on his lips.

"I hope you know I will miss you terribly."

"Not as much as I will miss you my darling," he whispered.

Annabelle choked back a sob.

"Chester MacKittrick, you are the best thing that ever happened to me."

Her husband smiled warmly and pulled her to him for one last embrace.

"Correction. We are the best thing that ever happened to each other," he murmured softly in her ear.

With one last squeeze, he released her and slipped out the door. It took Annabelle a moment to collect her emotions before she returned to securing the remaining trunks for the carriage. The driver had loaded Alexandra's baggage, and she was saying her farewells to Kishma on the veranda. The two young women wept and held each other tightly.

"I'm gonna miss ya so much," Kishma said between sobs.

"And I will miss you as well, but this is not forever. I shall come back to visit," Alexandra said, pushing aside the tears streaming down her cheeks.

Annabelle positioned her hat on her head as she followed her trunks out the front door, and Chester watched the men load them.

Turning to her niece and Kishma, she said, "Alexandra, we must be leaving to make the ship."

Never Leave My Arms

The two young women hugged one more time before Alexandra and Annabelle climbed into the carriage. Chester took his seat next to his wife, while his niece sat across from him. As the driver snapped the reins and the horses dug into the earth, the laden carriage slowly moved down the long drive. Kishma stood on the porch and waved to Alexandra until the coach disappeared from sight. Wiping her tears, she turned to see her mother, Lidy, standing behind her. The older woman wrapped her distraught daughter in her arms as they cried. Alexandra had brought a lightness to their lives they would never forget.

Elizabeth H. Franklin

St. Kitts
Basseterre
September 10, 1774
...two hours later

The heavily laden vehicle pulled up to the wharf in Basseterre. The area teemed with activity despite the storm from a week ago. Ships filled each of the slips, the package ship being one. Due to lack of room at the docks, other vessels remained anchored in the bay, the Saltire Wind being one.

Neatly stacked wooden crates lined the quay, waiting for horse-drawn flat carts to load them for transport to the marketplace and across the island. The carriage came to a stop in front of the package ship. Chester alighted before the driver could open the door and offered his hand to assist Annabelle and Alexandra.

"I will make the arrangements for your baggage while you and Alexandra check in with the Captain's clerk at the gangplank."

Although the couple had said their farewells in private at home, Annabelle gave her husband a soft kiss on the cheek and murmured something that brought a flush of red to his face.

As she pulled away, he cleared his throat uncomfortably and, in a brusque tone, said, "Safe and peaceful travels, you two."

Before joining her aunt, Alexandra gave her uncle a brief hug.

"Thank you so much for everything Uncle Chester."

Until that moment, the older man had not realized how much brightness and life Alexandra had brought to their home. Her absence would leave a void.

"I wish you all the happiness you have brought your aunt and me."

With her own emotions threatening, Alexandra gave him a trembling smile and one more quick embrace before rushing to join her aunt in line to board the ship. Before disappearing from the gangplank into the vessel,

Never Leave My Arms

Annabelle looked back to see her husband standing on the dock, waving to her. Smiling brightly, she blew him a kiss and then disappeared through the entrance on the side of the ship. Once aboard, she and Alexandra located their quarters. At least an hour would pass before the staff delivered their trunks to their cabins.

In the interim, Annabelle suggested they go on deck to take in the last bits of the trade winds when they set sail. Alexandra gave her aunt a faint smile. Until now, she had been distracted by travel preparations and the hurt of Pierce's deception. The true impact of actually leaving St. Kitts and Pierce behind pressed on her. She would never see him again. She could not; he had a wife. Despair threatened to envelop her, but she tamped it down. Although flooded with mixed emotions about leaving, she was eager to see her family and home.

"That sounds lovely."

The two women made their way up the stairs to the main deck, where some of the other passengers were milling about. Alexandra had returned to wearing her London wardrobe. She wore a stylish yet simple English travel gown in dark blue, with a corset and fitted bodice. The long skirt fell over her petticoats, and pleats shaped the back. The elbow-length sleeves and lightweight camlet fabric made travel in the warmer climes more comfortable.

To keep her long light-blonde hair contained, she wore it pulled back from her face and secured with decorative hair combs. She had purchased them the day she first saw Pierce in the village marketplace. Once she had secured her hair, she tucked it under a wide-brimmed straw hat and tied it with a ribbon at her chin.

A group of deckhands scurried about, neatly readying ropes at the base of the large masts and securing the crates with large woven ladder-like covers. A handful of passengers wandered about trying to find a location with the best vantage. Annabelle and Alexandra made their way towards the bow and found a space along the rail. The spot had an expansive view of the bay and the Basseterre wharf. There were countless vessels anchored, and Alexandra wondered if one of them was Pierce's.

"Stop it you fool. He used you," she thought viciously to herself.

Tamping down her emotions, she wandered to the front of the ship. A crew member leaned precariously off the side. Alexandra cautiously approached the rail and glanced towards the water. She saw a thick tether slowly cutting through the water as the sailor guided the anchor up from the ocean floor.

Standing on tiptoes, she leaned forward for a better view. A strong gust of wind pulled her loosely tied hat from her head, sending it sailing into the water and setting her long hair blowing freely in the wind. Alexandra scrambled to collect the platinum mass. Pulling it over her shoulder, she plaited it into a single braid and tied it off with a ribbon her aunt had found in her bag.

Annabelle was not the only one who noticed the incident. Nials Bissett stood at the bow of the Saltire Wind, surveying the ships entering and exiting the bay when he spotted Alexandra's hat landing in the water. Following the direction of where the hat came from, he espied her unusually light blonde hair flowing in the breeze.

"Oh, tiens!" the Frenchman exclaimed.

Pierce and a crew member had finished repairing a portion of the rail when he heard Nials.

"What do we need to see?" Pierce asked casually.

"A beautiful woman with ze most magnificent hair I 'ave ever seen," Nials raved.

Pierce frowned as he took the spyglass from his friend.

Never Leave My Arms

"She is at ze bow of de package ship," Nials said, pointing toward the slow-moving vessel.

As the image of Alexandra braiding her hair came into view. Pierce swore under his breath, "Bloody hell."

At first, he did not understand where she was going until he saw Annabelle step up and hand her something. It was then he realized Alexandra was leaving St. Kitts and that her aunt must be escorting her home. Her sudden departure confused him.

Pierce thought they had turned a corner that night. He had planned to tell her everything so there would be no more secrets to keep them apart. He had made sure Annabelle and Chester knew he would return when the ship's repairs were completed. More importantly, he specifically asked them to tell Alexandra of his impending return as well. What could have caused this sudden departure?

While his mind raced, Nials noticed that Pierce was not the only one taking an interest in the lovely passenger. He spied the pirate, Lucrete, at his own bow with his spyglass trained on the package ship. Pierce quickly placed the magnifier to his eye and spotted the nefarious marauder following Alexandra's every move, then suddenly barking orders that sent his crew scattering. A pit developed in Pierce's stomach. He knew Lucrete's plan; to go after the craft and take Alexandra. There was no way he would allow that to happen.

"Nials, how close are the repairs to being done?" Pierce asked sharply.

Sensing the urgency, Nials replied quickly, "We could lift anchor and go out with ze tide at sunset tomorrow evening."

From the looks of the activity on Lucrete's ship, the pirate planned to leave with the sunrise tide. Pierce knew the Saltire Wind could catch the package ship if they left no later than sunset tomorrow. He had not accepted any cargo, and the only weight the ship carried was the concealed cannons

243

in the hull. Lucrete's vessel, while slightly larger, carried a heavy load based on its high waterline, slowing it down.

Pierce knew it would be a close race to Alexandra, but he would not allow Lucrete to reach her without a fight.

"Capt'n," Alasdair called as he approached Pierce on deck. The Scotsman had just returned with supplies on the skiff.

"Mr. MacKittrick give me this ta give ta you."

Pierce took the sealed envelope and before opening it, he stepped away from the two men for privacy. It contained a letter from Chester as well as the first missive Pierce had received from his father upon his arrival at St. Kitts.

Chester's letter read as follows:

Pierce,

I thought you should know that Alexandra insisted on returning to Middlesex immediately. While I wanted to tell you directly, she made it clear she did not want you to know. Now that she and Annabelle are on their way, I am no longer bound to that promise of silence.

As you may know, I am not a man who inserts himself in others' personal affairs, but I feel it is important for me to provide you some information that may be helpful to you in setting this situation right.

Neither Annabelle nor I understood Alexandra's rush to return home nor her adamance of severing all ties to you. However, I came to learn last night it is because she became aware of your marriage. I will spare you all of the unnecessary details, but I have enclosed the letter she found in your room from your father. To respect your privacy, I have not shared the letter with anyone, including Annabelle.

I presume you will want to leave directly and return to England to make this right. Thus I have taken the liberty of

Never Leave My Arms

having your things brought to your ship this afternoon by my overseer.

I wish you and Alexandra well and hope you are able to find your way back to each other. Safe travels.

Yours in friendship,

Chester MacKittrick

Elizabeth H. Franklin

The Lesser Antilles
At Sea
September 12, 1774

The Saltire Wind sliced through the stormy waters of the Caribbean, its white sails fully extended and taut from the strong southerly wind. Ships that had come from the east and made port at St. Kitts the following morning reported a tropical storm brewing and gaining strength. One well-traveled captain warned that it had the potential to become a hurricane by the time it reached the Leeward Islands.

As Pierce looked out over the sea, with the wind tugging at his hair and plastering his clothes to his body, he feared the reports could be accurate. The further north they sailed, the higher the swells, the stronger the winds, and the more torrential the rains. He worried about Alexandra and her fear of storms, and how she would fare on a ship during a hurricane.

The memory of her paralyzing fear that day at the mill, and in her room that night they spent together, flashed through his mind. She had been inconsolable. He needed to reach her before the storm unleashed its full fury, but more importantly, before Lucrete.

As expected, the marauder's ship had set sail at sunrise, giving it a ten-hour lead on Pierce, while the package ship had at least a one-day head start. Thankfully, the Saltire Wind crew completed repairs early, allowing them to lift anchor sooner than expected.

Nials approached Pierce on the bridge. He knew what he was thinking.

"Lucrete's too heavy to make good time."

The British-Scot nodded silently. He stood broad and tall at the wheel, his booted feet braced apart and hands steady on the helm. His expression remained unchanged; determined and intensely focused on ensuring Alexandra's safety.

246

Never Leave My Arms

As they sailed further northeast around the islands, the storm's intensity increased. By mid-afternoon the next day, they spotted Lucrete. It had somehow caught up with the package ship. Based on their position, it appeared the two vessels were in a narrow channel between islands, providing some shelter from the high winds.

Using his spyglass, Pierce saw that the pirates had taken the passengers aboard their ship. The small group was on deck with Lucrete and his men. At first, he did not see Alexandra and her aunt, but as he scanned the travelers, he caught sight of her light hair and Annabelle standing beside her. The two women clung to each other as the wind and rain pelted them mercilessly.

Pierce yelled over the howling storm to Nials, "Bring her starboard."

Calling to Alasdair one deck below, he instructed, "Al, ready the cannons, and wait for my order."

Alasdair quickly did as directed and disappeared below.

Although Pierce wanted to unleash everything he had on the pirate ship, he did not want to risk harming Alexandra or any other passengers. However, he needed to send a message to Lucrete that his intentions were serious. Thus, he ordered Alasdair to fire a warning shot just short of the bow.

The blast of gunpowder cut through the sounds of the hurricane, and the kick of the cannon jolted the ship as the heavy lead ball soared high into the air, landing with a large splash within ten yards of Lucrete's vessel. Pierce watched the kidnapper's reaction through his spyglass, smiling with satisfaction at his expression of shock. Now that he had his attention, Pierce ordered two more shots aimed to land short of the ship, but close enough to let them know they would not be leaving.

247

While Lucrete ordered his crew to turn away from the Saltire Wind in an attempt to put the package ship between them, Pierce had Nials bring them around and raise the sails to close the distance.

What the pirate had not counted on was encountering another vessel in the channel sailing directly in their path, blocking his escape. Pierce recognized the other ship immediately. Wiping the rain from his monocular, he chuckled as he spotted Mame at the bow, her magnifier trained on him.

As soon as they recognized each other, she gave him a thumbs-up, signaling her intent to assist him. He also saw his friend Greene standing next to her. Apparently he had been unsuccessful in convincing the young woman to leave her seafaring days behind. Pierce could hardly believe his good fortune. He signaled for her to keep Lucrete pinned in and to send out a small crew to meet him near the shoreline. She understood his request and readied her crew to fight if necessary.

Because the channel provided protection from the powerful wind gusts, this allowed Nials to maneuver the ship in such a manner that Pierce, Alasdair, and several crew members could launch a skiff undetected and meet up with Mame's crew.

While the two small boats made their way to their rendezvous point along the edge of the choppy channel, Lucrete and his men fought to keep their ship steady. The storm's waves made it difficult for them to transfer much of the package vessel's cargo and passengers to the marauder's vessel.

As Lucrete struggled to strip the small ship bare of its possessions and people, the two small boats convened at the shoreline. Surprise registered briefly on Pierce's face when Greene stepped from Mame's small craft to his. Neither man said a word to each other. There was an unspoken loyalty between the two that they would follow each other into whatever situation lay ahead without explanation or question.

Never Leave My Arms

Pierce addressed the female captain as their respective crews listened intently.

"Lucrete has approximately two dozen passengers, one of which is very special to me. I am certain he will likely take her to his cabin. We need to get aboard, get everyone out, and then I will signal to have Lucrete's ship sunk along with he and his crew."

Mame was quite familiar with how the villainous pirate operated. She had rescued a number of his captives. For those he took a special interest in, he kept them aside and imprisoned them in his quarters. One could draw their own conclusions as to what occurred behind that door.

"He keeps most of his prisoners in the hull, but the ones that catch his eye are taken to his cabin." She continued. "We can provide the distraction while you get your friend, but we will need two of your men to help us get the passengers from below."

Pierce nodded.

"Let's get going. Nials can only continue to conceal us for a few moments more, and we need to board Lucrete's vessel without being detected."

While the small rescue group set off to carry out their strategy, Lucrete had plans of his own.

"Get all the prisoners down in the hull," he barked to three members of his motley crew. As they herded the small group, Lucrete's hand snaked out and yanked Alexandra from the pack.

"Except you," he said, giving her a leer that made her shudder. He turned to his first mate.

"Put her in my cabin. I will tend to her after sinking these two ships."

When Annabelle tried to intervene, the first mate struck her viciously across the face, knocking her to the ground. A fury unlike anything Alexandra had ever known welled up inside her. She yanked free of Lucrete's grasp and kicked the grimy sailor as hard as she could in the groin

249

with her large, buckled leather shoe, bringing him immediately to his knees on the hard wooden deck, howling and gasping for air.

Regaining his hold on Alexandra, Lucrete jerked her hard against him. Lucrete snarled, his face inches from hers.

"Looks like someone needs to be tamed. I'll take care of this one myself,"

Alexandra's stomach turned at the smell of his rancid breath and the sight of his blackened, rotten teeth. Shoving her forward, he glared back at his injured crew member with disdain.

"Get up you lazy tar and get those prisoners down in the hull."

Alexandra fought fiercely to free herself as the marauder dragged her up the stairs to his cabin. Try as she might, she could not pry her arm from his vise-like grip. When he opened the door, the smell of urine assaulted her. She gagged as the bile rose in her throat. The pirate laughed at her reaction.

"You'll get used to it," he said cruelly as he shoved her through the door. Alexandra landed on the filthy floor several feet inside the room. Scrambling to her feet, she whirled on Lucrete, her eyes blazing, ready to fight. Laughing, he mocked her spirit.

"You'll fetch me a hefty price with that light colorin, but I plan to put that fire in you out first."

Tears sprang to Alexandra's eyes as he squeezed mercilessly and tried to force her to her knees. She fought the pain and refused to concede to his implied command as she stood unyielding. Her obstinance incited his rage and he lifted his hand to strike her. Alexandra, turned her face and waited for the blow. She could hear the sound of the storm as it raged outside and the thud of the torrential rain striking the wooden deck. So focused on the impending blow, the sound of clanging metal did not register with her. It did with Lucrete. Swearing under his breath, he suddenly released her and shoved her back.

"Alas, that will have to wait until I attend to some pesky business first."

Never Leave My Arms

As he reached for the door, he turned and looked appreciatively at Alexandra.

"When I get back, you best be sitting on the bed and not wearing anything," he said in a deadly tone before yanking the door closed.

Lucrete laughed at the thud of the urn when it struck the wooden entry as he turned the key to lock it. Inside, Alexandra looked at the large metal pot lying on the floor, and began to shake uncontrollably.

As she picked her way about the disgusting cabin looking for a weapon of any kind, Pierce and Mame had already set their own plan into action. The two boats had fought the choppy waters and high winds, struggling to reach the side of Lucrete's ship.

Mame's crew boarded first and hurriedly made their way up the tethered lines. Once on the main deck, the small group maneuvered easily among the cluttered area, concealing themselves behind wooden crates that had broken free and were scattered about. Thankfully, the weight of the cargo kept the ship from pitching too much and the blinding rain kept the visibility low so they were able to move undetected.

Pierce, Greene, and their team were on Mame's heels. Once aboard, they fanned out in the opposite direction of the female crew, taking out the few bandits that were not below with the prisoners.

Mame signaled to Pierce and Greene they were clear to find Alexandra before she and her group slipped below to rescue the prisoners and draw Lucrete out.

The two men fought the wind and pelting rain as they climbed the stairs to the captain's quarters. Pierce tried the door handle but it was locked. Greene stepped aside as Pierce lifted his leg and kicked the wood door. The frame split and broke free as it swung inward and came to rest, hanging precariously from one hinge.

251

A cry of terror flew from Alexandra's lips as the cabin door burst open and a large figure filled the doorway, blocking the storm's fury behind him. Water dripped from his soaked hair and clothing. It was Pierce!

At first, Alexandra thought he was an illusion; something she had conjured. But when she heard his voice, she knew he was real and flew into his arms, calling his name. He pulled her tightly to him, whispering her name, as the strength in her legs gave out.

She sobbed, "Is it really you?"

He answered her with a tight squeeze before pulling her away.

Pierce shouted over the roar of the storm.

"We don't have much time. I need to get you off this ship and to safety."

So many questions raced through her head, but they could wait.

"My aunt. They took her below with the rest of the prisoners."

Pierce nodded.

"They are being rescued as we speak."

Pushing her behind him to shield her, he glanced around the door jam. Although unable to see the person, Alexandra heard Pierce say, "Have Mame take her to the island, and I will join later."

"Who is Mame?" Alexandra wondered.

Suddenly, a tall, slender man with dark hair appeared outside. Like Pierce, he was soaked through. He had a blanket slung over his arm and a stuffy British affect.

"Madam," he said in greeting.

Pierce grabbed Alexandra by the arms and turned her to him.

"This is my trusted friend Greene. He will ensure your safety on an island close by. Your aunt and the prisoners will join you there."

Her eyes widened with concern and fear.

"What about you? Why can't you come with us?"

"I will be along shortly. I have unfinished business."

Never Leave My Arms

She opened her mouth to argue when he pulled her roughly to him and kissed her. Alexandra did not struggle or push him away. Instead, she released all the fear, anxiety, and elation bottled up inside her. Melting into his arms, she accepted him fully.

Oblivious to Greene, who had turned away out of propriety, she wrapped her arms tightly around Pierce's neck and pressed herself to him. Taking her signal, he slipped his tongue into her mouth, deepening the kiss. Alexandra greedily sucked and played as though this were the last time they would ever see or feel each other.

Her fear of the tempest outside lifted as the sound drifted into silence and she fell deeper into their passion. Suddenly, Pierce broke away and pulled her from him. They stood staring at each other, chests heaving, both trying to catch their breath. He wanted to go with her but knew he could not; not yet.

"You must leave with Greene now," he said haltingly. "I will meet you on the island shortly."

Turning to his friend, he said sharply, "Get her off this ship now."

Pierce did not look back as he disappeared down the stairs toward the main deck.

Greene shook open the blanket draped over his arm and placed it around Alexandra's shoulders.

"Miss Alexandra, you must cover your head to conceal your light hair."

Alexandra immediately complied, pulling the material around her, even concealing her face. Greene instructed her to remain behind him at all times and to hold on tightly to his coat. Keeping her head down, she tucked in behind him, her eyes fixed on the wooden floor of the ship. The moment they stepped out of the cabin, the whipping wind struck them, almost knocking her off her feet.

"Hold tight," he called to Alexandra above the howling wind.

253

She pulled on his coat to signal she heard him. Greene quickly guided her on a circuitous route through the ship until she found herself descending a rope ladder to a waiting skiff. The small boat pitched violently, nearly crashing into the hull. Twice, Alexandra came unseated. She gritted her teeth and clenched her fists as she fought to suppress her panic.

The wind roared in her ears, and she barely heard Greene.

"Sit down on the floor."

She obeyed and huddled, wedged against the side, with the soaked blanket tightly around her. Greene and two sailors struggled to pull their oars through the choppy water toward land. It felt like they would never reach the island. Then suddenly, the skiff stopped abruptly as it ran aground. Pulling the blanket back from her face, she looked out through the rain and saw a thick forest of tropical trees and vegetation.

A movement to her left caught her attention, and she made out the figures of passengers from the package ship climbing out of another boat on the beach. Her breath caught in her throat when she saw her aunt, with the help of another woman, making her way down a path into the trees.

Between the rain, wind, and weight of the blanket, Alexandra had difficulty getting to her feet. Suddenly, she felt a hand at her elbow and looked up to see Greene assisting her. She was about to climb out of the small boat when a pirate rushed toward them, calling to Greene.

Alexandra blinked several times trying to bring the figure into focus. As they approached, her eyes widened in surprise. The young woman, dressed as a pirate, could not have been more than twenty.

"This must be Alexandra," she said, the howling wind making her yell to be heard.

Greene nodded as he turned to Alexandra.

Never Leave My Arms

"This is my dear friend Mame. This is her island, and her crew lives here. She will take you to her home. You will be safe there. Your aunt is already on her way."

Even though Alexandra had many questions, she did not waste time and simply nodded.

Directing his attention back to Mame, Greene said, "I am going back to get Pierce."

Mame knew it would be fruitless to discourage Greene. Nothing could shake his loyalty to his friend and family, not even his own safety, so she did the next best thing and said, "Be careful. Hurricanes make the seas merciless."

Greene responded with his classic dry look. Mame shook her head and chuckled in response before turning her attention to Alexandra. The two women watched as the stiff Brit and two sailors pushed their small craft into the rough seas they had just navigated.

"Come along," Mame yelled over the howling winds to Alexandra as she guided to the opening in the trees. "My home is not far from here."

A clap of thunder and a flash of lightning made Alexandra jump. She hadn't realized she had screamed. Mame turned to see the fear in the young woman's eyes and tried to assuage her worries.

"Once we are off this beach, the forest will shield us."

Alexandra gave her host a shaky look and quickly followed behind her. Once inside the protection of the thick vegetation, she could see clearer, but the wind still thrashed, bending some of the trees almost sideways.

Relief and a sense of awe washed over her as they stepped into a clearing where a large white two-story home stood. It looked like something from the English countryside. A long veranda stretched across the front, and a large wooden double door marked the entry. To prepare for the storm, someone had closed and latched the wooden shutters on the first and second-floor windows and emptied the flower boxes on the window ledges. Each side of the home had second-story balconies with wooden doors leading inside, and a stone walkway led to the front steps. It was an unexpected and grand home for such a remote place.

While Greene successfully secured Alexandra's safety and Mame tended to her comfort, Pierce found himself not only battling nature, but Lucrete. The notorious and cruel trafficker had managed to escape Mame's crew. He watched with fury as Pierce took his prize possession from his cabin. Filled with rage, the criminal launched an attack but Pierce easily deflected his attempts, disarming him of his saber and subjecting him to numerous blows about his face and body.

Even though Lucrete was at least fifteen years older and nowhere near as fit as Pierce, he put up a good fight. The loss of his crew, cargo, and captives fueled his anger. The two men struggled among the cluttered deck. Lucrete latched onto anything he could use as a weapon, but Pierce was too quick and strong for the older man. Finally, as the criminal lay on the ship's deck, exhausted, his breathing heavy, his face bloodied and barely recognizable from the beating Pierce had given him, he managed to croak out, "Enough."

Pierce stepped back and straightened as he looked down with disgust at the bandit, debating for only a second whether he should finish him or let his cannons do the deed. Remembering the look of terror on Alexandra's face when he found her, Pierce stepped over to the rail, raised his arms, and gave Alasdair the signal to fire the cannons. He had less than a minute to get off the ship and could see Greene in the distance coming back for him.

As he turned to repel down the tether, he felt a sharp pain in his side and looked at the dagger embedded in his flesh. Lucrete had pulled it out of the hand of one of his dead crew members as he stumbled to get to Pierce.

His bloodied mouth curled into a sneer at Pierce's look of surprise. The villainous pirate's satisfaction was quickly replaced with horror as his enemy pulled the very same knife from his side, inserted into Lucrete's chest and twisted it.

Lucrete collapsed on the deck of the ship, dead before he struck the ground. Pierce, weak and bleeding, fell backwards over the rail into the rough waters.

Alasdair and Greene looked on in horror as their friend fell overboard. They put all of their strength into getting the small boat out to their friend and retrieve him from the sea.

Chapter Seventeen

The Lesser Antilles
Veilwind Island
September 12, 1774

Alexandra stared in amazement at the massive home. Based upon the island remoteness, she thought any inhabitants, especially pirates, would live in crude thatched huts, certainly not such a stately residence.

Incredulous, Alexandra asked, "This is your home?"

Mame smiled with pride at her guest's appreciation.

"Certainly is. My crew helped me build it."

Once inside the front door, the house did not disappoint. The furnishings were impeccable. They were a mixture of styles from the islands, England, and France.

Mame reached to remove the soaked blanket from Alexandra's shoulders.

"Here. Allow me to help you with that."

Once rid of the heavy soddened cover, Alexandra shivered and rubbed her hands up and down her arms to try and warm herself.

Mame gestured for her guest to follow her down a hallway to a staircase.

Never Leave My Arms

"Come. Let me show you to your room."

Once they reached the second floor, Mame continued to the end of the corridor and opened the door to a bedroom. The room rivaled Alexandra's at the MacKittrick estate.

Mame reached to light a lantern at the side of the door.

"Normally it is quite bright in here during the day, but we had to secure the balcony doors and shutters because of the storm."

Crossing the room, she lit two more lanterns. Between the three, they fully illuminated the room, exposing well-appointed furnishings. The grand bed, the room's key feature, was positioned to allow one to enjoy the view through the balcony doors while resting. It had an ornate wooden headboard, and folds of muted gold and rose-colored fabric cascaded from the ceiling down the wall behind it, collecting at each corner. The polished floors featured plush decorative rugs. The doorway to the balcony was adorned with pristine white sheers draped across a decorative rod, flowing down each side and pooling on the ground. The room included every amenity, such as an upholstered dressing screen for changing and an ornate vanity with a matching padded bench.

"'Tis beautiful," Alexandra whispered, running her hand along the finely crafted piece.

"Thank you," Mame replied. "I selected each of these pieces myself."

Alexandra turned to look at Mame, who appeared to be close in age to her but carried herself with mature confidence. Tipping her head, Alexandra gave her a quizzical look.

"For a pirate, you have excellent English. I'm guessing you're not from around here."

Mame smiled at her guest's perception.

259

"You are correct. I am originally from England, but I haven't been there for many years. Alas, that's a long story, and you'd likely catch your death if you stayed in those clothes for the duration of it."

Alexandra looked down at her bedraggled, soggy appearance and frowned.

With a sheepish grin, she asked, "I don't suppose any of my things made it off the package ship?"

Her hostess laughed softly.

"Not that I'm aware of, but I have something that might fit you."

Pulling open the large wardrobe, Mame removed a simple light green dress. Although dated in style and long, it would do.

"Thank you so much," Alexandra said.

Mame shrugged casually.

"You're welcome, but it's only an old dress."

Alexandra shook her head.

"Not just the dress. Everything. Taking me in, my aunt, and all the travelers. I cannot thank you enough."

Uncomfortable with the sentimental direction of the conversation, Mame cleared her throat.

"Lucky we came upon you when we did and that we saw the Saltire Wind and its intentions."

Looking questioningly at her host, Alexandra said, "I don't understand."

Mame filled her in.

"The weather made us late returning to the island. We spied the package ship with Lucrete bearing down on it. We knew his intentions. We then saw Pierce's vessel close behind. Greene realized something was awry and then I saw Pierce's signal. Although precarious, we managed to get a skiff off along the shoreline where we met up with Pierce and some of his crew in a small boat. He explained what had happened. Once we had a plan together, Greene joined Pierce and the two groups headed for Lucrete's ship."

Mame gave Alexandra a serious look.

"The moment I saw the unusual color of your hair, I knew exactly why Lucrete pursued the ship. You would have obtained a heavy price, regardless of what you would have suffered at his hands before being trafficked."

Alexandra rubbed her bruised arm and shivered at the thought of the vile criminal. The warnings her aunt and Kishma had issued played over and over in her head.

Slipping behind the privacy screen, Alexandra tossed the green frock over the top and began stripping off her clothes.

She didn't want Mame to think her unappreciative of the risks taken by her, her crew, and Greene.

"You all risked your lives for me, for us, and I can't thank you enough."

Mame accepted her guest's thanks graciously.

"Tis Pierce you should thank. His determination to get to you knew no bounds."

The hurt and humiliation she felt over learning of Pierce's marriage and duplicity welled up inside Alexandra. She fought to suppress her emotions and stayed focused on the present.

Trying to redirect the conversation, she asked lightly, "How do you know Pierce?"

While Alexandra pulled the dress over her head, Mame collected the wet clothes from the top of the screen and shook them out. A smile slipped out at her guest's cloaked interest in what Pierce meant to her.

"I met him on his way to St. Kitts earlier this year," she said absently.

Alexandra worked to pull the gown into place, getting it settled on her hips. Except for the additional three inches of fabric at the bottom and the tight bodice, the dress fit her fairly well. She stepped around the screen and presented her back to Mame.

Pulling her long, wet tresses over her shoulder, she asked, "Could you help with the fasteners?"

Mame tossed Alexandra's wet clothes over a chair and set to work hooking the remaining loops while her guest continued the questions.

"So, Pierce stopped at your island on his way to St. Kitts?" Alexandra asked, unknowingly holding her breath for the response.

A lopsided grin formed on Mame's lips as she thought of how to answer her question. Clearly, Alexandra cared for Pierce, and he for her. He risked his life, crew, and ship to find her.

Mame looped the last dress fastener and turned her attention to the wet clothes she had set over the chair.

"We met when my ship stopped his and liberated some supplies we needed from him."

Alexandra's mouth dropped open, and she spun around, her eyes wide with surprise and a touch of mirth.

"You robbed him! she exclaimed in amazement.

Mame looked directly at Alexandra and nodded. The two women simultaneously broke into laughter; Mame out of a sense of pride and Alexandra at the thought that a woman had bested Pierce. She listened intently as her host regaled her with the story of how she and her all-female crew intercepted his ship, something they had done many times with passing vessels.

"We lifted every piece of furniture in this house from merchant vessels sailing through our channel."

That impressed Alexandra. She had never heard of female pirates, let alone a crew of them living on their own island. Certainly not ones who effectively amass goods to comfortably sustain themselves.

Never Leave My Arms

"How do you recruit your ship's crew?" Alexandra asked curiously.

Mame chuckled at her question.

"Why? Are you looking to stay on?"

Her guest laughed lightly and then pushed down the sadness that threatened to overtake her.

"No. I'm heading back home to Middlesex, to my parents and sister. I miss them terribly and have been away from them for almost a year."

A shadow fell over Mame's expression as tumultuous memories of her own family and childhood tried to creep into her thoughts.

Shaking them off, she nodded.

"This life is nothing like that of the gentry or aristocracy."

Mame explained that most of her crew were women and surprisingly, some men that they had rescued from Lucrete's trafficking. They could choose to stay and join the community or accept transport to catch a vessel on a nearby island. Some stayed while others moved on. The passengers from the package ship would be offered the same options.

"Did Greene decide to stay on instead of continuing to St. Kitts with Pierce?" Alexandra asked.

Mame shook her head and chuckled as she tried to imagine the stuffy Brit making a life for himself on the island sustained by thievery at sea.

Alexandra learned Greene's presence was to convince Mame to turn away from her life of crime and return to England. Although short on details, she shared that the two knew each other from a young age. Her mother and sister perished when their ship sank while on a journey towards France, but Mame survived.

"Greene recognized me through the spyglass when we stopped them. Imagine my surprise!"

"How serendipitous!" Alexandra exclaimed. "I take it his reform efforts have been unsuccessful?" she asked, smothering a giggle.

263

Mame liked her new guest. "Correct. Although I believe he still holds out hope," she said with a chuckle.

Giving Mame a tentative look, Alexandra asked softly, "So Greene knows Pierce very well?"

"From what I gather, Greene and his family have close ties to Pierce and his parents that go back at least two generations."

A knock at the door brought their conversation to an abrupt end when Bert arrived, dripping wet and out of breath.

"Cap'n, I need a word in private."

Mame looked at her bedraggled next-in-command and stepped into the hallway, pulling the door almost closed behind her.

"What is it Bert?"

"There's an Alasdair from the Saltire Wind downstairs wanting to speak with you. It's about his cap'n. They can't find him."

Before Mame could respond, Alexandra yanked the door open. She had overheard the first mate's comments.

"What do you mean? Pierce is missing?" she demanded.

Although the two had not met, she knew Alasdair was one of his closest friends. Pierce had often mentioned him during their times at the cove. Panic rose in her as she thought of Pierce somewhere out at sea, struggling to stay above the waves or worse.

"Where is Alasdair?" she asked as she pulled up her skirt and raced toward the stairs. Mame was fast on her heels while Bert struggled to hurry, her extra-long saber scraping on the floor.

"Alasdair'!" Alexandra called as her bare feet barely touched the steps.

"Yes miss?" he answered tentatively, standing just inside the front door, his hat held tightly in his hand.

"What is this about Pierce missing?" she demanded.

The man looked confused, caught between the two women. He knew Mame but did not recognize this beautiful light-haired, blue-eyed woman.

Stammering, he said, "He, he, he fell in the sea, and me and Greene lost sight of him. The boys are in a skiff searching, but we need more help."

Mame shot a look at her first mate.

"Bert, gather as many strong swimmers as possible and have them meet us at the beach immediately."

Alasdair looked confused, his gaze shifting from Mame barking orders to Alexandra tying the skirt of her dress up so she could move freely.

Casting a look at her host, she announced, "I'm going down there now."

Then, turning to Alasdair, she said firmly, "Take me to where you saw him last."

Disregarding the torrential rain and wind, Alexandra opened the front door and pushed her way through, staying closely behind Alasdair. Mame shook her head in disbelief. Pierce had told her and Greene that the blonde beauty was terrified of storms, but you would never guess it. Alexandra certainly did not allow them to get in her way when it came to Pierce Tennyson.

Elizabeth H. Franklin

The moment Alasdair and Alexandra cleared the trees near the beach, the intensity of the rain and wind increased. Twice, the gusts knocked Alexandra to her knees. The rain stung her face, and her gown was soaked through. No shelter on the beach existed to escape the hurricane. Shielding her eyes with her hands, she tried to look out over the white-capped sea. Dread set in as she realized the impossibility of finding anyone in the high, undulating waves.

She spotted the Saltire Wind anchored in the center of the channel. The seas beat mercilessly against its massive hull, but it rolled with each wave, always returning upright. Surprisingly, the package ship remained erect one-hundred yards up the channel. They were forced to drop anchor when Lucrete captured them.

At first, Alexandra did not see any sign of her kidnappers' boat until she noticed its main mast protruding from the water further north. She surmised Pierce's ship had sunk the vessel. Loud blasts of cannons broke through the roar of the storm after Greene got her to the beach and into Mame's care.

Fighting the wind, Alexandra remained determined and focused on finding Pierce. She pushed her way toward the shoreline across from Greene and the skiff.

"He went overboard there," Alasdair yelled above the wind, pointing toward the marauders' ship wreckage.

Nodding, she scanned the beach. Focusing on the direction of the tide, she turned right and carefully made her way through the trees and vegetation along the waterline. Even though the rough surf made navigation difficult, she pressed on, covering at least fifty yards while constantly stopping to search the waves for any sign of Pierce.

Her legs felt like lead as she fought against the weight of her soaked dress and the soft floor of the surf. With each gust of wind and clap of thunder,

Never Leave My Arms

her mind battled the terror that threatened to overwhelm her. She refused to give the storm power over her.

Alasdair followed a short distance behind, keeping a close eye on her. He knew Alexandra meant a great deal to his friend and captain. He witnessed a deadliness descend upon him he had never seen in Pierce as they hurried to prepare their ship to pursue Lucrete and ensure her safety.

Although never confirmed, he surmised she was the young woman who had captured his friend's heart in St. Kitts. Pierce had described her as a local beauty with unusual blue eyes and a love of the water. The British Scot was not one to engage in discussions about his personal life, but Alasdair had drawn his perspective from the marked change he had witnessed in his friend during his stay in St. Kitts. Even the crew members had noticed.

The quiet anger Pierce carried from London had vanished. He even laughed at jokes that included him as the punchline. This young woman's influence had affected him. Although something must have happened between the two in the past week that seemed to have cooled their budding romance, Alasdair hoped they would have the opportunity to resolve the matter so he could see his friend happy again.

He caught sight of Alexandra as she waded around a small inlet and then disappeared inside. Suddenly, above the howl of the wind, he heard her calling for help. Greene's head snapped up as he too heard Alexandra, and he immediately turned the skiff toward her. Alasdair lifted his knees as high as his short frame allowed and jumped through the shallow rough water to get to the inlet.

The moment Alexandra had made her way through the watery vegetation and trees, she saw Pierce lying face up, eyes closed, and the surf pushing him against an old tree trunk. Sinking to her knees beside him, she grabbed his shirt and pulled him closer.

"Pierce. Can you hear me!" she cried.

Placing a hand on his bearded cheek, she felt the coldness of his skin and then noticed the large red stain on his chest. As she pushed the fabric aside for a better look, Alasdair and Greene appeared.

"It looks like he has been stabbed," Greene said.

Alexandra pressed her face against Pierce's and whispered his name softly as she placed her hand on his chest. She felt the steady thud of his heart.

"He is alive!" Alexandra exclaimed.

The three of them and the small crew made haste and carried an unconscious Pierce out of the marshy area, through the relentless storm to Mame's home.

Observing the situation from her vantage point on the beach, the female swashbuckler sent several of her crew ahead to prepare for Pierce's care.

Alexandra remained focused on him, drowning out the sounds of the surrounding storm, her determination to ensure he lived her only aim. With each step, she recited a silent prayer asking for his life to be spared.

There was no time to waste when they reached the house. Alasdair and Greene carried their friend to a bedroom on the second floor, where the waiting healer began tending to his wounds. The group gathered by the door and watched the old woman as she assessed Pierce's condition.

"At the very least, he has a knot on his head and a knife wound on the side of his chest. I will know more about the extent of his injuries after we get him out of these wet clothes."

Her next order did not sit well with Alexandra. She directed her to find bandaging and fresh water. While she was gone, Greene and Alasdair could help get him out of his drenched clothing. Mame noticed the stubborn set of her young guest's mouth and took her aside.

"He will be fine. You and I can gather what the healer needs while Greene and Alasdair get him cleaned up."

Never Leave My Arms

Alexandra looked at Mame for a moment before finally relenting. She needed to prioritize Pierce's needs over her own.

"Very well," she said. Then, turning to the older woman and Greene, she continued, "We won't be gone but a few moments."

Greene nodded, exchanging a knowing look with Mame. Thankfully, while they worked to gather the supplies, Mame convinced Alexandra to change out of her sodden gown. She did not have another dress that would fit her guest, so she offered her a pair of sailor togs; drawstring burlap pants and a blouse with a simple belt cinched tightly at her waist.

Alexandra looked at her reflection in the mirror. She barely recognized the young woman looking back at her. With boots and a headscarf or hat, she could pass as one of Mame's crew. Running her fingers through her long hair to remove as many tangles as possible, she quickly plaited it into a single braid before rushing back to Pierce's room.

Greene and the healer had made quick work during her absence. They had removed his wet clothing and propped him up against the headboard. Fluffy sacks were placed behind him buffering him from the hard wood and his chest was bare exposing the angry wound. A crisp white sheet and thin blanket covered him from the waist down.

A pit developed in Alexandra's stomach as she noted Pierce's pale pallor. He had lost a significant amount of blood from the knife wound. While the head injury was concerning, his lack of consciousness spared him as the old woman carefully stitched the deep gash on the left side of his chest. After completing the treatment, she spread a dark salve on the incision and wrapped bandages tightly around his torso.

Standing back, the healer surveyed her work.

"I've done my best. Now we need to watch for a fever."

"I will stay with him," Alexandra announced.

269

Greene stood stoically looking at her, while she returned a look that brooked no argument.

"Very well," he relented. "I shall be outside the door if either of you needs anything."

Based on what she knew of Greene, she expected he would argue with her. His acquiescence surprised her. She accepted his consent graciously, nodded, then pulled a chair to the side of the bed and sat down to give Pierce her undivided attention.

Never Leave My Arms

The sound of birds chirping drifted in on the tropical breeze through the bedroom window. Alexandra was amazed that just a day ago, a tempest had swept across the island, threatening to take everything in its path, only to be replaced by bright sunshine and cool air. She could hear the movement of people below as they worked to clear away broken tree branches and debris near the home.

The healer had stopped to check on Pierce's progress. He had slept through the night but had not yet regained consciousness. A small amount of blood had seeped through his chest bandage, but it was not a cause for concern. Although he did not feel feverish to the touch, the older woman suggested keeping cool compresses on his forehead and behind his neck. Alexandra followed her advice and returned with a basin of cold water and wrappings just as Greene and the healer adjusted Pierce's pillows.

"Miss Alexandra, I can stay here so you can take a few moments for yourself," Greene offered.

"Thank you, but that won't be necessary," Alexandra replied, soaking the cloth in the water and carefully wringing it out before placing it on Pierce's forehead.

Greene debated insisting she take a break, but something told him she would not listen anyway. The one person who might get through to her knocked lightly on the partially opened door. Alexandra turned at the distraction, and her eyes lit up at the sight of her aunt. The young woman flew across the room into her waiting arms.

"I am so glad to see you," she said, tears filling her eyes.

Annabelle hugged her niece tightly.

"My dear, I am so glad to see for myself that you are well."

Alexandra pushed herself back just far enough to see her aunt's face.

"I had planned to find you as soon as I made sure Pierce would recover."

271

Mame, with Greene's help, had arranged to move Annabelle to a bedroom down the hall from Alexandra's late last night. When the crew informed Mame of the aunt's concerns, she honored them immediately. Even though they assured Annabelle that her niece was safe, she wanted to see for herself. Moreover, the host knew her young guest might benefit from having family close at hand.

"I do not mean to interrupt," Mame said to her two guests, "but there is tea and a hot breakfast downstairs for you."

Before Alexandra could decline, Annabelle grasped her niece's hands.

"Come. You need a change of scenery, and I bet you haven't eaten in quite some time."

Biting her lip nervously, Alexandra looked at her aunt.

I don't know whether I should leave just now."

She glanced over her shoulder at Pierce. His color had improved, but he still had not regained consciousness.

"Nonsense," Mame interjected. "The cook opened the kitchen before dawn and has prepared a feast. You two go downstairs, and Greene and I will watch over Pierce."

Annabelle took the cue and pulled Alexandra along. Before closing the door behind them, she said to her niece, "We won't be gone long, and they will take good care of him."

Keeping her young charge close and distracted, she chattered as they made their way down the hallway to the stairs below about how kind everyone had been to her and the passengers.

"Early this morning, when the rain stopped, people immediately set about cleaning up the debris."

Annabelle had learned that the crews of the Saltire Wind and the package ship were also part of the effort. They wanted to clear the path to the sea so they could return to their ships, assess the damage, and start making repairs.

Never Leave My Arms

Alexandra and Annabelle stopped in their tracks when they turned the corner and found themselves in a grand dining room. It should not have surprised them, considering the beauty of the few areas of the home they had seen.

Like the main living room and upstairs bedrooms, the décor reminded the two women of England, with its finely woven area rugs and Chippendale furniture. The long dark mahogany table had slender legs and claw feet. It could comfortably seat twelve. The light window treatments and local fresh flowers in vases softened its heaviness.

Alexandra slipped into a finely upholstered chair at the end of the table while her aunt poured steaming hot cups of tea for both of them and took the seat to Alexandra's right.

As Annabelle added a teaspoon of sugar to her cup, she kept an eye on Alexandra, noting her reaction when she casually said, "Our host told me this morning that they hope our ship can set sail within the next three days and resume our trip back to London."

Alexandra absently stirred her tea and nodded. All of those feelings of pain and betrayal hovered at the surface, threatening to emerge. Determined to remain focused on getting Pierce better as soon as possible, she pushed them down. Once she was certain he was on the road to recovery, she needed to return to London and look to her own future without him. Taking a sip of her tea, she set the fragile cup down in its matching saucer and reached for a biscuit.

"The sooner, the better," she said.

Annabelle frowned at her niece's response. Before they had left St. Kitts so abruptly, she had not pressured Alexandra to explain her haste in leaving. She had hoped she would willingly share her reasons, but did not. Annabelle surmised it had something to do with the ruse surrounding Alexandra's identity and Pierce's anger over being duped. Yet, something told her there

273

was more to the issue. The fact that the man risked everything to get to her spoke volumes. Before they arrived in London, nay, before she left the island, she planned to find out the truth.

Alexandra pushed herself from the table.

"I must be getting back."

Exasperated, Annabelle replied, "But you've only had a bit of your tea. That is not enough to keep your energy up."

Alexandra placed an affectionate kiss on her aunt's cheek.

"I will be fine."

She then slipped from the room and rushed down the hall to the stairway.

Never Leave My Arms

Mame found Annabelle alone a short while later still seated at the grand dining table. From the expression on her guest's face, she sensed something troubled her.

"Is something amiss?" Mame asked with concern.

Annabelle jumped at the sound of her hostess's voice. So engrossed in her own thoughts, she had not noticed anyone entering the room. Composing herself, she smiled warmly.

"No. Perhaps. I am uncertain." Then she laughed at her own indecision.

Mame took the seat next to Annabelle that Alexandra had vacated.

"Perchance I can help," she offered.

Annabelle looked curiously at her hostess. She knew Mame had a connection to Pierce but a closer connection to Greene, who seemed to have a long history of friendship with the British Scot. Perhaps during his time on the island, the two had discussed Pierce in greater detail, and Mame could help answer Annabelle's questions.

"If you could tell me why my niece could not get far enough from Pierce several days ago and now won't leave his side, that would be a start," Annabelle joked.

Mame looked at the older woman with surprise. "Really? Although my conversations with her were brief, she seemed nothing but devoted to Pierce and his well-being."

"Now I am even more confused in light of how quickly she wants to leave once the ship is ready to sail in the next few days."

That revelation surprised Mame. Alexandra gave every indication she wanted to stay for as long as Pierce needed her. In fact, it appeared she cared deeply for the man.

"That does not seem to make much sense," Mame pondered.

Annabelle nodded.

"My feelings exactly."

275

She shared with the female pirate about Alexandra's disguise, how she and Pierce had met in St. Kitts, grown close and then an irreparable misunderstanding seemed to tear them apart.

"Chester, my husband, noted a significant change in Pierce as the months progressed. He seemed happier and lighter than when he initially arrived."

Continuing, she said, "Pierce confided in him about meeting and growing close to a beautiful native girl. His description of her raised Chester's suspicions. He grew even more wary when he learned she shared the name of our cook's daughter and Alexandra's close friend. He and I put it together. I confirmed it when Alexandra admitted she was the young woman."

Not much surprised Mame, but Alexandra's ingenuity bowled her over.

"I take it Pierce found out her true identity?"

Annabelle nodded.

"The surprise in all of this is that from the time Pierce arrived, I had tried many times to introduce the two because I thought they would enjoy each other's company. They both have roots near London and come from well-respected families."

Upon realizing Alexandra was the young woman who had caught Pierce's eye, the Chester and Annabelle decided that she had not been fair to Pierce and needed to admit the ruse.

"When Alexandra confessed to the subterfuge, she confided that she had done it out of concern for her safety. She had no idea he was our houseguest. Over time, as their friendship grew and her feelings deepened, she felt guilty and planned to tell him. Before she could, he discovered her charade."

"Neither knew each other's true identity when they met?" Mame said incredulously. "How is that even possible?"

Annabelle shook her head.

"It sounds unbelievable, but it is true. They happened upon each other at a private cove in the far corner of our property, struck up a conversation and introduced themselves by their first names. Alexandra, being cautious and true to her native disguise, used the first name of our cook's daughter, Kishma.

"His name did not register with her?" Mame inquired.

"Looking back, when I informed her of his impending visit, I only said our visitor was a business associate of her uncle. I did not give his name because that is all I knew at the time."

Annabelle went on to explain the moment the ruse was revealed.

"Much to Alexandra's dismay, Chester and Pierce returned home sooner than planned and the matter was brought out into the open quicker than she expected."

"Pierce must have been angry," Mame surmised.

Annabelle was hesitant to believe the damage was irreparable.

"Yes. But Chester and I could tell they both had a strong bond and felt they could work through the issue.

Mame listened intently about how Chester had taken it upon himself to visit Pierce on his ship and advocate for the two to talk to each other.

"We were hopeful when we ran into him the day after a storm had kept us overnight in Basseterre. He indicated he would be returning to the estate," Annabelle said.

She shook her head as she recalled Alexandra's emotional state upon their return to the plantation.

"Once the roads were passable and Chester and I could finally get home, Alexandra was hysterical and insisted we return to London immediately. I tried to elicit a reason, and all she would say is she wanted to go home."

"Curious," Mame replied.

Annabelle looked hopefully at her hostess.

"By chance, has she shared with you the reason for her haste in returning to London?"

Mame shook her head.

"No, she has not."

The older woman frowned with disappointment.

"Well, I am determined to discover what is behind this rush to leave."

Mame gave Annabelle a sympathetic smile and wished her well in her effort before leaving the house to check on the island clean-up efforts. She even made a special mental note to speak with Greene about this later.

That opportunity arose when Mame and Greene retired to their room later that night. While waiting for her to join him in bed, Greene replayed the events of the last two days in his head; that moment when he climbed into Pierce's skiff in the rocky seas and followed his friend to help him reach someone in danger on Lucrete's ship. Not one to explain himself, and Greene not one to question Pierce, he did so without further inquiry.

When the two men found Alexandra locked in the marauder's cabin, the stoic Brit silently drew his own conclusions. He saw the intensity between the two. Pierce and Greene had grown up together. He knew Pierce better than anyone. He had never seen his childhood friend react to a woman the way he did with Alexandra, let alone risk his ship, crew, and life in a raging storm to save anyone, unless they were someone he loved.

After the wounds inflicted by Helene and her duplicity and cruelty, it would take someone exceptional to break through the walls Pierce had built. Clearly, Alexandra had reached his friend in a deep and meaningful way. Greene gleaned from Alasdair that the British beauty had captured Pierce's heart the moment he laid eyes on her the day he made port in St. Kitts.

In the months that followed, they became very close as evidenced by their reaction to each other when they found her in Lucrete's quarters. Thus, her presence on the package ship confused Greene.

Never Leave My Arms

"We had little time to speak before Alasdair interrupted us to find Pierce," Mame said as she slipped beneath the covers and pressed herself against him, resting her cheek on his chest.

Greene wrapped his arm around her soft shoulder and pulled her close after placing an affectionate kiss on her forehead. Running her finger along the thin line of dark hair that ran from the center of his bare chest and trailed down his stomach, she asked, "Do you think she is hiding something?"

He casually caressed her well-toned arm as he pondered her question.

"I do not believe so, but there is a piece to this puzzle that is missing."

Maury, as Greene preferred to call her, was an enigma. She had an athletic body from working her ship, regularly exercising her saber, and laboring alongside the residents of the island to build an impressive community.

Her drive to succeed and protect her crew and friends knew no bounds. She could be ruthless when necessary yet exhibit a level of compassion that could bring one to tears. She viewed the island as a sanctuary for those seeking peace and safety, ergo the name *Veilwind*

So much had transpired between the two since Greene's arrival. What had initially been his personal quest to turn her away from a life of crime, had resulted in him seeing Maury not as a thieving pirate, but as a special person. The first sign arose one month after his stay on the island.

She and her crew had intercepted another human trafficking vessel, similar to Lucrete's, and rescued the prisoners. Maury provided for each person and offered them an opportunity to remain and become part of the close knit group. If they did not want to stay, she transported them to Tortola, which was close by, so they could secure passage to anywhere they wished.

To protect the island's privacy, the departing rescues had to remain blindfolded and in the ship's hull once it set sail. This ensured no one could trace their location.

279

Every day, he watched her work from dusk until dawn on either a ship or the island; no job was too menial. This house, her home, she personally designed and built, working shoulder to shoulder with her community. As new residences needed to be added, she ensured homes were constructed, tirelessly making certain everyone had their own space. Their relationship developing into an intimate one surprised them both.

Chapter Eighteen

The Lesser Antilles
Veilwind Island
September 15, 1774

Pierce thrashed about, the heat from his fever consumed him. A sudden coolness on his brow momentarily brought relief, and he calmed. The respite lasted only a short while, and then the nightmares returned.

Her face flashed before him. She laughed with cruel delight as he called out her name through the inferno he fought.

"Helene," Pierce mumbled.

Greene, who had been summoned to the room with Alasdair, glanced at Alexandra at the mention of the woman's name. She tried to appear unaffected, as though she had not heard him. Inwardly, she gathered that "Helene" must be Pierce's wife. Alexandra rang out another cool cloth and placed it on his feverish brow, easing his movements and gibberish.

For over two hours, she had been applying compresses to reduce the heat affecting his body and mind, but it did not help. The healer had warned that an infection could set in his wound. They called the older woman to help.

At her direction, Greene and Alasdair attempted to hold Pierce down while she doused the wound with strong liquor to clean out the infection. Through his delirium, he bellowed at the pain of the harsh intoxicant on his bare flesh. The two men could barely hold him down. Once satisfied with her efforts, she placed another poultice of healing herbs on the wound, which instantly calmed Pierce.

"Keep applying the cool compresses. The fever needs to break," the healer instructed Alexandra before leaving the room.

As directed, she complied and continued to lay freshly soaked cloths on his brow, all the while Helene's name slipped from his lips. Her first instinct was to flee the room, but Alexandra remained determined to see him through to recovery; then she would leave for London.

Alexandra went to refill the basin with fresh water and discovered the ewer empty. Turning to Greene and Alasdair, she said more tersely than she intended, "I won't be but a few moments."

Greene seized the opportunity to speak to Alexandra privately and rushed to open the bedroom door for her. He stepped into the hallway behind her and closed the door.

"Miss Alexandra, if I may," he said to get her attention.

Alexandra stopped and looked questioningly at Pierce's friend.

"Some things are not as they seem. He sacrificed everything to save you. At least give him a chance to explain before you condemn him."

"There is nothing to explain. He is married and never told me. I will ensure he is on his way to recovery." A lump lodged in her throat and her voice cracked. "It is the least I can do to repay him so he can return to his wife."

Overcome with emotion, she left Greene no opportunity for him to respond. Tears filled her eyes and she instantly turned away and rushed down the stairs, disappearing from sight.

Never Leave My Arms

"Well, at least you now have the missing piece," a familiar voice said.

Greene turned at the sound as Mame stepped out of the shadows of a doorway.

"I have the full picture, but regrettably, she does not," he replied in his usual dry delivery.

Although she knew the answer to the question, Mame asked it anyway.

"Are you going to tell her?"

Greene gave her his usual dry stare.

"Tis not my place."

Reaching to open Pierce's door, he stopped and turned.

"Nor is it yours, Maury."

Mame understood his subtle warning.

"You are right. If it is meant to be, they will find their way back to each other."

Shaking her head, she went downstairs to find Bert and check on the status of the repairs to the package ship.

Alexandra rushed around the corner with a full bowl of water and almost ran into her host. She was clearly distracted and hurrying to return to Pierce. Mame's quick movements spared them from getting soaked.

"Easy," Mame said with a chuckle.

A crimson blush stained Alexandra's tanned cheeks.

"Oh dear. How careless of me," she said.

Mame steadied the basin in the young guest's hands and smiled warmly.

"Tis no harm done. A little water never hurt anyone."

She felt sorry for Alexandra. Mame could see her exhaustion and anxiety.

"Let me bring the water upstairs and have Greene and Alasdair take care of Pierce while you take a break and rest. You have not slept in days."

Alexandra refused to release the basin and shook her head, tamping down the lump in her throat.

283

"No. I am fine. I need to do this, but thank you anyway."

Mame shook her head as Alexandra rushed past her.

"She is as stubborn as her father," Annabelle said, stepping out of the dining room after hearing the exchange between her niece and Mame.

"Running herself into the ground will not help her or Pierce," Mame replied.

Annabelle nodded.

"She still plans to leave when the package ship is ready to sail."

Mame raised an eyebrow.

"She won't be sailing anywhere at the rate she is going."

"I still do not understand her haste in leaving. She refuses to talk to me about it," Annabelle said.

Mame looked at the woman, trying to decide whether to reveal Pierce's secret. If she did, it would cause Alexandra embarrassment, and she did not want to hurt the young woman more than she already had been.

"Perhaps once you are at sea, she may open up to you," Mame offered.

"Perhaps," Annabelle said.

Eager to be about her business, Mame placed a friendly hand on the woman's arm.

"I really must check on the status of our repairs. Please let me know if there is anything else I can do for either you or Alexandra."

Annabelle gave her an appreciative smile and made her way upstairs to check on Pierce and her niece.

When she opened the door, she saw Greene seated in an overstuffed chair by the open window and Alexandra on the bed next to Pierce, placing a fresh cloth on his flushed face. His normally well-groomed beard had grown longer and desperately needed a trim.

Glancing over her shoulder at her aunt, Alexandra said anxiously, "He still hasn't regained consciousness."

Never Leave My Arms

Greene went to stand beside his friend's bed, his normally expressionless face filled with concern.

"The healer said we need to break his fever, but it does not appear Miss Alexandra's efforts are showing much promise."

Annabelle pushed up her sleeves

"I think I can be of help."

Giving Pierce an assessing look, she said, "We need to cool more than his brow. Alexandra, I know you won't like what I'm going to say, but I must insist. You cannot be in the room while Greene and I work to lower his body temperature because it would not be proper."

Alexandra opened her mouth to disagree, but Annabelle shook her head.

"No. You and Alasdair can be of the greatest assistance by bringing buckets of the coldest water on the island with a stack of clean bath sheets."

Again, her young niece tried to object, but Annabelle silenced her. Taking the cloth from Alexandra's hand, she gently pulled her niece from the side of the bed and guided her to the door.

"Greene and I can handle this. Go find Alasdair and bring the supplies to us as soon as possible. Quickly. Time is of the essence."

Alexandra reluctantly complied and rushed down the hall to the stairs to do as instructed.

Pushing herself away from the closed door, Annabelle wasted no time in taking control of the situation. She and Greene stripped off Pierce's bedcovers, leaving only a light muslin sheet across his hips for modesty, exposing his upper body and legs.

They saturated the cloths in the basin and placed them across every inch of his exposed skin, behind his neck, in his armpits and groin. As Greene placed the last cloth, Alexandra and Alasdair arrived with the buckets of water and bath sheets. Annabelle and Greene quickly relieved them of the supplies and then shooed them out of the room to collect more water.

285

The two set to drenching the bath sheets in the buckets full of icy well water, cocooning him from the top of his head to the soles of his feet. At first, the heat from his skin was so intense, the muslin became dry to the touch in a matter of minutes. After working for hours, constantly replacing the fabric with freshly saturated full-body cold compresses, Greene and Annabelle finally saw the fever easing. Pierce began to rest more comfortably.

While they tended to Pierce, Annabelle insisted her niece remain outside, even enlisting the help of Mame and Alasdair to keep her at bay. Alexandra was no match for her host, but Alasdair was an easier mark. As she was about to push past him, the door opened. Her aunt stood with a broad smile.

"His fever has finally broken."

Wishing to see for herself, Alexandra rushed to Pierce's bedside and placed her hand on his cool forehead. Although he had not regained consciousness, he no longer thrashed about. Her aunt and Greene had placed fresh linens on the bed after the healer checked his wound and applied a fresh dressing.

"He needs to rest now," Annabelle said.

Alexandra pulled a small chair to the side of the bed and sat down, determined not to leave until she saw with her own eyes that he had passed the worst. Physically and mentally exhausted, Annabelle smiled and shook her head at her niece's obstinance.

Barring her from the room for those few hours annoyed Alexandra. Casting a parting glance at her niece, she turned to Greene before leaving the room.

"Come and get me if the fever returns."

Never Leave My Arms

Alexandra looked over her shoulder at her aunt and nodded, her eyes filled with emotion. Greene quietly thanked Annabelle for helping his friend as he escorted the older woman out of the room.

Before going below, Annabelle turned to Greene with an exhausted smile.

"If the fever does not return by morning, he is past the worst and well on his way to recovering."

Alexandra awoke with a start, momentarily disoriented by her surroundings. As her eyes adjusted, she realized she was sitting next to Pierce's bed, her cheek resting on his hand. She was unsure how long she had been asleep, but her back and neck felt stiff.

Suddenly, she noticed his skin was cool to the touch, and she sat up abruptly to see if he had finally regained consciousness. She inhaled sharply when their gazes locked. His eyes showed no sign of delirium, and his color appeared normal, but his lips were dry and cracking.

Pierce had woken just before dawn to the sensation of something soft pressed against his hip. In the muted light of the room, he saw a mass of familiar light blonde hair flowing beside him. He made out the silhouette of Alexandra's sleeping face. Her cheek rested on his darkly tanned hand.

Pierce longed to feel her soft tresses between his fingers but fought the urge to free himself. He did not want to wake her. Then, as if sensing he stirred, she suddenly looked up and captured his gaze. He noticed something different in her expression.

Breaking free from his transfixing stare, she reached for a mug beside the bed and filled it with fresh water. Someone, likely Greene or her aunt, must have brought it in during the night. As she raised it to his lips, he lifted his hand to stop her. Their eyes locked and he attempted to speak, but she interrupted him.

"Don't try to talk. You need water," she said, pushing his hand aside and pressing the cup to his lips.

He frowned in annoyance but complied, glaring at her over the rim of the mug. The cold liquid quenched the dryness of his throat. As he lowered it from his lips and went to say something, the room began filling with guests.

"This is a pleasant sight," Annabelle chirped as she entered and took in the scene of her niece offering water to a wide-awake Pierce Tennyson.

Never Leave My Arms

Alasdair, Greene, and Mame followed closely behind, each wearing a broad smile. Grateful for the distraction, Alexandra stepped back from the bed as they surrounded Pierce and drew his attention. When the healer entered the room a moment later, Alexandra seized the opportunity to quietly slip out and return to her own room.

Once inside, she leaned against the closed door and released a ragged breath. Uncertainty about Pierce's recovery, combined with her lack of sleep in the past days, and the impending departure of her ship to London, frayed her nerves. She couldn't leave him without knowing he would recover, but when their gazes locked that morning, she sensed he had passed the worst and just needed rest to regain his strength.

Surrounded by his close friends and crew, she felt confident he would make a full recovery, allowing her to leave without further concern for his health. Beyond the clarity that had returned to his eyes, she could see he wanted to talk, but there was nothing more to say; he had a wife.

Alexandra knew she needed to return to London and move on with her life. Pushing away from the door, she brushed a tear from her cheek. She needed fresh air and sought the comfort of the balcony.

The bright morning sun felt rejuvenating as she closed her eyes, inhaling the fragrance of tropical flowers and the sounds of chirping birds. A light breeze gently tugged at the tendrils of hair framing her face, tickling her skin. She allowed herself to reminisce about the moments when Pierce had appeared in the doorway of Lucrete's cabin.

The intensity of that moment flooded her with emotion. Never had she imagined he would risk himself, his ship, and his crew to find her. The safety she felt in his arms and his fierce kiss made her knees buckle. However, it was short-lived. After Pierce had Greene whisked her off the vessel to safety, her anxiety grew with each passing moment he had not arrived on the island.

He had stayed behind to fight Lucrete amid the raging tempest. Alexandra felt assured that Pierce would prevail.

Alas, when his crew could not find him, she instinctively set aside her fears and raced into the eye of the hurricane without regard for her own safety to locate him. Her focus remained on his well-being, even at her own peril. Thankfully, she found him, and he was now recovering from his injury. She had accomplished what she needed to do. The time had come for her to leave, but for now, she needed to rest.

As she returned from the balcony to her room, a soft knock on the door caught her attention.

"Alexandra dear. It's Annabelle."

Seated on the edge of the bed, Alexandra replied, "Come in."

Annabelle eased the door open.

"I thought you would be sound asleep."

Alexandra offered a tired smile.

"Actually, I was about to lie down for a bit."

Annabelle noticed her niece's red eyes and guessed she had been crying.

"Of course dear. I don't want to keep you awake. I just wanted to let you know the healer said Pierce's fever has not returned and his wound looks much healthier. She expects he will be well enough to get out of bed in a day or two, but he'll need to limit his movements for at least a week to avoid breaking the stitches."

Annabelle watched Alexandra's reaction closely at the news.

Alexandra pulled back the coverlet and sat on the edge of the bed, letting out a sigh.

"That is wonderful to hear."

Curling up on her side, she yawned.

"Has the captain of the package ship set a departure date yet?"

Never Leave My Arms

Annabelle frowned, having thought Alexandra had changed her mind about leaving for London so quickly.

"The last I knew, they planned to leave in two days."

Alexandra closed her eyes and nodded. Exhaustion had settled in.

"I will make certain I am ready to leave then. I am eager to get home," she said before drifting off to sleep.

Annabelle shook her head, hoping that some rest would provide her niece with a new perspective. In the meantime, she did her best to make Alexandra comfortable by closing the balcony doors. She adjusted the louvers to block the light but still allow the breeze to flow into the room. Satisfied with her efforts, Annabelle quietly slipped out, casting one last glance at Alexandra's sleeping face.

Elizabeth H. Franklin

The Lesser Antilles
Veilwind Island
September 19, 1774

"Don't you think you should at least say goodbye to him?" Mame asked, lightly fingering the hem of the dress Alexandra had recently folded and placed on the bed.

Without looking up, she replied, "He needs his rest. Besides, there's nothing more to say."

Mame casually leaned against the dressing table. She watched Alexandra gather her few belongings and carefully tuck them into the small valise her aunt had brought her that morning.

"He seems to think otherwise. He keeps asking for you."

Trying to focus on her packing, Alexandra absently waved off the comment.

"We cannot always have what we want."

Nodding, Mame decided it best to drop the subject. She frowned because she knew Greene would be disappointed that she did not push the young woman harder.

The stoic Brit had asked her to approach Alexandra again about seeing Pierce before she left. Given the bond the two women had developed, he hoped she could convince her to stay.

Conflicted by his commitment to discretion regarding his friend's personal affairs, Greene could see the undeniable connection between the two. He knew that if Pierce could explain his situation, Alexandra would understand it wasn't as she assumed. Thus, he hoped Mame could help bring them together.

Regrettably, the frown on Mame's face as she left Alexandra's room dashed his hopes. When their eyes locked, she saw the question in Greene's gaze and slowly shook her head.

Never Leave My Arms

Annabelle had also tried her best to draw her niece out about her feelings for Pierce, but it fell on deaf ears. She was determined to leave the island and had no intention of saying goodbye to him.

On several occasions, Greene and Alasdair had to dissuade Pierce from seeking out Alexandra. Even though his recovery exceeded expectations, he was still weak and needed to minimize his movements to avoid reopening his wound.

For the first two days following his return to consciousness, they placated his inquiries about Alexandra's whereabouts by explaining she was overly exhausted and catching up on her rest. By the third and fourth days, when it became clear that their efforts to keep him distracted were failing, Greene knew he had to break the news to his friend. The opportunity arose sooner than he expected when he found Pierce knocking loudly on her door.

"Alexandra, open the door," he demanded. "You can't keep avoiding me. We need to talk."

Greene cleared his throat to get Pierce's attention; he did not want to have this discussion in the hallway.

"You really shouldn't be moving about so much."

Pierce snorted in derision.

"I'm tired of being told what I can and cannot do and where I can and cannot go."

Greene fought to suppress a smile that threatened to emerge. He had never seen this petulant side of Pierce; his annoyance at his lack of control over the situation was evident.

"Alexandra is not in there," Greene said, then turned to walk down the hall. He wanted his friend to have the privacy of his room when he received the disheartening news. Pierce paused for a moment and then followed Greene.

"Where is she? Is she with her aunt?" Pierce asked.

293

Greene closed the door of Pierce's room and looked at his friend with that all-too-familiar stoic expression. Inside, a knot had developed in his stomach. He knew he was about to deliver upsetting news.

"She and her aunt left for London yesterday."

The silence hung in the air as Pierce stared at him. Although he resumed his usual unreadable expression, Greene knew him well; the news struck him to the core.

"What is the status of the repairs to the Saltire Wind?" Pierce asked in a deadly voice.

"Alasdair or Nials would have the specifics."

Pierce sat down in the chair next to the open window and looked out into the bright sunlight at the cloud-free sky. Its brilliant blue mirrored the color of Alexandra's eyes. He briefly closed his own, remembering the look in them when he found her on Lucrete's ship. Mentally shaking himself, he directed his attention back to Greene.

"Have one or both come here immediately with a full report on the ship's status."

Greene gave a curt nod and left. Within the hour, the men returned and briefed Pierce on the projected timeline for completing repairs and being ready to sail. Although the vessel did not fare as well as the package ship, the moment the weather cleared, the crew, along with several of Mame's workers, immediately set about starting the needed work.

A few local craftspeople were currently working on the larger restorations to the hull, while another group assembled to mend two of the large sails. Thankfully, they could salvage pieces from Lucrete's partially sunken vessel, but that proved time-consuming. In total, Nials and Alasdair estimated another three weeks before they could resume their trip back to London.

"I would like it to be sooner, but if not, so be it," Pierce said to the men.

Never Leave My Arms

A blush, almost the color of his unruly red hair, crept into Alasdair's cheeks as he sheepishly asked, "Did the healer feel you would be fit to leave so soon?"

He had witnessed how close to death his friend and captain had come. Pierce knew Alasdair's question stemmed from concern, and he could not take him to task for it.

"I will be fit to leave long before that, and I'll be working alongside you to complete the repairs."

"Very good," Alasdair said with a smile.

Nials was pleased as well, while Greene remained stoic at the news. The two crew members saw nothing unusual in Greene's typical bland expression, but Pierce knew his friend faced a difficult decision much sooner than expected: did he want to leave Mame and the island to return to London?

Perhaps Greene had succeeded in convincing Mame to abandon her days of crime on the high seas and return to the British societal life she was born into. Pierce had observed their interactions over the past few days and noted the admiring glances between them when they thought no one was looking. Clearly, they had grown very close, but to what extent that influenced their respective decisions for the future remained to be seen.

Chapter Nineteen

Landon Estates
Middlesex England
December 15, 1774

Alexandra sat on the window seat with her knees tucked under her chin and arms wrapped around her bent legs. The upcoming social season in London was the last thing on her mind. She had a much bigger issue than filling her dance card at some stuffy ball.

"It has been almost a month since you returned home, and you have not accepted a single one of these party invitations," Penny complained as she sifted through the stack of envelopes on Alexandra's bedside table. "Your season will be starting in the Spring and you haven't even selected your gowns."

Alexandra could not seem to pull herself out from under the heaviness of losing Pierce. Initially, she thought her constant exhaustion and queasiness stemmed from the anxiety of her trip. However, the nausea persisted even after she returned home and found her land legs. She could no longer deny condition.

Never Leave My Arms

She had successfully hidden it from her sister, despite Penelope's constant presence in her room, but their mother had taken notice. Late one morning Cherisse took her eldest daughter aside for a private conversation.

Shortly after their unexpected return home, Annabelle had told Cherisse and Brenton about Alexandra's stay on the island. She thought it important to share the tangled relationship between their daughter and Pierce Tennyson, pointing out how well they actually suited each other.

Taking all of it in, Cherisse closely observed her daughter in the week following her return. Alexandra had withdrawn into her room, limited her time at family meals, and expressed no interest in any holiday celebrations or preparing for her London social season.

Understanding the gravity of the situation, Cherisse surprised Alexandra with a visit after lunch. Not unexpectedly, Penelope was already there, having brought her sister a tray of food that sat untouched on the bureau.

"Penny luv. Would you give Alexandra and me a few moments to speak in private?" Cherisse asked warmly.

Her youngest child smiled cheerfully.

"Certainly, Mummy."

Cherisse waited until she heard the click of the door latch before turning to her daughter. Perched on the window seat, Alexandra looked at her mother questioningly.

Giving her daughter a warm smile, she ran her finger along her daughter's soft cheek.

"You and I have not had much time to talk about your trip to your aunt and uncle's. Annabelle told me you had quite the adventure and made some friends. She mentioned you became close with their cook's daughter, Kishma, and helped her family by caring for her sister's children."

Alexandra nodded, her voice shaky.

"Yes. That kept me quite busy."

297

Cherisse pulled a chair closer to the window seat and looked lovingly at her daughter, placing her hand on Alexandra's.

"I also understand you became quite close to a young man from London who was also a guest at your aunt and uncle's. Annabelle said his name is Pierce Tennyson?"

The mention of his name brought a lump to Alexandra's throat, making it impossible for her to respond. Instead, she could only nod as tears welled in her eyes.

"Your aunt also mentioned he became very angry when he discovered you were not who you presented yourself to be. Is that right?"

That was all it took. The floodgates opened. Although her words came out in gasping sobs, Alexandra recounted the story, at least most of it, leaving out their night together. She started with the reason for her disguise and ended with her intention to tell him before he found out on his own.

"He would not let me explain and stormed off."

Cherisse knew her daughter held something back.

"Is that why you wanted to leave so suddenly?"

Alexandra could not look at her mother. Instead, she focused on her tightly folded hands in her lap and gave an evasive reply.

"I could not understand how we could have such a close bond of friendship, and he wouldn't give me the benefit of the doubt."

Her mother pressed her.

"If being near him was too painful, and he left, then why the rush to cut your trip short?"

Alexandra stared silently, her head down. How could she tell her mother that she and Pierce had been intimate, that he had withheld the fact that he was married, and that she now carried his child?

Taking a different approach, Cherisse placed her hand on her daughter's cool forehead.

Never Leave My Arms

"Luv, I know you have not been feeling well." Noting the untouched tray of food on the bureau she continued. "You have barely sampled your meal. Perhaps I should get you some hot tea?"

Offering a plausible explanation to assuage her mother's concern, Alexandra replied, "I still feel a bit under the weather from the journey home, but I had tea and a bit of a biscuit earlier."

"Hmm," Cherisse pondered. "Tea and biscuits were all I could tolerate at first when I was expecting you."

Alexandra's head snapped up, and her mouth opened, but nothing came out as she stared at her mother in disbelief.

Taking her daughter's hands in hers, Cherisse's eyes filled with emotion.

"You were not home two days that I suspected. When your aunt told me about Pierce, I knew at that point. I had hoped you would come to me and tell me."

Alexandra threw her arms around her mother and sobbed. Cherisse held her child tight, comforting her. She knew the fear and anxiety her daughter had been carrying these past weeks were overwhelming.

"We will figure this out. Don't you worry," Cherisse soothed.

Pushing herself away from her mother, Alexandra shook her head as she tried to collect herself.

Choking back a sob, she managed to say, "There is nothing to work out. He is married. He never told me, and by the time I found out, it was too late. That is why I wanted to leave St. Kitts and come home early."

Cherisse wiped the tears from her daughter's cheeks and allowed her to calm down as she processed the shock of her news. The Tennysons were a well-known and respected family not only in England but also in Scotland. She found it hard to believe that Larena and Nathaniel would raise their son to treat a well-bred young woman so callously. Unless, their intimacy had occurred while he believed her to be an island native, a young woman he

299

could dally with, free from worry about the consequences. Some men believed such reprehensible behavior was acceptable. She would reserve judgment on Pierce Tennyson until she had the opportunity to call upon Larena and Nathaniel.

In the interim, she needed to speak with Brenton who was already in London on business. Before arranging her impromptu trip to see him, Cherisse needed to know one important thing from her daughter. Lifting Alexandra's chin gently, she asked, "Annabelle said you told her you had fallen in love with him. Is that true?"

Alexandra looked away in shame.

"Yes, but I feel like such a fool."

"Darling, you are not a fool," Cherisse eased.

Alexandra's eyes filled with tears and her voice cracked.

"He kept trying to speak with me after the kidnapping incident, but I knew if I let him, I would get drawn in further."

"Do you think he was trying to tell you then?"

"Possibly. I don't know. What would it matter? He is married."

Cherisse patted her daughter's hand and kissed her affectionately on the forehead as she stood up.

"I am going to have some fresh tea sent up, and I want you to relax and get some rest. I need to think about everything you told me so we can talk more and decide on an appropriate course of action."

Alexandra's eyes widened as she grabbed her mother's hand.

"Please don't tell Papa."

Cherisse squeezed her hand and gave her a reassuring smile.

"Your father is in London, but he will have to be told sooner rather than later."

Tears returned anew at the thought of how disappointed her father would be.

Never Leave My Arms

"He will never forgive me."

Cherisse held her daughter's face in her hands and looked at her meaningfully.

"My sweet child. Your father will understand."

Alexandra did not grasp the full implication of what her mother was trying to convey. Brenton understood because he and Cherisse had experienced the same thing when they too fell in love.

Elizabeth H. Franklin

The Landon Townhome
Westminster, London
December 17, 1774

Cherisse wasted no time arranging transport to their Westminster townhome in London to meet with her husband. She also had a messenger rush a note to Larena and Nathaniel Tennyson, asking to meet with them as soon as possible upon her arrival in the city. Although the two couples were not close friends, she knew they would accommodate her request, especially when she indicated that the matter was urgent.

Before leaving, she decided it was best to keep her plans from Alexandra and left word that she had been called out to an emergency to help a young family. Neither of her daughters thought it unusual, as their mother routinely offered assistance to members of their community.

"I should not be gone for more than a couple of days, perhaps less. The staff have my instructions, and Annabelle is here as well," she said, kissing each of her daughters on the forehead.

Cherisse looked pointedly yet warmly at her youngest.

Penelope, please spend your time productively and practice your stitching. If needed, use your father's study for some quiet so you can focus. I would like to see some progress when I return."

Her youngest grimaced and nodded.

"Yes, Mummy."

Turning her attention to Alexandra, she pressed her cheek to hers and whispered so only she could hear, "We will figure this out when I get back. I promise."

Tears formed in Alexandra's eyes as she nodded. Cherisse fought back her own emotions as she slipped out the front door to the waiting carriage.

The normally tedious two-hour ride to London flew by as the concerned mother contemplated how to tell her husband about their daughter's situation. She knew he would be disappointed and likely angry, but she needed to remind him that they had been in a similar situation when they were young lovers; the glaring difference being that he was not married.

Cherisse was abruptly shaken from her thoughts when the carriage had barely stopped in front of their Westminster townhome, and the door was yanked open by her husband.

Brenton Landon had the same intoxicating effect on her as he did over twenty years ago. She found it easy to get lost in the depths of his warm brown eyes. He towered over her at just under six feet tall, with a well-toned physique that he maintained by engaging in weekly pugilistic events at his club. His skills were unrivaled, and often his fellow members sought him out for advice on honing their own abilities. While his opponents felt the power of his rock-hard fists, Cherisse experienced the strength of his love through those very same hands during their most intimate moments.

The frantic look on his handsome, chiseled face made her cringe. Perhaps in her haste to write her note to him, she may have been a bit dramatic.

"What has happened? Are the girls well? What about Annabelle? Has something happened to her?" he asked rapidly.

After helping her alight, she placed her hand gently on his cheek and smiled lovingly.

"Darling, everyone is fine. Can we please go inside so we do not have this conversation on the sidewalk in front of our neighbors?"

Realizing his overreaction, Brenton took a calming breath, smiled affectionately at his wife, and tucked her hand inside the crook of his arm as he escorted her to the open front door.

"Of course. Your note had me worried."

Cherisse removed her gloves and placed them on the small entry table before turning to her husband and giving him a sweet kiss.

"I am sorry I worried you."

She glanced down the polished wood-lined hallway and scanned the stylishly decorated parlor.

"Who from the staff is here?"

Brenton frowned at her question. "Just Mae. She is in the kitchen."

"Perfect," Cherisse said.

Its location was one floor below them, and they could have the privacy they needed.

"Let's go to your study."

Nodding, he guided her a few steps down the long hall and closed the door behind them. Turning to his wife with a concerned expression, he asked, "Cherisse, what is this all about?"

Taking his hand, she pulled him down next to her on the large leather sofa.

"It's about our Alexandra."

Recalling her initial reassurances, Brenton looked attentively at his wife, waiting for further explanation.

"She has fallen in love with someone she met in St. Kitts, and we know his parents."

Brenton looked expectantly at his wife.

"It is Nathaniel and Larena Tennyson's son, Pierce."

Much to her surprise, he gave her a blank stare.

Cherisse gave her husband an impatient look.

"Darling, Pierce married a young woman from Scotland earlier this year."

His one-word reply brought her to her feet in exasperation. "Yes," he replied.

Emotion and frustration overcame Cherisse at her husband's lack of reaction. Before she knew it, she blurted out, "Alexandra is carrying his child."

Never Leave My Arms

Her hand flew to cover her mouth and her eyes widened with shock at how she had revealed the news.

Now it was Brenton who was on his feet, his eyes burning with anger.

Cherisse immediately tried to temper the situation.

"Darling, I am sorry. I did not mean for you to hear it that way."

Brenton began pacing.

"My preference would have been a softer approach, but regardless, it would still have been equally shocking."

"I sent word to Larena that we wanted to speak with her and Nathaniel," she said.

Suddenly he stopped pacing and looked squarely at his wife, his jaw set with determination.

"Pierce has compromised our daughter, and he will marry her posthaste."

Opening a bottle of whiskey at the sideboard, he poured a generous amount of the amber liquid into a crystal glass, downed it in one swallow, and then poured another.

Cherisse looked at her husband in disbelief. For a brief moment, she thought her husband had lost his senses.

"Brenton, dear, Pierce is already married to some young Scottish girl."

As he fought the burn of the fine liquor, he waved off her concerns.

"Pierce had Nathaniel annul his marriage immediately after it happened. I do not have all the details, but word around the club is the bride committed, among other things, fraud."

A blend of relief and shock flooded Cherisse. She quickly sat down before her knees gave out. Her daughter thought she had fallen in love with a married man and would never find happiness because he belonged to another. Come to find out, there could be a future for the young couple if Alexandra would talk to Pierce. She just could not understand why the young man had not told her daughter. She had a right to know.

305

"I have so many questions for the Tennysons," Cherisse said, wringing her hands with worry. "They should have received my note by now about meeting."

Brenton sat on the edge of the sofa arm, swirling the remnants of the whiskey in his glass.

"They are in London. I saw Nathaniel leaving the club yesterday."

Although they both wanted to rush over to the Tennyson residence, the concerned parents decided to settle in and await their reply, hoping it would arrive by early morning.

Never Leave My Arms

The Tennyson Townhome
Mayfair, London
December 18, 1774

"Larena, your home is absolutely lovely," Cherisse said, taking in the elegance of the drawing room.

The auburn-haired Scottish beauty smiled warmly as she poured a cup of tea for her guest before taking a seat next to her on the settee. Their husbands sat in two finely upholstered high-back armchairs on either side of their wives, enjoying a fine Scotch.

"It was very kind of you to invite us for dinner. We did not want you to go to any trouble," Cherisse said.

Larena placed a friendly hand on her guest's arm.

"Nonsense. It's no trouble. Besides, we've been intending to have you over for quite some time."

Holding the delicate China, she focused on stirring the hot liquid. A faint frown touched her brow as she recalled everything that had occurred over these past many months.

"Unfortunately, this year has been quite demanding with travel and Nathaniel's work. Thankfully, things have settled down."

Larena turned the conversation to her guests.

"You must be busy with your eldest's season. They grow up so fast. She must be terribly excited."

Cherisse seized the opportunity to broach the subject of Pierce and Alexandra. Taking a sip of her tea and a calming breath, she eased into the reason for their visit.

"Time has passed swiftly. Our Alexandra is nineteen now," Cherisse said, a hint of melancholy in her voice. Looking to her husband for strength, she continued, "Your Pierce must be close to his mid-twenties?"

307

"Twenty-five," Larena said softly, recalling the chain of events set into motion from that very birthday.

Nathaniel saw the shadow fall across his wife's face and quickly intervened to lift her spirits, pride filling his voice.

"Our Pierce has become a captain of industry. His maternal grandparents turned over the running of Fraser Shipping to him. We are thrilled he decided to relocate the headquarters to London. I have spent these many months assisting him in getting things settled while he traveled to the Leewards to visit a friend of mine."

Brenton cleared his throat and asked casually, "Would that be the MacKittricks?"

Larena and Nathaniel looked at each other in surprise.

"Yes. Do you know Chester and Annabelle?" Larena asked.

"Annabelle is my sister, and Chester is my brother-in-law."

"My word. How serendipitous," Larena exclaimed.

Although not immediately detected by his wife, Nathaniel noted the serious glances exchanged between Cherisse and Brenton.

Cherisse shared the details of their daughter's plans.

"After much discussion and pleading, we conceded to Alexandra's request to spend a year with Annabelle and Chester at their home in St. Kitts. When Annabelle returned to the islands early this year, Alexandra joined her. They surprised us a month ago when they returned several months earlier than planned."

Larena gave her husband an excited expression.

"Then she and Pierce must have been surprised to discover their families connection."

Nathaniel had exchanged a few letters with Pierce, updating him on the status of his efforts to annul the marriage and matters related to Fraser Shipping. He never shared specific personal details from their son, but in his

Never Leave My Arms

last two letters, Pierce mentioned he had met a beautiful island native. The young woman had renewed his faith in women. She challenged him in ways no other had and possessed a warmth and insight like his mother. He described her as having striking eyes unlike any he had ever seen, especially among islanders, and that her name was Kishma.

Instinctively, Nathaniel began to assemble the pieces. He carefully observed his guests reaction to the next bit of information he shared.

"In the few letters I exchanged with Pierce, he mentioned meeting a young island woman with whom he was quite smitten. He said her name was Kishma. Did Alexandra meet her by chance?"

Cherisse had to give credit to Nathaniel. He, too, knew how to present an opportunity to elicit a specific response. Perhaps she said it too quickly, but Cherisse nodded.

"Alexandra is Kishma."

Larena looked at her husband in confusion while Brenton gave his wife a supportive glance.

"I don't understand," Larena said.

Cherisse explained.

"The short story is our two children met, and I cannot speak for Pierce, but Alexandra fell in love with him."

Not giving away too much from what he had shared in his letters between he and his son, Nathaniel interjected, "I believe the same is true for Pierce."

Larena gave her husband a questioning look.

Not wanting to keep his wife in the dark, he explained.

"He mentioned meeting this young woman, Kishma, in his last two letters. He seemed quite taken with her. Chester even mentioned in his last correspondence how much better Pierce seemed under her influence."

Pierce's parents worried he would never come out from under the cloak of anger he carried over what Helene and his grandmother had done to him.

309

Nathaniel initially had concerns that this young island native woman was only temporary, serving his son's physical needs. However, as he reflected on Pierce's letters, he recalled how he focused on her emotional attributes, a young woman of principle, warmth, and strength.

Larena rose and looked among the three. "Could someone please fill me in?"

Nathaniel smiled and drew her over to the seat he had just vacated. She declined his invitation to sit down. Instead, she stepped behind the high-back chair and held onto the top. She listened to her husband explain all their son had shared about this wonderful young native island woman named Kishma.

"She worked wonders in helping him get past the damage from earlier in the year."

Brenton and Cherisse made a mental note to explore that comment further but gave no outward reaction.

"And this Kishma is actually Alexandra?" Larena asked, looking among the small group.

All three nodded.

"Why wouldn't she just tell Pierce her real name? Why the charade?" she asked.

Cherisse explained that her daughter took on the disguise as a safety measure to move about the island more freely. Her light hair and eye color made her a target for pirates who trolled the islands looking for young women to kidnap and sell, or worse.

Expounding further, she went on to share that neither Alexandra nor Pierce knew their connection when they first met. During Pierce's first weeks on the island, his time was monopolized with his ship's continuing journey to other islands, its return, and working with Chester. Meanwhile Alexandra helped her friend from dawn till dusk prepare for a new addition to their family. It was not until their respective commitments eased that the two happened upon each other near the ocean one afternoon. They only exchanged first names.

"Annabelle had only told her a business associate of Chester's would be arriving. Alexandra presumed the man was much like her uncle, likely his age, and would have nothing in common with her."

A blush crept into Cherisse cheeks at the allusion to her brother-in-law's penchant for stuffy pursuits.

Nathaniel and Larena were impressed with Alexandra's ability to pull off such a convincing charade and understood her reasons.

Larena had little doubt her son would find fault once she provided her reasons.

"I am certain once she explained it to Pierce, he completely understood."

Nathaniel did not share his wife's optimism. The scars Helene and Maisie inflicted with their deceptions cut their son deeply. For Pierce to allow himself to trust again only to be duped, even for a legitimate reason, would be crushing.

Cherisse and Brenton did not share Larena's view either. They relayed that Annabelle had told them Pierce refused to allow Alexandra to explain and shut her out. He even stayed on his ship to put distance between them.

Although Chester was not one to involve himself in others matters of the heart, he even paid a visit to Pierce to help him understand things from Alexandra's perspective.

Chester thought he got through to Pierce. He and Annabelle had run into him at the docks the day after a severe storm struck. The couple had spent the night in town and were heading home. Pierce told them he would be returning to the estate once he had completed the repairs to his ship. They presumed he had cooled off and wanted to hear out Alexandra. When they reached the plantation, Alexandra was upset and insisted on cutting her trip short to return home, saying only that Pierce had set her aside."

Larena frowned in confusion. It sounded as though the two were on their way to resolving the issue.

"I wonder what could have possibly happened to make her want to leave so suddenly. Now that she has returned home, has she given you any idea why?"

Brenton looked to Cherisse and gestured to share what she learned from Alexandra.

"Quite honestly, that is the reason we wanted to speak with you two."

Nathaniel and Larena exchanged wary looks.

Cherisse glanced to her husband for support. Brenton nodded slowly for her to tell them everything.

Stating it as delicately as possible, Cherisse shared her discussion with her daughter.

"Alexandra told me that the night of the storm, Pierce returned to the plantation. The two worked through his upset and hurt over her charade, and declared their love for each other."

Larena dropped her head, and Nathaniel closed his eyes.

Cherisse continued.

"The next morning, she awoke to find him gone. When she went to his room to look for him, she saw a piece of paper on the bureau and thought he had left her a note. As she began to read it, she realized it was a letter to Pierce about his wife. Devastated, she ran back to her room, and when Annabelle returned, she insisted on going home immediately."

Larena wiped a tear from her cheek. "That poor child."

"Indeed," Cherisse said. "Alexandra is carrying your son's child." Referencing the four of them, she added, "Our grandchild."

Larena looked at her husband with emotion-filled eyes.

"Nathaniel, we need to tell them everything."

Never Leave My Arms

Brenton and Cherisse exchanged glances, uncertain they could take any more surprises.

Nathaniel nodded. He knew gossip had circulated about Pierce marrying in Scotland earlier in the year, but as is often the case with rumors, there are usually only a small amount of truth to them.

Before launching into the specifics, Brenton refreshed his and Nathanial's drink. Both men were surprised when their wives insisted they have a generous amount of whatever they were drinking as well.

Once everyone had their spirits and were comfortable, Nathaniel recounted the saga of all Pierce had suffered and what led him to St. Kitts.

Brenton and Cherisse sat slack jawed, hearing what Pierce had endured. They completely understood why the young man had such a strong reaction to Alexandra's charade, but concealing the marriage concerned them.

"Why withhold the fact of the marriage, particularly if an annulment was in process?" Cherisse asked.

Nathaniel tried to explain from his son's perspective.

"Even though Pierce believed himself relieved of Helene and the marital bonds before he left for the Leeward Islands, the fact it was not formally and quickly disposed of weighed heavily upon him. I thought he would have told Alexandra once he received my letter with the proof."

Withholding the personal feelings Pierce shared with him in his correspondence, Nathaniel felt it important to tell the Landon's how Pierce felt about their daughter.

"My son and I exchanged several letters during his stay in St. Kitts, and I must tell you that your daughter came into Pierce's life at a time when he needed her the most. She broke through the walls he had erected, to allow himself to be happy and it appears, to fall in love with her. Chester MacKittrick wrote me as well and confirmed as much."

313

The four parents sat quietly for a moment. There was much to absorb. Finally, Cherisse broke the silence.

"Where do we go from here?"

Before anyone could answer, Larena and Nathaniel were approached by their family steward, Geoffrey Greene.

"Pardon the interruption," he said, inclining his head to his employer and their guests, "but dinner is ready."

"Thank you, Geoffrey," Larena said.

Pausing for a moment, he quietly inquired of his employer, "Sir, Madam, if there is nothing else you require from me this evening, would it be acceptable for me to retire a bit early? My son has returned from his trip, and my wife and I would like to spend time with him."

"Certainly," Nathaniel said, then stopped the man before he could leave.

"Geoffrey, when did Llewellyn return? Is he here?"

Giving his employer a quizzical look, he nodded.

"He arrived this morning, and he is in the kitchen at the moment."

"Excellent. Could you send him here? I need a brief word."

The steward bobbed his head.

A moment later, Llewelyn Greene entered the drawing room tentatively.

"Sir, my father said you wished to speak with me?"

"Yes, thank you," Nathaniel said with a friendly smile. "I understand you and Pierce returned from your trip to the islands. When did you arrive?"

"This morning sir."

"Did Pierce say he would come home today, or did he plan to stay on the ship?"

"He didn't say sir. He left the ship shortly before noon to ride to Middlesex."

Cherisse and Brenton exchanged glances. They surmised Pierce was going to the estate to see Alexandra.

Never Leave My Arms

Nathaniel did not want to make the young man any more uncomfortable than he already seemed.

"Thank you Llewellyn, and welcome back."

"Thank you sir," he said as he excused himself.

Brenton looked among the small group and held up his glass for a toast.

"It appears Pierce has determined the next step."

Chapter Twenty

Landon Manor
Middlesex, England
December 18, 1774
...later that afternoon

Pierce had arrived at Landon House in the late afternoon demanding to see Alexandra.

"She does not wish to see you," the staff informed him at Alexandra's direction.

He had no intention of being put off. Insistent and his voice elevated, he replied, "I need to speak with her. It is urgent."

Pierce raised such a ruckus that Penelope heard him all the way down the corridor in her father's study. When she quietly came to investigate and peered around the corner, she was shocked to see a tall, well-built man towering over the family's steward. The stranger did not look menacing, just firm in his purpose.

Certain he could not physically throw Pierce out, the family representative chose a more diplomatic route. He sought out Annabelle in the hopes that she could calm their unwelcome guest and encourage him to leave.

"If you will step into the drawing room, I will see if Mistress Annabelle is available."

Pierce gave a quick nod and stepped into the room as directed. He chose not to sit down. His emotions were running high. He needed to see Alexandra, tell her everything, and make her understand.

Annabelle found Pierce pacing in front of the drawing room fireplace, a scowl on his face.

"Pierce, the staff say you are refusing to leave unless you speak with Alexandra."

She sympathized with him and with her niece. Whatever the cause of the estrangement, she firmly believed they would work past it. They were meant to be together.

Seeing a familiar friendly face sent a wave of relief through Pierce.

"Thank goodness. Annabelle, I think I know why she left St. Kitts so suddenly and why she would not speak to me on Veilwind island. I need to explain it to her."

Annabelle sat down on the settee and indicated the vacant seat next to her.

Pierce did as she asked and took the seat next to her, his hands resting nervously on his knees.

"I can see how much you care for Alexandra. I saw it in St. Kitts, and you demonstrated it when you rescued us from Lucrete at your own peril. I also know that Alexandra cares deeply for you, dare I say, loves you. Give her time. In the interim, I will impress upon her that she should listen to you."

Pierce sat quietly, digesting Annabelle's words. He knew she championed his pairing with her niece and that she would do her best to encourage the relationship. While he appreciated her aunt's support, he needed to find some way to get through to Alexandra sooner. With each passing day, the wall Alexandra built between them grew thicker and more impenetrable.

He needed to regroup. Perhaps enlist the insight of his father. Accepting short-term defeat, Pierce let out an uneasy breath and rose. He extended a gentlemanly hand to help Annabelle from her seat.

"Thank you. I appreciate whatever you can do."

Squeezing his hand affectionately, she tucked hers into the crook of his arm, and the two walked together to the front door where they said their goodbyes. Neither saw Penelope slip from sight and rush down the corridor to her father's study.

The cold December air felt refreshing to Pierce as he walked toward the path where the stable hand had taken his horse and carriage. The crunching sound of his boots along the stone driveway kept his mind sharp as he contemplated how he could reach Alexandra.

It took a few seconds for the soft whistle coming from the corner of the home's façade to break through his thoughts and make him stop to determine its exact location. His eyes scanned both sides of the large circular drive but saw nothing. Glancing back toward the grand home, Pierce skimmed each of the windows on the upper floors and found none were open. As his attention turned to the main floor, a flash of color caught his eye at the farthest corner near a series of hedges bordering a garden. A windowed door was partially open, and a young girl, with a blanket around her shoulders, stood in the entry motioning for him.

Pierce looked around to ensure that no one was about and swiftly made his way across the drive. At her insistence, he stepped inside, and she quickly closed the entry behind him, pulling the curtain closed as well.

As he went to speak, she placed her finger to her lips then listened for anyone approaching down the corridor. The location of the room appeared

Never Leave My Arms

to be at the far end of a wing. Satisfied they were safe from interruption, she motioned for him to follow her to the farthest corner of the room by a set of French doors.

At first, he thought she planned to go outside, but instead, she gestured for him to sit down in a chair next to the large fireplace. It appeared someone, likely the young girl, had been working on some needlework, as her efforts lay on the seat of a chair next to him. Smiling broadly at him, she pushed the sampler aside and introduced herself.

"It is nice to finally meet the man who swept my sister off her feet. I predicted that, you know. I am Alexandra's younger sister, Penelope. My friends call me Penny."

At first, Pierce presented her with his usual unreadable expression as he assessed her. Although she shared Alexandra's petite stature and smile, that is where the resemblance ended. The younger girl's hair and eyes were dark, while Alexandra's were light, and she was far more forthcoming with information than her older sister.

Penny instinctively sensed that Pierce was mentally comparing the two siblings.

"Alexandra favors my mother, and I favor my father," she explained.

Pierce immediately regrouped at the young woman's perceptiveness and relaxed.

"You must forgive me. Alexandra never told me she had a sister, especially such a sharp-witted one."

The young woman blushed and giggled at the compliment.

"I gather from the chaos you caused that you want to speak with my sister, but she does not seem to want to speak with you. She can be stubborn to her own detriment sometimes."

Pierce began to feel he had found an ally in this young girl.

319

"I believe if I could speak with her for just a few moments, this entire matter could be rectified."

"So I heard, all the way down the corridor," Penny said with a lopsided grin.

Immediately, Pierce's expression tightened, and she realized he was not in the mood to be teased. Clearing her throat, she adopted a more serious tone.

"So, after you speak with her and the situation you reference is corrected, what then?"

Pierce pushed himself out of the chair and grumbled, "This was a mistake…" when Penny added, "I will only help you if you came because you love my sister and want to fight for her."

Towering over the young girl, he stared hard at her trying to discern if she viewed this as a game. It surprised him that she remained steadfast and returned an equally intense look; a similarity she shared with her sister.

"Yes," he said simply. No explanation, no elaboration.

Penny nodded. "Very well. Come back at dark to the door I let you in, and I will take you to her. Leave your horse and carriage at the house by the road. It is empty, and there is a stable in the back where it will be safe."

Never Leave My Arms

As promised, Penny waited at the study door for Pierce as night fell. When he arrived, she quickly led him through the French doors at the far corner of the room and into the garden. To ward off the cold, she pulled her shawl tighter around her shoulders.

Retrieving the small lantern she had placed on the ground, she guided him down the side of the grand home to a concealed doorway. It led to a staircase to the wing she shared with Alexandra.

Before opening the door to their corridor, Penelope whispered, "Alexandra's room is the first one on the right, and mine is across the hall."

Pierce glanced down the passageway. There several wall lanterns providing enough light to make out four other doors along the corridor.

Frowning, he asked in a barely audible whisper, "Are there any other rooms occupied in this wing?"

Penny shook her head. "No. Just mine and Alexandra's."

After giving her a quick nod, she extinguished the lantern, and he followed her out of the stairwell, stopping at Alexandra's door.

Penny smiled brightly and whispered, "Good luck," before slipping into her own room.

Pierce nodded and mumbled, "I may need it."

Before turning the handle, he looked at the bottom of Alexandra's closed door and saw a faint light. Easing it open, he peered inside and quickly scanned the room. The expansive space contained a large bed draped in light-colored fabric across from him. It was centered between a set of doors on the left that led out to a balcony and an oversized window to the far right. Floor to ceiling draperies partially concealed the seat below the window.

Seeing no immediate sign of Alexandra, he slipped inside the room and silently closed the door. Pausing for a moment, he pressed his back against it and looked more closely around the space. He frowned when he still could not see any sign of her.

As he pushed himself away from the door, Pierce slowly made his way past the bed when a movement from behind the draperies at the window seat made him stop in his tracks. He held his breath as a pair of bare feet and shapely women's calves appeared then stepped onto the lush decorative carpet.

A second later, Alexandra emerged, dressed in a soft pink flowing nightdress and matching robe. Her long light-blonde hair flowed freely over her shoulders and down her back. Initially, she did not look in his direction. Instead, she reached back to pick up something from the seat she had just vacated. Suddenly she froze and stared at the window.

Pierce frowned and then realized what held her attention, his reflection in the glass.

It seemed like minutes, but it was actually only seconds before Alexandra reacted with a gasp and whirled around to confirm she had not seen an apparition.

Afraid she would try to flee, he rushed forward and pulled her into his arms. At first, the surprise of his presence paralyzed her, and she did not resist his embrace. Then, the memory of deception crashed down on her, and she fought to free herself.

"Let me go," she demanded as she struggled against his unyielding grasp.

"Alexandra, I will let you go if you promise to listen to me," he said rationally.

"There is nothing you have to say that I am interested in hearing. Go back to Helene. your wife," she bit out as she continued to struggle.

Whether it was the mention of Helene's name or his frustration with Alexandra's stubbornness, something inside Pierce snapped. Grabbing her roughly by the shoulders, he pulled her face inches from his. His hazel-green eyes flared, and his jaw ticked as he kept a tight rein on his annoyance.

Never Leave My Arms

"I have chased you thousands of miles and almost lost my life in the process of saving yours. The least you can do is grant me a few moments to tell you what I have wanted to say since that night we spent together. If you are not willing to listen, I will gag you and tie you to that chair until you do. The choice is yours," he ground out.

Alexandra had never seen Pierce this angry. Looking into his eyes now, she recognized it as the flicker of emotion she had glimpsed their first day at the beach. He had kept it in check then and never disclosed what haunted him.

Curiosity got the best of her, so she relented. She would give him an opportunity to speak in the event he wished to finally share it. Then, she would order him out.

Giving him a mulish look, she said crisply, "Have your say, but it will not make any difference."

Rolling his eyes in exasperation, he released her. Alexandra quickly sat down in the small armchair by the window, crossed her arms, and looked at him with icy expectancy.

Pierce decided it best to block her path of escape should she try to run past him, so he positioned himself on an ottoman directly in front of her.

"Alexandra, I am not married." Before she could fire off the retort on the tip of her tongue, he continued. "I was married for less than one day and had it annulled."

Although less biting, she replied, "Even if that is the case now, I saw the letter from your father. You were married while you were in St. Kitts, and you never told me. I deserved to know. For all I know, you could still be married."

Without giving him a chance to respond, she reminded him of his hypocrisy.

323

"You walked away from me when you discovered I had been in disguise; something I did for my safety. You refused to listen."

Pierce found it hard to argue against her point; his intractability had been unfair.

"Rage, hurt, and distrust consumed me, and that is no excuse. But I want to tell you everything that happened to me that led to this."

Alexandra looked at him with surprise.

By now, her resistance had eased, but she remained adamant. Anything he had to say would not change how she felt. Still, she was open to hearing him out.

"Very well."

Steeling himself, he started at the beginning. He explained his maternal grandfather's dying wish was to give Pierce Fraser Shipping when he turned thirty. Before his passing, and unbeknownst to Pierce, his grandparents set special conditions on his twenty-fifth birthday. The terms were contrived to keep Pierce tied to Scotland permanently. They involved a pact made with a neighboring clan that he marry their oldest granddaughter, run Fraser Shipping, and after five years of marriage, on Pierce's thirtieth birthday, he would take sole ownership of the company.

"Helene being the granddaughter?" Alexandra inquired.

Pierce nodded and continued, his emotion evident as he relived the hurt of his grandmother's manipulation. She not only stripped him of the choice of his life partner, but made it clear he would be responsible for a potential clan war if he refused to fulfill the pact.

Shaking his head, he said, "All because she wanted me to remain permanently in Scotland. She hated my father and my English heritage."

Alexandra could never imagine her parents allowing such a thing to happen. They always encouraged her and her sister to make their own decisions and pursue their own happiness.

Never Leave My Arms

"I take it your allegiance to keeping peace among the two clans won out?" she asked quietly.

"I tried to tactfully beg off from the wedding."

He relayed his conversation with Helene, noting that he sensed she had eyes for another boy, but she insisted she would not shame her grandparents and would see the pact through.

"Little did I know," he said cryptically.

Feeling trapped by his grandmother's manipulations, he took control of the one thing he could: Fraser Shipping. He secretly arranged to relocate its operations to London.

"That must have set your grandmother's teeth on edge," she said, a touch of admiration in her voice.

Pierce nodded and flashed her a lopsided grin.

"Indeed. I made my grandmother sign the transfer documents after the ceremony and directed Helene to gather her things because we were leaving for Inverness. Only my parents knew of my plans to sail from there to London."

Pierce released an apprehensive breath as he struggled to relate what happened on the wedding night. Although Alexandra seemed to have softened after hearing the details thus far, he knew it would not be easy for her to hear about his and Helene's night together.

Sensing his struggle, she placed a caring hand on his as she captured his gaze, her eyes filled with compassion. Although all this happened long before Alexandra and Pierce met, she would be dishonest to say she did not feel a twinge of pain at the thought of him with another woman.

"I can handle whatever you need to tell me," she murmured.

Clearing his throat, he summoned his courage and pressed on, sharing how Helene had drugged him. She needed to incapacitate him to carry out her and her lover's plan to dupe him into believing she was chaste. When

325

the effects of the drug wore off sooner than expected, he discovered her deception.

Pierce held his head in his hands.

"I cared naught about her virginity. What mattered to me was that she had lied about it and had tried to trick me. I told her to pack her things and that she would be returning to her grandparents, where she would end the marriage pact and set me free. She tried to manipulate me by claiming we had consummated the marriage, yet I have no clear recollection of such and it would not have mattered regardless."

Even as he recounted the story, he could not make sense of all that had happened between them under the effects of the drug that night. He recalled flashes of Helene looking down on him and laughing, then darkness overcame him. She would reappear again in a dreamlike state, her head thrown back, moaning, then Pierce would lose consciousness again.

Alexandra was dumbstruck by Helene's actions. She could not understand why the woman insisted on going through with the marriage. Surely it could not be out of a sense of obligation to her family; her conduct bespoke selfishness, not altruism.

The next bit of information answered Alexandra's questions. Much to Pierce's surprise, Helene had no intention of returning to her family in shame. Her lover and his cousin arrived shortly after Pierce discovered her deceit and knocked him out with a sharp blow to the head.

Alexandra gasped in shock and outrage as she listened to what unfolded. Although bound and gagged after coming to, Pierce heard the cousins discussing the entire plan: drugging him, knocking him out, transporting him to the Firth, and dumping him in its icy waters to drown. Then, once his body was found, Helene would claim the Fraser fortune as the rightful heir.

"They had not realized that the only ships at the docks that night were Fraser vessels, so once I freed myself from the ropes, I had enough strength to bang on the hull of the Saltire Wind. Alasdair was on deck at the time and fished me out."

Once aboard and dried off, Pierce had Alasdair collect his father at the castle and bring him back to the ship, where he explained the chain of events. He and Nathaniel crafted a plan to force Helene to annul the marriage or face shame from her clan. In the meantime, Pierce and the Fraser fleet would be well on their way to their new headquarters in London and out of further attempts on his life.

Pierce sighed in exhaustion.

"My father is friends with Chester and thought the journey and warm weather would do wonders for me while he worked to secure my freedom from Helene."

Alexandra could not speak. She could never fathom that this was the pain he carried daily and concealed. The fury rose in her at the thought of what this woman had done.

Pierce took a moment to gather himself. He sat silently before Alexandra on the low stool, his elbows on his knees, head down, staring at the floor. His concealment of this from her had nothing to do with selfish ulterior motives. Rather, he was not prepared to relive the pain, particularly when he had not yet received word from his father about his freedom. Every day that this secret hung between them weighed heavier on him.

So wrapped up in his own thoughts, he did not immediately notice that Alexandra quietly slid from the chair to position herself between his legs. Pierce raised his head and found himself captivated by her beautiful blue eyes, no longer filled with hurt and anger. They were deep pools of compassion and emotion. Neither spoke as she slipped her arms around his neck and buried her head in his shoulder. Reacting instinctively, he pulled her close, and they both held each other tightly.

"Forgive me?" he whispered miserably.

A sob escaped Alexandra's trembling lips when she pulled back to look at him, acceptance in her eyes. A tear slid down her cheek as she nodded. Pierce gently kissed the droplet and brushed a stray tendril from her face.

"There is one more bit of information you need to know," he said softly.

Alexandra's eyes widened. She could not imagine what more Pierce had to endure at the hands of this woman and her lover.

Running his hands softly up and down her arms, he said, "The morning after our night together, I returned to my ship to find a letter from my father. It took six weeks to reach me. He told me the nightmare was over and I was an unmarried man. So, you know what that means?"

Alexandra paused for a moment. For once it was Pierce faced with an unreadable expression and he was at a loss. Mistaking it for trepidation on her part, he nudged softly, "I am hoping my marital status will change soon if you will say yes."

Alexandra's expression softened as she stroked his beard and looked deeply into his eyes but still remained silent. Pierce raised an eyebrow at her hesitation and gentled pushed for her answer. "Alexandra, it means we can marry and have a life together."

She lowered her eyes and murmured softly with an accepting smile, "It also means you were not bound to another when we conceived our first child."

At first, he felt as though he had the wind knocked from him. However, he quickly recovered and gave her a broad smile before pulling her to him in a happy embrace.

Never Leave My Arms

Landon Manor
Middlesex, England
June 1811

Three hours swiftly flew by as the older couple shared what brought them together, carefully omitting the details of their intimate moments. Falling silent after revealing their reconciliation, the two looked at each of the faces of their family to gauge their reactions. Much had transpired that had ultimately brought them together, and they expected their sons and wives would have questions.

Surprisingly, the inquiries did not center on them. Rather, the primary source of interest was Greene and Pirate Mame. To hear that their steward, the unflappable, exceedingly private, and intense protector of the family, had fallen in love with a female swashbuckler piqued even Reece's interest. For as long as they could remember, the sons always recalled Greene being present but knew nothing about his past. He and his parents were thought of as members of the Tennyson family.

Sarah posed a question first.

"Obviously, Greene returned to London, but whatever happened to Maury? Did the two ever see each other again?"

Greene and his parents' relationship with the Tennyson family went back many years, and although he worked for them, Pierce grew up with him and considered him a close friend. As such, he did not feel it was his place to discuss the man's personal relationships.

"You know Greene," Pierce said cryptically.

Kat and Sarah looked at each other.

Kat gave a bewildered look. "Apparently not."

"Exactly," Pierce said with a wink.

The two got their father-in-law's point. Nudging Kat with her elbow, Sarah chuckled.

329

"I believe he is telling us we will never know."

This brought a laugh from the group.

Alexandra cleared her throat to gain Pierce's attention, her expression serious.

"Dear, there is one more piece of the story you need to share," she murmured.

The brothers and wives looked questioningly at each other. The parents had endured so much. What other tests were they put through?

"Your mother is right."

Pierce gazed down at his wife.

"The most important piece of this story needs to be told. It is something we discovered ten years ago."

It took some time, but over the years, the wounds healed between the Fraser and Cameron clans. In fact, relations had softened so much that when Robbie died ten years ago, Pierce's cousin went to the Americas to help Helene. Her combative behavior and long-time addiction to alcohol caused the cousin to cut the trip short.

Before they began their journey back to the Highlands, Helene bragged about how she carried Pierce's child when she left Scotland after marrying Robbie. When pressed for information, Helene would only say the girl had run away when she was sixteen and presumed dead.

Pierce's voice cracked with emotion as he thought about the daughter he had never met.

"When we heard the news, I asked McCoy to investigate. He met with Helene's other daughter who confirmed the story. He followed several leads, but the trail went cold. She had disappeared without a trace"

Alexandra could see how draining rehashing these difficult memories were for her husband and stepped in to bear some of the burden.

Never Leave My Arms

"McCoy kept at it. He discovered a lead in Philadelphia not long ago. It led to London and he found the young woman. Her name is Kristina."

Each brother reacted differently to the news that they had an older sister. Reece, true to form, remained unreadable. Alex's initial silence turned to a chuckle and then a shake of his head.

"We have a sister," he said aloud as he looked between his brothers. Christopher kept quiet and his head down.

Alexandra worried about her youngest's reaction to the news. She made a mental note to seek him out after the family retired for the night and speak to him.

Pierce cautiously shared the rest of the information.

"I met with McCoy this week, and he is trying to broker a meeting with Kristina. He doesn't believe she knows Robbie is not her father."

Excited by the thought of having a sister-in-law, Sarah asked, "What did McCoy find out about her? Is she married? Does she have a family?"

Alexandra answered with matched exuberance.

"Kristina is a successful interior designer. She owns her own company which was established in Philadelphia. She expanded to London a few years ago and opened a small shop. From what McCoy tells us, she is devoted to her business and success and has never married."

His half-sister's ambition impressed Reece, and he saw that as a common thread they could relate to and help ease the introduction.

"I would be happy to accompany you and McCoy when you meet with Kristina. Perhaps we can do it at the Fraser Shipping office."

A faint smile touched Kat's lips as she squeezed her husband's hand. Her father-in-law needed to know his son supported him.

Alex was quick to offer his encouragement as well.

"Count me in too if I can be of help."

Much to Pierce and Alexandra's surprise, Christopher spoke up too.

331

"If it would make things easier on you to have all three of us there, let me know the time and I will be there."

Tears filled Alexandra's eyes, and she placed her fingers over her mouth to conceal her trembling lips. Pierce struggled to push down the knot of emotion threatening to emerge. Neither parent expected such a resounding positive reaction from their sons to the news.

Pierce had dreaded telling them he had fathered a child before meeting Alexandra, particularly under the circumstances it occurred. She tried to reassure him they would understand, but even she was caught off guard with Christopher's immediate acceptance.

Kat could see her in-laws overcome with emotion and decided it would be helpful to add some levity to lighten the mood.

"Four Tennyson men against one Tennyson woman? That sounds like a fair match."

The group could not help but laugh, especially as they all formed a mental picture.

"I think Kat is on to something," Pierce said. "Let's not overwhelm ourselves just yet."

As the men stood in preparation to break for the evening, Sarah and Kat remained seated and looked at each other. They had one final question of their in-laws.

"Did you ever go back to St. Kitts and visit the MacKittricks and Kishma?" Kat asked.

Alexandra and Pierce shared a loving glance. Leaving this part of the story to his wife, he inclined his head with a smile.

"As a matter of fact, we did," she said with a wistfulness.

Never Leave My Arms

The three brothers immediately returned to their seats. They were equally curious, especially if they could learn more about what happened between Greene and Pirate Mame. The thought of their stoic steward intertwined with a female buccaneer was worthy of their admiration and further inquiry.

Elizabeth H. Franklin

Journey to St. Kitts
Late October 1775

Pierce and Alexandra made their return to St. Kitts shortly after Reece's first birthday. The small family sailed from London on the Saltire Wind because of its comfortable accommodations for the three. The ship also had concealed cannons should they run into pirates. Alasdair and Greene accompanied the trio.

Alexandra insisted they make a brief stop at Veilwind Island to visit Mame and bring a cargo load of supplies for the community. It was a small gesture for the kindness the female captain had extended them in their time of need. Their stop also gave Greene an opportunity to reconnect and stay, if he wished, while the young family went onto St. Kitts. They could retrieve him on their return home in the Spring.

"She must have been surprised to see you two with Reece and Greene," Sarah said.

Alexandra nodded with a soft smile as she recalled being greeted by Mame, someone she considered a friend. In spite of their initial meeting where his ship was liberated of some supplies, Pierce had come to think of her as a friend as well. The extent of his appreciation for helping to save Alexandra, the services of their healer to treat his injuries, and providing immeasurable assistance repairing his ship, could not be quantified.

When Mame received a report the Saltire had moored in their channel, she instantly knew who she should expect to see.

"I remember her greeting us on the beach," Alexandra said, shaking her head as she recalled the young woman's appearance.

If she were not dressed as the swashbuckler they all remembered, Pierce and Alexandra would not have immediately recognized her. Greene, however, knew her instantly. Instead of her long auburn hair pulled back and

334

Never Leave My Arms

plated into a single braid, she wore it loose, flowing freely about her shoulders and down her back. A welcoming smile lit up her sun-kissed face and her eyes twinkled with excitement greeting her guest. Her grin deepened when she espied Pierce walking behind Alexandra, carrying a small child. Her expression softened when she noticed Greene following not far behind the young family.

Although they had not planned to stay more than a day or two before journeying on to St. Kitts, Mame convinced them to remain a week. Because of the circumstances of their initial visit to the island, they could not see much of it. This time, their host made certain they were able to enjoy their stay on Veilwind.

"Did Greene remain while you went on to St. Kitt's?" Reece asked.

Not only Kat, but his brother's and Sarah looked at him in shock. Even Pierce and Alexandra paused for a moment. Not because of the question, but because of who asked it. They all knew Reece to be the man who looked down on asking those types of inquiries. He always gave off an air of being above what he would describe as trivial personal things. Apparently, something had shifted in him when it came to Greene and his involvement with the female pirate.

Recovering, Alexandra nodded.

"Yes. We picked him up on our return.

Not surprising, Greene remained under the auspices of continuing his campaign to reform the female pirate. He wanted to convince her to turn away from her life of thievery and return to London society where she belonged. Pierce and Alexandra knew otherwise, but kept it to themselves out of respect for Greene's privacy.

The group sat expectantly waiting for further elaboration, but none came. Pierce chuckled. He had to give them credit. They were trying their best to extract as much information about Greene and Mame's relationship.

335

"They parted on friendly terms and anything more than that is personal," Pierce said.

Although somewhat disappointed, the family loved and respected Greene. They did not want to invade the privacy of a man who clearly kept things to himself.

Trying to redirect the conversation, Sarah interjected, "The MacKittricks must have been so happy to see you."

Alexandra's eyes began to water with emotion. She vividly recalled her aunt's reaction when their carriage arrived at the front steps of the plantation estate.

"Annabelle was particularly thrilled to meet Reece."

Her aunt and uncle were standing on the veranda waiting to greet their guests. Kishma's father, their estate supervisor, had ridden ahead to let them know the young family were on the way. The moment the carriage stopped, Annabelle squeezed Chester's hand in excitement and rushed down the stairs, scooping the babe from Alexandra's arms and hugging him close.

Although Annabelle had stayed for Pierce and Alexandra's wedding, and would have loved to help see Alexandra through her pregnancy, she missed Chester. Before departing for her return journey, she extracted a promise from her niece that they would come for a visit as soon as they could manage.

After Reece's first birthday, Pierce had overheard Alexandra speaking with her mother about her desire to make the journey to St. Kitts after the stormy season. She wanted to see Mame again and have her and Annabelle meet Reece. She decided to postpone approaching Pierce about the idea until after work had eased for him. Fraser Shipping's business boomed from the changes he and his father had made, and it would likely be difficult for him to pull himself away.

Pierce glanced over to his wife with a loving smile.

Never Leave My Arms

"I had wanted to make the trip back there as well but held off suggesting it to Alexandra. I thought she would think Reece would be too young."

Recalling the moment he surprised her with news of the journey brought a soft laugh from her. He had told her at breakfast, and in her excitement, she had accidentally dumped his plate of eggs and kippers in his lap, creating a mess.

"He took it in stride. Without so much as a grumble, he gently brushed away the food, replenished a new plate with fresh fixings, and returned to his seat."

Sarah and Kat smothered giggles, while the brothers shifted uncomfortably and cleared their throats, trying to fight off a burst of laughter.

Taking it in stride, Pierce refocused the conversation on their arrival at the MacKittrick's.

"With the help of Annabelle and Chester, we were able to surprise your mother shortly after getting there."

Giving his wife a wry grin, he quipped, "Thankfully, I had finished my meal at the time it unfolded."

A soft flush appeared on Alexandra's cheeks at the reminder of her excessive exuberance at the news of the trip. She swatted at him playfully and smothered a smile.

Pierce had asked Annabelle to swear Lidy and her husband to secrecy about their visit. He wanted to re-unite Kishma and Alexandra. The native couple eagerly agreed to remain mum. They knew the special bond the two young women held. Lidy and Annabelle came up with the perfect ruse to effectuate the reunion.

On their third morning at the plantation, Lidy arranged for Kishma to come to the estate under the ruse she needed her to help prepare for guests due to arrive in the coming days. As expected, Kishma eagerly agreed to

337

help her mother and the MacKittricks. They had always been kind to her and her family.

When she arrived at the grand home, she went straight to the kitchen to greet her mother. Lidy smiled warmly at her youngest daughter. She barely held her excitement at the thought of how happy seeing Alexandra would make her. Keeping her emotions in check, she directed the young woman to find Annabelle in the dining room for direction on what she needed done before the guests arrived.

Annabelle, Pierce, Lidy, and Chester had arranged it so the group would be having their morning meal. They were all gathered around the table with the baby asleep in a cradle in the corner when Kishma stepped into the doorway of the dining room.

Alexandra had her back to the entry and did not see her friend. Kishma, however, recognized the light head of hair immediately. Her jaw slackened and eyes widened at the shock. She stood motionless and speechless.

Annabelle's eyes shimmered with emotion as she witnessed the moment. Chester cleared his throat while Pierce looked squarely over the top of his wife's head, his eyes locking with Kishma's.

Pierce's adeptness at keeping his expressions unreadable came in handy when Alexandra looked among the group, and then at her husband. Annabelle's misty eyes and her uncle's sudden discomfort perplexed her. Pierce gave nothing away except his eyes were fixed on something behind her.

No one said a word, not even Kishma. Finally, exasperated at the silence, she tossed her napkin on the table in front of her, and turned around to see what had caught her husband's attention. A squeal peeled from her lips that woke the babe, and he immediately began to whimper. While Annabelle tended to Reece, the two women held tight to each other.

Never Leave My Arms

Alexandra introduced Pierce and Kishma. Surprisingly, in all of the time he stayed as a guest, she had never met him. She later told Alexandra that he was even more handsome up close. More importantly, as she watched the two interact, she could see their devotion to each other.

The two friends spent numerous hours during the course of their three-month visit catching up. Kishma had also fallen in love and married. She met the young native man while on a trip with her sister to a neighboring village. The two were expecting their first child in five months. Her sister and their children were thriving, thanks in part to the care Alexandra had provided those first few months after her arrival.

"Chester and Annabelle ensured we had a wonderful time and Reece did not lack for attention, especially where Annabelle was concerned," Pierce told the group.

The older woman showered Reece with attention at every opportunity. Annabelle insisted she and Chester could watch the babe while the young couple could enjoy their stay on the island, just the two of them; something they never had an opportunity to do their first time there. Alexandra had no concerns leaving Reece with her aunt and uncle. She trusted them implicitly with her son's care.

"It was a wonderful time for everyone," Alexandra said.

"Do you still keep in touch with Kishma," Sarah asked with some hesitation. She did not know if something had befallen the young woman in the years that had passed, particularly in a climate that has such dangerous storms.

Alexandra nodded.

"To this day, we still exchange letters. Kishma and her family are thriving; all six children: two boys and four girls and twenty-one grandchildren between the lot."

339

Sarah and Kat looked at each other. They both had two children and that was a handful with help from Millie and the governess. The thought of managing twelve children between them seemed overwhelming.

"Kishma has my undying respect," Sarah quipped.

Kat and Alexandra both smothered laughs but were brought up short when Pierce said, "The sound of a dozen sets of small feet running through this huge manor sounds good to me."

Never Leave My Arms

Landon Estates
...that same night, after the family meeting

Alexandra had taken an extended period of time readying herself to retire for the night. While Pierce was propped up in bed engrossed in a book, Alexandra sat at her dressing table and removed the combs from her hair, releasing the long, light blonde and silver-gray mass. Pierce had freed the fasteners of her gown, but she had not yet doffed the garment. Instead, she wanted to brush out her hair.

Staring into the mirror, she slowly ran the brush through her mane. Her thoughts wandered back to the time of their return trip to St. Kitts. It felt wonderful to relive those memories of seeing Kishma, and enjoying those months with Pierce on the island together as a couple and a family.

A soft smile touched her lips as she thought about one secret she and Pierce withheld from the family about that return trip. A deeply personal one that would remain only between the two of them.

Elizabeth H. Franklin

St. Kitts
The MacKittrick Estate
March 1776

For the first two months of their stay, the young couple's days were filled with activity. Alexandra regularly visited Kishma at her new home in the village and helped her get ready for the arrival of her first child. She also stopped at Kishma sister's home for a visit. They were ecstatic to see the British beauty, and she had brought Reece with her as well. He enjoyed playing with the younger children, and slept all the way home, barely waking long enough for Alexandra to feed him before putting him to bed.

For ease and comfort, when she and Pierce arrived on the island, Alexandra had chosen to don native clothing and wrap her hair in a scarf. Although Lucrete was dead, the threat of other traffickers remained. Thus, Pierce insisted she be escorted either by him or Kishma's father. Alexandra had not wanted to interfere with Pierce being able to enjoy himself, so her friend's father graciously agreed to be her chaperon.

While busy catching up with Kishma, Chester and Pierce made their rounds on the island visiting neighbors. His host wanted to show him the results of their efforts with creative watering over these past two years. The systems he designed worked splendidly and crops far exceeded expectations.

On one particular day when Pierce and Chester left early to journey to Basseterre, Annabelle had suggested Alexandra enjoy the grounds while she watched Reece. The young mother had not had any time to herself since arriving.

Before she had an opportunity to make up an excuse to stay, her aunt took the babe from her arms and shooed her niece out the door, but not before she ensured Lidy packed a basket of goodies to take with her.

Alexandra laughed when she opened the carrier and saw it filled with enough food to feed a family of four. Shaking her head, she closed the lid

342

and set out on her walk. As she meandered along the path that led away from the house, she espied the trail that went to the horse barn. A thought struck her.

Since arriving, she had not been to the cove. The warm temperature and cloud-free blue sky made it a perfect day for a swim. Picking up the pace, she rushed down the dirt road to the stable. In a matter of minutes, she emerged astride a horse and steered it towards the route to the lagoon.

Once reaching the familiar tree line, she remained on the mount and picked her way through the overgrown area. It appeared no one had been there for some time. Glimpsing a break in the trees, she found the opening and guided the animal through the narrow space. As she emerged from the thick vegetation, a smile broke from her lips at the sight of the crystal blue lagoon. The lush surrounding landscape cradled the body of water as it shimmered in the bright early afternoon sun. It was as beautiful as she remembered.

Alexandra dismounted on a boulder close by and situated her horse in the shade, close to the high grass where it could graze easily, then set her basket close by. She wandered around the edge of the cove, stopping to run her hands through the warm silky water. Chewing her lower lip, she contemplated whether to give into her desire to enjoy a dip. It had been over two years since she enjoyed the lagoon, and she had the place all to herself.

Giving into her desire, she removed her clothing and waded into the warm crystal water. Upon reaching the point where she could no longer feel the bottom, she kicked her feet and pulled herself through the velvety liquid, and then submerged fully, breaking the surface with her hair sopping wet and small water droplets speckling her face.

Alexandra had no sense of time as she dived to the bottom. She played hide and seek with the small colorful fish that darted in and out of the submerged watery vegetation. She imagined Pierce had enjoyed the lagoon much the same way. It was a shame the two had not been able to enjoy the water together.

She remembered that day she came upon him after their first kiss on the beach. He had gotten too forward, and she stayed away for over two weeks. A slight flush crept up her face at the memory of him emerging from the water naked, his broad muscular back and perfectly shaped buttocks slowly appearing with each step. He had no idea she watched him.

Wearing a wistful smile, she stretched out on her back and floated. Her breasts peeked out above the surface, while her long hair spread out around her head and shoulders. Alexandra loved the feel of the sun caressing her nakedness and the lull of the muffled ocean surf that rolled yards away.

"The ladies of the London ton would find this shocking if they ever knew," she thought amusingly to herself.

While Alexandra enjoyed her uninhibited sunbathing, it was not shock but desire her husband felt as he stood silently, concealed in the shadow of the trees, watching his wife, the beautiful water nymph.

Pierce and Chester had returned home shortly after Alexandra left for her afternoon of venturing about the estate. Pierce frowned at the news that his wife went alone but relaxed somewhat when Annabelle assured him she had donned her native island attire. His anxiety increased, however, when she absently mentioned Kishma's father saw Alexandra on horseback, headed towards the abandoned mill and cove. She knew that would propel Pierce to seek out his wife.

Seconds after their guest disappeared out the door, Chester looked at his wife with a raised eyebrow.

Dismissing her husband's silent rebuke, Annabelle shrugged and commented, "I am just presenting opportunities."

Chester shook his head as he walked away.

Never Leave My Arms

Pierce rode at breakneck speed to reach the cove. He followed the freshly broken path Alexandra had made. Even though Lucrete no longer served as a threat, there were always predecessors waiting to step in and take his place. However, as he jumped off his horse and rushed through the screen of trees, he was brought up short. He had to blink several times to ensure his eyes were not playing tricks on him.

There, in the center of the pristine lagoon water lay his wife, uninhibited and naked. His loins instantly tightened at the sight of her creamy, glistening body. Her light blonde hair fanned out around her shoulders and arms, and every few seconds, he would catch a glimpse of her hands gliding across the glassy surface.

Alexandra lay facing away from him, oblivious to his presence. Wearing a naughty grin, he quietly removed his clothes and eased unseen into the water. Once immersed to his chest, he silently slipped below the surface and pulled himself through the depths, until he reached her.

He had not realized Alexandra heard him the moment he entered the water. So focused on his efforts, he failed to notice her peering through hooded eyes as she admired his masculine physique, particularly his erect manhood. Her stomach flipped with excitement at the thought of making love outside, in the water and in the place they fell in love.

She had suspected her Aunt had set this entire situation in motion, particularly when the older woman had shoved the large basket of food at her before she left. Most likely, Annabelle also manipulated Pierce into making the trip to the cove so he would "happen upon her". Her mother would refer to it as "presenting opportunities."

Not wanting to spoil her husband's efforts to surprise her, she played along and acted momentarily shocked as he swam up underneath her, slid his hands around her waist and pulled her against him as he surfaced.

345

Alexandra relaxed instantly at the sound of his voice. She relished the feel of their naked wet bodies entwined, and his excitement pressed against her.

"What a sight you are," he whispered in her ear with a passion-filled husky voice that sent shivers down her spine.

Alexandra turned in his arms to face him.

"So are you," she murmured before he claimed her lips.

While the two shared a fiery kiss, Pierce guided her legs around his hips, signaling Alexandra to hold on as he slowly maneuvered them close to a shallow area. Once his feet reached the lagoon bottom, he broke free of her lips and began a slow and methodical assault of her body. Using his tongue, he started at her ear and worked his way down her neck to her shoulder, branding her with each flick of his tongue and nibble of his teeth. While his mouth worked, his free hand did not remain idle. He kneaded a plump breast and teased the sensitive hardened peak. Her body arched in an involuntary reaction.

Alexandra laid back across his arm as he held her at the surface. Her hair spread out in the water and drifted around her shoulders as his lips traveled to the other mound and captured the crest. She moaned softly at the waves of pleasure he sent to her womanly core. Her legs still around him, she began to move against his hardened shaft, creating a friction that furthered her desire.

Pierce did not give into her cue. Instead, he slid his finger inside her, a smile of satisfaction on his face as her body jerked at the invasion. Her vibrant blue eyes held his, their message clear. She wanted him.

Still unyielding to her unspoken demand, he gently rubbed the sensitive nub while his finger wreaked havoc inside her, and he taunted the buds of her breast with his tongue. He could feel her body tighten around his finger, and she squirmed in frustration.

Never Leave My Arms

The water should have suppressed the heat of her excitement, but it did not. She felt like she would burst into flames.

Certain he had pushed her to her limit, Pierce momentarily ceased his passionate onslaught. Her legs were still wrapped around his waist as he carried her out of the water and placed her down on a soft grassy area close to shore. Water dripped from his hair and body as he hovered over her, their bodies barely touching. He unhooked her legs from around him while he placed soft kisses on her swollen lips.

Alexandra waited with anticipation, her eyes beseeching him, her breath shallow from desire, but he made no move to enter her. Instead, his lips and tongue traced streaks of fire over her breasts and down her stomach to the folds of her womanhood. Every fiber in her body felt alive.

Pushing her legs open, he exposed the tiny sensitive nub and flicked it with his tongue, over and over. Once again, she felt the penetration of his finger, and it pushed her even closer to the edge.

Her body reacted on its own as she lifted her hips. She grabbed handfuls of the thick cool grass as she fought for control over the sweet ecstasy of his attack. With each brush of his tongue and stroke of his finger, he pushed her further to her zenith.

Sensing she was about to reach her breaking point, he dropped back on his knees and positioned his engorged shaft at the entrance to her core. Looping his arms under her legs, he leaned forward, and easily slid into her.

A soft moan escaped her lips and her eyes fluttered closed as she reveled in the feel of him filling her. Alexandra opened her eyes wide with alarm when Pierce pushed her legs forward, completely immobilizing her. Her concern was short-lived when she felt him embedded in her at a depth she had never felt before.

The sensation was so intense, Alexandra quickly reached her climax, but Pierce would not let her descend. Instead, without losing their connection, he had her turn onto her hands and knees. Then, with slow and rhythmic thrusts, he revived her arousal.

With each stroke, her sheath constricted tighter and hotter around him, giving the sensation of a velvet-gloved hand trying to pull his seed from him. Unable to hold back, he wrapped his arm around her waist and sat back on his knees as he took her with him, impaling her while he found his release.

The pair rocked back and forth, their bodies still connected, as they rode their passionate wave and drifted back to reality. Neither made a move to separate. Pierce enjoyed the feel of his wife's soft naked body molded to his, and Alexandra welcomed his strong, muscular arms pressing her tightly to him.

A short while later, the young couple availed themselves of the savory lunch Lidy had packed. Alexandra had donned Pierce's shirt to protect her skin from over-exposure to the sun. The oversized garment fell to her knees and the neckline hung so low, he could see the curves of her breasts. Her sparse state of dress made it difficult for him to focus on the food.

His distraction did not go unnoticed by Alexandra. She slowly slipped the garment off announcing she wanted to enjoy another swim before returning. Pierce tried his best to remain unaffected, but his loins stiffened at the sight of his wife's swaying hips and naked bottom as she slowly waded into the blue water. Giving into his urges, he joined her.

The young couple finally returned home several hours later, as the sun began to set.

Their second child, Alexander, was born nine months later.

Chapter Twenty-One

Fraser Shipping Offices
London, England
July 3, 1811

Pierce stood staring out the window of the Fraser Shipping London office. Kristina had been on his mind more often than usual; every day, sometimes several times a day, especially since he and Alexandra shared their story with the family.

Although she claimed to understand, he did not feel right discussing her with Alexandra. She never said so, but he thought Kristina might be an uncomfortable reminder of his past with Helene. Even though she always maintained a brave face at the mention of his daughter's name, Pierce knew it must affect his wife deeply. It cut him too, but in a different way.

Pierce never allowed himself to imagine that Kristina would accept his invitation to meet. He had to sit down when Davis told him she had replied affirmatively. The two men agreed it was best to arrange their introduction at the Fraser office in London, as Reece had suggested, and to have his oldest son present.

349

The light rap on the office door put all three men on alert. Pierce's written invitation had arrived two days earlier at Kristina's hotel, asking her to attend a meeting regarding a family matter. Her first instinct was to tear up the invitation. She had severed ties with her family after leaving home abruptly eighteen years ago at the age of sixteen.

The abuse she suffered at the hands of her parents drove her away. Kristina had put that part of her life behind her and never looked back. She had made a new life for herself and done quite well.

Nevertheless, receiving this missive out of nowhere, all these years later, piqued her curiosity. If she were much younger, with the wounds of her childhood still fresh, she might have thought differently. Now, as a grown woman, she felt more emotionally equipped to deal with the pain of her past.

About ten years ago, word had reached her from her sister Marjorie that their father, Robbie Clyne, had died. Somehow, she had stumbled upon someone who knew Edith Hall and she in turn, shared the news with Kristina. The two women had grown close over the years and Kristina had shared some of the details of her unhappy and abusive childhood at the hands of Robbie. Thus, when word reached Edith of the man's passing, she felt compelled to share it with her young friend.

Apparently, his drinking had finally caught up with him. Marjorie had expressed a desire to reconnect with Kristina, but she never reciprocated. Seeing her sister would only reopen old wounds, and she did not want to relive the past. She had no use for her father or mother, and his death had no effect on her.

Nonetheless, curiosity got the best of her when she received a mysterious invitation to meet with representatives of the Tennyson family. The fact the request originated in England, far from Boston, where she was born and lived until her mid-teens, increased her interest. Besides, she now spent

Never Leave My Arms

some of her time in London launching her new shop, so it was no inconvenience on her part to inquire into this mystery.

The click of the door handle broke through Kristina's thoughts. A handsome, middle-aged man with salt-and-pepper hair opened the door. He had kind eyes and was slightly taller than Kristina's five feet, ten inches. He greeted her with a warm smile as he stepped aside to usher her into the office.

Kristina had chosen a conservative outfit for the meeting: a simple emerald high-waisted gown with cream accent trim that embellished the dress's V-neck and hem. She had swept her long wavy dark auburn hair up, with silky tendrils falling next to her ears and soft waves flowing past her shoulders in the back. Clearing her throat, she offered him a bright smile and announced herself.

"Good afternoon, my name is Kristina Fraser. Mr. Tennyson is expecting me."

She relaxed immediately upon hearing the man's American accent.

"Good afternoon Miss Fraser. We are so glad you came. My name is Davis McCoy, and I work for Mr. Tennyson. Please follow me; we are meeting in his son's office."

Kristina took a few steps but stopped. Although the gentleman appeared pleasant enough, she felt apprehensive about proceeding until she had a clearer understanding of what the meeting entailed.

"Excuse me Mr. McCoy, but I don't know you or Mr. Tennyson. Before I go any further, I would like to discern specifically what this meeting is about."

McCoy stopped and turned to face her, his expression understanding.

"Certainly. My apologies for the lack of specificity. That is completely my fault. I work for Mr. Tennyson, and he wanted to meet with you regarding your Scottish heritage. You have a familial link to him."

Although vague, his words piqued her interest in discovering more about her heritage beyond her parents. She nodded, and McCoy took that as a cue to escort her to Reece's office.

Pierce had paced nervously for the past hour. Reece watched helplessly as his father came close to wearing the wood stain from the floor in front of his desk. He had never seen him so unsettled.

Pierce was uncertain whether Kristina would even attend the meeting, but when he heard the knock at the front door and a woman's voice, his anxiety increased exponentially. Although he had years to prepare, Pierce suddenly found himself at a loss when the moment arrived.

Davis could see that his employer needed to gather his emotions. The investigator and friend graciously offered to greet Kristina and usher her in, allowing Pierce to collect his thoughts before meeting his daughter for the first time. It helped immensely.

By the time McCoy led Kristina into the office, Pierce appeared outwardly calm and welcoming, though his insides were a different story. He presented a charming and exceedingly handsome figure, bestowing a beautiful smile that lit up his eyes as he reached to take her hand, his daughter's hand.

"Miss Fraser, thank you so much for agreeing to meet with me. I am Pierce Tennyson, and this is my son, Reece."

He gestured toward the desk where Reece had been seated until she entered the room.

Kristina nodded politely, quickly assessing the man. He bore a striking resemblance to his father, albeit younger. In looking at him, she concluded there was no doubt, he was his father's son, with one exception; an errant bang that hung above his right eye. Quite handsome in a roguish way.

Pierce also gestured to McCoy.

"Of course, you met Davis already."

Kristina nodded and gave a friendly smile as she replied. "Yes."

Pierce directed her to the wing chair by the window.

"Won't you please have a seat?"

Although awestruck by the man dressed in a dark patterned kilt, high collared shirt, with a complementary fitted jacket and leg and footwear, Kristina concealed her feelings well. Slightly taller than Davis, he possessed a strapping physique that exuded masculinity. Despite his size and commanding presence, he did not come across as intimidating. Rather, if she didn't know any better, he looked at her with a hint of affection.

Kristina smiled tentatively and accepted his invitation, sitting on the edge of the chair across from him. McCoy sat off to the side while Reece returned to his seat behind the desk, his expression indecipherable.

It took Pierce a moment to collect his thoughts. Seeing and meeting his daughter for the first time overwhelmed him. His heart swelled at the sight of the beautiful young woman before him. She looked significantly younger than her thirty-four years.

Surprisingly, prior to her entering the study, he had never allowed himself to imagine what she might look like. To his astonishment, she resembled Helene only in her nose and oval face shape. Her deep mahogany hair and sparkling green eyes traced back to Pierce's mother, and she had inherited her height from him.

Pierce collected himself and casually leaned on the edge of the desk, his hands braced on either side of his hips. Smiling warmly at his daughter, he asked cryptically, "Where to begin?"

"The beginning is always a nice place to start," Kristina said warmly as she removed her gloves and placed them demurely in her lap.

Pierce floundered for a moment, letting out a nervous laugh before regaining his composure.

Returning her smile, his eyes twinkled.

"Yes of course. My invitation must have sounded puzzling."

Capturing his gaze, she replied candidly, "I must be completely honest. My initial thought was to decline."

She explained that she had lost contact with her limited family eighteen years ago when she left Boston, omitting the painful details of her departure. When she saw the names Tennyson and Fraser, it piqued her interest; she recalled hearing them occasionally by her parents. Kristina left out that Helene and Robbie had mentioned them during their alcohol-fueled fights.

"I presumed they originated in Scotland, perhaps kin to my parents."

Unbeknownst to her, Kristina provided the perfect opening for Pierce.

"Actually, Tennyson is my father's family name. He was from England. Fraser is my mother's family name; she was from Scotland and the daughter of the leader of Clan Fraser."

Kristina listened intently as Pierce shared a brief history of his parents' love story. He explained he spent much of his childhood in Scotland as the oldest grandson of the clan leader. Kristina frowned when he recounted the prearranged marriage pact his maternal grandmother had made. Although she kept her thoughts to herself, Kristina found his grandmother's actions cruel for taking away the choice of whom he would marry.

As Pierce's tale unfolded, she nodded in understanding, then frowned in confusion.

"I am uncertain how this involves me, Mr. Tennyson."

She explained, though omitting certain parts.

Never Leave My Arms

"My last name at birth was Clyne. I changed it to Fraser after leaving home," once again omitting the reason, and how she arrived at that particular name.

Pierce knew the next bit of information would open a box he could not close again. He kept a careful eye on his daughter for her reaction to the next bit of news.

"You do have a connection to Clan Fraser. I am the first-born Fraser grandson, and your mother, Helene Cameron, was the first-born granddaughter of Clan Cameron's leader."

Taking a moment to digest this new information, Kristina's frown deepened.

"You were married to my mother?"

Pierce nodded slowly.

"Aye. Very briefly. Almost thirty-five years ago."

Absent the notion that Pierce Tennyson was some evil ogre, which he clearly was not, Kristina thought her mother had made a poor choice when she ended her marriage to the strapping Scotsman..

Kristina believed she had surmised the connection—albeit severed when the marriage ended.

"So, how are you and I connected if you and my mother ended your marriage?"

Not wanting to be evasive or cryptic, he launched into a more definitive explanation, revealing Helene's deception and how her plan backfired when he discovered her duplicity. He spared her the details of her parents' attempt to murder him on their wedding night.

Pierce went on to explain about securing the annulment, and that within two months, Helene married Robbie Clyne. Realizing she could not repair the damage they had done, they eloped to Gretna Green and slipped off to the Americas.

355

"I left Scotland the day after we were married and sailed to the Leeward Islands shortly thereafter."

Glancing down at his folded hands, he added softly, "Helene never told anyone she carried my child."

Something briefly flickered in Kristina's eyes at his statement, but she maintained her quiet attentiveness. Pierce pressed on recounting his cousin's visit to Boston years later when Robbie passed away.

"During that visit, Helene revealed her firstborn was my child.

As his expression changed to one of comfort and emotion, Pierce's eyes met Kristina's, holding her gaze.

"As soon as I found out, I began searching for you. It was one of the happiest days of my life when Davis finally located you."

Slowly, as each piece of the puzzle fell into place, Kristina's expression shifted from confusion to shock, then to disbelief. Watching her processing the emotions, Pierce reached for his daughter's hand, but she recoiled sharply. She suddenly stood and stepped around the chair, putting distance between them.

Her head spun as the blur of her childhood came into focus. All the abuse and rejection she suffered washed over her, stealing the breath from her lungs. Blinding tears filled her eyes as she gasped, trying to find the words, but they would not come. Concerned, Pierce tried to reach for her and guide her back to the chair to explain further and comfort her, but Kristina pulled away.

"Don't," she said firmly.

Angrily swiping the tears from her cheeks, she took a steadying breath and straightened her back. Kristina then looked at the strapping Scotsman, truly looked at him. She was incredulous. How was it possible that this man was her father? He was everything Robbie Clyne was not. This had to be a mistake or a cruel joke.

Never Leave My Arms

"That's what it is," she thought desperately. *"This is some evil game my mother is playing."*

Pierce looked between Davis and Reece, at a loss for what to do or say. Reece understood this was tearing his father apart and tried to be a voice of reason.

"Miss Fraser, if you would please give him the opportunity to explain, this might make better sense."

Other than a cursory glance at Reece when she arrived, Kristina had not truly scrutinized him. Pinning him with her bright green eyes, she slowly took in every inch of his face.

"How old are you?" she asked quietly.

Reece met her stare with his own intensity.

"I turned thirty-six in June of this year."

Kristina quickly ran the numbers through her mind. Six months in age separated them.

"You are my younger half-brother?" she whispered in a hollow voice, just before taking a sharp breath as the realization registered.

Reece nodded.

"My brother Alex is thirty-two, and Christopher, the youngest, is twenty-nine."

Kristina's eyes widened in shock. *"I have three half-brothers,"* she thought in disbelief.

Shaking her head to rid her mind of the confusion, Kristina's hand trembled as she reached for her reticule and gloves on the chair. The room had become suffocating; she needed air to clear her mind.

Pierce could see the revelation was too much for his daughter. He did not want her to leave in such a state of upset. He hated being the cause of her pain.

"Lass, please don't leave."

Despite her resistance, she felt an undeniable pull towards Pierce Tennyson. She wanted to stay but could not. Even if what he was telling her was true, too much time had passed for them to establish a paternal relationship. She had outgrown the need for a father many years ago. Drawing from deep within herself, Kristina reined in her emotions.

As her gaze locked with Pierce's, she experienced a moment of uncertainty. She fought the urge to rush to him and feel his protective embrace; something she had never felt with Robbie. Pushing down all the fanciful dreams she had of receiving a father's love and affection, Kristina put up her wall.

"Mr. Tennyson, I fear there is some mistake. It is not possible that I am your daughter."

"Yes, you are," Pierce said firmly.

Before Kristina opened the door to leave. She stopped, her forehead resting on the wooden frame, eyes closed, unable to look at him.

"The little girl who longed for the love of her father died many years ago."

Kristina then quickly slipped out the door and rushed to hail a waiting hack.

Once inside the vehicle, her emotions released, and the tears flowed freely down her cheeks. Meanwhile, Pierce sank into the chair across from Reece, wordless, staring blankly at the floor. Silence filled the room. Reece did not know what he could say to console his father. Davis shook his head in disappointment.

Never Leave My Arms

Kat and Reece's Townhome
London, England
July 10, 1811
...one week later

Pierce and Reece had retired to the study to discuss business. Alexandra did not want to disturb them, so she informed Greene that she had an errand to run and would not be gone long. Truth be told, she could have stopped in to tell her husband she was leaving for a brief outing, but she knew he would ask where she was going. Alexandra did not want to lie to him. If she mentioned she planned to see Kristina, she knew he would try to stop her.

Quietly, Alexandra slipped out of the London townhouse and into the waiting hack.

"The Blackburn Hotel," she called to the driver as she stepped inside and closed the door.

She had overheard Davis McCoy tell Pierce where Kristina was staying. City traffic moved quickly in the mid-morning hour, and within fifteen minutes, the carriage pulled up in front of the luxury hotel. Dressed in a simple dark blue satin dress with a matching hat, her ensemble conveyed class and wealth—the type of clientele the Blackburn catered to.

As she gazed absently out the window, watching people bustle along the busy London sidewalks, Alexandra pulled on her gloves and waited for the bellman to open the carriage door. She mentally rehearsed what she would say.

Upon alighting from the carriage, the bell captain opened the lobby door and greeted her with a tip of his hat.

Good morning, Madame."

Alexandra returned his greeting with a bright smile.

"Good morning," she replied, quickly making her way through the vacant lobby to the front desk.

359

The older gentleman at the counter had his head down concentrating on writing when she approached.

Sensing her presence, he asked without looking up, "May I help you?"

"Yes. I would like to speak with a guest, Miss Kristina Fraser."

The clerk sighed in exasperation, immediately regretting it when he looked up and saw Alexandra Tennyson before him. Almost everyone in London knew or had heard of the Tennyson family, as well as Alexandra's parents, the Landon's.

"Forgive me Mrs. Tennyson."

Giving him one of her best smiles, she sought to allay his embarrassment.

"No offense taken dear. Is Miss Fraser in?"

The clerk straightened his back and adjusted his fitted jacket, offering her the respect she deserved.

"Miss Fraser is still in residence."

"Excellent."

Alexandra pulled a small envelope from her bag and handed it to the clerk.

"Could you please have your man deliver this to her? I will wait for his return with her answer."

"Of course," the clerk said with a nod and promptly motioned to an employee, handed him Alexandra's note, and instructed him to return with Miss Fraser's response.

Thankfully, the lobby was empty. Alexandra found a comfortable chair tucked in a corner, hoping to avoid running into anyone she knew. She did not want word to reach her husband that she had gone to the Blackburn Hotel. He would quickly surmise she sought out Kristina.

She remembered how their first meeting had crushed him. Later that night, he had only opened up a little to her; it was too painful for him to discuss.

Never Leave My Arms

Lost in her thoughts, Alexandra did not notice the bell captain standing in front of her until he spoke.

"Madame, are you well?"

She gave him a warm smile to assuage his concern.

"I am fine. Were you able to speak with Miss Fraser?"

"Yes, madame," he said as he offered his hand to assist her from her chair. "If you would follow me, I will take you to her suite."

Alexandra graciously accepted his assistance and followed him up the enormous marble staircase to the second floor. Once they reached the top, the wings of rooms split off in two directions, except for Kristina's. Her suite was straight ahead. Above the entry an engraved plaque read, "Blackburn Suite."

The bell captain lightly rapped on the door, and within seconds, a lovely dark auburn-haired woman answered.

"Miss Fraser, may I present to you Lady Alexandra Landon," he announced.

Kristina immediately focused on the petite woman beside the hotel employee and smiled brightly. Reaching out her hand, she opened the door wider.

"My lady, please come in."

Kristina made an instant impression on Alexandra. Presenting the young woman with a beguiling smile, she inclined her head and stepped inside the suite.

"Thank you dear, and please call me Alexandra."

As Kristina spoke with the bell captain, Alexandra quickly scanned the well-appointed room before turning to regard her husband's daughter. Pierce had only mentioned that Kristina resembled his mother's family and she was quite lovely. Alexandra had expected such knowing she favored Larena. Kristina appeared to have inherited much of her father's height, standing just

361

shy of six feet, and she was slender, with stunning green eyes and rich, dark auburn hair.

Alexandra pulled herself from her thoughts as Kristina closed the door and turned to face her.

Presenting the young woman with a bright smile, she said, "Thank you for seeing me dear. I hope I did not catch you at an inconvenient time."

"Not at all. I recognized the Landon name immediately as one of my company's best clients."

A flicker of confusion crossed Alexandra's face, which did not go unnoticed by Kristina.

Sensing she might have confused Alexandra with a family other than the Landon's of Middlesex, Kristina asked, "Are you related to Cherisse and Brenton Landon?"

Alexandra's mind raced, trying to place how Kristina Fraser would know her mother and father.

"Yes, they are my parents."

Relief washed over Kristina's face, thankful she had not made herself look foolish.

"Your mother's referrals helped build my design business into what it is today."

Gesturing for Alexandra to take a seat by the window, Kristina shared how the original owner, Edith Hall, had gifted her the company ten years ago shortly before passing away. She carefully omitted the fact that Edith had taken her in at sixteen when she escaped Helene and Robbie's abuse.

"After arriving in Philadelphia, I inquired for work with Miss Hall. Interior design interested me and she needed help in her shop. She brought me on and helped me see my creative potential."

Although factual, Kristina withheld much with regards to her efforts and struggles to find work. Few jobs were available for girls her age outside of cleaning and sewing. Through a stroke of good timing and luck, Miss Hall spotted Kristina walking down the main street, bag in hand, stopping at businesses with employment announcements in their windows. The shop owner watched sympathetically as the young girl entered establishments with a bright smile, only to exit with disappointment. After each rejection, Kristina collected herself and approached the next business renewed, but the outcome remained the same.

Admiring Kristina's determination, Miss Hall invited her to rest and have tea. The two instantly connected. For the first time, she felt a warm bond with someone. The older woman offered her room and board in exchange for keeping her cottage clean and sweeping the shop after hours. Kristina eagerly accepted, and after a few months, she showed a real promise in interior design, impressing Miss Hall with her critical eye for high-end creations. Business surged with interest from wealthy aristocrats in London and Paris. Cherisse Landon was the customer who opened the door for the shop's expansion into the London market.

"I had the pleasure and honor of meeting your mother about fifteen years ago when she visited the Philadelphia location," Kristina said.

Alexandra was captivated. She had never realized there was a connection between Kristina, her husband's child, and the Landon family.

"What a splendid coincidence."

Kristina nodded as she poured their tea. Handing Alexandra a cup, she smiled and asked, "How can I assist you?"

Setting the delicate China on the table, Alexandra took Kristina's hands in hers, her eyes cast down as she struggled to find the right words. A frown formed on Kristina's face as she watched her guest grapple with her thoughts.

"My Lady?"

Alexandra looked up and smiled.

"Please dear, call me Alexandra."

Kristina corrected herself.

"Alexandra. Is there something troubling you with which I can help?"

Broaching the subject slowly, she nodded.

"Actually, yes. I understand you recently met with my husband and son."

Kristina paused to take inventory of the various meetings she had during her two weeks in London. Alexandra observed the young woman's face as she mentally ticked through her memories. At first, Kristina recalled business meetings, but when her thoughts shifted to personal encounters, there was only one, the encounter with Pierce Tennyson and his son. The expression on Kristina's face changed to shock at the memory of meeting the man who claimed to be her father.

Alexandra did not want Kristina to shut her down immediately, so she quickly explained.

"Dear, I am Alexandra Landon Tennyson. Pierce Tennyson is my husband, and Reece is my oldest son."

Kristina shifted uncomfortably as a knot formed in her stomach. Looking more closely at Alexandra, she noted her exceptional beauty and effervescence. This was the woman she could see Pierce Tennyson falling in love with, not Helene.

"Mrs. Tennyson, I mean Alexandra, I do not want to discuss this issue with you."

Not one to be easily deterred, Alexandra gently continued.

"Dear, I did not come here to upset you. Pierce and I have no secrets from each other. I have known about your existence since he…"

Kristina tried to correct her. "I don't believe your husband is my father."

Alexandra smiled sympathetically, understanding that Kristina was fighting the truth. While she thought her defiance stemmed from loyalty to the man she had known since birth, nothing could have been further from the truth. Kristina could not entertain the idea that Pierce was her father, as that would bring the unbearable pain of knowing she could have had a parent who truly wanted and loved her throughout her childhood, her life.

Tears gathered in Kristina's eyes as she looked at Alexandra.

"Dear, I am not asking you to accept Pierce as your father, even though I know he is and desperately wants to forge a relationship with you. My husband never gave up hope of finding you after all these years. Since he returned from your meeting, the light has dimmed in his eyes. Although he tries to present a brave face, I know he is heartbroken."

Kristina sat quietly, absorbing Alexandra's words. In truth, she too felt a heavy weight on her shoulders since abruptly leaving their meeting. She was at odds with herself, which was uncharacteristic. Kristina led a focused and determined life.

Sensing she had made progress, Alexandra did not want to push further.

The two women stood, and before drawing Kristina into an embrace, Alexandra said quietly, "Please do not close the door on this. Take the time to put the pieces together. You will see the truth. When you do, my husband, I, and our entire family will be waiting to welcome you."

Alexandra then pressed her cheek to Kristina's affectionately as she fought back the emotions that threatened to surface. Giving her a tremulous smile, she slipped out of the room. Kristina battled her own feelings until she heard the door shut. The tears she had been holding back released.

Chapter Twenty Two

Helene Cameron's Residence
Boston, Massachusetts
December 1811

Four months had passed since Alexandra visited Kristina at her London hotel. The older woman had made her realize that turning away from the possibility that Pierce Tennyson truly was her father only hurt herself and him.

When Alexandra first arrived at the hotel, Kristina did not know she was related to Pierce, let alone his wife. She had given the front desk her maiden name, Landon, unaware that Kristina knew her mother, Cherisse. Alexandra's admission that she was Pierce's wife knocked the wind out of Kristina. Once past the initial shock, Kristina felt a curiosity about the woman Pierce Tennyson had fallen in love with and married.

To her delight, she discovered that Alexandra was nothing like Helene. She possessed not only a breathtaking outer beauty but also a genuineness that touched one's soul. It was clear to Kristina that Alexandra adored her husband. Because of that meeting, Kristina made a life-altering decision: she needed to return to Boston and confront her mother. The following morning,

Never Leave My Arms

she left London and headed back to America, determined to get answers from Helene.

After returning to Philadelphia, Kristina spent two days attending to business before journeying north to Boston to face Helene. Her mother still resided in the same house where Kristina had grown up, but she never considered it her home. The house held nothing but terrible memories for her. In truth, she never felt she had a home until Edith Hall took her in.

When Helene answered the door, she looked critically at Kristina standing on the front porch. Age had not been kind to her mother, likely due to her drinking habits, as evidenced by the half-empty bottle of whiskey on the table and the smell of it on her breath. The deep scowl on Helene's face made it clear she had not changed. She was still her usual judgmental self, scrutinizing her daughter from head to toe.

The tall, confident, well-dressed woman standing before her looked nothing like the teenaged daughter who ran off without a word. Kristina wore her thick shiny hair in the current style accentuating her perfect bone structure and bright green eyes. She pulled the mass off her face, leaving tendrils at each ear, and secured it at her nape in a knot with decorative combs.

"Well, you've changed since the last time I saw you," she said with a sneer.

Kristina was no longer afraid of Helene, as was evident from her crisp, sarcastic response.

"Eighteen years will certainly change a person. Would you like to have this conversation in front of the entire neighborhood, or will you let me in? I assure you, I won't take up much of your time."

Her mother pushed the door open and retreated to her chair and bottle of whiskey, not even inviting her daughter inside. Shaking her head, Kristina

367

realized that time had changed nothing. Helene sat down in a well-worn chair in the small parlor, looking at her daughter with a raised eyebrow.

"I'm busy. What brings you here?"

Kristina went straight for the jugular.

"I had the pleasure of meeting a charming Scotsman while in London recently. His name is Pierce Tennyson; he claims to know you intimately," emphasizing the last word.

She observed her mother's reaction. Helene had lost her ability to control her feelings years before Kristina left home. Her mother used to be adept at delivering very convincing performances, easily transitioning from sweet and kind to vicious and cruel at the snap of a finger. Since drowning herself in the bottle, she lost her ability to conceal her true feelings, especially when caught off guard.

Not surprising, the older woman had nothing but nasty things to say about Pierce. Kristina vividly remembered the loud fights between Robbie and her mother. They often escalated when she mentioned Pierce's name, although she had never heard it stated alongside Tennyson until her recent trip.

Once her mother had worked herself into a lather about how terrible Pierce was, Kristina went in for the kill.

"Is he my father?"

Helene sneered with disgust.

"Of course he is. You look just like those bloody Frasers."

Her mother made no apologies for never telling her the truth. She smirked with cruel satisfaction at the hurt that briefly registered on her daughter's face.

"Your very existence made our lives miserable. You were a constant reminder of the man who shamed me before my clan, and Robbie despised."

Kristina looked at her mother in disbelief.

Never Leave My Arms

"If you hated me that much, then why didn't you just give me away?" Helene let out a short, caustic laugh as she glared at her daughter.

"What better revenge than to have something your enemy holds dear, knowing he will never have it?"

That was the final straw for Kristina. A wave of nausea washed over her as she looked at the old haggard woman before her. Between Helene's cruelty and the stale air in the room, Kristina felt she had to leave. Standing abruptly, she gave her mother one last glance before walking out the door without a word. As far as Kristina was concerned, Helene Cameron was dead. There was no reason for her to see that hateful creature again.

Kristina returned to Philadelphia and tried to continue with her life, throwing herself into her design business. For several months, she fought the urge to return to London and see her father. Ingrained self-doubt pressured her to stay away, but her heart urged her to go. After all, what did she have to lose? A father she never had?

Alexandra's words replayed in her mind: "You will see the truth. When you do, my husband, myself, and our entire family will be waiting to welcome you."

Rallying her confidence, Kristina decided to return to London and arrange to meet with her father again. Although their first exchange had gone badly, she hoped he would be receptive to seeing her. She needed to explain her reaction to his revelation and what her mother had told her. Thus, she arranged for immediate passage to England.

369

This trip would also provide an excuse for her to complete the arrangements for expanding her London location. Discovering Pierce was her father and confronting her mother had pushed those plans aside. Returning to London would allow her to finish the project, making it possible to split her time between America and England and hopefully build a relationship with her father.

Never Leave My Arms

Landon Estates
Middlesex England
Mid April 1812

Kristina's ship reached London in six weeks. She checked into her usual suite at the Blackburn Hotel. Through inquiries, she discovered that the Tennysons were at their Middlesex country estate, a two-hour ride from the city. In short order, the hotel arranged transportation, and she was on her way to see her father again.

By the time she reached Landon House, Kristina's nerves were completely frayed. Anxious and uncertain, she worried that Pierce would decline her attempt to establish a congenial relationship. How could she blame him after she had rejected him at their first and only meeting?

Greene answered the door. Kristina quickly ceased wringing her hands and looked up at the stoic steward.

"Good afternoon. My name is Kristina Fraser. Is Pierce Tennyson here by chance?"

The normally expressionless man briefly raised an eyebrow in surprise. He knew she was his employer's daughter and that he had not been the same since their meeting. The light seemed to have gone out of his eyes after she had suddenly left London last year.

Without a word, Greene stepped aside and gestured for Kristina to enter. After closing the door, he nodded and motioned for her to follow him down the long corridor to the study. When he reached the doorway, he stopped short, blocking her from entering. His tall presence concealed her from the view of the occupants, Pierce directly across the spacious room with his back to the door and Reece to his father's left, seated at the large wooden desk, reading.

Greene cleared his throat to indicate his presence.

"Mister Pierce, you have a visitor," he said in his usual bland manner.

371

Pierce stood at the French doors, dressed in his traditional Scottish regalia, his arm resting on the wood frame as he stared out into the gardens, his mind elsewhere. Since Kristina had left without a word after their terrible meeting, he had been at odds. With each passing month and no word from her, he slowly gave up hope of ever seeing her again. According to Davis McCoy, she had booked passage to the Americas shortly after their disastrous meeting.

For so many years, he had searched for his daughter, and when he finally found her, albeit well into adulthood, she wanted nothing to do with him. He carried the crushing weight daily.

Pierce did not turn around; he called over his shoulder in response.

"Who is it?"

Greene moved away from the doorway and gestured for Kristina to enter the study. She looked at him questioningly but stepped inside as directed. To her confusion, he quietly pulled the door shut behind her.

Reece looked up from his work when he heard the click of the latch and saw Kristina. He recognized her instantly. A flicker of surprise crossed his face, then his expression returned to impassive but not unwelcoming. He quietly rose from the desk, collected his papers, and slipped through the French doors to his right, wanting to give his father and half-sister privacy.

Pierce glimpsed Reece's departure and frowned. When he did not receive an answer from Greene, he turned around to ask again but stopped in shock. Nothing could have prepared him for what he saw. Kristina stood across from him, only a dozen feet away, more beautiful than he remembered.

She wore her hair pulled up on the crown of her head, secured with decorative combs, while two long tendrils hung softly at each ear. The violet empire waist gown with white lace trim around the scoop neck complemented her light green eyes and highlighted the auburn tones in her mahogany hair.

Never Leave My Arms

As quickly as the breath left him at the sight of her, his broad chest thrust forward as he refilled his lungs with air and his heart with hope. A combination of joy and uncertainty washed over Pierce as he took in the sight of her. His heart urged him to go to her and pull her close, but he hesitated, unsure of how she would react after their first and only exchange. He did not want to drive her away. Indecision was readily visible on his face.

Thankfully, Kristina broke the barrier. Looking down at her tightly folded hands, she slowed her racing thoughts. Her eyes glistened with tears as a flood of emotions overwhelmed her. All those years of feeling unwanted by her mother and Robbie released inside of her. For the first time in her life, she allowed herself to shed the heavy burden of their abuse. Trying desperately to keep her emotions in check, she looked up at Pierce, tears falling freely down her face.

"Their hate stole us from each other."

Pierce could see the suffering in his daughter's eyes, and his heart broke for her. It was because of him that she was in pain. He followed his instincts and swiftly closed the distance between them, enfolding her tightly in his arms.

Resting his cheek against her head, he whispered miserably, "I thought I lost you forever lass."

Kristina choked back a sob.

"I am so sorry."

"Nonsense. You have nothing to be sorry for," he soothed.

Pierce had waited ten years to hold his only daughter and had no intention of letting her go anytime soon. Likewise, Kristina had no desire for him to release her. For as long as she could remember, she had dreamed of being held by her father, of feeling his love and protection. It was everything she had imagined and more. She had never felt so wanted and safe.

After what seemed like an eternity, Pierce set her back from him without letting go. He wanted to see her; truly look at her for the first time. Cradling her face in his hands, he gently swiped the streams of tears from her cheeks and took in every inch of her face. He looked affectionately into her sparkling green eyes, his own glistening with emotion.

"You have your grandmother Fraser's eyes and hair."

Kristina looked away and choked back a sob. She had never experienced this type of warm parental attention. Pierce pulled her close to him again, pressing her head to his shoulder. He hated to see her so distressed.

"Lass, please don't cry."

Since confronting her mother, Kristina's emotions had been at the surface. She never imagined it would be so difficult to hold her composure. For over eighteen years, she had not allowed herself to feel the loss. Now it washed over her like waves.

"I can't help it."

Pierce gave her a gentle squeeze and whispered softly, "Then cry as much as you need lass. You're entitled after everything you have been through."

Kristina drew back from him and turned away, her embarrassment evident. He would not allow it; he refused to relinquish his hold. She had no reason to be ashamed. What she did at sixteen to escape such unspeakable suffering at the hands of Robbie and Helene was something not even a thirty-year-old could do. What courage she had to face her future with no one to lean on.

Pierce knew both Helene and Robbie had filled Kristina's childhood with rejection and abuse. In Davis's last report, he told Pierce he had spoken with her younger half-sister, who witnessed it firsthand. Kristina often caught the backhand or even fist of Robbie, particularly when he was drinking. As she got older, the mistreatment escalated.

Never Leave My Arms

When she was a small child, it took little on their part to make her cry. However, as a teenager, they had to make more of an effort; slaps became punches. It became so intolerable for Kristina that she packed her things one night and slipped away without a word.

Unbelievably, she found her way from their home in Boston to Philadelphia. Although it was unlikely her mother and Robbie would look for her, she made certain to sever all ties with the name Clyne, changing her name to Kristina Fraser. Pierce would later learn she chose the name because, when well into his cups, Robbie would go into fits of rage at the mere mention of the name Fraser. For Robbie, the name represented a well-respected, powerful Scottish clan and served as a reminder of Pierce, the man Helene lusted for and gave herself to. For Helene, it was a reminder of the man who rejected and shamed her. Interestingly, Kristina had not known that it was actually Pierce's maternal grandparents' name.

Taking her hands in his, Pierce could feel her trembling. He steered her to a chair by the fireplace. Stepping to the nearby sideboard, he splashed a bit of whiskey into two glasses. Holding them both in one hand, he pulled a low table closer to Kristina, handed her one drink, and took a seat on the table's edge in front of her. Pierce noted how her hands shook as she raised the glass to her lips and took a sip of the burning liquor.

"It will help calm your nerves."

Kristina smiled weakly and relaxed, welcoming the effects of the alcohol while it slowly washed over her. As Pierce gazed fondly at his daughter, he still could not believe she sat before him. So many questions were on the tip of his tongue, but he held back for fear of driving her away. Setting the glass down on the table next to her chair, she looked at her father with hesitation.

"I could use some fresh air. Would you mind if we took a walk?"

Pierce smiled understandingly and patted her hand.

"Of course lass."

She accepted his extended hand to help her out of the chair, but once standing, Kristina did not let go. Instead, she laced her fingers through his and glanced at him with uncertainty. Pierce had a difficult time controlling his feelings. His eyes moistened, and his heart swelled as he wrapped his fingers tightly with hers, squeezing her hand affectionately while they made their way out the French doors and into the garden.

Never Leave My Arms

Father and daughter walked in silence through the manicured grounds, wandering along the winding path lined with beautiful flowers and greenery. The fresh air brought a sense of renewal for both of them. Although Pierce was eager to learn as much about Kristina as possible, he did not want to push; he wanted her to lead the conversation. He knew she must have a myriad of questions for him. Kristina kept her eyes down but held tightly to his hand. She couldn't bring herself to look at him yet, her anxiety still too close to the surface.

Finally, she whispered softly, "Did you love her?"

Pierce owed his daughter an honest answer. He stopped walking and turned her to face him, shaking his head.

"No lass. I did not want to marry her, and she knew it."

He guided her to a small bench surrounded on two sides by hedges, where they sat as he explained the long, complicated story. Kristina listened intently as he recounted how he and Helene were forced into marriage, the deceptions of her and Robbie, Helene drugging him, and their attempt to kill him.

Nathaniel, Kristina's paternal grandfather, worked tirelessly to secure an annulment at Pierce's request while he traveled to St. Kitts. Even though Helene gave an impressive performance, insisting she was innocent and wanted to reconcile with Pierce, Nathaniel's relentless efforts on behalf of his son, coupled with the damning evidence, exposed the two cohorts' duplicity.

"She tried to make my father out as a liar until he made good on my threat and produced proof of her fraud and Robbie's attempt on my life. For a brief time, the clan elders believed her."

When Nathaniel sought out legal assistance that threatened, among other things, Clan Cameron's financial windfall from the Fraser Shipping expansion agreement, Helene's grandfather stepped in and made the decision to break the marriage bonds.

"Knowing my mother, she must have been furious not to have the upper hand," Kristina said.

Pierce nodded, his expression grim.

"She tried to gain it another way, and it had a lasting impact on everyone's lives, particularly yours."

Robbie and Helene realized her grandfather would not sacrifice the lucrative financial deal between the two clans to benefit the two of them under any circumstances. The cohorts anger over their humiliation seethed in them. It was not just Helene caught in the storm. The cloud of suspicion Robbie carried from his attempt to kill Pierce threatened the fragile peace among the clans as well. This weighed heavily with the leaders against him continuing to live among his fellow clans people and family. The elders were ordering his exile.

To the surprise of their families and Nathaniel, Helene suddenly agreed to the annulment without further argument. Within hours of signing the paperwork, she and Robbie eloped to Gretna Green and left for the Americas without a word.

Ten years ago, shortly following Robbie's death, Pierce's cousin made the journey to Boston to see Helene. The estrangement between the two clans had subsided over the years, and they had mended fences. While there, he tried to offer Helene moral support and extend condolences on behalf of the Fraser family. In return, she railed against the Frasers and Tennysons.

"From what I was told, Helene's anger at me never subsided. She blamed me, for among other things, her miserable marriage to Robbie."

Over the course of consuming a bottle of whiskey, Helene delighted in sharing her and Robbie's plan to strike back. It started when she discovered she carried Pierce's child. Robbie became furious. However, with some convincing from Helene, he saw it as an opportunity for one final malicious act that would pay dividends in exacting revenge on Pierce. The two planned to claim Pierce's child as Robbie's and instill in it a hatred of the Frasers and Tennysons, particularly Pierce.

Helene coped with the plan better than Robbie. After the baby was born he saw the close resemblance to the Fraser's and it ate at him. Each year, as the child matured, she reminded him more and more of his enemies. In an effort to soothe Robbie's festering fury, Helene kept pushing spirits at him to repress his anger. At one point, she even offered to give the child away. Initially, Robbie agreed, but then changed his mind. As rage churned inside him and alcohol muddled his brain, he relented and saw that the best way to get even with Pierce and his family was to take the one thing he would love the most: his child.

Pierce shook his head, his expression grim.

"To lash out, she gleefully told my cousin about you. She said you disappeared one night, never returned and were probably dead."

Kristina could not help but be affected. She grew silent. She knew Robbie hated her, but to hear her mother used her, a child, as a weapon and then could so callously cast her off, made her stomach turn. She recalled Helene's parting remarks when she last saw her before returning to London. Deep down, Kristina wanted to believe Helene said those things out of hurt and anger. She wanted to believe that her mother, somewhere in the depths of her being, had a least a modicum of maternal affection towards her. What parent is devoid of any care or warmth for their child? Apparently a soulless one like Helene Cameron Clyne.

Kristina's voice cracked with emotion.

"I asked her why she kept me if she hated me so much."

Pierce sat down and took her hands in his.

379

Her eyes were filled with emotion as she looked up at her father.

"She told me there was no better way to inflict pain on someone you despise than by taking from them the one thing they love the most."

Before Pierce could process the enormity of Helene's actions, Kristina pulled herself from the despair that threatened to pull her down. She took a deep cleansing breath and gave him a caring smile to set him at ease.

"I learned a long time ago that Helene and Robbie's abuse knew no bounds."

Not wanting to press, Pierce allowed Kristina to decide what information she wished to share about her childhood and the years after she left home. He knew that bringing up her past would open deep wounds. Through her half-sister Marjorie he had heard about some of the abuse Kristina suffered at the hands of Robbie and Helene.

Kristina initially thought she could not speak about her mother and Robbie's mistreatment. Until she met Pierce Tennyson, she had become adept at burying those feelings. She had never spoken of all she had endured as a child, not even to her close friend Edith Hall.

Sitting here now with her father, she felt a sense of comfort and protection in sharing her life experiences with him. Even without saying much, she knew he wanted to know everything she had endured, and she felt at ease sharing it with him. Squeezing his hand affectionately, her green eyes shimmered with emotion.

"I want to tell you about my life with Helene and Robbie, and after I left them, with the understanding that you will not pity me. Their cruelty drove me to make the decisions that shaped who I am today, and I am very proud of that person."

Pierce looked at his daughter in awe. From what Davis had told him about the abuse Kristina underwent, she would be well within her rights to seek sympathy and pity for what she withstood. Yet, remarkably, she viewed the pain as the force that helped her find her own life and happiness. Pierce took a breath, placed his hand on her soft cheek, and looked deeply into his daughter's beautiful eyes.

"Lass, you will always have my outrage and sympathy for what you suffered at Helene and Robbie's hands, but never pity. I can see you are too strong a woman."

A lone tear slipped from Kristina's eye. "Thank you."

As Kristina shared her memories of childhood abuse, Pierce tried his best to restrain his emotions. A few times, he had to stand and move about to fight off the physical urge to strike something, anything, especially when she told him about the beatings she received when Robbie and Helene were drunk.

As she grew older, she became mindful of when they started drinking and snuck away to a hiding spot where they could not find her. Sometimes she would stay hidden for hours. Her half-sister Marjorie would steal her into the house after the two had passed out in a drunken stupor. Other times, she slept outside, hidden in the heavy brush behind their home. In the early morning hours, certain they were sleeping off their late-night drinking, she slipped inside, cautious to stay out of their way.

It was after one particularly volatile fight with Robbie that Kristina could not escape, she decided to leave. She could no longer evade their anger, and their drinking worsened. Nursing her swollen lip and blackened eye, she waited until Helene and Robbie passed out, then collected what few belongings she had, and crept out in the middle of the night.

To spare her younger sister from lying, Kristina left without saying goodbye. At sixteen she had no one to turn to for help, but armed with a strength for survival and a desire for a better life, she left home without a trace.

The knot in Pierce's throat would not go away as he listened intently. His emotions came at him from different directions: fury at Helene and Robbie for their abuse and cruelty; helplessness that he could not have been there to protect his child from them; admiration for her determination and resilience under such horrible conditions.

"The moment I walked away from that nightmare, my life began," she said softly. "I went as far away as I could get from Boston and even changed my name to ensure they could not track me down."

Pierce looked at his daughter questioningly, a curious smile played on his lips.

"How did you choose the last name Fraser?"

Kristina smiled impishly.

"Over the years, when Robbie and Helene fought, I heard the name Fraser mentioned many times as they raged. Something within me made me pick that name out of spite towards them, but also because it seemed to suit me. I cannot explain it."

Pierce smiled to himself as he processed his daughter's words.

"It most definitely suits you. You look just like my mother, your grandmother, Larena Fraser. I wish you two could have known each other."

The thought of her resembling her grandmother made Kristina smile. For the first time, she realized she had never believed she belonged to any family, particularly Robbie and Helene. Now, all these years later, it felt renewing that the pieces of her true familial puzzle were coming together.

Giving her a tentative look, he offered her a suggestion.

"If you could indulge me, I would like to show you some of the Fraser and Tennyson family portraits. My wife had them all carefully hung in the North wing of the manor."

Kristina nodded quickly and smiled.

Never Leave My Arms

"I would love that. I would also like to speak to Alexandra to thank her. Is she here?"

Pierce looked puzzled. "You met my wife?"

"Yes. She came to visit me in London after our initial meeting at your company office last year. She convinced me to find the truth. It is because of her that I am here."

A slow smile broke across Pierce's face.

"Alexandra, you little minx," he thought wryly to himself. *"Once again, you presented opportunities and produced wondrous results."*

Epilogue

Landon Estates
Middlesex, England
December 24, 1812

The din of the small group in the drawing room carried into the grand foyer of Landon House. Alexandra, dressed in a rich burgundy gown with jeweled trim, flitted among family members and close neighbors spreading holiday cheer.

Fresh garland wound through the rails of the manor's massive main staircase and hung over the entryways that led to various areas of the grand home. The fragrant decoration, each accented with large red bows as centerpieces, filled the air with the scent of evergreen.

The Tennyson grandchildren played happily by the newly cut Christmas tree. The small fir sat atop a round pedestal table in the large front window of the drawing room. Their little faces were enraptured by the shiny trinkets and strings of dried fruits and gingerbread hanging from its limbs.

Kat and Sarah kept a close eye on the three youngest while Maddie, the oldest granddaughter, sat quietly drawing in her book of pictures in a chair by the fireplace. Her love for painting and drawing had emerged at age five when her uncle purchased a painting set for her.

Alexandra spied her husband positioned near the front window, periodically peering outside. She smiled lovingly. The family was missing a few members who should have arrived days ago. The unusual snowy weather had slowed all travel by land and sea.

Alex and Christopher had been gone for almost four months on a Landon Stables business trip to Pennsylvania. Kristina left two months later on a trip to France to shop for fabric for her London and Philadelphia stores. James Masters planned to catch passage on one of his ships from Charleston, South Carolina. Alexandra frowned at the thought of Kat and Sarah's father's absence. He should have arrived at least two weeks ago.

Alexandra softly slid her hand up her husband's broad back to gain his attention.

"Luv, the weather has slowed everyone down, but they will be here."

Pierce turned at the sound of his wife's voice and smiled down at her. Slipping his arm around her shoulder, he pulled her close, giving her an affectionate squeeze. He could always count on her to lift his spirits.

Nodding, he replied, "I know. I just wish it were now."

"Me too," she said as she slipped her hand in his and pulled him away from the window.

"Come, let us spread some holiday cheer to our guests."

Pierce laughed lightly at his wife's enthusiasm.

"Very well," he replied, then smiled wider as he glimpsed his grandson, Landon, trying to reach for a gingerbread man on the Christmas tree. He scooped the toddler up before the child could pull it off the table. The little boy laughed infectiously as his grandfather redirected his attention by tickling his tummy and breaking off a small piece of the goodie to give to him.

Kat, busy with her youngest Alison, shot her father-in-law a grateful look for his quick reflexes.

Never Leave My Arms

Reece approached his father to relieve him of his young grandson, but the older man waved him off.

"Leave us be. We are fine," he said, laughing as Landon grinned while enjoying his piece of gingerbread.

Suddenly, the sounds of the room grew louder as Alex, Christopher, and James entered the drawing room with a stranger in tow. The group erupted in cheers as the men entered. Greene was there to help them remove their winter attire and secure the packages they had brought, except for a box Christopher held back.

Sarah and Maddie rushed to Alex while Alexandra hugged Christopher, and Pierce shook James hand. Gesturing to the tall, lithe stranger standing off to the side, Alex introduced him.

"This is Jace Garrett, owner of Heritage Hills Thoroughbreds. He is joining us for the next few months. We are going to be working together on two new bloodlines."

Alexandra and Pierce extended their welcome and insisted he stay with them.

"There is plenty of room in this home," Alexandra said.

Inclining his head, Jace replied with a hint of a smile. "That is very kind. Thank you."

The American had a mysteriousness about him. He had a soft raspy voice with purposeful inflection. Alexandra did not find it unsettling, rather, intriguing. She also noted he squinted slightly when conversing. His penetrating gray eyes seemed to analyze everything about you and what you were saying, as though he was quietly judging you but not in an offensive way. His contributions to the conversation were not rushed; they were measured and deliberate, always on point. Alexandra felt he would fit in well doing business with her sons.

Setting aside her assessment of their guest, she turned her attention to James, and smiled brightly. Alexandra and the American Southerner got along splendidly.

"I take it you were delayed by the weather as well?"

The slow talker from South Carolina chuckled.

"Actually, the delay was because I made a stop in Philadelphia to pick up these gentlemen," he said, referring to Christopher, Alex, and Jace.

"The passenger ships were taking longer routes because of the weather, so they caught a ride with me on one of my merchant vessels."

Pierce clapped James on the back and laughed.

"Thank you for ensuring they got home safe and sound in time for the holiday."

A pang of disappointment tugged at Pierce because Kristina had not yet arrived, but he pushed it aside and focused on those in attendance.

Alexandra encouraged the men to relax with the rest of the guests in the drawing room.

"Please come in and enjoy something warm. Dinner will be served shortly."

The four easily assimilated into the group, each enjoying a glass of fine liquor. As the excitement of their arrival subsided, the front door caught Greene's attention once again to greet Davis and Sallie McCoy.

The couple had journeyed from their London home with their two year old twins in their arms, Grace and Quintin. Greene happily assisted the parents with doffing the little one's coats and boots so they could play with the other children.

Sarah and Kat waited patiently to greet their close friend and her husband. Kat hugged Sallie first.

"We are so glad the snow did not keep you from coming."

Sarah looked her friend over from head to toe and grinned mischievously.

Never Leave My Arms

"You look wonderful."

Sallie immediately blushed and smothered a giggle. Kat looked bewildered at first then quickly put the puzzle together when Sarah lowered her voice and whispered, "How far along?"

"Shush. Not so loud," Sallie murmured. Looking about to see if anyone overheard, she whispered, "Almost three months."

Sallie had befriended Sarah years ago when she worked for her brother. Their friendship became so close, Sarah even had her escort Maddie from Charleston to London. While on that trip, she met Kat and the two became instant friends. Neither realized her connection to Sarah until much later.

Sallie had prepared herself for a life of living for others and was happy with such. But then, she and Davis McCoy met through his association with the Tennysons in London. A deep friendship developed, and the two fell in love.

While the adults socialized and conversed, Maddie took in the excitement of the room and set aside her picture book when she spotted the box Christopher had brought in. She thought she saw it move. Approaching it slowly to investigate, she saw it had holes on top and was made of wood.

Pulling on Christopher's hand to get his attention, she asked, "What's in the box?"

The youngest Tennyson brother smiled down at his eight-year-old niece. Placing his finger to his lips, he quietly led her over to the container and dropped down on his haunches

"This is a Christmas gift I brought back from Philadelphia. Mr. Garrett gave it to me, and I was hoping you could help me with it."

Maddie's eyes lit up with excitement as she nodded quickly. Lifting the lid, she squealed with delight at the sight of a chubby, butterscotch-colored puppy with big brown eyes and a jet black nose. The little creature looked up at Maddie in wonder as she gently lifted it by its round pink belly. It's small tail wagged rapidly and it immediately began licking her face the moment she held it close, eliciting a giggle from the little girl. Maddie's excitement captured everyone's attention in the room, and they all gathered to meet the newest addition to the Tennyson family and Landon Stables.

"Does it have a name?" Maddie gushed as she sat on the floor, the puppy in her lap.

Christopher smiled at his niece's exuberance.

"No, she doesn't. What do you think would be a good name?"

The little girl sat for a moment, contemplating the puppy's face, when Landon, her two-year-old cousin, still in his grandfather's arms, blurted out, "Shibby," pointing at the puppy. While the adults chuckled at the toddler's suggestion, Maddie thought it was a great name.

"Shibby fits her perfectly," the little girl said with a big smile.

"Welcome to the family, Shibby," Pierce declared with a laugh.

At Maddie's insistence and her parents' reluctant agreement, they allowed the pup to stay with her in her room just for the night. Christopher promised to make arrangements for more permanent accommodations the next day.

Never Leave My Arms

Christmas morning, Tennyson family members, minus one, along with their neighbors, and Jace Garrett gathered at the small church on the estate for a holiday service. Afterwards, they congregated at the grand home for brunch.

While Alexandra continued her efforts to spread the season's cheer, she could see her husband struggled with Kristina's absence. Their close neighbors even noted that the recent snowfall had made local travel difficult for them as well and was likely responsible for her delay returning from France.

As the large group gathered in the drawing room, waiting for the late morning brunch buffet to be set out, Alexandra caught sight of Greene rushing through the foyer to the front door. A moment later, she heard murmurs and went to investigate, quickly covering her mouth to stifle a gasp. Tamping down her excitement, she casually called out to her husband, "Pierce, luv. Could you come here for a moment?"

He had been speaking with their neighbors, the Trebelcock's, while the family warmed themselves at the large fireplace. Pierce politely excused himself to join his wife in the foyer.

"Is something amiss?" he asked as he approached her.

He only saw Greene near the front door assisting a guest he presumed was part of the group returning from the church.

"Nothing at all," she said, a mischievous smile playing on her lips.

As Greene stepped aside, a figure dressed in a full-length wool cloak, looked up, and locked eyes with Pierce. A broad smile broke across his face as he immediately recognized the familiar green eyes and auburn hair peeking out from the raised fur lined hood.

"Kristina," he breathed happily, pulling her into his arms and hugging her tightly.

vii

Pierce gave her no time to doff her cloak before he immediately guided her into the large gathering in the drawing room.

"Look who is here!" he exclaimed.

The entire family rushed over to welcome her. Sarah and Kat insisted on spending some quality time discussing her thoughts on the new French dress styles and fabrics. Maddie excitedly told her about the new puppy, and her half-brothers each gave her affectionate welcoming hugs. Pierce then introduced her to their neighbors who expressed their happiness that she had joined the Tennyson family.

Jace Garrett stood off to the side quietly taking in everyone as they happily gathered around the young woman. The American had a comfortable casualness about him as he watched the group interact. Christopher noticed his new friend and business associate and wanted to include him in the festivities. Grabbing Kristina's hand, he drew her away from the group to their guest.

"Kristina, I want you to meet someone who hails from your area of the Americas."

"Really?" she replied curiously as she allowed her younger half-brother to pull her away from the fray.

"Alex and I are partnering with him on two new bloodlines."

As Kristina approached the tall stranger, she sought to free herself from her warm, heavy cloak. Distracted by her efforts to release the fastener, she did not immediately look at him. Once she lowered the fur trim hood and swept it from her shoulders, she gasped when their eyes locked.

A lopsided grin appeared on his lips and his twinkled with affection.

"Jace?" she whispered.

"It's great to see you Kris. You look wonderful," he said in his slow, raspy voice.

Never Leave My Arms

The End...For Now

Stay Tuned For The Next Installment:

The Tennyson Series: Book Four

Race the Storm

(Due for Release in Late 2026)

Elizabeth's Other Reads:

The Determined Pursuit

Love's Unforgettable Flame

Purchase, New Release & Contact Info Available At:

www.regencyromanceandsecrets.com
or
www.elizabethhfranklinbooks.com
(Don't forget the second "h")

Follow her on Facebook
(Elizabeth H. Franklin Author Page)

Tiktok (ehfranklinauthor)

Instagram (Elizabeth H. Franklin Author)